The Crystal Cavern

*Also by Hannah Alexander
in Large Print:*

Missouri: A Living Soul: Variety Is the
Spice of Romance in the Show-Me State

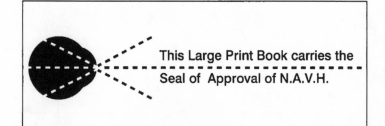

This Large Print Book carries the
Seal of Approval of N.A.V.H.

THE CRYSTAL CAVERN

*A place of refuge . . .
or a deadly trap?*

Hannah Alexander

Thorndike Press • Waterville, Maine

This book is a work of fiction. Names, characters, places, and incidents are either products of the author's imagination or used fictitiously. Any similarity to actual people, organizations, and/or events is purely coincidental.

Published in 2006 by arrangement with
Barbour Publishing, Inc.

Thorndike Press® Large Print Christian Mystery.

The tree indicium is a trademark of Thorndike Press.

The text of this Large Print edition is unabridged.
Other aspects of the book may vary from the original edition.

Set in 16 pt. Plantin by Ramona Watson.

Printed in the United States on permanent paper.

Library of Congress Cataloging-in-Publication Data

Alexander, Hannah.
    The crystal cavern : a place of refuge or a deadly trap? / by Hannah Alexander.
        p. cm. — (Thorndike Press large print Christian mystery)
    ISBN 0-7862-8414-5 (lg. print : hc : alk. paper)
    1. Ice storms — Fiction.   2. Women physicians — Fiction.   3. Caves — Fiction.   4. Ozark Mountains — Fiction.   5. Large type books.   I. Title.   II. Thorndike Press large print Christian mystery series.
    PS3551.L35558C79 2006
    813'.54—dc22   2005036797

Dedicated to the memory of a true local hero, who was killed making sure others reached safety during the tornado that destroyed downtown Pierce City, Missouri, on May 4, 2003.

May the memory of James Dale Taunton continue to bless the citizens of our hometown.

As the Founder/CEO of NAVH, the only national health agency solely devoted to those who, although not totally blind, have an eye disease which could lead to serious visual impairment, I am pleased to recognize Thorndike Press★ as one of the leading publishers in the large print field.

Founded in 1954 in San Francisco to prepare large print textbooks for partially seeing children, NAVH became the pioneer and standard setting agency in the preparation of large type.

Today, those publishers who meet our standards carry the prestigious "Seal of Approval" indicating high quality large print. We are delighted that Thorndike Press is one of the publishers whose titles meet these standards. We are also pleased to recognize the significant contribution Thorndike Press is making in this important and growing field.

Lorraine H. Marchi, L.H.D.
Founder/CEO
NAVH

★ Thorndike Press encompasses the following imprints: Thorndike, Wheeler, Walker and Large Print Press.

For I am convinced that neither death nor life, neither angels nor demons, neither the present nor the future, nor any powers, neither height nor depth, nor anything else in all creation, will be able to separate us from the love of God that is in Christ Jesus our Lord.

ROMANS 8:38–39

Chapter 1

"Who do you think you are?" The dark voice curdled through the moist air and ricocheted along the passage of the cavern. "I'll kill you!"

He reached for her and she scrambled away, uttering a cry that froze in her throat. . . .

Sable Chamberlin awakened to the sound of her own voice as it spiraled across the room. Her eyes flew open and she sat up, sucking in air between clenched teeth, stumbling from the sofa where she had fallen asleep. The tendrils of the nightmare clung to her. She clamped her fingers over her lips to keep from crying out again. Gradually, the familiar surroundings of her living room brought the world back into focus.

"It was a dream," she whispered. "A dream." She murmured the familiar litany Grandpa had given her when she was a child. "Dreams will always go away, then everything will be okay."

She waited for the relief those words had brought her in years past, but this time it

9

didn't work. The nightmare was too close, and after months of struggle it seemed to be haunting her even more often.

And Grandpa wasn't around to make the truth of his words stick.

She stumbled through the dimness of the living room to the kitchen, rubbing her eyes, wishing she could sleep for the next month. Instead of turning on the overhead light, she peered out the window into the darkening sky over the small town of Freemont, Oklahoma. There must be a February storm coming in.

For the past six-and-a-half months, she had tried to accept this place as her new home, but the only reason she had even come here in the first place was to be near Grandpa.

Now Grandpa was dead.

Her true home was deep in the Missouri Ozarks, on the old farm that held so many memories — most of them good.

"Grandpa," she whispered, her voice wobbly with the tears that had hovered near the surface all week, all through the funeral, all through the press of loving relatives surrounding her and her mother and brothers.

Clouds roiled outside, and she dashed the tears from her face as she saw a flash of lightning. As distant thunder began to roll across the sky, she was startled by the beep of her cordless telephone.

She gasped, then snatched it up, annoyed by her own jittery nerves. "Yes!"

"Sable, is that you?"

She shivered in the freezing room. She should have turned the heat up when she arrived here an hour ago. "Noah." Relief.

"What're you doing back in Freemont?" demanded her elderly friend.

"You know," she said. She still had to clear Grandpa's name. Josiah Kessinger's death on Monday — five days ago — had somehow opened the floodgates on a nasty rumor that he had defrauded some locals — Noah included — of their hard-earned savings. It was crazy, of course, but since Grandpa Josiah wasn't a native of this small, tightly knit mining community, he made an easy target for blame.

"You should've stayed in Missouri," Noah snapped.

Sable shivered, still fighting off the remnants of the recurring nightmare that had haunted her these past few months.

"But never mind that," Noah said. "I got this delivery while you were gone. I think you'll want to come out and see it. I'd bring it in, but I've got my truck in town getting the brakes fixed."

11

"What kind of delivery are you talking about?" she asked, dabbing one last tear from her face.

"Big package. You know, big manila envelope."

"And . . . there's a reason you need me to see it?"

"It's addressed to you."

"To me? Why is it —"

"It was sent in care of my address, but you're the person listed on the attention line. It's there, clear as day. It says, 'Doctor Sable Chamberlin.' I figure it's something important. I was going to forward it on to Missouri, but I thought I'd call your apartment one more time before I sent it. How's your family holding up after the funeral?"

"Not well, Noah." She glanced at the digital clock on the stove. It was just 6 p.m. Why did she feel as if she were taking a medical call in the middle of the night? Because she'd been driving for six hours, and she was tired.

" 'Specially you, huh?" Noah said.

"Especially me." She'd been closer to Grandpa than anyone else, even Mom. "Who's the package from?"

"Josiah."

"Grandpa?"

"It's his writing, I can tell you that. No

name on the return address, but it's Eagle Rock, Missouri, sure enough."

Fresh grief mingled with the hovering sense of horror that had convinced Sable to leave Oklahoma forever — just as soon as she got to the bottom of the nasty rumors.

She knew it couldn't be true. Josiah Kessinger would never willingly injure another living soul. It was true that he'd been strapped for money — it was the reason he'd come down here in the first place, to join an old buddy in a mining venture with the promise of riches. Grandpa and his dreams . . .

"Noah, could you open the envelope? If it's something important, I'll drive out to your place now." Sable looked down at the telephone recorder, which she had programmed to record every one of her conversations. Grandpa had given it to her two weeks ago, along with a stern warning to use it at all times.

Over the telephone she heard a ripping sound. Noah muttered something unintelligible under his breath, and then she heard an exclamation of surprise.

"Oh . . . Lord, help us all."

"Noah? What is it?"

Noah continued his muttering, as if he were reading out loud to himself.

Sable waited. She knew better than to rush Noah Erwin through anything. He'd been a patient of hers since her second day on the job, and he was nothing if not deliberate. In the past six months, he'd also become the most important human influence in her life. Because of Noah, she and Grandpa had found hope for the future and a whole new reason for living.

Fresh out of family practice residency in Tulsa, Oklahoma, she had taken the job in Freemont to be closer to Grandpa. His business partner, Otis Boswell, had made a special effort to fly her down on a chartered jet, gave her the grand tour of the town of three thousand, and impressed upon her how much they all needed a new physician.

Amazing how different the dream was from real life. As the designated company physician for Boswell Mining, she had endured six months of long hours and low pay, but she'd been determined to stick with her first job, in spite of Grandpa's apparent displeasure with her decision.

"Sable? You still there?" Noah finally came back on the line.

"I'm here." Her voice cracked with weariness.

"You better come out here." There was a hush in his voice.

"Why? What is it?"

She heard a rustle of papers over the line. "I'll tell you this much," he said, obviously reluctant to speak. "Looks like something big's been going on. I knew he was up to something, but the old rascal never was much for sharing his thoughts."

"Something big like what?"

There was a long silence.

"You should see the stuff he's dug up," Noah said finally. "All kinds of papers and letters about dirty deals, pictures, medical reports."

"Dirty deals? What kind of —"

"There's big bucks involved, that's obvious. Big, big bucks. And Sable? Better brace yourself, young lady. There's a note to you."

"I'll be right out."

"Better pack to leave," Noah said. "Come to think of it, maybe I oughta pack, myself. Here's one of those sticky notes. Says these are all copies. Originals back in Missouri. Have you got any idea where that might —" He broke off.

Sable heard a rustle of movement over the line. "Noah?"

"Just a minute." He spoke in his normal

15

voice now. "Thought I heard something."

She felt another chill. "If you think —"

"No . . . no . . . never mind. It's probably the wind picking up. Looks like a storm. Just get out here, okay? Josiah told me awhile back I oughta make believe Big Brother is looking over my shoulder, and —" He broke off again. "Hmm. What was that noise?"

"Noah?"

No answer, then, in the distance, "Hello? Who's there?"

She gripped the telephone and took a slow, steady breath. Just the wind.

Noah came back on the line. "Sorry about that."

"What's going on there?"

"Nothing. I'm just a little jumpy is all." But an undertone of worry gave the lie to his words.

"I'll call the —"

"No! Don't call the police. If this stuff is for real, some of them are dirty."

"But what if someone —"

"Paul Murphy's got his cell phone with him. I'll call him out, just to be safe."

"I'll be there in a few minutes," she said.

Freemont suddenly felt like a frightening place. She needed to see what Grandpa had sent. If they had to, they could both leave tonight.

16

"I'll be waiting. See you in about ten minutes." He hung up before she could say another word.

Sable replaced the receiver and watched the recording device stop. Noah lived four miles outside of town, in an old, rambling farmhouse. She'd better hurry.

She grabbed her car keys from the kitchen counter, pulled on her coat, and shoved her billfold into the deep right pocket. She ran out of the apartment, locking the door behind her. Automatically, her hand went up to the old pocket watch she kept on a chain around her neck. An enigmatic Christmas gift from Grandpa.

Ever since he'd given her the watch, he'd become jumpy, snappy, and especially secretive. He'd also become more adamant about her getting her Missouri medical license. Then, three weeks ago, he had told her, "Darlin', if anything happens to me, I want you to get out of Oklahoma. Don't look back. This isn't any kind of town for a young lady like you."

She jumped into her Camaro and backed out of the driveway. Soon, maybe this nightmare would be over.

Or maybe it had just begun.

★ ★ ★

The sudden brilliance of a flash of lightning shocked Sable to a halt at the gate to Noah Erwin's front yard. The storm split the clouds with its violence. She peered through the broken darkness at the outline of her friend's unkempt home.

She had to will away a cowardly shiver. Why hadn't Noah left any lights on in the house? Why hadn't he come out onto the front porch to greet her, the way he always did?

She unlatched the gate and pulled it open, wincing at the rusty creak of hinges. "Noah, I'm here!" she called with false bravado, stepping carefully along the flagstone path. Maybe the lightning had knocked out the power, the way it usually did out here when there was a storm.

"Noah!"

She stopped as another crack of lightning illumined the top step of the porch and the wide-open doorway. In that instant she felt a blast of shock at the sight of a human-shaped shadow. The elderly man lay sprawled across the threshold, his body blocking the heavy oak door.

Sable froze in horror. She forgot to breathe.

She clutched the side of the wooden structure for support. "Noah!"

The darkness threatened to overtake her as nausea and weakness caught her in their grip. She forced herself forward; there was no time for the luxury of emotion. Another flash illuminated the blood that had trickled from a hole in her friend's temple. His glazed, open eyes held the blank stare of death.

Swallowing hard, she sank to her knees and felt for a pulse at his throat, though it wasn't necessary. Whoever shot him had taken measures to complete the job. Noah's head fell sideways, revealing a mass of blood at the back of his skull.

"No!" She froze there, paralyzed by the sudden loss — and by the implications. She leaned against the doorframe for support.

Unwanted tears welled in her eyes in spite of her resolve to remain strong. The icy wind whipped her hair across her face in a blinding curtain. She brushed it back and stood up to peer into the living room beyond the doorway. Shadows lurked and jumped in every corner of the huge room as flicks of lightning outlined the sofa and chairs and Noah's old desk in sharp relief. Sable tuned her ears to the slightest sound, but the storm effectively drowned out any noise.

Scattered papers drifted across the foyer, blown by the wind from the open doorway.

The wind died down for a moment. A footfall echoed from the darkness near the kitchen door.

A movement! A black form separated itself from the shadows and lunged across the living room floor, stumbling over a footstool as the lightning revealed a human shape. Vestiges of Sable's nightmare returned as she screamed and skittered backwards over Noah's body. She fell on her side, then scrambled to her feet and raced down the porch steps.

The intruder, in hot pursuit, reached out a hand to snag the sleeve of her jacket. She screamed and yanked away, darting out onto the front lawn, past the bushes toward her car.

Heavy rasps of breath harmonized with the thud of running feet across the porch, down the steps, too close . . . coming too close!

Breaking her line of motion in order to gain ground, she dove sideways into a shadowed hedgerow prickly with thorns that scraped her exposed hands. She fought her way through the brambles that clung to her clothes with a vengeance, as if eager to assist her assailant.

She broke free just as the man who was chasing her reached the yard side of the thorny hedge. Angry, muttered curses informed her when the man followed in her wake through the thorn patch.

She pivoted back through another break in the hedgerow, but her right foot caught on a root, and she fell to her knees. The man grasped her sleeve again. She swung around to claw at his face . . . but he had no face! Then the lightning revealed what she should have expected — he was wearing a ski mask.

A sudden flash of headlights pierced the night, etching the outline of her attacker through the spiny branches of the shrubs. The rumbling power of an approaching SUV terrified her, but it also startled her attacker. He released her abruptly, swung away, stumbled, broke back through the hedgerow, and disappeared into the darkness.

Sable froze like a deer in the glare of the headlights for what seemed like an eternity, heart pounding in rhythm of the engine, breath coming in hard rasps. As soon as the vehicle passed, she turned and ran toward her car.

When she reached the Camaro, she yanked open the door, then looked back to find the SUV circling in behind her, pinning her in the glare of lights, blocking her escape. With a cry of fright she plunged into the blackness beyond the driveway.

"Hey!"

Sable ran faster, tripping over the uneven ground in Noah's garden. Again, she heard the sound of pursuing footsteps, but these were swifter and heavier. In a burst of desperate speed, she reached the level ground beyond the garden and raced toward the toolshed. There might be a weapon of some sort among the garden tools, maybe a hoe.

Large, strong hands gripped her shoulders and spun her around against the wall of the looming shed.

"No!" she screamed, jerking her knee upward until it hit something solid. "Get away!"

The man grunted, but he didn't release her.

"Let me go!" She raked her nails down the side of his neck, kicked at his legs. "Let go of me!"

There was another grunt. "Sable!" He grabbed her by the arms and pulled her tight against his solid chest. "Sable, stop it!

It's me. It's Murph!" He paused and groaned in pain. "Who are you fighting? What's happening? Who was that man?"

Gradually recognition of the voice and the broad expanse of shoulders seeped past Sable's panic. A sharp sob of mingled relief and shock burst from her throat. She looked up as the growing brilliance of the electric storm showed Paul Murphy's strong facial features. For several seconds she held her breath, afraid to trust her own senses.

"Murph." Paul Murphy, the paramedic who had been with the clinic for the past six weeks. Tears of horror and grief once more flooded her eyes. She slumped against him. "Thank You, God."

Murph held her steady. "Sable, what's going on? Where's Noah?"

She swallowed hard and straightened as the first fat drops of the storm splashed against her face. "He's on the porch. He's . . . he's dead."

His hands tightened on her arms, then he released her and sucked in air as if he'd been kicked. He turned to look toward the house, though there was nothing to be seen through the darkness.

"No." His deep voice roughened with shock. He took a step in that direction.

Sable's fear once more escalated. She grabbed his arm. "Wait! Don't go over there. He's been shot, and whoever was chasing me was in the house when I arrived."

He turned back to her. "Noah . . . ? Are you sure —"

"He's dead, Murph. I saw him. Believe me, he's gone." It was too much to bear. *First Grandpa, now Noah.*

Murph touched her arm. "Are you okay? Did the man hurt you?"

"No, you scared him off. I'll be fine as soon as we get away from this place."

Murph turned again toward the house. "We can't leave Noah like —"

"Noah wouldn't thank us for getting ourselves killed, Murph. He's already gone, and we need to get to help."

"Are you sure he's . . . ?" There was pain and pleading in his voice, and tears stung Sable's eyes once more. She couldn't believe it, either, but it was true.

"Yes. Please, Murph, we're in danger. We've got to get out."

"But the police —"

"No, we can't call them. Murph, you've got to believe me." She had to trust Paul Murphy. Obviously Noah had. Even Grandpa had said that Paul Murphy

24

seemed like "a reasonable man." He was also a smart man. Right now, apparently, shock and grief were dulling his instincts.

Sharp needles of icy rain splashed Sable's face. A brilliant flare of lightning lit up the yard and porch. Murph caught his breath in an audible reaction to the sight of Noah's dead body. He took a step toward the house, and another. Sable saw a white flash of papers rustle through the doorway.

The envelope? The copies of reports and pictures Noah had mentioned. With Murph's arrival, the killer had fled from sight. Maybe the envelope Noah had received was still in his living room. If so, they might be able to find out what was going on.

She followed Paul Murphy through the rain to the front porch. When he sank to his knees beside Noah, Sable stepped over the body, reaching inside for the light switch. It flipped up, but nothing happened.

Heart pounding once again, she plunged through the inky blackness, guided every few seconds by the lights from the storm. A crack of thunder shuddered through the house as Sable paused at a stack of papers, hesitated, then moved on.

"Sable?" Murph's deep voice called from

the doorway. "What are you doing?"

"Noah called me tonight and asked me to come out." Her words tumbled over themselves in her need to share the burden with another human being. "He received something in the mail this week, some evidence about an investigation Grandpa was conducting — apparently on his own. Bad stuff, Murph. I'm afraid that somehow someone knew about the mail and came to get it."

Murph stood up and peered inside. The strobes of lightning cast an eerie pall across his grief-stricken face. "What did Noah tell you?"

"To go back to Missouri. Same thing Grandpa told me."

"But why?"

"I'm not sure." She shrugged, looking helplessly around the large living room. No envelope. "I'm not sure of anything anymore."

She heard a beep and turned to find Murph opening his cell phone.

"What are you doing?"

"Calling the police."

"No!" She rushed across the room and grabbed the phone before he could dial. "Didn't you hear me? We can't call the police. Noah said it looked like some of them might be corrupt. Look, Murph, we can't stand here and argue about this. It isn't safe."

An especially bright burst of lightning illuminated a sheaf of scattered pages on the floor beside the telephone. She knelt and gathered a handful and shoved them into the deep left pocket of her coat. The day after Grandpa's death, while his body was being prepared for transfer to the family home in Missouri for burial, Sable had received a visit from Otis Boswell, accompanied by the police. While she was still reeling from the shock of Grandpa's death, Otis had stood in the living room of her apartment and accused Grandpa of salting a mine — planting ore in an unproductive mine in order to trick someone into purchasing the land.

She would never believe that of Grandpa. Maybe these pages could help prove his innocence.

She stepped gingerly past Noah's body.

Murph followed. "What do you expect to find back in Missouri?"

"I wish I knew." Her voice caught with quick tears. "Noah didn't get a chance to tell me."

There was another long crackle of chain-link thunder, and when the echo of it died away, it was replaced by the strident shriek of a siren.

Sable gasped and caught Murph's arm. "They're here. We've got to go now!" She jumped from the porch. "Murph, come on!" She raced toward her car. "Get in!"

The sirens were drawing close — within half a mile — when she jumped into the car, slammed the door, and turned on the key. The motor sprang to life with a rumble of reassuring power. As she put the car into gear, Murph slid in on the passenger side.

The wide tires of the Camaro tore up grass and slung mud high against the windows as they gripped the earth. Sable held her breath and pressed the accelerator to the floorboard. They cleared the bushes at the far end of Noah's front yard just as the red flashing lights of a police car lit the night sky. Dark as the night was, Sable didn't dare switch on her headlights, not if there was a chance they could get away unseen.

"So you believe me?" she said as she turned onto a straight stretch of road.

"Yes. Just drive!"

Sable obeyed, turning her attention to the road ahead.

Her ruse worked. They didn't see her

without the lights. As the sirens receded, she relaxed her foot for a moment on the accelerator. Headlights beamed into her eyes from the rearview mirror, but no cherries flashed.

"Someone's following us," she told Murph. "But it doesn't look like the police."

"Just keep driving, and get those lights on or we'll plunge into the canal."

Sable switched on her headlights and downshifted for a burst of power, bracing herself for the dangerous turn at the edge of the deep, water-filled canal less than a quarter mile ahead.

Despite her speed, the car behind drew closer. She gritted her teeth and tightened her grip on the steering wheel.

Only a few hundred feet from the sharp turn, the other car accelerated. Sable pressed her right foot to the floorboard, and the Camaro responded with a burst of speed.

High-beam headlights glared from the left-hand lane. She swerved to miss the oncoming car, then realized too late how close she was to the canal curve. She yanked the steering wheel hard left. The road was too wet and slick, even for the road-hugging tires of a Camaro. The car rammed sideways against a concrete abutment. Murph's door flew open. Sable screamed.

"We're going over!" Murph shouted, reaching for Sable's arm. "Jump!"

Instinctively, Sable dove across the seat toward the opening. The car bumped off the blacktop and plummeted toward the water.

Sable and Murph pushed themselves free from the car and plunged into icy wet blackness.

Chapter 2

Murph kicked his way to the surface, gasping for air in response to the shocking cold. Waves from the car's impact washed over him like ocean surf, and he fought to stay afloat. He strained through the darkness for a sign of Sable, but before he could call out, lights penetrated the night. Two sets of headlights on the roadway above.

Someone wanted Sable out of the way, which meant she posed a danger to them. But who was it, and why? Did she know something in particular?

Hampered by the force of the splash and by the drag of his down-quilted coat, Murph swam to the bank of the canal. A bush loomed above his head, and he grasped it to pull himself from the water. He still had not seen any sign of Sable. He opened his mouth to call out a soft query to her, but when he heard twin thumps, like car doors closing, he swallowed his words. He couldn't risk it now.

Then, in the wash of the headlights, he saw the outline of a dark form about ten feet to his right. Sable. He felt a rush of relief. Now if only she would remain still until —

Male voices rat-a-tatted across the water's surface.

"Who was it? Did you see?"

"Had to be Chamberlin. It was her car."

"I know that," the first man snapped. "Who was with her?"

"Some big guy."

"Murphy, then."

"Why's that?"

"It was his Bronco in the drive." The beam of a flashlight traveled slowly over the surface of the water, as if studying it for clues . . . or for victims. Murph didn't move from behind the sparse growth of winter brush.

"Anything out there?"

"No sign. What brought you out?" The beam continued its search.

"Heard some rumors."

"Let me guess, it was from a tap in Erwin's house?"

The answer was a grunt. "Josiah Kessinger was onto more than we realized."

"Sounds that way."

"What're your boys planning to do about it?"

"Trying to keep the Feds out of it. The rest is up to you. Think you can get that envelope of stuff from Erwin?"

"Have to."

"Either that, or we'll hightail it to Missouri and find out what the old codger's talking about."

"That won't stop him from taking what he's got to the Feds."

"No."

After a short silence, a new voice joined the others. "Hey! This just came over the radio. Somebody shot the old guy."

The flashlight beam stopped its methodical search of the water and was redirected to the roadway above. Peering up the embankment, where all the activity had suddenly focused, Murph saw three dark figures huddling together. The men lowered their voices as their conversation continued.

"Noah Erwin," the newcomer said softly. "Got him in the head."

There was a short pause.

"Won't have to worry about that one, then," said one of the others.

Murph gritted his teeth at the casual dismissal of Noah Erwin, as if he were some unwanted trash they had dumped on a garbage heap.

"And the envelope he was bragging about to his buddy?" one of the men asked.

"They didn't find it."

"So Chamberlin shot the old fool, took the evidence, and tried to get away."

"Some buddy she turned out to be."

"The chief has gotta be thrilled about this one," the speaker said dryly.

There was a short silence as Murph shivered in the icy air, and the flashlight beam began to play across the water again. Murph glanced to where he had last seen Sable, but he could no longer see her shadowed form. His chest clenched in panic.

The beam of the flashlight edged toward him. He closed his eyes and prayed, forcing himself to perfect stillness. Seconds later he heard a scuffle of footsteps.

"Find the car and get it out of the canal," came a terse command. "Tomorrow we'll release the news that the fleeing killers paid for the murder with their lives."

Once more the beam of light swept across the water, and once again he could see no sign of Sable.

Where was she? He had to get to her . . . as soon as the goons left. He waited, still afraid to do more than breathe, as the lights continued to probe the darkness.

"Looks like they both went down with the car. Let's go cover our hides before something leaks out about this."

The light retreated and the voices faded as the men walked away from the edge of the bank. When Murph heard the echo of engines from the roadway above, he scrambled quietly along the steep embankment toward the place he had last seen Sable. In the blackness of the night, he could see little, and what he could see came from the lightning that was slowly retreating from the area, taking the rain with it.

There was a loud splash followed by a surge of water, and a human form shot past the surface directly beside him. The distant lightning revealed Sable's white face emerging from the inky blackness of the canal, her dark jacket and jeans and the squiggly ropes of black hair plastered against her face and neck. She gasped desperately for air as she struggled toward the bank.

Murph grabbed her arms and pulled her from the water. "What happened? What are —"

"Are they gone?" she asked between gasps.

"They're gone."

"I had nowhere to hide, and the flashlight beam was about to reach me. I had to go under, b–b–but it was so horribly cold, and —"

Her teeth began a rhythmic chatter as her breath powdered the air with steam. "I held my breath as long as I could, but the c–current k–k–kept —"

"We've got to warm you up or you'll get hypothermia." Murph put his arms around her and helped her climb to a more secure position on the steeply sloped bank. "Are you okay?"

"Freezing," she said with a shudder. "I'm f–freezing."

He opened his coat and drew her against him, wrapping her completely within its protection against the wind. "Could you hear what they said?"

"M–most of it, until I went under."

Awkwardly, attempting to keep them both encased within the wet-but-protective folds of his coat, he drew her down the other side of the canal bank and onto the road.

"We've got to get out of here," Murph said grimly. "I'm going with you to Missouri."

Sable stiffened, her teeth still chattering.

"There's a bus station at Freemont, isn't there?" he persisted.

"Yes, but —"

"We can't go back to our apartments. Someone could be watching them, and right now they think we're dead. We want them to keep thinking that, at least until we're away from this place."

"D–didn't you m–move here from Wichita?" Her voice rose and fell as her whole body shook. "You said you had f–family there."

"A sister."

"Give y–yourself a break and get out of this mess," Sable insisted. "You're not a p–part —"

"I'm part of it now," he said. She didn't know the half of it . . . or did she? Maybe she knew a whole lot more than she was telling. "And stop trying to talk. You need to concentrate on warming up."

"Medically speaking, wh–whether or not a patient talks —"

"Sable, be quiet."

"L–look, I ap–p–preciate everything y–you're —"

"You're in no position to argue with me right now," he said as he snugged the coat more tightly around her. He had to go with her, whether she invited him or not.

A gust of freezing wind knifed through them, and Murph quickened his pace, drawing Sable along with him. "Whatever I decide to do when we get to Freemont, we've got to get there first. The least we can do is keep each other warm."

"What time is it?" Sable asked through still-chattering teeth.

"Seven-thirty, if my watch hasn't stopped," Murph said. About fifteen minutes had passed since they'd pulled themselves from the water, and they had traveled about a mile on this muddy, black stretch of road that ran parallel to the canal.

"We need to move faster," Sable urged. "We're at least another mile from Freemont, and the next bus to Tulsa leaves at eight." She stumbled, and Murph reached out to steady her.

"How do you know the bus schedule?" he asked.

"Grandpa took the bus back home on weekends sometimes. I always took him and picked him up."

"You don't think those goons could be watching the station?"

"We've got to try. Besides, you told me yourself, they think we're dead. I don't know any other way out of this —"

The sound of an automobile engine

scattered Murph's thoughts like rain in a river. "Sable."

"I hear it."

They ducked behind a concrete balustrade as headlights pierced the darkness above their heads. The car splashed through puddles barely fifteen feet from where they hovered in the dark night shadows.

Sable shivered again in Murph's arms.

"Why didn't you tell me your hypothermia was getting worse?" he asked.

"Why? You c–couldn't do anything about it anyway. Besides, we've got to keep going. Do you have any money?"

Murph reached for the right rear pocket of his slightly freeze-dried jeans. Empty. Feeling a fresh stirring of alarm, he patted the left pocket. Nothing. His billfold must have come out in the water.

"No," he said at last. He patted the left front pocket of his heavy chamois shirt. It was empty, but he felt the reassuring bulk of his holstered gun, which he wore strapped to his body when he wasn't on duty at the clinic or asleep in his bed at home.

"I have an ATM cash card," Sable said. "Everything else went down with the car."

"Then that'll have to do. Is there enough in your account to purchase tickets for us?"

"There's enough."

"Then let's go." He led her back onto the blacktop. Another mile and they'd reach Freemont. If they reached Freemont at all . . .

The meager lights at the edge of town barely shone through the black night. By the time they passed the city limit sign Sable was stumbling against Murph, even though he had removed his coat and wrapped it around her, buttoning it all the way to the collar.

After five minutes of stumbling along the shadowed, uneven roadside, they arrived at the bus station. Seeing no one around, Murph opened the door and held it for her.

"Murph, wait —" she said. "We probably look like a couple of drowned rats."

Murph gave her the once-over. "No, you look fine. My coat covers up everything. Don't worry about it." He motioned with his hand for her to step through the doorway.

Sable caught her breath, then gave a soft moan of relief as a blast of heated air greeted her.

He took her arm. "How are you feeling?"

"Cold." She fumbled inside her coat, brought out an ATM card, and stepped toward the clerk at the far end of the long,

40

narrow room that served as the town's bus station.

The balding older gentleman looked up from a desk cluttered with packages and boxes, and his face brightened. "Why, hello there, Dr. Chamberlin. What're you doing here at this cold hour?"

Murph felt a frisson of dread. Of course the man knew her. Everyone knew everyone in this town. How many more people would recognize her before they could get out of here?

"Hightailing it out for a break," Sable said casually as she leaned on the counter, her voice giving no hint of the horror she'd faced in the past couple of hours. As Sable joked with the clerk and purchased the tickets, Murph could have sworn she sounded as if she'd just spent a hard day at the clinic and was looking for a weekend getaway — until the man expressed his sympathy over her loss.

She hesitated for a second before thanking him for his concern.

Murph found the vending machine and purchased a cup of coffee, then turned to find Sable slumping into an old, plastic chair, eyeing him dubiously, damp tendrils of long, curly black hair fraying out around her cold-pinched face.

41

She held up the tickets, then shrugged out of his coat and handed it to him. "Two to Eagle Rock, departure in five minutes."

He gave her a grim smile and handed her the coffee as he took the coat. "What convinced you to let me go with you?"

"Fear." She took the cup and held it to her lips, closing her eyes as she inhaled the steam. "I'm scared, Murph. I don't suppose you have a water-resistant cell phone in one of those coat pockets."

He sank down beside her as the headlights of an approaching bus gleamed through the plate glass windows at the front of the station. "It's in the canal."

"And mine is ruined." She reached into her coat pocket and pulled out a tiny fold-up phone.

"Who would you call?"

"My brother, Peter. I want him to know what's happened here in case we don't reach . . . home."

Murph pointed to a pay phone in the corner of the room. "You might have time to use that if you hurry. Looks like they have packages to load first. I have some change in my —"

"I'll use my calling card number." She stood up and plodded wearily to the telephone.

Murph kept an eye on the desultory activity in the station while also watching Sable as she punched a long string of numbers into the phone.

Since he'd started working with her — and taking orders from her at the Freemont clinic six weeks ago — he'd grown to admire her kindness to patients, her quick wit, and her independent spirit.

That independence could sometimes come across as Missouri-mule stubbornness, but he didn't mind. He supposed it took a lot of stubbornness to complete university and med school and residency training and then to plunge neck-deep into a world dominated by men. In Freemont, a miner's town, the male population outnumbered the females by three to one, and he'd seen her face up to more than one domineering miner who seemed to have more on his mind than medical treatment.

She returned to the chair beside him and picked up the cup of coffee. "No answer at Peter's house in Kansas City. I tried to reach Mom at the house, but no answer there, either. I'm not surprised. She was planning to go home with Randy for a few days. He's my other brother." She looked up at Murph, and then glanced at the left side of his neck. Her eyes widened. "Oh, Murph, did I do that to you?"

He reached up and touched the welts. "Served me right for coming at you like that." He decided not to comment about the kick that had landed a wallop high on his left thigh. "What I'm worried about right now is you." He gestured toward her blue-white hands, which gripped the paper cup carefully, as if she were afraid she might drop it.

"I'll be fine in a few minutes. All I want is to get out of this . . . this place forever." Her voice wobbled. A tear escaped her right eye and trickled down her cheek.

"Sable?"

She shook her head and returned the coffee cup to the dilapidated plastic table beside her chair. "I can't believe this is happening. First Grandpa, now . . . now Noah." Her voice grew hoarse as more tears joined the first. "If you only knew what a wonderful person . . . what a truly Christian person Noah Erwin was."

"Yes," he said quietly. He knew very well. Much more than she realized.

"It's my fault he's dead."

"No way."

She sniffed and nodded. "You heard them back there at the canal. They tapped his telephone conversation to me. I made

44

him tell me why he wanted me to drive out to his house. I made him open that envelope. If I hadn't —"

"If you had gone out sooner, you might very well be dead, too." Murph glanced toward the clerk, who was assisting the bus driver with the packages. "Someone murdered Noah, and there's no way anyone could place the blame for that on you." He touched her hands, which were only a few degrees warmer than an ice cube, then clasped them between his own. "This isn't your doing, Sable. It's —"

"Time to board, folks," the clerk called to them from across the room.

Sable pulled her hands from Murph's and nodded to the man. "Coming, Bailey."

Chapter 3

To Sable's alarm, the southwestern Missouri weather, well known for its February fickleness, decided to show its high spirits across the Missouri Ozarks in the dark early hours of Saturday morning. The thick layer of clouds and bad weather seemed to have pursued Sable and Murph from Freemont, hovering at each station as if taunting them with further delays.

Now, four miles past Cassville on Highway 86, Sable closed her eyes and rested her head wearily against the pillow the bus driver had given her. No way could she sleep, but if she could just close her eyes for a few moments . . .

By the time they'd reached Joplin late last night, their layover at that station had been stretched another two hours because of a storm in Kansas that delayed their connecting bus. She and Murph had attempted to rent a car and drive to Eagle Rock, but that had proved impossible, with no credit card and in the middle of the night. During their uncomfortable wait,

Sable's stress level had shot through the ceiling of the station, fueled by a second cup of coffee and the packaged sandwiches she and Murph had purchased with cash they got from an ATM machine.

As each new passenger had entered the station, she had stiffened, and she'd sensed Murph's cautious wariness, seen his eyes narrow, watched him shift in his seat. She knew what he'd been thinking — had someone followed them from Freemont?

By the time they'd boarded the bus again at 3:30 this morning, Sable had been jumpy with paranoia, watching with suspicion the four other passengers who boarded with them, including a teenage boy and a gray-haired older lady.

By the time they'd reached Cassville, near the Missouri-Arkansas border, the temperature took a plunge, and rain began to freeze as soon as it hit the windshield of the bus. Sable knew from past experience that this accumulation could become very dangerous very quickly, especially amongst these hills. The February storm concentrated itself around the wilderness area of the Mark Twain National Forest; Sable watched the weather with ever-increasing worry.

Highway 86 was deserted except for

their bus as they struggled along the curving highway amid the bare, grasping branches of winter-stripped trees. The droning engine muffled the soft sound of falling rain; all she heard of the storm was the methodic *swish, swish, swish* of the wipers as they threatened to lull her closer to the edge of an uneasy, sleep-starved trance.

The bus driver's muffled grunt startled her from her thoughts. She frowned as the red-headed woman handled the steering wheel, her surprisingly muscular arms working back and forth with quick movements. The roads already appeared opaque with ice, and Sable hoped the driver knew what she was doing. She certainly knew how to talk. She'd held conversations with everyone on the bus — exchanging names and places of birth and destinations. She — and Murph and Sable — now knew everyone by name. The driver's name was Jerri.

When the steering wheel straightened and Jerri leaned back with relief, some of the tension eased from Sable's neck and shoulders — but not much.

"We're getting close," she told Murph, straightening in her seat. "Only a couple more miles now." At their present rate of speed, that would take about ten minutes. If they made it at all.

She wasn't aware of her tightly clenched hands until Murph touched them.

"It won't help to try to drive the bus for her." His steady baritone voice reassured her, as it had done often since he came to work at the clinic six weeks ago.

Paul Murphy had been a calming influence since the day she met him — a good quality for a paramedic to have. An especially good quality to have right now.

"The sooner we get off this road, the better I'll feel," she said.

"Same here. Apparently, this little freezing storm didn't show up on the weather reports, or we'd still be stranded in Joplin."

"Happens a lot in this area," Sable said. "I just hope the rain stops in the next few minutes, because we'll have to walk to the house in that stuff."

"There's no one we can call to come and pick us up?"

She shook her head. "With all the ice, the phone lines are most likely down by now, and we're out in the boonies, about five miles from Eagle Rock." Fortunately, they'd been able to persuade Jerri to let them off at the end of the quarter-mile drive to the farmhouse.

"You know this place well," he observed.

"I should. When Dad died, Mom sold our house in Eureka Springs, Arkansas, and moved here with me and my two brothers. I was sixteen at the time, so this is home." She reached up and grasped the pocket watch that dangled from a chain around her neck. Sadness overwhelmed her.

"I don't think I've ever seen you without that watch," Murph said.

She nodded. "Grandpa gave it to me for Christmas this year. I still remember the pride in his eyes when I opened the package and pulled this out. When I was a little girl I loved to sit on his lap and wind this watch and listen to it tick. It doesn't tick anymore, but the memories are still the same."

"Remember the good times," Murph said. "That's your treasure to keep."

She looked up at him, and once more her attention was caught by the red welts on his neck, caused by her fingernails. Again, she felt remorse. "I guess we both took a beating."

He reached up and fingered the scratches, and he gave her a slight grin. "You have a few skills, but I could show you more aggressive — and effective —

techniques if you promise not to use them on me."

"I promise, as long as you identify yourself before you grab me." She kept her voice soft. "Do you think anyone else here," she gestured to the others with a jerk of her head, "hails from Freemont?"

"Could be. I admit I'll be relieved when we make it to the house."

"Me, too, but you heard them at the canal last night. I'm the primary suspect." She lowered her voice and gave a quick glance around the bus. "The police will be after me, and they'll know where to look."

"Don't borrow trouble."

"It might be a good idea to be prepared in case it comes our way." She glanced out the window. "If only I knew where to look for answers." She had lost that handful of papers when they landed in the canal. She was at ground zero.

"We'll just have to take the time to search," Murph said.

She nodded. "Noah wanted to come with me." She looked at Murph again. "Just like that, he wanted to help. That's the kind of person he . . . he was."

"I . . . could see that about him." Murph took a deep breath and let it out slowly. His attention remained focused on Sable.

"Knowing that, you must know he wouldn't have blamed you for all this."

She frowned at the measured cadence of his words, as if he were holding back emotion. "You and Noah really took to each other, didn't you?"

Something about Murph's demeanor changed, some infinitesimal tightening of his shoulders, a slight quickening of his breath. "He's . . . he was a special person." He paused for a moment, then said, "He never blamed Josiah for the problem with the Seitz mine."

"He talked to you about that?"

"Sable, this week everyone's been talking about it."

She felt the rush of pain again. Grandpa wouldn't do anything like that. It was true that he had been financially strapped for years, and that in the past year or so he had finally seemed to get on his feet. That could also be, however, because all three of his grandchildren were finally out of college and supporting themselves. He had insisted on paying for all of their higher education. Sable's had been the most expensive.

"I still don't understand why your grandpa, Noah, and Boswell decided to sell the mine," Murph said. "Why not work it themselves?"

"Grandpa didn't talk to me about it much. I do know he and Noah needed a quick turnaround on their investment. Grandpa couldn't afford to go deeper into debt. He was a prospector, not a business manager."

The bus slid sideways with a whine of brakes. Sable caught her breath, her hand automatically closing around Murph's forearm. After an uncertain moment, they glided to a stop at the edge of the road. Sable's heart rate gradually grew steady again. Only another mile or so, and they would be off this bus. She would rather walk in the freezing rain than risk an accident on the cliffs up ahead.

"A prospector?" Murph asked softly as the bus driver eased her foot from the brake and inched the vehicle forward.

Sable gave Murph an irritated glance. She knew he was only trying to distract her from the road, but she'd overheard several comments around Freemont about Grandpa's questionable intentions when he agreed to go into debt yet again to purchase the Seitz mine.

"He didn't salt that mine," she said. "He and Noah were misinformed about the layout of the land when they purchased it. They should have checked it out more completely, but they didn't panic and plant ore in it later to save their own necks. That isn't what happened."

"Then it stands to reason that their third partner had some input."

"Their third partner was Otis Boswell. Our employer," she stressed. The man had plenty of money already.

"How well do you know him?" Murph asked.

Sable shrugged. "He and Grandpa knew each other for many years, and they went hunting together sometimes. You knew Boswell was from the Ozarks originally, didn't you?"

Murph shook his head.

"That's how Grandpa first went to work for Boswell Mining. Boswell had been a neighbor. Grandpa and Otis weren't the best of friends, but Grandpa never could turn down a hunting trip." Her voice caught, and once again she felt the sting of tears in her eyes. Ordinarily, she didn't cry this easily, but the events of the past week had left her feeling lost and vulnerable.

Murph put his hand over hers. Strangely, he reminded her of Noah — not that he looked like Noah in any way, but there was a sensitivity about him that appealed to her.

"Murph, why did you come with me?" Sable asked.

For a moment, he didn't reply.

"Not that I don't appreciate your help," she added. "It's just that I haven't met a lot of people who would risk their lives the way you have."

"Noah would have done it," he said quietly. He turned and looked at her, and those forest green eyes touched her with an almost tangible force, even in the dim overhead light. "I couldn't let you try to get here by yourself," he said. "What if you'd been followed?"

"I have a gun at Grandpa's," she whispered. "I'm not afraid to carry it."

His expression didn't change. "Carrying it and using it are two separate things entirely. Using it is hard." He held her gaze. "Hard."

She watched his face with growing interest. "Had some experience with that, have you?"

"Some. About a week after I came to work at the clinic, I heard you joke with the nurses about hunting. You complained about your grandpa killing innocent animals when he went hunting with his buddies."

"I was teasing."

"I knew that, but I also know you're an animal lover, so your statements had some grounding in truth. You're a doctor, Sable. How much more strongly would you feel about killing humans?"

"To protect myself or someone else against a killer, I could do it."

"Are you sure? What would you do if you held Noah's murderer at the business end of your gun barrel, and he appealed to your compassion by crying? Could you pull the trigger?"

She straightened and looked at him more closely. "You really do sound as if you've had some experience with this sort of thing." She waited for a moment, and when he didn't reply, she shrugged. "We're off the subject a little, aren't we? You've only known me a month and a half; why put yourself at risk for me?"

"You hold the key to Noah's death."

"So? You didn't know him any longer than you've known me." When he remained silent she leaned toward him. "Did you?"

He stared out the window, obviously avoiding her gaze. "Tell me, how is the house set up for security?"

She frowned at the obvious change of subject. "It isn't. We've never had any

56

reason to need security." She shrugged. "The house is built over the mouth of a cave. I guess you might say it could serve as an escape if necessary."

He didn't seem satisfied. "I'm curious about the evidence your grandpa gathered. Evidence about what? About whom?"

"Good question."

"Wouldn't he have left something like that in a safe deposit box?"

"Not necessarily. He came home often on weekends, and if he had papers or letters, he would've brought them with him."

"So they'd be in the house somewhere."

"Maybe. There's a safe upstairs in the attic, but I don't know if he used it." She didn't know everything about Grandpa. He could be close-mouthed about some subjects.

"Sounds like the safe would be the place to start," Murph said.

"It isn't as easy as it sounds. He was the only one with the combination. He was one of those people who didn't believe anything bad could ever happen to him." Dear, stubborn, impulsive Grandpa.

"Then it's up to us to discover what really happened," Murph said.

"Exactly." She put her hand on the seat in front of her to pull herself up. "We're almost there. I'd better go up to the front to tell the driver."

Murph pulled their coats from the overhead compartment and followed close behind Sable as she made her way to the front. Four rows along, a chubby man by the name of Perry something-or-other snored softly, his arm flung out in front of them. They slipped past quietly.

The bus lurched and Sable grabbed the seat beside her, earning a glare from the hard-muscled man who sat there. Simmons was his last name, if she remembered correctly.

With a quick apology, she passed on. She seldom traveled by bus, but when she did she was always amazed by the cross-section of humanity on display.

The driver glanced into the wide rear-view mirror as Sable and Murph approached. "It's getting worse. Better grab a spot and have a seat."

Sable took a place beside the gray-haired woman, directly behind the bus driver. "Jerri, you can drop us off just around the next curve, past the speed limit sign," she said.

The driver nodded.

Sable's seatmate flashed a smile and reached out a hand. "You're getting off at the old Kessinger Cave?"

"You know the place?" Sable asked.

"Who doesn't? I had a summer cabin in the Eagle Rock area." She held her hand out. "I'm Audry Hawkins, and —"

The bus lurched sideways in a long, icy glide. The darkened tree line swept toward their window in a smooth arc. There was a collective gasp from the passengers.

Sable stared past a sheath of icy limbs outside the window. She knew that beyond those limbs, there was nothing. The ground dropped steeply into darkness. She held her breath as the bus slid toward that darkness with almost casual ease.

Jerri's face was white in the rearview mirror as she wrestled the steering wheel and pumped the brake. The bus slowly straightened, once more parallel with the center line when it came to a stop.

Again, Sable thought about the cliffs ahead. The next time the bus lost traction, they might not be so fortunate.

"If there was another way to get where I'm going," Audry murmured softly, "I'd have taken it."

"Where are you headed?" Sable asked.

"My nephew is getting married down in Eureka Springs," Audry said. "Thorncrown Chapel. Why he chose the worst month of the year to get married I couldn't tell you,

59

except his bride wanted to be married on Valentine's Day."

The muscle-bound man with the steel gaze — Simmons — came forward along the aisle, carrying his duffel bag. "In case you hadn't noticed," he said to the bus driver in a gravel-barrel voice, "this road is dangerous. If they're getting off here, so am I."

"Agreed," came the high-pitched, nervous voice of the chubby man behind them. "I don't relish plunging to an early death in these hills. Couldn't we just park here until this blows over?"

Jerri shook her head. "Mr. Chadwick, do you really want to camp out here for two or three days? It could take that long before the road gets cleared. I have a responsibility to get my passengers to their destinations, and —"

"Alive," Simmons snapped. "Doesn't your license say anything about that?" He peered at the photo ID displayed prominently at the front of the bus, then muttered a curse and leaned closer. "That's not even your license up there. It isn't your picture. What's going on here?"

"Relax, the driver who was scheduled for this run called in sick," Jerri explained, "and there was a last-minute substitution."

"But you've driven this route before," Chadwick said.

"Not exactly," Jerri replied. "This is a new route for me."

"A new route?" Audry exclaimed. "You don't know the route?"

Perry Chadwick groaned. "I really don't want to hear this."

"So let me get this straight," Simmons growled. "It's raining Popsicles outside, we've got a road that bends like a pretzel, and a driver here who's driving it for the first time? I don't suppose you've noticed that the skating rink out there isn't open to the public? There hasn't been another car on this road since we left Cassville, unless you count the pickup truck in the ditch back there."

Sable cleared her throat and spoke into the tense silence. "Perhaps we could stop for awhile." She did not want to do this, but what choice did she have? What choice did any of them have? "I do know this road," she continued, "and I've seen a couple of cars after they plunged off the cliffs up ahead."

Jerri hesitated. "But we can't just pull over and stop, or we'll freeze. I guess we could try to make it back to that old schoolhouse we passed a couple of —"

"The drive to my —" Oh, brother, was this absolutely necessary? "The drive to my grandfather's house is a couple hundred feet ahead, before we reach the cliffs. You really don't want to tackle those cliffs on this ice." Sable hesitated, then gave in to the inevitable. "There's room at the house for everyone." This was crazy! But she couldn't allow the bus to continue on this road. She wouldn't be able to live with herself if five innocent people plunged off the side of a hill.

Innocent people? At least she hoped they were all innocent.

Chapter 4

Paul Murphy had long ago learned to cover his alarm with a look of calm detachment, but he struggled with it this time. It would be criminal, of course, to allow the bus to continue on this impossible road, but he had been counting the minutes until he and Sable could reach her grandfather's house alone, without the presence of others — any one of whom might be dangerous to them.

"Are you sure about this?" the driver asked Sable. "No telling how long we'll be stuck here if we stop now."

One look at Sable's face told Murph she was just as unhappy about the dilemma as he. On the other hand, he reminded himself, there was safety in numbers. If someone had truly overheard Noah's conversation with Sable, they would be coming from Freemont in search of that evidence.

But what was the likelihood that any of these particular passengers on this particular bus could be from Freemont?

Perry Chadwick cleared his throat. "I would prefer to stay in a house indefinitely over the possibility of plunging off a cliff to our deaths. I vote we stay."

"No voting to it," Simmons said smoothly. "It's all we can do."

Murph studied each man in turn. There was a likelihood he and Sable had been followed, if someone knew they were still alive and had taken the bus. In fact, these same people had all arrived at the Joplin bus station long after he and Sable. What better way to find the secluded Kessinger place, and the evidence stored there, than to follow Josiah Kessinger's granddaughter?

On the other hand, the men at the canal had seemed convinced that he and Sable had gone down with the car.

Audry reached forward and patted the driver's shoulder. "This highway is treacherous in bad weather, especially if you aren't familiar with it. I know it well. Now let's get to this house of yours, Sable, before the road collects more ice."

Sable gestured to the large mailbox spotlighted by the bus headlights. Beside it was a long, narrow gravel driveway that curved downhill between naked deciduous trees and green cedars. "You can pull the bus alongside the road, Jerri." She turned to

64

the others, who hovered near the front in silent tension. "We'll have to walk from the mailbox."

"Walk?" Chadwick's voice rose to a squeak, his triple chins jiggling in alarm as Jerri maneuvered the big vehicle forward. "How far?"

"A little over a quarter of a mile."

"Why can't we drive there?" the chubby man protested.

"The bus simply won't fit," Sable said in a voice Murph had often heard her use when dealing with a recalcitrant patient. "There's a cliff on one side that overhangs the drive, and the other side drops about two hundred feet into a rocky ravine."

Jerri parked the bus at the edge of the road. "Okay, folks, looks like we're on our own from here."

For a moment, everyone hesitated.

Simmons reached down for the duffel bag he had dropped to the floor in front of his feet. "That ice isn't melting, in case you hadn't noticed. Let's get this over with."

A muttered query reached them from the center of the bus. The brown-haired boy, who was about fifteen, poked his head over the back of a seat and peered at the others with sleepy brown eyes. "What's going on?" he asked. "Are we there already?"

"No, I'm sorry, Bryce." Jerri set the hand brake and unbuckled her seat belt. "We won't be there for awhile. Get your coat and umbrella, if you have one. We're going on a little walk."

"In the dark?" Bryce protested. "In the rain?"

"In the freezing rain," Chadwick stressed. "In the storm."

"That's right." Jerri scanned the tiny group, and her gaze fell on Murph. "Mr. Murphy, would you please check the overhead compartment in the back for umbrellas? I think we have a few that have been left by passengers. Does anyone have a flashlight?"

"Only my little one," Audry said. She pulled a penlight from her purse and showed it to the others. "Amazing what a little beam can do in the darkness. I wouldn't be without this thing."

"Better save it," Jerri said. "We might need it later. I have one here on the bus. Everybody gather up your things while I try to call dispatch."

Five minutes later, after Jerri had tried the radio and a cell phone to no avail, they knew they would be out of touch with the world in the static of these hills.

"We can try to make contact again when we get to the house," Sable said.

Perry Chadwick returned to the front with a long coat over his arm, pulling a hard-sided case with wheels and a telescoping handle. "I can't believe we're doing this; I can't walk on that ice. Did you see those limbs? The ice must be an inch thick. And how do you propose I carry my luggage?"

"Your complaints aren't helping," Jerri snapped. "I suggest you carry only the bare essentials, an overnight case if you must, but no more." She indicated his suitcase. "That's too much."

Chadwick scowled at her. "This goes where I go."

"Those wheels won't be any good to you on the uneven ground."

Chadwick arched a pale eyebrow, surprisingly resolute. Jerri shrugged and shook her head. She flicked off the bus lights and turned on her flashlight. "Sorry I don't have any more of these, folks. We'll have to stay close together." She pulled the door open to an invading wall of wind and ice.

Murph stepped out first, catching his breath as the rain pelted his face and neck, slapping softly against the hardening surface of the ground. He stomped into a pile of ice-coated leaves and was dismayed by how solid the ice was. He stomped again, breaking the ice and found a grip for his feet in the thickness of leaves beneath.

"Watch your footing," he told the others. "It's slick out here." Bracing himself against the bus, he turned to help Sable.

She hesitated before she took his hand, and he could see the tension in her eyes.

"Stay close," he said as she stepped down beside him.

"I will."

"Come on, let's keep it moving," Simmons snapped behind her.

Evading Murph's outstretched hand, the muscle-bound man with the gravel voice landed on the ground with surprising grace.

Chadwick came next. When Murph reached up to help him with his suitcase, he jerked it back. "I'll take it myself," he murmured, allowing Murph to steady him as he stepped down. "Delicate equipment."

One by one, they stepped from the bus and gathered in a huddle beneath a clump of cedar trees, which sheltered them from the worst of the rain as they opened umbrellas. Except for Jerri's flashlight, the frigid darkness was absolute.

Murph couldn't help comparing this pre-dawn experience to the one he and Sable had gone through last night. How much more would they have to endure?

Chadwick took an umbrella and braced himself with it as he lurched to Sable's side. "Are you sure we're at the right place? We could freeze to death out here."

"We're definitely at the right place," Audry assured him.

Sable turned to the older woman, curious.

Audry shrugged at her. "Everybody in these parts knows about the Kessinger Cave. Now, Mr. Chadwick, what was your first name again?"

"Perry. Not that it'll do us any good to be on a first-name basis if we turn into ice statues."

"Could we socialize later?" Simmons urged. "Let's go! Head 'em up, move 'em out, or whatever the hillbillies say around here. We're not waiting for spring."

"We should let Jerri lead the way with her flashlight," Sable warned. "There's a dangerous ledge a few hundred feet ahead."

As she scrambled for traction along the dark drive beside Murph, icy needles of rain stung her face, whipped by the wind beneath the protection of the umbrella. In spite of her earlier protests, she was thankful for his presence — especially now, with company.

It would take time to search the house for the evidence Grandpa had collected; she didn't need all the extra eyes watching her. At least with this storm, surely no one else could reach them here for awhile — maybe even a few days, depending on the weather.

She cast a sideways glance at Murph, whose footing seemed secure and steady, especially compared to Perry Chadwick. With the suitcase clutched in his arms, the overweight man stumbled and slid with every step. By the time they reached the cliffs, a couple of hundred feet from the highway, he was puffing and gasping for breath.

From here, the road dipped in a sharp decline, hugging the hillside in a hairpin curve, and exposing them to the ravine below.

A sudden gust of wind snaked across the road from that ravine, shocking Sable with a blast of cold sleet, attacking her umbrella, nearly jerking it from her grip. Audry cried out. Chadwick stumbled and fell to his knees.

Sable lost traction, and she instinctively reached for Murph's arm.

He caught her and steadied her. "Are you okay?"

"Yes, but it's getting worse. This ice is almost impossible, and the ravine —" She'd warned everyone about it, but they needed to be careful. "Everyone stay as close as possible to the hillside," she called to the others. "And take your time. You don't want to lose your footing now."

They had only walked a few more yards along the driveway when Perry Chadwick gave a startled grunt and stumbled against Jerri, knocking the flashlight from her grip. It clattered to the ground, and in a spiral of rotating rays, slid over the edge of the cliff into empty, black space. In the startled silence, the spatter of rain was so loud they didn't hear it hit bottom. The darkness rushed to engulf them.

"You idiot!"

"Oh, no, what are we going to —"

"Now calm down and stay put!" Jerri shouted from ahead of them. "Audry, where's your penlight? Looks like we're going to need it."

"Okay, but could someone please help me hold my umbrella for a moment?"

Murph released Sable and stepped backward just as someone else — Bryce? Chadwick? — cried out and fell.

In the blackness, the wind attacked Sable's umbrella again, wrenching it from her grasp. Then someone shoved her from the right. Hard.

Instinctively, she flung her arms out as her feet flew out from under her. She screamed as she fell, hitting the edge of the ice-packed drive hard on her left side. She continued to slide, her body gaining momentum down the side of the steepening slope toward the ravine.

She screamed again, grasping desperately for a tree, a bush, anything in the darkness that would stop her descent. Slick stones and spindly brush gouged her arms and legs. The rocks gave no support, and the brush uprooted in her grasp.

"Help me!" she cried as the ground steepened. She knew she was nearing the cliff's edge. "Help!"

"Sable!" Murph shouted.

"Help me!" She flung a hand out, groping blindly through the darkness.

Her body rammed against a boulder, knocking the breath from her lungs, stunning her for a few precious seconds as she felt herself tumble sideways like a lifeless mannequin. Her hand smacked against something, and she instinctively grabbed it. Her grip closed around the trunk of a sapling, halting her slide with a jolt just as her left foot kicked out into open air.

She tried to gain traction with her right foot, tried to dig the toes of her shoe into the earth to gain a foothold, but she could not climb up. She heard the scatter of rocks and debris tumble into the ravine.

"Sable!" Murph called down from above. "Grab something and hold on!"

"I . . . I am," she rasped. But she couldn't hold on much longer. She reached up with her left hand and tried to reinforce her grip, kicking frantically against the ground.

The sapling snapped. She screamed as she fell.

Chapter 5

Once again she struck something solid, landing hard on her back on a narrow ledge. Digging her fingers into the rocky earth, she paused to catch her breath.

She clung to the ledge and caught her breath. "I'm here," she tried to call, but her voice was barely more than a whisper. She cleared her throat and tried again.

"Murph? I'm here!" But for how long? The water-coated ice gave no traction. She couldn't even hold on; how could she climb back up to the others or prevent herself from plunging deeper into the ravine?

Sharp rocks dug into Sable's legs. "Murph, help me!"

"Hold on!" he yelled down to her. "I'm coming down."

"You'll fall and kill us both. Stay where you are!" she called. "There's rope at the house. If you could just get there and . . ." But how could she hold on that long? Her hands were already growing numb.

A small light flickered from above, and Audry called out, "Hang in there, honey,

74

we'll get you. How far down do you think you are, about fifteen feet?"

"At least." That meant she still had a long way to fall. She forced her thoughts from that possibility.

"Can you climb any distance at all?" Murph asked.

"No, it's too slick. It's solid ice down here."

She heard voices above her, a frightened blur of voices she couldn't understand. "What are you waiting for? Just bring me a rope!"

"We've got something that I think will work," Murph called down. "Hold on for another moment."

She was going to die. She could feel herself slipping, could almost feel the icy fingers of the darkness groping for her from the ravine below.

"Okay, now reach up, Sable," Murph called.

"What is it?"

"It's a rope . . . of sorts. Reach up, and I'll try to place it directly into your hands."

Balancing cautiously, she groped upward with her left hand and waited, terrified that the ledge would give way, terrified that the wind would whip her from her unsteady perch.

"Where is it?" she asked.

"It's not long enough," she heard Audry say. "How can we make it longer? Hurry, people, think, or she's going to fall!"

"Sable," Murph called down. "Can you try to climb just a little way?"

"That's crazy!" Sable shouted. "You try climbing on this ice!" But she felt along the icy hillside for any handhold. Her feet kept sliding, and she had to scramble for traction that wasn't there. She reached upward in desperation, scrabbling at ice-coated stubble and imbedded boulders. Thank goodness for Audry's penlight, or the darkness would have been complete.

"Hold the line steady," Murph told the others. "I'm going to use it to climb down to her."

"No!" she cried. To her amazement, her fingers discovered a dry patch of earth over her head, where the ice must have broken loose with a scattering of rocks. She dug into the soft mesh of roots and dirt, gained a handhold and pulled herself upward a few more inches.

Again she reached above her head, and this time her fingers caught the end of something dangling down from above. She stretched her arm and grasped the tip. It felt like leather. Was it a belt? "I've got it!" she shouted.

Murph called down to her, "Wrap it around your arm and let me pull you up."

"It isn't long enough. I can barely reach it." She tightened her grip and balanced on one foot as she kicked into a layer of ice to reach the dirt beneath. Miraculously, she gained a toehold and stepped up. Just then the ledge beneath her other foot crumbled. She grasped the belt with both hands and kicked again at the hillside in one more desperate attempt to gain traction. To her relief, she found another place where the ice hadn't accumulated so quickly.

She wrapped the leather around her arm, gripping it tightly in her hand, and held on, praying that the leather wouldn't break, that Murph and the others wouldn't drop her.

"Pull me up," she gasped, as her arms began to quiver from the ordeal. She could find no more soft earth, no more toeholds. Her arm quivered from the violent wrench she had suffered. All she could do was hold on as her shoulders protested in pain and the rocky cliff gouged at her legs and arms. Every second, she expected to lose her grip and go plunging to her death at the bottom of the ravine.

"Sable, you're getting close," Murph

called from directly above her. "Reach up and I'll grab your hand."

With help from Audry's light, Sable could make out the dark length of Murph's form as he reached down for her. She shoved against the slick trunk of a cedar with her foot and reached up to grab Murph's hand. Her foot slipped from the cedar, and she lost her grip. Dirt crumbled from beneath her other foot. She felt herself falling backward, and she cried out.

"Grab me!" she heard Murph call out to the others. Amazingly, his hands caught her arms, and he pulled her up against him. Over his shoulder, she could see Simmons, Bryce, and Jerri holding onto Murph.

With reassuring strength, and with the help of the others, he pulled her up over the edge of the road and into his arms. For a long moment she buried her face in the wet material of his coat front, digging her fingers into its softness, unable to let go as she gave in to panic at last.

"Sable, what happened?" he asked.

She clung to him until her breathing eased and the horror lost some of its sharpness. "I'll tell you about it later. Right now, let's get to the house."

★ ★ ★

Murph and Sable stepped onto the huge, sheltered front porch of the farmhouse. The others joined them quickly. Due to the ice, it had taken them three times as long to reach the house than it ordinarily would have.

"Home," Sable murmured, still breathing heavily from exertion. She looked up at Murph. "Something about this place soothes me."

"I thought we'd never make it," Perry Chadwick muttered. "How anyone could live at the back of —"

"Mr. Chadwick," Audry cut in, "if you don't mind, I've heard enough of your complaints to last me the weekend. Sable was kind enough to invite us to stay here, or we would still be up in that bus." The lady peered through one of the diamond-paned windows, then turned to Sable. "Honey, is someone at home? Looks like there's a light in there."

Sable and Murph glanced through the same window. The glow came from a fire in the fireplace, and it flickered in rich hues against the paneled walls.

"Maybe Mom didn't go to Randy's, after all." Sable hesitated, glancing quickly at Murph. "She might have been out when I called."

"Do you mind if we go on inside?" Chadwick said with a trace of sarcasm in his voice. "We'll find out soon enough who's here, and I'm getting pneumonia."

Murph tested the door. It swung open into the cozy warmth of a large, paneled living room, complete with a hearth and a mantel at least ten feet in length. He led the way inside, peering cautiously up the huge, curved staircase, studying a hallway that led toward the back of the house from the far right side of the room. Light glowed from the end of the short hallway. There was a closed door to their left, and another door stood ajar at the end of the hearth.

"Better come in and gather round the fire," Jerri advised the group. "We'll want to change into dry clothing as soon as possible."

"Now this is more like it." Perry placed his suitcase against the wall carefully, then rushed toward the fire that flickered and crackled from the stone hearth.

"Come on, folks," Jerri said. "Sidle up to the fireplace. Let's get these wet coats off."

There were soft exclamations of relief as the others gladly followed the driver's instructions. Murph stood back, observing, on sharp alert as Sable moved to stand beside him.

"I don't like this," he murmured under his breath.

"Let's find out who's here." Without removing her coat, Sable strolled toward the hallway. "Hello? Anybody home?" she called.

Murph quickly pulled off his coat and dropped it beside the others as he followed Sable. He wanted better access to his weapon in case he needed it.

The kitchen light was on, but the room was empty. Murph barely caught a glimpse of it before Sable pivoted past him and stepped into the family room across the hallway. In a very few minutes, he received an abbreviated tour of the huge house, following behind Sable as she switched on every light in every room, along the upstairs hallway, and even gave a cursory glance up the attic steps. They didn't find anyone.

He could almost feel Sable's increasing tension as she led the way back along the upstairs hallway to the staircase.

"Is there anyplace else they might be?" he asked.

"I haven't looked in the basement." She shivered and hugged herself. "Or the garage. It's cold up here."

"Why don't you let me check the basement and garage while you join the others at the fireplace. You've been through a lot, and we can't afford to have you sick."

"I'll be fine. I'm not —"

"Sable, be quiet and just listen to me for a change."

"We've got to find out who's here, before —"

He grasped her by the arm and stopped her before she could reach the stairway landing. She blinked up at him in amazement.

"What are you doing?"

He slid the soaked sleeve of her sweater up her arm and felt the goose bumps on her flesh. He felt a quiver run through her and noticed how cold her hands were.

"Stay right here," he said. Before she could protest, he opened the nearest bedroom door, grabbed an afghan from the end of the bed, stepped back into the hallway, and wrapped it around her shoulders. "You're going downstairs to the fireplace right now, and I'm going to complete the search."

To his surprise, she didn't protest as he led her down the stairs.

Sable held her numb hands toward the fire, sure she would never feel warm or safe again. She shivered beneath the folds of the afghan Paul Murphy had forced on her. At her directions, he was checking the garage for automobiles. She should have thought about that immediately when they arrived, but she'd been distracted by the cold . . . and by fear.

Perry leaned toward Jerri at the hearth, and Sable heard him mumble an apology for the accident with the flashlight.

Jerri forgave him with a pat on his broad, fleshy shoulder. "We're alive, that's what counts," she said, then pointed down at his leather-soled, black dress shoes. "Next time you travel out of the city, may I suggest a pair of lug-soled boots?"

Sable sighed with frustration. Was she panicking? Maybe the push had been an accident. Someone else could have lost his balance and shoved against her to stabilize himself. But somehow she would have expected such a person to at least say, "Excuse me for pushing you off the mountain."

No. Someone had pushed her.

"While we're waiting to discover the identity of our mystery host," Audry said, "why don't you put me to work gathering towels and blankets for everyone? The fire is nice, but we're going to need —"

The basement door at the end of the

hearth flew back suddenly, and a tall, dark-haired man stepped through the threshold. His heavy brows tipped in surprise at the sight of the small, bedraggled crowd huddling together around the fireplace.

"What on earth is —"

Sable recognized him immediately. "Craig!"

He jerked around and his brown eyes clouded with confusion. "Sable? What are you doing back? What are all these —"

"You might say we had a little . . . accident," Simmons murmured from the far end of the hearth.

Sable rushed forward and gave her friend a quick hug, suddenly overwhelmed by relief. She felt his surprise at such an affectionate welcome, especially since she'd just seen him at the funeral less than two days ago.

"So you're the culprit," she said. She couldn't tell him how relieved that made her. "What are you doing down from the mountain? Did you and my brothers decide to do a little cave exploring?"

"Not this time." He glanced at the rest of the group, and then at Murph, who was returning from his foray through the kitchen to check the garage.

Sable took Craig's arm and turned to the

others. "Meet our nearest neighbor, Craig Holt. We can probably thank him for the fire and the unlocked door." She caught Murph's suddenly intent look. "He's a family friend," she explained, turning back to Craig. "I tried calling here last night, but no one answered. I couldn't reach Peter, either."

"Weather got bad yesterday, so your mom drove to Eureka Springs to stay with Randy," Craig explained. "And there's a phone line down. But what are you doing back so soon?" He gestured toward the others. "It isn't the best of weather for a house party."

"They were passengers on our bus. The road got too bad to continue."

"Bus?" Craig said. "In this weather? Why would you take a bus when you —"

"I'll explain it all later," Sable assured him.

Craig shrugged. "Suits me. Your mom wanted me to keep an eye on things while she was gone. With the ice storm, I thought I'd just stay for a couple of days. No use trying to climb home from here, and I'm sure not going to try to drive the Jeep in that mess out there."

"So that's your Jeep in the garage?" Murph asked.

Craig nodded, giving Murph a silent once-over.

Audry stepped forward. "Is there room for us to stay here until the storm breaks up?"

"That's up to Sable," Craig said. "And it looks like she's already invited you." He gestured toward the broad staircase. "In fact, I was stoking the fire down in the wood furnace when I heard the floorboards squeaking up here. I'll just go open up the second floor bedrooms and bring down some towels. You all look a little wet. You walked from the highway?"

"You mean to tell us there's another way down here?" Simmons growled.

"Not on that ice," Craig said. "Unless you've got ice skates."

Audry cleared her throat. "Sable discovered that the hard —"

"Craig, why don't you get those towels?" Sable interrupted. "We can't afford to have everyone sick on us, not when we're unable to get out of here."

Craig shrugged, nodded, and took the steps two at a time and disappeared into the upstairs hallway.

Sable was glad she hadn't bothered to discard the old clothes she and her brothers had accumulated in the attic over the years. Many of the things would fit the guests. If the weather didn't let up, she would take them to the attic to rummage around through the stacks of boxes for extra clothing — it might keep them occupied for a few hours.

She thought about the old safe, also up in the attic, buried deep behind the antiques and near-antiques stored up there. Of course it was the logical place for Grandpa to conceal any evidence he might have brought back here. She would check it out as soon as possible, even though she had never known the combination for it. She had never paid much attention to it, except when she and her brothers had played up there as children, imagining the heavy old safe to be stuffed with stolen cash or gold pieces or treasure maps.

At this point, she could only hope it contained something more precious than any of those things — proof of Grandpa's innocence, if only they had the combination. It might also lead to the culprit who murdered Noah.

While Sable and Murph helped the others spread their wet things over the bricks of the raised hearth, Sable glanced instinctively toward Murph from time to time, as if to assure herself that he was still nearby. In the time he had worked at the clinic, she had found him to be kind to patients, detail oriented . . . and good looking. Nobody could deny his attractiveness — from the dark-lashed green eyes to the dark auburn hair to the broad shoulders. Patients and staff alike trusted him.

He was a naturally caring person, willing to help his colleagues without a need for personal credit. She'd also sensed something more about him, as if he weren't as open and uncomplicated as he seemed on first impression. Today, however, he represented solidity in a world of shifting foundations.

Sable pulled off her shoes and socks, rolled up the legs of her jeans, and sank her bare feet into the warmth of the deep carpet while she watched Murph interact with the others. When he turned toward her, she looked away. She had allowed herself to be attracted to the wrong kind of man a few months ago, and her poor choice had endangered her life. She still seemed to have little control where physical attraction was concerned, but this time would be different. She liked Murph, admired him, and right now she depended on his protection. She knew, however, that this kind of volatile situation could exaggerate emotions.

Audry readjusted her coat over the far corner of the hearth, inspected an antique brass planter containing a thick silk fern, then stepped to a "favorites" cabinet, featuring some of Grandma's antique figurines. "Some of these things are older than I am. Probably in better working order, too. Whoever decorated this place did a good job."

"Thank you," Sable said.

The older lady stepped to the display case that contained Grandpa's rock collection. "You did this? And the drapes, the paneling, those mirrors in the corner?"

"The paneling has been here as long as I can remember. My grandfather and mother and I decorated the house together last summer. I just finished the final touches over the Christmas holiday." Sable hesitated. "I supervised. Mom did the sewing, and Grandpa did the heavy stuff." She studied the fist-sized rocks in the case, turned to Audry, then frowned and looked back at the rocks. There was something about them. Something different . . .

Craig came back down the stairs with an armful of mismatched towels. "Come and get 'em," he invited.

Audry reached for a small hand towel and gave it to Sable. "Honey, I think you need to step closer to the fire. Your hair is still wet." She took Sable's arm and gently urged her forward. "Where is your grandfather now?"

"We . . . had his funeral this week."

Audry caught her breath in a quiet gasp and released Sable's arm. Her face paled, noticeable even in the dim flicker of the fire.

"Audry? Are you okay?"

For a moment, the woman didn't respond. She pressed her hands against her cheeks, closed her eyes, and took a slow, deep breath. "Forgive me. I . . . suppose the excitement must have upset me more than I thought."

Out of habit, Sable asked, "Do you feel weak? Are you having any kind of pain?"

Audry shook her head and opened her eyes. "I'll be fine. Don't worry about me." She sighed. "I'm so sorry to hear about your grandfather."

Murph stepped forward and placed a hand on Sable's shoulder. He squeezed gently. "Where can I find some blankets?"

"Back bedroom upstairs," Sable said. "Turn right at the top of the staircase, then left along the next hallway. There's a chest at the end of the bed."

Murph glanced down at her rolled-up

jeans and black wool sweater. "You still look wet. Did you leave any of your clothes here?"

"Yes, and there's more in the attic, plenty to go around." She gestured to the others. "Craig, would you show everyone where the extra clothes are? I'm going to change quickly and make something warm for us to drink to knock off the chill."

Those who had brought overnight cases with them went upstairs to change, while Craig led the others to the attic. Sable stepped into her mother's bedroom, which connected to the living room through a set of double doors left of the front entrance.

The bed was unmade, and as she pulled on a pair of dry slacks from her mother's closet, she caught sight of a faded, pea-green backpack tossed into the far corner of the room.

It was Craig's — she'd seen it many times when he, her brothers, and her grandfather had gone hunting together. For a brief moment she felt uncomfortable about anyone — even a family friend — moving into her mother's bedroom while she was away. It made sense, however, for Craig to stay in the room closest to the fire, and since Mom was gone, it shouldn't matter to Sable. After all, Craig had spent nearly as much time here as anyone else, hanging out with her brothers, listening to Grandpa's stories, exploring the Kessinger Cave.

She pulled on one of Mom's long-sleeved, blue silk blouses, far too lacy and frilly for Sable's taste, but it would have to do.

She reached for the telephone atop Mom's bedside stand. The line was dead, as Craig had told them. For a moment longer, however, she hesitated. Mom kept all her recent correspondence in the top drawer of this stand. What if there was something here?

The drawer was a disorganized mess, totally in character for Mom during times of crisis. Grandpa's death had hit her hard, as Sable had known it would. Sympathy cards were mixed with grocery receipts mixed with bills. Most of the unopened envelopes were most likely sympathy cards, but they could be anything. Sable's mother had never handled grief well, and she was prone to depression. When Dad died, Mom's meticulous world had collapsed for many months afterward, which was why they had moved in with Grandpa. Sable and her brothers had learned many years ago that they didn't talk about it when a loved one died.

This past week, Sable had attempted to explain to Mom the change of heart — the change of life — that Grandpa had experienced at Christmas when Noah Erwin had explained to them the true power of Christmas, and the faith by which Grandpa had lived the final few weeks of his life. On Christmas night, less than two months ago, Sable and Grandpa had become followers of Christ.

Mom had refused to listen. "If that gives you comfort, Sable, then you cling to that," she'd said gently. "I'll remember my father in my own way."

Grandpa's new faith did give Sable peace.

In the messy stack of Mom's correspondence, Sable found two clusters of pages from different letters, one from Randy and one from herself. Beneath these were some old grocery lists, a recent letter with Grandpa's Freemont return address — which Sable slid into the front pocket of her slacks — and a bank statement. She found nothing unusual, replaced everything else into the drawer and closed it.

If only she could open Grandpa's old safe. Why, oh why, hadn't he given anyone the combination? Dynamite couldn't blow that thing out of the concrete wall he'd built for it years ago.

The second drawer in Mom's bureau contained tax records that Sable had organized at Christmas. But on top of all that was a business envelope with Grandpa's characteristically flamboyant scrawl across the front, "If I should die before I wake . . ."

There was no address. Sable opened the envelope, took out a folded page, unfolded it, and then nearly dropped it. It was a letter to his family. She stared at the barely legible writing, and her eyes blurred with tears.

My Dear Family,

I'm not sure what words to use that will explain what I'm doing. I only hope that someday you will forgive and accept. It's been more than eleven years since Grandma died, and I've never looked back, never considered anything like this before.

By the time you get this letter, you will have heard the story. I'm sorry for the trouble this will cause you. I'm sorry I'll miss Sable's birthday party this year, because I know how she loves them. You'll have to combine the watch I gave you for Christmas as a birthday gift, as well, Sable. Don't try to take on my own guilt. I'm no

longer afraid of the truth. Don't worry,
I'm safe in the afterlife.

I now ask my partners to forgive me
for the fraud connected with our pur-
chase and attempted resale of the
mine back on the old Seitz place. To
our misfortune, the buyer checked the
mine more thoroughly than I had an-
ticipated and discovered what others
had overlooked. The walls were
salted with sphalerite and galena from
elsewhere. I must confess, and I
leave my guilt in the hands of Christ.

But still, there is so much more in-
volved here.

May God Help Me,
Josiah D. Kessinger

"Oh, Grandpa," she whispered, her voice
catching. "You did it? You really did?" She
sank onto her mother's bed, doubling over
with the pain that overwhelmed her.
"Grandpa, no," she moaned.

Grandpa, who had always been there for
her. Grandpa, whom she had admired and
loved, who had shared his heart and home
with her, with her whole family.

Grandpa . . .

This past week, she had comforted herself with the assurance that the Josiah

Kessinger she knew wouldn't do what Otis Boswell and the police had accused him of doing. She'd been so sure his name would be cleared in the end because of the integrity with which he'd lived.

Now where would her comfort come from?

She stuffed the note into the front pocket of her slacks. She couldn't think about it right now. She couldn't believe it!

She heard a squeak of floorboards just outside the room. She had pulled the latch that locked the ancient doors, of course, but the knob of the right door turned slowly.

She stiffened and held her breath.

Chapter 6

"Who's there?" she called sharply.

The knob stopped rattling, and the floor creaked again. Sable rushed to the door and jerked it open to find Craig Holt backing away.

"Sorry, Sable, I thought you'd be changing in your own bedroom upstairs."

"It's okay, no problem." She gave her heart a few seconds to find its normal rhythm again. "I'm just a little jumpy right now."

"Guess it was a little slick getting here. You okay? You don't look your best."

"Thanks," she said dryly. This was the Craig Holt she knew, who at the age of twenty-nine retained many of the boyish qualities her brothers had outgrown after marriage. Craig was still terminally shy around most women, he preferred hunting and fishing to anything else in life, and he was a diehard spelunker. A few years ago he had made a few awkward attempts to ask her out on a date. At the time she was too busy learning the complex intricacies of medicine to pay much attention.

"Where's your car?" he asked. "Why'd you take the bus?"

"The car's . . . I wrecked it."

"What! You wrecked that Camaro?" He made it sound like a personal affront. "When?"

"Last night."

"How bad?"

Sable shook her head at him. Typical. "Thanks, Craig, I'm fine, but I appreciate the concern."

"Sorry, but you're obviously okay."

"The Camaro's gone. It went into the canal down by Freemont. I'll tell you all about it later. Right now I think I'd better see to our guests."

"Oh, yeah, sure." Craig turned toward the front door. "Well, I think I'd better bring in some more wood for the furnace."

Sable shivered when he opened the outside door. She heard the hiss of the rain slapping on the icy ground. It would be light soon — the darkness was already lifting, though deep in this valley it would be hours before they saw the sun. Sable could only pray the clouds would lift and it would warm up quickly. A check of the thermometer gave the outside temperature at twenty-nine degrees . . . and the rain continued to fall.

The thicker the ice, the longer they would all be stuck here.

Simmons came down the stairs, his curly brown hair hanging in wet ringlets around his face. He wore an old, red plaid shirt that had once been a favorite of Sable's brother, Peter. Simmons's thick, muscular neck prevented him from closing the top button, but the shirt hung in folds around his midriff.

"Somebody get overheated?" he complained as he reached for the door to close it.

Just then Craig came barreling through with an armload of wood. "Oh, good," he said when he saw Simmons standing there. "You look like you could carry a few sticks of wood without much trouble. Want to bring in another armload or two?"

"Not a problem," Simmons replied, stepping outside.

As the two men worked, Sable went to the kitchen. Already she missed the peace that had always greeted her when she came home to the family farm. Tonight, home didn't offer the feeling of safety and seclusion she needed so desperately. She felt stranded. She was stranded. And vulnerable.

Her mind went back to the questions that had been nagging at her ever since she had fallen on the way to the house: Who had pushed her? Why would anyone do such a thing unless they had followed her and Murph from Freemont? And yet, it could have been an accident. Couldn't it?

The kitchen held the sweetest memories for her as she recalled the hours she and Grandpa had put into the renovation. From the smooth brick floor to the heavy, dark oak beams on the ceiling, she could feel his presence. Grandpa had carved the beams himself. He had always liked to work with his hands. There was a woodworking shop attached to the house, and he'd made good use of it.

The pain of loss filled her again. Grandpa. How she missed him, and how she ached to clear his name of the shame that had been attached to it. But was that even possible now?

She leaned against the work island in the middle of the large kitchen and noticed the dust that had accumulated on the copper utensils hanging above the breakfast bar. She marveled again, as she always did, at the beautifully inlaid counters that Grandpa had made. Through the dining room she could see the corner of the rustic table with split log benches, also hand-made by Grandpa. Everywhere, the reminders both saddened her and warmed her heart with memories.

There was another fireplace in a cozy family room across the hallway from the kitchen, but it lay cold and empty. The family was gone now; Sable, Peter, and Randy were involved in their own lives, and Mom lived alone in this huge house. How would she feel about staying here now?

Sable brushed her fingertips along the dark oak of a cabinet, then picked up a copper kettle and carried it to the twin sinks. Waxing nostalgic, she grasped the bright red handle of the old water pump and worked it up and down. A healthy stream of water splashed from the spout into the sink. She filled the kettle from the pump and carried it past the antique woodstove to the modern electric stove on the far wall. Both the pump and the woodstove came in handy during bad weather. The electricity in this old house wasn't always the most reliable.

After turning on the burner, Sable left the water to heat and went upstairs. She needed to at least make a cursory check of the attic and make sure the old safe was still terminally locked. Even if she couldn't get into it, no one else would be able to, either.

The long, L-shaped upstairs hallway glowed with the light of electric lamps in three of the small alcoves. Colorful oil lamps stood on polished wooden shelves at intervals on both sides of the paneled hall — ready for use in case of a power failure.

The house was well insulated, recessed into the hill behind it, which helped keep it warm in the winter and cool in the summer. Sable had fond memories of the tricks she'd played on her brothers when they were children. During games of hide-and-seek, she had discovered the benefits of climbing from the sewing room window on the second floor onto the cliff that was just inches from the window ledge. Then she'd scale the rocky crag up one floor, scamper over to the attic window, and climb back inside.

After the third or fourth time she'd tricked her brothers this way, Peter caught on, and he locked the windows, leaving her outside on the ledge. She had perched on that ledge for at least ten minutes, screaming at the top of her voice, until Grandpa heard her and let her in. Poor

Grandpa'd had his hands full when he was left to baby-sit three rowdy kids.

In addition to the sewing room, the second floor had four bedrooms and two bathrooms. The floor below had two more bedrooms and a bathroom. Enough space for plenty of people to stay without getting in each other's way too much, for which Sable was glad. She had always cherished her privacy.

She caught sight of Murph standing beside the dresser in her old bedroom at the end of the hall, perusing an old photograph album. He looked up when she entered and held the book up for her to see.

"I recognize Otis Boswell and your grandfather." He indicated the photo on the top right corner of the left page. "Who's this other man?"

She took the album from him. There was the familiar, beloved face of Grandpa in his old billed cap, grinning broadly as he held his rifle balanced across his shoulder. To his right stood Otis Boswell, at least six inches shorter and twice as broad. The third man was the tallest of the three, with black hair and a familiar, warm smile.

"That's Reuben Holt," she said. "Craig's father."

"Craig's father was also friends with Boswell?"

"Neighbors. I wouldn't call them friends, exactly. Grandpa and Boswell hunted on Reuben's property a few times, with Reuben's permission."

Murph's green eyes focused more intently on Sable. "So Craig is living out here in the middle of the Mark Twain National Forest by himself? A young man like him?"

"His parents, Reuben and Wanda, moved to Jefferson City a few months ago. Reuben is running for the state senate. Craig stayed on the farm, and he's all alone in a huge house, plus he owns a boat dock down by Eagle Rock."

"You know Craig pretty well?" Murph asked.

"Sure . . . at least I used to. Holts have always been Grandpa's closest neighbors, and Craig was good friends with both my brothers. It seems like he was always hanging around here."

"How well did Craig know your grandfather?"

"Very well."

"Did Craig know Boswell?"

"Yes, but the Holts — he and his folks — didn't seem to care much for Otis Boswell.

Murph, do you mind telling me why the questions? What are you thinking?"

"I'm just wondering if maybe the Holts might know something we don't know."

"About what?"

Murph took the album from her. "It's a gut instinct, maybe not significant, but if Josiah Kessinger didn't salt that mine, and Noah Erwin didn't salt it, it stands to reason their other partner did. That would be Boswell."

"Or it could have been salted before they purchased it," Sable said. "Maybe they were all duped." With a pang, she thought about the note in her pocket. Grandpa had condemned himself with his own words. Some people might say there was no reason now to even try to clear his name. But she would search for the evidence Grandpa had collected, anyway. She needed to find out who had killed Noah. She also needed to clear her own name, and if Grandpa truly was guilty — something about which she still wasn't convinced — she needed to know the extent of his guilt.

"I'll ask Craig what he knows," she said.

"Not tonight. I don't think we need to tell anyone about all this yet." Murph's expression softened. "Sorry, I don't want to worry you; I just opened the chest looking for blankets and found this photo album lying on top. We'd better get the blankets down to the others while they're still needed."

The pleasantly aromatic scent of cedar enveloped them as Murph helped Sable pull out two stacks of quilts and blankets.

Sable closed the chest, awash once more in her memories. "Grandpa made this chest for me years ago. I wanted him to make it out of cedar, and he wanted to work with oak. We argued about it for three days, until he gave in. After all, as I put it, if it was a gift for me, I should have my choice."

"So you inherited your strong will from your grandfather."

"You might say that." She inhaled the fragrance of cedar again. "So, Murph, you think Boswell could be a suspect?"

"All I know is that someone killed Noah, and someone tried to kill you, and no matter what else your grandfather might have been blamed for, he sure didn't do that."

"Us," she said. "They tried to kill us."

"You were their target last night, you heard them. But . . ." He hesitated, obviously reluctant to continue.

"But?" she prompted.

"Boswell spent some time questioning us in the clinic while you were gone this week."

"About what?"

"I don't know about the others, but he wanted to know if I'd noticed Josiah spending any time in the clinic with you, or if I'd seen you carrying any papers home with you after working hours."

"Papers from the clinic?" she exclaimed. "But that doesn't have anything to do with the Seitz mine."

"No, it doesn't."

She slid her hand into the front pocket of her slacks and touched the corner of the note, which she had found in Mom's drawer downstairs. "There's something else going on there, Murph. I know there is."

"Is that the loving granddaughter talking, or the logical mind of Doctor Sable Chamberlin?"

"Gut feeling. You have those, so can I. I know how it looks. I hate what happened to Noah, and that was another thing that convinced me that Grandpa didn't salt the mine. Noah was a friend — a good friend. He just wouldn't do something like that to Noah." Would he? She picked up on

Murph's uncharacteristic silence. "What else is on your mind?"

He didn't meet her gaze. "You know how worthless rumors can be."

Rumors again. That was one thing she hated about some small town mentalities. "Just tell me what you've heard. Let me decide for myself if it's true."

He shook his head. "I don't think it would do anyone any good."

She watched him, allowing her imagination, and the knowledge she had about the gossipy town of Freemont, guide her. She came up with a doozy. "I can guess, Murph. Is it possible they're saying the wreck that killed him was on purpose, that he did it to himself?" When Murph didn't reply, she added softly, "That it was suicide, because they caught him?"

"It doesn't do any good to think like that."

"But that's what they're saying." She swung away, disgusted. "Let me tell you something, Paul Murphy. I'll do all I can to uncover the truth about Grandpa's involvement with the mine, and if I find proof that he did salt that mine, I'll do anything it takes to see that the injured parties are compensated, even if I have to pay for it out of my own pocket. But listen to me on this: There's no way the Josiah Kessinger I knew would ever have given up and killed himself, and I knew him pretty well. No way he would do that. It wasn't in his nature, even less so since Christmas. That was when he became a believer in Christ, thanks to Noah's influence. That was when I became a believer, as well." She turned and looked back at him. "Grandpa was sold out. Dedicated."

There was a discernible softening of Murph's expression, a tenderness in his eyes. "Leave it to Noah," he murmured, his voice husky. He turned away abruptly and stepped to the window.

She followed him. "Murph?"

He cleared his throat, took a slow, deep breath and released it. "Looks like it's up to us to find what we need to find here."

She wanted to show him the note but couldn't bring herself to do it. Not yet. The sting of Grandpa's words was too fresh and too shocking.

Murph looked down at her, and his attention focused on the watch Sable wore around her neck. He reached out and touched the antique working of the metal. "Beautiful craftsmanship. You say it no longer runs?"

She shrugged. "I don't use it as a timepiece." She caught his look of curiosity. "Sentimental value. Grandpa carried it in his pocket for years."

"You loved him very much." It was an observation, not a question.

"He became my father after my own father died."

He glanced once again out the window at the predawn gray of the sky. "He did a great job."

"Thank you." She allowed the comfort of his words to seep into her heart.

"Since the two of you were so close, did he ever mention anything to you about his concerns in Freemont? Any hints about what he was doing, what evidence he was collecting?"

"Nothing. He was one of those tough guys who doesn't like their women and children to worry." *What else were you hiding from the women and children, Grandpa?*

He nodded. "I know the type. It runs in my family, too, but that means we have to start from scratch."

"Yes, and I think we're going to have to do it without letting the others know."

"Of course." Apparently, he caught some inflection in her voice, and he frowned at her.

"Murph, I didn't slip down that cliff tonight. I was pushed."

A pulse of adrenaline snapped through Murph like a horsewhip. "Pushed! Who —"

"I don't know."

"Why didn't you say something when it happened?"

"What good would it do? Ever since it happened I've tried to convince myself that I imagined it, that it was an accident, but what if —"

"— what if someone followed us?" Murph finished her sentence for her. He exhaled a long, slow, deliberate breath. "This changes things a little, doesn't it? I wish you'd told me sooner."

"How? In front of the guests? I haven't had a chance to tell you."

"They aren't guests, they're passengers from the same bus. We don't know who they really are." And right now he wanted to find out, and fast. "Maybe I'll have a talk with Jerri."

"Do you think she can keep her mouth shut? If someone did follow us, we can't afford to alert them to our suspicions."

Murph controlled his impatience with difficulty. "Whoever pushed you knows that you know."

Sable turned away, her blue eyes narrowing in thoughtful concentration. "I'm not even sure it was intentional. I keep hoping it wasn't."

"We can't take that chance." He felt an overpowering need to protect her, and, so far, he hadn't been doing a very good job.

"Well, we can't panic the whole house on a suspicion." Her chin jutted slightly forward in a characteristic display of stubbornness as she stared out the window. "I don't want to say anything about it yet."

"Then we'd better do some hard praying," Murph said.

She glanced at him over her shoulder, then nodded. "Murph, there's something I need to show you." She reached into her pocket. "You probably need to read this —"

"Hello! Knock, knock." Audry's brisk voice rang out from the doorway of the bedroom.

Murph recoiled in surprise, and Sable caught her breath in an audible gasp.

"Audry," Sable said, removing her hand from her pocket. "You startled me."

"Looks that way." Audry stepped through the doorway. "Sorry, honey. I wondered what was taking you so long. Need some help? Got something I can carry down for you? Here, let me have

112

some of those. Everyone is still chilled." She reached for some of the blankets and carried them out.

"You were saying?" Murph prompted, as Audry's footsteps faded.

"Later. I'll show it to you later." Sable picked up a stack of blankets and handed them to him. "If you would carry these downstairs, I'd appreciate it. I'm going to check the attic, then I'll be right down."

"Alone?"

"Why not? As long as the others are downstairs I'm perfectly safe."

He continued to hesitate.

She nudged him from the room. "Just go. I'll be down in a moment."

Chapter 7

Sable didn't feel as courageous as she'd pretended to be, but she took comfort in the fact that the house was full of people. She knew Murph would keep a close watch on the others to make sure they stayed downstairs.

She opened the squeaky attic door and glanced over her shoulder as she turned on the overhead fluorescent light. The hallway was deserted. Safe.

Quickly, she climbed the steep attic steps, grimacing at the familiar creak on the third step and again on the seventh and eighth. The overhead lights, installed less than a year ago, bathed the stacks of furniture and boxes, old lamps and mattresses, in a glow as bright as daylight. Grandpa had gotten a little carried away when he installed the fixtures, saying he'd gotten tired of all the gloom.

As she rushed between stacks of boxes as high as her waist and old pieces of furniture that loomed like sentries throughout the huge room, Sable silently thanked her grandfather for getting so carried away.

She found the big old safe at the far end of the attic, behind a hanging rack of old shirts and dresses. It was as ancient and heavy as the hills that surrounded this place. When she lived here, the family used to tease Grandpa that if this house ever burned to the ground or if a tornado ever struck, the safe would be the only thing still standing.

She checked the dial and jiggled the handle, just to satisfy herself that the safe was locked. When it predictably refused to budge, she redistributed the clothing on the rack to disguise the front of the safe, then gingerly made her way back down the attic steps, resisting the urge to start her search this morning. Right now she was so tired she didn't think she would recognize what she was looking for even if she had a map that led her to it.

In the living room, Perry Chadwick and Jerri moved among the others with mugs of steaming coffee and cocoa while Audry handed a blanket to Bryce. Murph was standing in the middle of the room, still holding a pile of blankets. When he saw Sable coming down the stairs, he allowed himself to relax. He raised an eyebrow in a silent inquiry, to which she gave an infinitesimal shake of her head. She'd found nothing.

"Special brew for our hostess," Perry said, his fleshy cheeks stretching in a grin as he handed Sable a mug of hot chocolate. "You probably saved our lives and nearly lost yours, so you get the last cinnamon stick we could find in the kitchen."

Audry took part of Murph's load. "No need for you to be running around taking care of the rest of us, Murph. We all might as well make ourselves useful." She shot an impatient look at Simmons, who was sprawled across the sofa, staring into the fire, apparently oblivious to the activity around him.

Murph ambled across the room, his whole mind and body on full alert as he studied Craig Holt's tall, lanky frame, which was bent over the fireplace. He glanced at Bryce, who was stacking logs onto the hearth, then looked at Simmons.

He turned again to Sable, who peered at the others through the steam rising from her mug. Her expression reflected his own uneasiness.

"Do you have a farm, Sable?" Bryce gestured toward a picture on the wall of the black Angus bull Peter and Randy had raised for a 4-H project when they were teenagers.

"Not anymore. Mom sold all the farm animals."

"All but the dog," Craig said. "I've been watching him." He glanced out the window at the gray, storming sky, then sat on the hearth beside the stack of logs. "Looks like we'll be here for awhile, but we can keep a teenager entertained. Sable's got an honest-to-goodness cave here, with ghosts to go with it."

Murph suppressed a smile at Craig's youthful exuberance — though he was nearly twice Bryce's age.

"Ghosts." Bryce's tone left no doubt about his disdain for the subject.

"Ask Sable," Craig said. "Her family lived with it for years."

Bryce looked at Sable, who took another sip of her chocolate and sat down beside Craig on the hearth — close beside him, though of course that made no difference to Murph . . . none at all. "He's talking about a story that accompanied the cave when my grandpa bought this place thirty years ago," Sable explained. "Two men moved here from New York in the early forties and bought the cave, intending to mine it for zinc and lead. Unfortunately for them, the man who sold it to them had convinced them it had rich deposits of ore."

"You mean they bought it without checking it out?" Bryce asked.

"No, they checked it and found galena and sphalerite, the lead and zinc ores, but later they discovered they'd been tricked. Someone had planted it in the cave. That's what they call 'salting a mine.'"

"How'd they do that?" Bryce asked.

Sable hesitated. "They probably used a shotgun to shoot it into the walls to make it look like it was imbedded."

"But when the men explored further," Craig said, obviously impatient to continue the story, "word got out that they'd discovered silver."

"Silver!" Bryce exclaimed.

"Craig, don't lead him on like that," Sable warned. "It was just a rumor."

"Maybe so," Craig said, "but rumors spread like fever, and somebody offered the partners an outrageous amount of money for the cave."

"Hey," Sable protested, "whose story is this?"

"Sorry." Craig didn't look at all repentant.

"Every tale about this cave is different, anyway," she said. "The two partners disappeared. Everybody just figured they'd gone back to New York for a visit, and nobody paid much attention, because this part of the country had a flood about that time, and the community was preoccupied with the rising rivers. . . ."

While Sable told the story, Murph surreptitiously studied each face in turn. Craig sat watching Sable with rapt attention, like a love-struck schoolboy . . . or maybe that was Murph's imagination.

"Neighbors searched for the men," Sable continued. "They even wrote to New York, and they received no reply."

Murph looked at Simmons, who hadn't moved from his seemingly comatose position on the far end of the sofa. Audry wandered around the room, looking at family pictures, studying figurines. Perry Chadwick had returned to the kitchen.

"One of the partners had a nephew," Sable continued, "who inherited the place after they were declared dead, and he sold it in the late fifties to a man who later sold it to my grandpa. The nephew, and the man he sold it to, both insisted the cave was haunted."

"Legend has it that the ghosts of the two men guard the treasure," Craig said, making his voice dramatically spooky.

"What legend?" Sable razzed him. "There's no legend."

Craig chuckled, ignoring her. "Sable's grandpa wasn't afraid. I don't think anything ever scared him. Besides, he figured it out. Both of the previous owners had had a cabin over the mouth of the cave, but they'd obviously never been around caves before. The barometer rises and falls in a cave just the way it does outside, creating a draft. That caused the door to open and close all by itself."

Bryce's shoulders slumped. "You mean that's all there is to it?"

"Sorry to be such a disappointment to you," Sable said dryly. "I've never seen anything haunting around here." She glanced quickly at Craig. "Or almost nothing," she said softly.

Craig gave her a barely perceptible nod, which Murph, feeling highly perceptive all of a sudden, noticed immediately.

"Can I explore the cave?" Bryce asked.

Sable hesitated. "Maybe we should wait and see if the weather improves in the next few hours. You may be able to finish your bus trip."

"But if not, can we go exploring?"

Again, Sable hesitated. Murph noticed Craig watching her closely.

"Maybe if we're stuck here long enough," she said.

"All right!"

"And if you want to study a map first," Craig said, "there's one up on the wall in the attic. Josiah did all the research and drew it up himself. It's pretty close to scale."

Jerri strolled into the room, her muscular arms crossed over her chest and her red hair spiked as if she'd been combing it with her fingers. "I just radioed in. Thanks for the use of your equipment, Sable. We've got to stay put for the time being."

"But for how long?" Audry asked. "My family will be so worried."

"No problem," Jerri assured her. "The dispatcher will contact everyone's destination point and pass on the information about where we are and our circumstances. Your families and friends will all know you're safe."

Perry sauntered in behind her, yawning and stretching like a plump cat. "I think I'll prepare for bed, if nobody minds."

Audry gulped the last of her hot chocolate. "Sounds good to me. Let me take some of these cups into the kitchen, and then I'm ready to turn in, too."

The others agreed, and Sable assigned

rooms to everyone. Because Craig was using Mom's bed, Sable gave the other downstairs bedroom to Bryce. The adults she settled upstairs.

"If you don't mind, Sable," Perry said, "I'll use the cot in the sewing room upstairs. I've been told I snore like a semi truck. It's the weight, you know." He patted his triple chins.

Murph agreed to share a room with Simmons, though he hated the thought of sleeping with the pistol gouging his ribs. To his dismay, the room had bunk beds. His six-foot-one-inch frame did not fit easily into a bunk.

A duffel bag sailed past his left elbow and landed on the lower bunk.

"First dibs," Simmons called. He flopped onto the mattress, shoes and all. "I hate heights. Mind turning off the light?"

The sound of footsteps and muffled voices upstairs diminished as Sable settled onto the plump, comfortable sofa in front of the living room fireplace. She allowed herself the peaceful luxury of distant memories. How often she had sat flanked by her brothers, staring into the undulating flames while Grandpa perched on the stone hearth across from them, his blue eyes sparkling with eager anticipation and just a hint of mischief. He could weave an exciting tale for them at the spur-of-the-moment when Mom had one of her headaches and the kids needed to be distracted for awhile, or when depression incapacitated her and she couldn't handle three rowdy children clamoring for attention. Grandpa was always there.

The stories he told the three of them were always fiction. At least, the ones he called stories were fiction. That way Sable could always tell if he was relating something that had really happened or letting his imagination spin a tale of adventure. He told the stories when the boys were here, but when she was there alone with him, they shared something better than fiction. They shared dreams. Grandpa's dream had always been to send his grandchildren to college.

He'd paid to see those dreams come true — had he paid with his reputation and his life in the end? For the first two years of pre-med, Sable had been awarded a scholarship to MU in Columbia. Unfortunately, in her third year she had received a D in organic chemistry — which two-thirds of the class had flunked — and lost her scholarship. Grandpa took out a loan for her final year and insisted on supporting her through medical school. With Peter and Randy both in school, as well, Grandpa somehow found the money to support them. Only later did Sable discover that the tuition money had come from his business partner, Otis Boswell.

She wished everyone had known the side of Grandpa she remembered best. Her brothers had always idolized him as a tough, masculine man, like the person Craig had described tonight. Maybe it was because she was his only granddaughter that he had allowed her to see the dreamer in him, the gentler side of his personality. He was there to share her tears when she was a teenager in need of a mother — and her mother had shut herself away in her bedroom.

Sable pulled out the letter she had stuffed into her pocket along with the confession note. Thrusting the note from her, she scanned the first two pages of the letter Grandpa had written to Mom, dated the twentieth of December. The last page caught her attention. "I have a surprise for you and the kids," he had written. Grandpa always had a surprise of some kind. "Not sure about it yet, but I know it's there. Don't want to ruin it." The remainder of the letter, written in his usual, flamboyant style, said nothing more about it.

Sable read through it again. What could he have been talking about? Maybe the Seitz mine. It made sense, didn't it? He'd been so sure they would sell it, and he would be out of debt for good. But that was no secret.

A quiet movement from the staircase startled her, and she turned to find Murph standing on the third step from the bottom. His auburn hair had dried, and he wore jeans that were too short for him. An old, faded blue turtleneck of Peter's peeped out from beneath a baggy, ragged denim hunting shirt that had belonged to Grandpa.

"Nice fashion statement," she teased. "That shirt must be at least twenty years old."

"Hey, I'm a paramedic, not a male model." He chuckled and shoved the sleeves of the shirt up to his elbows as he padded barefoot across the carpet to join her.

He sat down next to her and rested an arm across the back of the sofa. The weight and warmth of his body surrounded her with a special kind of assurance. "How are you holding up?" he asked.

"Part of me is so tired I want to crawl into my bed upstairs and sleep for a week. Another part tells me I may never sleep again."

"It was rough up on that cliff," he said quietly. "For a moment I was afraid we'd lost you."

"So was I. I was also afraid you'd try to come down for me, and that we'd both go plunging into the ravine. It would have killed us."

"Then we can thank Bryce for our rescue, because I was on my way down when he suggested fastening our belts together for a rope."

"That was Bryce's idea?"

He nodded. "Good thing Perry Chadwick has a big waist, too, because our rope barely reached as it was."

"Just barely."

He reached forward and gently touched a place on her chin.

She winced and drew back.

"Sorry," he said. "It's turning a pretty shade of purple. Did it happen when you fell?"

"It must have. It wasn't there last night."

"Do you have any medical supplies here in the house? The way things are going, we'll definitely need them."

She grinned. "Oh, do we ever have medical supplies. I have a treasure trove in my bedroom." She examined the scratches on his neck. "You could use some peroxide on those."

His green gaze warmed on her with gentle teasing. "Yes, boss."

"And some antibiotic."

"Will do." He reached down and touched some scratches on her hand. "Physician, heal thyself."

Sable knew she was reacting with pure emotion because of her exhausted mental state, but the touch of his hand, the feel of him beside her, and the safety of his arm along the back of the sofa made her want to snuggle close and never leave his side. And even though she knew it was the danger and fear talking, something inside told her he wouldn't mind her company.

They sat in weary silence for several moments. Then Murph caught sight of the letter she had placed on the arm of the sofa. "Is that from Josiah? Looks like his handwriting."

She picked up the pages. "How do you know what Grandpa's handwriting looks like?"

He took the letter from her and sat forward to read. "Hey, I knew Josiah. Look at that wild scrawl. Nobody wrote with as much flair as your grandpa." He fell silent as he deciphered the pages. Sable read over his shoulder.

When he finished, he sat back. "Sounds like he was up to something in December."

"What's that supposed to mean?" she asked, then instantly regretted her tone.

"Sorry, poor choice of words," Murph replied. "But it does look like he was excited about something. Do you remember if he said anything? Any hint about what the surprise might be? Did your mom or your brothers say anything?"

"Not that I recall. I'll talk to Craig about it tomorrow."

Murph hesitated. "Are you sure that's a good idea?"

"I've known him most of my life. His father is running for political office. If I can't trust him, who can I trust?"

He quirked an eyebrow at her and handed her the letter. "Better put this where nobody will find it, just in case. The way I see it, we're looking for hard evidence that could incriminate someone not only for the Seitz mine debacle and for Noah's death but also, possibly, for Josiah's death."

Sable digested this in silence. Then

slowly she said, "You mean you think . . ."

"I don't think Josiah would have caused his own death, even if he was guilty — which I'm not saying he was."

"You mean someone might have caused the accident?"

Murph nodded. "Any idea where, besides the safe, we might find something? Maybe he mailed a package or letter from Freemont."

"It isn't as if I'm into the cloak and dagger mentality," she said.

"We just need to be on the lookout for anything unusual. We've got to be cautious, examine everything without preconceived notions."

Sable thought about that for a moment. "Preconceived notions? So you're saying we can't allow personal feelings to become involved."

"Right. We can't dismiss evidence that might make Josiah look guilty, or accept too quickly evidence that might make him look innocent. We're not playing games here; our lives could be in danger."

"Don't you think I'm aware of that?" She stood up and paced across the room.

"I'm sorry, but I'm trying to be thorough." Murph stood up and approached her. He placed his hands on her shoulders.

His voice grew tender. "I can't forget that your life could depend on it. I don't want to hurt your feelings, but we can't take chances."

"Your life could be in danger, and if not for me, you wouldn't be in this mess," Sable said. "I've asked this before. Why did you come here with me?" She stepped over to the hearth and sat down on the flat, raised stonework, arms still crossed over her chest, her back to the fire.

He turned and sat once more on the sofa, then leaned forward. His eyes darkened. "Somebody killed Noah." There was a catch in his voice. Sable recognized the sound of grief. Again, she wondered what was behind it.

She recalled the events of the previous night and Murph's shock and horror when he discovered Noah was dead. Even later, when he talked about it, the emotion expressed in his voice and his words seemed to go deeper than a six-week friendship with the older man would have warranted.

"How long did you know him?" she asked slowly.

He was silent for so long she decided he wasn't going to reply.

"What is going on, Murph?" she asked. "What haven't you told me?"

He closed his eyes and leaned back. With a deep sigh, he rubbed his face with his hands, then looked at her again. "Noah was my uncle."

Chapter 8

The heat from the fire grew a little too warm, yet at the same time there seemed to be a sudden cold draft through the room as Sable struggled with the impact of Murph's words. "Oh . . . ," she breathed.

"One of the hardest things I ever did was leave his body like that," he said.

"Oh, Murph," she whispered. Suddenly, many inconsistencies made sense — the lingering traces of grief and horror she'd seen in his eyes and his insistence on coming here with her.

"But I don't understand," she said. "Why didn't you let anybody know you two were related when you first arrived at Freemont? All this secrecy . . . why?"

"Sable, please." He cocked his head in the direction of the bedroom where Craig was presumably asleep. "Keep your voice down. I can explain." He joined her on the raised hearth. "Noah called me in November when the position opened up at the clinic. He knew I was in between jobs because the ambulance service where I worked in Kansas went belly-up. He wanted me to do some investigating."

"Into what?"

"Into Boswell Mining. Noah had invested his life's savings into that Seitz property, and then he became concerned about some information he accidentally discovered when he was looking at an old copy of a title to the property — a different title."

"Different?"

Murph didn't meet her gaze. "According to the old title, there had previously been productive galena mines in a circumference around the Seitz land."

Sable's interest sharpened. She caught her breath. "Are you sure about that?"

"I checked, which was what Josiah, Noah, and Boswell should have done before they bought the mine. Why didn't they?"

Oh, Grandpa, what have you done? "If there was ore all around their property," she said, "that means the land in the center would probably have been barren." It was common knowledge among geologists.

"Exactly. The land had been misrepresented. Then Boswell gave an agent orders to sell. The agent misrepresented it, and the new prospector became suspicious and checked it out."

"But Grandpa took the blame."

"And he died. And so did my uncle."

"Do you think Boswell is next?" Sable asked.

"It's possible," Murph said slowly. "Noah told me about some things that have happened in Freemont recently. The mining accidents, shoddy safety standards . . . a couple of people have disappeared. If I were Boswell — and if I was innocent — I'd be surrounded by armed guards."

Sable leaned forward wearily and rested her elbows on her knees. It didn't make sense. If Grandpa accepted the guilt for the deal gone bad, why did he die? He would not commit suicide. And why was Noah dead?

Hesitantly, she reached for the note and unfolded it. "You need to be aware of this, Murph." She felt like a traitor to Grandpa, but if she didn't share this information and something happened to Murph because he didn't know all the facts, she would be guilty.

"What is it?" he asked, taking it from her.

"I found it in an unopened envelope in my mother's bedside stand." She closed her eyes, braced herself, and took a deep breath.

They read it together.

My Dear Family,

I'm not sure what words to use that will explain what I'm doing. I only hope that someday you will forgive and accept. It's been more than eleven years since Grandma died, and I've never looked back, never considered anything like this before.

By the time you get this letter, you will have heard the story. I'm sorry for the trouble this will cause you. I'm sorry I'll miss Sable's birthday party this year, because I know how she loves them. You'll have to combine the watch I gave you for Christmas as a birthday gift, as well, Sable. Don't try to take on my own guilt. I'm no longer afraid of the truth. Don't worry, I'm safe in the afterlife.

I now ask my partners to forgive me for the fraud connected with our purchase and attempted resale of the mine back on the old Seitz place. To our misfortune, the buyer checked the mine more thoroughly than I had anticipated and discovered what others had overlooked. The walls were salted with sphalerite and galena from elsewhere. I must confess, and I leave my guilt in the hands of Christ.

But still, there is so much more involved here.

May God Help Me,
Josiah D. Kessinger

Sable folded the note and put it in her pocket. As before, when she read the words the pain seeped past every barrier she attempted to erect. She knew it was Grandpa's writing, she knew his flamboyant style, which couldn't easily be forged. She just couldn't stand to consider the truth of his words — and the fact that it did indeed sound like a confession and a suicide note.

Grandpa, how could you?

Murph cleared his throat, leaned forward, and sighed. "What an awful blow this has been to you just before your birthday. When is it?"

"The day after Valentine's Day."

"Tuesday. How old? Or is it impolite to ask?"

She knew he was just trying to divert her attention, to ease some of her pain. She felt the tears burn her eyes, and she forced them back. "Thirty-one, going on seventy, the way I feel." She sat for a moment fingering Grandpa's other letter. "Listen to me and my self-pity party."

"You're allowed." Murph reached up and cupped her chin with his hand. "This has been a rough week for you."

Sable hated the tears! Hated them! And yet they were never far away. She straightened, frowned, and pulled the note out of her pocket and unfolded it again. "Tell me if you think this is emotion talking, but something about this doesn't ring true."

Murph leaned over her shoulder. "Why?"

"It isn't Grandpa's style. I mean, he's rambling about things that don't make sense, and his letters have always been logical and direct."

"You don't think the turmoil of his pending confession might have something to do with it?"

"He kept his head about things, especially in an emergency."

"Did he ever face this kind of scandal before?" Murph asked gently.

She studied the note a moment longer, then folded it and put it back in her pocket. "Never. Maybe I'm just trying too hard to excuse away these words. It's like a nightmare, and I keep expecting to wake up and discover he was playing a big practical joke on all of us."

"Your grandfather influenced your life in many ways, Sable, and he still does. Something you've got to remember, though, is that the Josiah Kessinger who died in that wreck was a new man, a different person. If I were to make a guess, I think the guilt he felt about what he'd done could have been what drew him to Christ in the first place."

"And so I'm supposed to be happy about what he did?" She regretted the bitterness that crept into her voice.

"No, you can't be happy about what he did, but God has forgiven him. You will need to do the same."

"Just like that? He devastates the whole family, and I should just say, 'Oh, no big deal. Don't worry about it'?"

"None of us is without guilt, Sable. Your grandpa's already been forgiven by the One who matters most."

Murph's words, spoken with quiet sincerity, didn't ease her pain. "I never thought I'd be ashamed of being Josiah Kessinger's granddaughter."

Murph was silent for a moment, then he said, "Never be ashamed of who you are. You might have inherited your grandpa's impulsive nature, too." He grinned, in an obvious attempt intended to distract her again. "Along with a strong dose of independence and hardheadedness."

She allowed the diversion this time. She sighed and willed away the oppressive pain. "That impulsive nature may have saved our lives last night."

"True. I wonder who those goons reported to."

"So do I."

They fell silent for a moment, staring into the flames as if some message might come to them from the crackle of fire or the spiral of smoke that drifted lazily upward. Sable didn't want to think about what might have happened if Murph hadn't insisted on coming to Missouri with her. Would she still be alive? If he hadn't been out there on that cliff tonight when she fell . . . when she was pushed?

Something thumped against the front storm door with a startling impact. Sable lunged to the side and grabbed the fireplace poker. Murph leaped to his feet and pivoted, placing himself between Sable and the door.

The thump came again . . . then a familiar scratching on the screen. Sable lowered the poker as she remembered to breathe. "It's Dillon," she said, weak with relief. She stepped around Murph and rushed to the front door.

The big, furry head of a drenched German shepherd shoved inside as soon as Sable opened the door. He barked, jumping up to splash her around the waist with his drenched paws. His tongue flicked out and caught her across the mouth before she could pull away. She laughed, hugging him in spite of the water, in spite of the smell of wet dog. He thumped his tail against the paneled wall.

"That's enough, Dillon," she said, pushing him down. "Remember your manners."

Murph stepped forward. Dillon saw him and froze. His lips drew back in a challenging display of sharp, white fangs. His wet hackles sprang up as a low growl rumbled from his throat.

Murph eyed the dog with cautious admiration.

"No, Dillon," Sable ordered. "It's okay. He's a friend." She rested her hand on his head. "Friend."

Dillon relaxed. His fangs disappeared, and he looked up at her with trusting eyes. She couldn't prevent a smile of pride as she straightened to look at Murph. "Sorry about that. He's very protective."

"He needs to be." Murph remained in place. "Is he going to bite me if I try to pet him?"

"Not now. He knows what the word *friend* means." She reached for one of the clean towels Audry had stacked beside the door earlier. She unfolded it and knelt in front of the dog. "Feet, Dillon. You know the routine."

Dillon sat and raised his left front foot, then his right one, for Sable to pat dry. When she finished them he stood at quiet attention and allowed her to work on his back feet and coat. By the time she was finished, the towel was soaking wet, and Murph and Dillon had bonded while Murph petted him and talked with him softly.

At Sable's command, Dillon stretched out in front of the fire with his head on his paws, his honey-brown eyes occasionally flicking toward Sable as she and Murph returned to the sofa.

"Impressive," Murph said. "He's beautiful. Does he understand everything you say?"

"Sometimes it seems like he does."

"How long have you had him?"

"Grandpa got him for Peter and Randy after I started university, but he and I have always had a special friendship."

"Obviously."

"He seems to know what I'm thinking

most of the time. He can sense my moods. Sometimes he's an embarrassing barometer of the way I feel about guests in the house." She fell silent. Sometimes Dillon showed better insight about people than she did.

"Noah told me you have a way with animals," Murph said.

"I like them. I guess they can tell."

He leaned forward and stroked Dillon's fur, then turned and looked at Sable over his shoulder with a grin. "You have a way with me," he said softly. "Does that mean you like me?"

"Of course I like you," she said dryly. "You're handy in car wrecks and ice storms."

He chuckled and sat back, and for a few moments they were content to listen to the crackle of the fire and the hiss and slap of the rain outside.

"You said you were between jobs when you came to Freemont," Sable said at last. "What are your plans after you get out of this . . . mess?"

"*If* we get out?"

"I thought we were supposed to be thinking positive," Sable said.

"Sorry."

"You didn't answer my question."

"I liked working in the clinic setting, although I realize there aren't a lot of clinics that hire paramedics," Murph said. "But I also like the adrenaline rush of the ambulance or emergency department. How about you? What do you plan to do?"

"Solo practice . . . somewhere around here, if I can build one."

"I doubt you'd have a problem."

"I want to do just what Grandpa and I talked about when we sat in front of the fire this way years ago. I want to be a country doc who knows all the patients she passes on the street, knows their kids' names, their parents' names, and recognizes half her patient load at the ball game on Friday nights."

"Football lover?"

"High school basketball," she said.

Murph turned to look at her, and the firelight gave a smoky glow to the strong outline of his face, bathing his hair with red-gold highlights. "Could the ambulance service here use another paramedic? Or maybe you could use an office assistant. I make a mean pot of coffee, and I can even type forty words a minute."

"We'd go broke."

"Don't sell yourself short." He paused. "Don't sell me short, either. You've lived

143

here for how long? Since you were six-teen?"

"I lived here two years before I left for college. Not enough time for people to know me well."

"But everyone knows your grandfather . . . knew him. I come from a rural community, myself. For the most part, they're under-served by the medical profession."

Sable yawned. "I wouldn't count on building a practice around here quickly."

"Now who's the pessimist? Tell me about your grandmother," Murph said. "How old were you when she died?"

"Don't take this wrong, but aren't you sleepy?" Sable asked. "Don't you think it would be a good idea to get some rest?"

"You can go on up if you want. I think I'll sit here for awhile and wait for the sun to show itself."

"Standing guard?"

"Something like that."

"You could crash here on the sofa if you want."

Murph grimaced at her. "Poor word choice."

"Sorry. Okay, about Grandma. She ran a restaurant in Eureka Springs, which is about a thirty-minute drive from here. She was a great cook, and a good business manager. She was a good grandma, too, when she could spare the time for us." Sable hesitated. "She died of cancer when I was eleven. Actually, the cancer was the beginning of Grandpa's financial problems. When he retired from his job, he thought he was set for life, but there was a glitch with his insurance coverage. Someone made a mistake, and Grandma's name wasn't included on the policy. He had to borrow the money to pay Grandma's medical bills."

Murph stroked Dillon absently. "And your father died five years later?"

Sable nodded.

"I'm sorry," Murph said. "That had to be difficult for your family."

"I think it made us closer. Mom didn't handle it well, but our moving here was the best thing in the world for Grandpa. At least, that's what he always told me."

"I'm sure he meant it."

She nodded, taking another surreptitious look at him in the growing light of morning as it crept through the front window in a cloud of pearl gray.

When Murph first came to work at the clinic, her initial impression of him had been one of humor. He'd been laughing at something one of the nurses had said. The fine, attractive laugh lines attested to his quick grin. Sable knew from his employee file that he was thirty-three. His thick, dark brows showed a serious side that balanced out his nature.

"Now that I know you're Noah's nephew," she said, "I don't understand how I missed the family resemblance. It's in the eyes . . . and in your broad shoulders, and . . . you're a Christian?" she asked softly.

"That's right, I am."

"There was something I wanted to ask Noah before he died, but I never had the nerve."

Murph leaned forward, elbows on knees, with his hands clasped together. "Ask me whatever you want, Sable. I'll try to answer — not that I'm exactly a genius."

"Have you ever lost someone close to you? I mean, besides Noah? Someone who was not a believer?"

He nodded in understanding. "My grandfather."

Sable reached for Dillon and buried her fingers deeply in his drying fur. Maybe she should stop while she was ahead. Maybe she didn't want to ask this question and hear his answer.

"It was about four years ago," Murph

said quietly. "It hit me especially hard because I was on the ambulance crew that transported him to the hospital, where they pronounced him DOA."

"That had to be painful."

"Very."

"I don't like thinking about it," she said.

"Then don't."

"It was something Grandpa and I talked about. One of the hurdles of faith for me was accepting the concept of heaven and hell, and wondering if I'd be separated from my loved ones for eternity."

"You trust Him with your eternity, trust Him with your loved ones. You can't know the condition of another person's heart at the time of death."

She digested that for a moment in silence, her mind fogging with overwhelming thoughts from too many directions. Combined with sleep deprivation, it was too much. She needed to go to bed.

Murph watched Sable's face reflect the light of the flickering fire, watched her eyelids droop, saw her shoulders slump forward.

"You'd better go upstairs before you collapse," he said.

Her eyes fluttered open, and she straightened her slender shoulders. "You, too."

"And if we have been followed?"

"Dillon will sleep outside my room. He always does."

"Are you afraid someone will try to check out the attic while we're asleep?" Murph asked.

"Not with Dillon standing guard."

"Do you have a sleeping bag? I could post myself outside your room, at the door," Murph suggested, watching for her reaction.

Sable blinked, and a tinge of color touched her cheeks. As Noah had told him, Sable Chamberlin had spent the past few years studying to be the best doctor she could be, which meant she had very little social experience, particularly with the opposite sex.

According to Noah, she'd had a bad dating experience not too long ago, but he hadn't gone into detail about that. All he'd seemed interested in talking about was the wonders of Sable Chamberlin.

"I didn't mean to embarrass you," Murph said. "I just want to make sure you're protected."

Dillon raised his head and yawned, then stretched luxuriously before licking Murph's hand and closing his eyes once more.

"Okay, I get the message," Murph told

the dog. "I don't suppose it would be possible for me to go through Josiah's things in the attic while everyone else is asleep."

Sable groaned and stretched her arms out in front of her. "Maybe later this morning, after we've both had a nap. Be realistic, Murph, you need sleep as badly as anyone else."

"When this morning?" Murph asked.

She got up, stifling a yawn. "Right after brunch. Sleep first."

Murph stood with her. Dillon stirred briefly, then settled back with a contented growl as the warmth of the hearth beckoned. Firelight undulated against the heavy oak paneling of the room as Sable turned toward the fire.

Murph couldn't stop looking at her. She was a pretty woman, with delicate features, finely arched black brows, and thickly lashed eyes. He knew her appearance misled patients to think of her as fragile. She wasn't. He knew that from experience. This morning she was watchful, quieter than usual. That didn't stop his growing attraction to her, even under the circumstances . . . perhaps because of the circumstances.

Slowly his gaze caressed her soft, very feminine face, the high cheekbones, the firm, defiant chin, the delicately arched brow.

Without thought, he moved to touch her, then hesitated and dropped his hand. What was he doing?

Sable turned around and smiled at him with wise-innocent eyes.

Her smile faltered, and she glanced toward the stairs. "You *are* going to nap?"

He nodded. "Be careful. Lock your door."

"I will." She returned his gaze for a moment, and he saw the fear that still lurked there. She turned away. "Good night."

Murph watched her as she went up, her bare feet silent on the carpeted steps. The black ringlets of her hair formed a halo around her shoulders from the soft lighting in the second floor hallway. Maybe it was the storm or the late night or the excitement of the past week, but something about her affected him with increasing impact. After she disappeared from view, his last image of her lingered. If only he could do something to ease the fear that haunted her eyes. If only he could be sure he was capable of protecting her. He wasn't even sure he could protect himself.

He stepped over to the fire to throw on another log. Dillon still dozed, and Murph touched the soft, fire-warmed fur on the dog's neck. He closed the tempered glass doors of the fireplace, then stepped outside to check the weather. Wind and rain met him like a glacier wall, limbs crashed in the gray distance — the ice was overloading the branches already. He stepped back inside and closed the door. The ice glaze must be at least an inch thick by now. Worry tautened the muscles in his back and shoulders. They were trapped inside prison bars of ice, solid as steel.

The lamp by the window flickered out as he crossed the living room. The electric lines must be down. That wouldn't be a problem. He'd seen plenty of oil lamps upstairs, a hefty supply of batteries on the basement landing, and a wood furnace in the basement. Later today they would see about chopping some more wood.

"Come on, Dillon," he called softly. "Upstairs. You need to keep an eye on Sable."

The dog stretched to his feet from his comfortable perch by the fire and followed Murph up the stairs in the meager light of a stormy morning.

After seeing Dillon to Sable's door, Murph stepped into the bedroom he was sharing with Simmons. He did not want to sleep, but he needed rest.

The moment he stepped through the door, he saw Simmons's outline in the gloom.

"Who is it?" Simmons snapped, sitting up.

"Your roomie. Paul Murphy."

"Where've you been?" the man grumbled.

"Downstairs watching the fire. Sorry if I disturbed you." Murph wished he could get out of these clothes and get comfortable, but that didn't look like a possibility for the near future. He noticed Simmons did not lie back down but braced himself up on one elbow, watchful, alert.

"You headed somewhere in particular?" Murph asked.

"No, I just hopped on the bus for a joyride," Simmons snapped. "What do you think?"

"So where are you headed?" Murph kept his voice conversational, blaming the man's irritability on fatigue.

"Home to Fayetteville," Simmons said at last. "My mother's dying in the hospital there, and my sisters called me yesterday to tell me to hurry." Simmons still sounded resentful, almost belligerent, and Murph wondered if he was telling the truth. Then he felt ashamed for wondering.

"I'm sorry to hear that," Murph said. "Maybe this ice will clear up and we can get you on your way before long."

"And you?" Simmons asked. "Seems you and our hostess are friendly enough. Could be you were hoping for a lot less company."

There was no missing that insinuation. "Perhaps more to the point, we were hoping for *different* company," Murph snapped as he climbed onto the top bunk.

He was immediately contrite as his own words echoed in his head, but when Simmons didn't reply, he remained silent, as well. He lay on his side facing the room. He could find out more later, but Sable was right, he couldn't go without sleep. He hated going to bed with a gun strapped to his chest, but he couldn't afford to leave it lying around. Maybe later this morning he could find a good hiding place for it.

He allowed himself to relax into the pillow and reached upward for his real source of strength. *Lord, You brought me here. I know You did. Now please guide me, guide Sable, and heal us both from the pain we've suffered. Help our faith to grow strong, and show us how to depend on You alone. . . .*

He was still afraid to sleep. He couldn't afford to . . . but his eyes felt as if he'd been in a desert windstorm . . . and even this dinky bunk bed felt so good . . . so seductively comfortable. Maybe he could shut his eyes for a few minutes. He could hear Simmons's breathing, hypnotic and deep, its rhythm keeping perfect cadence . . . like a metronome, ticking off the seconds, blending with the whisper of the rain outside. . . .

Chapter 9

A low rumble of thunder burst from the darkness and reverberated through Murph's chest, jolting him awake. He smacked his forehead against the head-board of the bed. His legs were cramped, reminding him of his surroundings. He was in an upper bunk . . . with a Detonics Pocket 9 pistol strapped to his chest so tightly it felt as if it had embedded into his flesh.

He'd fallen asleep in a room with a man he didn't trust.

At least the pain reassured him that the small gun remained in place. He reached up to make sure he was still covered, and his fingers encountered the cotton fabric of the shirt he'd rummaged from a box of old clothing in the attic last night. Ragged as it was, it was the only piece of clothing he'd been able to find that fit him loosely enough to conceal the body-hugging holster and pistol.

The rumble came again, and he sat up in bed, listening. It wasn't Simmons snoring

— no sound came from the lower bunk. It couldn't be thunder, because outside the window an invisible sun had turned the shrouded sky from pale gray to brilliant blue. The storm had passed.

Yes! Maybe the thaw would come soon.

The rumble metamorphosed into the familiar cadence of a dog's growl. Dillon must be out in the hallway intimidating the guests. With a rush of relief, Murph tossed back the warm blankets and climbed down from the top bunk, taking note as he did so that Simmons was already gone — and that the room was cold.

Shivering, Murph opened the bedroom door to find Sable's big German shepherd standing guard three doors down along the unlit hallway. Sable's room. The dog whirled around with a snarl when Murph stepped out.

"Quiet, boy."

Dillon fell silent and his pointed ears relaxed as soon as he recognized Murph.

"What is it? Do you need to go outside?"

Dillon whined and wagged his tail, then trotted over and thrust his wet nose into the palm of Murph's right hand.

"Okay, but let me get my shoes and socks on first. I don't have as much fur on my feet as you do." With Dillon shadowing his steps, Murph returned to the bedroom to see if his socks had dried overnight. They hadn't. He should have spread them out in front of the fire before he went to bed, but he'd had other things on his mind. He could remain barefoot a little longer this morning, though; he had no intention of going outside.

With shoes and socks in hand, he stepped over to the uncurtained window and looked out. The winter scene washed him with a chill of foreboding. Eighteen-inch icicles clung to the eaves of the house like sharpened spears. The dim shapes of crystal trees and rock cliffs seemed to hover over the valley in a supernatural glow. This hollow in the forest was one of those places depicted in Ozark postcards, all hills and valleys at sharp angles, and this morning every inch of it was coated with ice. He could see no safe way out.

Dillon growled again.

"I'm coming." He trailed downstairs after the dog, who showed no interest in the front door, but instead waited patiently for his new human friend to spread his socks on the hearth.

Unfortunately, there wasn't enough heat to do much good. A few live coals continued to glow amid the ashes, but their warmth didn't reach far. The temperature in the house must have dropped overnight into the low sixties, maybe lower. Murph pushed aside the glass fire screen and rebuilt the fire with wood from a rack beside the hearth. Soon the rekindled flames shot their warmth out into the room.

Meanwhile, Dillon's interest was drawn to the basement door at the far left of the long fireplace. He sniffed, pawed at the door, then whined and looked up. Murph felt a prickling of tension.

"What is it, boy?"

With a growl deep in his chest, Dillon scratched the dark wood of the door.

"Okay, I guess I could let you have a look." As soon as Murph opened the door the dog leaped down the narrow steps with a growl of warning that increased in intensity as he disappeared into the darkness. Murph took a flashlight from the shelf at the head of the stairway and followed. He found Dillon hovering at the far end of the twenty-by-thirty foot concrete basement, his pointed nose working overtime at a short doorway about three feet square. The door stood open. Past that was the gaping, rocky mouth of the cave.

For a moment, Murph forgot his tension. His love of caves had always attracted him to the state of Missouri, because it boasted more caves than any other state. Since his early teens he'd done his best to become acquainted with all their hidden wonders. The story about this one fascinated him. More important right now, it seemed to hold a powerful fascination for Dillon.

Murph looked down at his bare feet, then back toward the entrance. He should have put on his shoes and socks, wet or not, but what would it hurt to step in and look around for a moment? If nothing suspicious turned up, he could send Dillon back to Sable's door for further guard duty.

From here, the cave floor appeared fairly smooth, and his feet were tough. He could wipe them on the mat at the top of the stairway when he came back out.

He dropped to his knees and crawled through the cave mouth, shining his light ahead of him. A sound of shuffling reached him from the darkness, but before he could stop his movements and identify what it was and where it came from, Dillon barked.

Murph turned to find the dog still hovering, with hackles raised, at the cave mouth. He had apparently decided not to enter. "Coward," Murph muttered under his breath. He waited for a moment, listening for the sound again, but it didn't come. Bats, maybe? Was there another entrance to this cave? Sable had said the cave would provide an escape if necessary.

A few feet farther, he discovered that the narrow mouth opened into a wide cavern. He stood up and paused, inhaling the moist scent of the air while he played his light over gray and white formations. He shone the beam of the light along the obvious path that generations of footprints had scoured into the solid, limestone floor. The trail wandered past a regal column of white to a ledge of stone about twenty feet ahead. This natural wall blocked his view and cast the cavern into patches of shadow that danced in an undulating, macabre rhythm with the movement of the beam over uneven surfaces.

The sound came again, a shuffling noise . . . like the cautious tread of a human foot, and it seemed to come from behind the rock ledge.

"Hello?" Murph called, his hand tightening on the flashlight.

No answer.

"Sable? It's me. Murph. Are you back there?"

Silence.

He stared into the shadows for a moment. He knew the sounds of bats and falling rocks and rushing water. He also knew the sound of stealth. He reached beneath his shirt and slid the holster into position, then crept forward, ducking past a long stalactite as he kept his eyes focused at the far range of his beam. The shadows fell away, and he stepped past the rock ledge, his tension mounting, his senses tingling as the cavern opened once more into another room.

Dillon's bark from close behind him scattered his concentration. Someone darted out from the shadows of the ledge and stumbled against a boulder. Dillon snarled and raced past.

The sudden glare of a flashlight split the darkness. "No! Get back!" The broad-shouldered figure straightened, and he aimed his light at the charging dog. "Get away!" The man's eyes were wide with fear.

"Down, Dillon! No!" Murph called.

The dog slid to a stop several feet from the man, but his deep growl continued to rumble with threat.

"Back! Get him away from me." Panic edged Simmons's voice.

"He's not touching you." Murph kept his

voice steady and conversational, hoping his own tense suspicion was not obvious. "Out for a morning stroll?"

Simmons kept his light trained on the dog. "You got a problem with that? We can't go outside. I'm not staying cooped up in that house with a bunch of strangers."

"Did you ask permission to come down here?"

There was an annoyed silence. "Did you?"

"Not unless you count Dillon's invitation." Something about Murph's casual attitude must have reached Dillon. Though his attention stayed fixed on Simmons, he stopped growling.

Murph leaned against a boulder and aimed his light around the walls of the cave. "Interesting place, isn't it?"

"Weird place," Simmons muttered. Murph took special note of the muscles that bulged beneath the long-sleeved T-shirt the man had found in the attic last night. He had a very muscular build — he was probably about 5'10" — about three inches shorter than Murph — and weighed about 190, without an ounce of fat.

"I love caves," Murph said, aiming his light at some soda straw formations to the far right of the room. "It amazes me what

God can do even in the absence of light."

Simmons gave a sudden snort. "You like to hang out with bats and talk about God?"

"If you don't like bats, what are you doing down here?" Murph asked.

The other man didn't answer right away but lowered the beam of his light toward a black pit that gaped at them from Murph's right, about ten feet from the passage. "This place is dangerous."

"You have to be careful," Murph agreed.

Simmons ambled over toward the pit and stopped at the rocky edge to peer down into it. "I bet this is what happened to those two guys Craig and Sable were talking about last night." He kicked a loose stone, which echoed as it fell into the pit. "Probably fell off a ledge, or maybe into a pit like this one. Maybe drowned in a pool, you think?" He reached up and brushed his fingers through his curly brown hair, which had frizzed from the moisture in the cave. "Think any of the passages lead anywhere? You know, like to civilization?"

"No one mentioned it last night, but it wouldn't hurt to ask. I know you're in a hurry to get to the hospital."

Again, Simmons didn't reply but continued to wave the flashlight around the edges of the pit, then up the side of the cave wall.

"I hope your mother's doing okay." Murph held the man's gaze for a moment, fighting another prickling of discomfort. Perhaps it was the paleness of the man's eyes, or the way he tended to look past a guy, instead of meeting his gaze straight on. "I'm sorry you're stuck here, when you need to get out so badly."

Simmons nodded. His flashlight lowered. He gave a long, deep sigh. "Now I wish I'd driven instead of taking that bus."

"Maybe we'll have a quick thaw, and you can be on your way." Nothing would make Murph happier.

"Whatever." Simmons sounded suddenly bored with the subject. "Guess we could go prospecting while we wait."

"Prospecting?"

"You know, for silver. Think there's anything to that story they told?"

"I doubt it. Missouri isn't known for silver mines, only galena and sphalerite — the ores for lead and zinc. You know how easily stories get started."

"Wouldn't hurt to look, though, would it?"

Murph shrugged. "With permission from the owners."

Simmons raked the sides of the cave with his light once more, then ambled away from the side of the pit. "Like I said, this place is weird." He stepped over some scattered rocks and onto the path.

As he drew closer to Murph, Dillon stiffened and snarled.

Simmons aimed his light into Dillon's eyes.

The growl deepened with menace.

"Dillon, get back," Murph said.

The dog obeyed.

"I hate dogs," Simmons muttered as he walked past them toward the entrance, perhaps thirty feet away.

Murph could imagine that most animals returned the sentiment. Simmons was not exactly a likable man, but then people reacted differently to stressful situations.

Dillon whined and looked up at Murph, then lowered his head, perked his ears, and followed Simmons from the cave.

Murph nodded. "Good boy. Go to Sable. I'll be out in a moment." But first, he wanted to check out the pit that had so impressed Simmons. He shone his light around the glistening walls and ceiling, stepping cautiously along the rock-strewn limestone. The pit seemed to swallow light, except for the jagged boulders around the rim, like teeth in the mouth of a giant serpent. They splayed the beams of Murph's flashlight into undulating shapes across the white wall behind them.

The mouth they surrounded was big enough to swallow a small car. Murph's light barely touched the rocky bottom, about thirty-five feet below. Instinctively, he took a step backward. Anyone who fell down there could be badly injured — even killed.

"Better be careful over there," came a man's voice from behind him.

He spun around. The beam of his light illuminated Craig Holt's frowning features from the cave entrance.

"Thanks for the warning." Murph picked his way carefully back toward the path. "That's quite a drop."

Craig shoved his hands into the pockets of his jeans and strolled forward. "Sometimes there's water in it, depending on the weather. If there's a drought, it's dry, if it's rainy or we have a lot of snow melt, it's filled with water."

"You grew up with the Chamberlins?" Murph asked.

Craig nodded. "My sister and I used to come over all the time when we were younger. Even before Sable and her brothers moved in with Josiah, they came here a lot. About every time they came over, they'd call my sister and me, and we'd come over and help them get into mischief."

"You weren't afraid of the ghosts?"

Craig laughed. It had a tight sound, as if he wasn't as relaxed as he wanted Murph to think. "Even when we were children we knew that was just a story. Rumors spread easily across these Ozark hills."

Murph peered back along the passage into the inky darkness. "Is the cave very large?"

"We thought it was. We could spend a whole day down here and not cover it all. It's changed with the drought we've had the past few years. Some of the pools have dried up. Actually, from the house to the end of the main passage it's about a half mile, but there are other passages that branch away from the main one." He glanced down at Murph's bare feet, and his straight, black brows drew together. "Plan to do some exploring?"

"Not at the moment, but later, maybe. Spelunking is a favorite hobby of mine."

Craig turned and strolled ahead of Murph toward the house. "It used to be one of Sable's, too. I guess she told you all about what happened here a few months ago."

"I heard she was attacked by some crazy guy, but I didn't get the details. I didn't realize it happened in this cave."

Craig shrugged. "Guess she wants to forget all about it. She can tell you more if she wants you to know." There was a thread of challenge in his voice — was that jealousy?

Murph suppressed a smile as Craig knelt down to crawl out of the cave. "I'll be sure to ask."

Chapter 10

An echo of splashing water reverberated against the black cave walls, punctuated by a glittering swirl of light against over-hanging stalactites. The glow from Sable's lantern did little more than shape columns and stalagmites into lurking monsters.

One shadow undulated across the rocky path in rhythm with her footsteps, and she gasped, freezing in place for a tortured moment as she raised the lantern higher. The shadow dissipated. Another illusion.

Even though Sable knew these forma-tions were inanimate limestone, unable to break away from their stone foundations, she couldn't suppress the sense of fore-boding that held her in its grip as she crept forward again.

A rattle of rock shivered toward her from somewhere in the darkness ahead, but this time she didn't stop. Obviously, it was an-other illusion. She wanted out of here.

The rattle echoed again. She continued forward, picking her way carefully over a scrabbling of loose stones.

She sidestepped a boulder, raising her lantern high to locate the cave entrance. The shadows of formations danced, but when she stood still one pool of darkness continued to move.

She gasped, stepping backward. Her heel caught on a ledge as a scream exploded from her throat, but it was instantly absorbed by the heavy, white mist that surrounded her. Silence.

The formation took the shape of a man, who lunged forward with a look of dark anticipation on his furious face. "Who do you think you are, Sable Chamberlin?" His voice curdled through the moist air and ricocheted along the passage. "I'll kill you!"

He reached out for her and she scrambled away, uttering a cry that froze in her throat. She whirled and plunged into the wall of fog behind her. The light from the lantern reflected back at her in a confusing array that served only to blind her and advertise her location. She switched it off and felt her way along the well-used passage, depending on her memory.

"I had your life in my hands!" he shouted, close behind her. "I could have killed you! You're —"

Sable threw the lantern at him and ran.

His shout of pain and rage thundered around her, becoming one with the darkness. She heard a familiar splash of water to the left ahead of her — the whirlpool — and she darted toward it, automatically hearing in her mind all of Grandpa's dire warnings about venturing too close.

She hesitated, imagining, for a short second, the pool sucking her down.

A footfall echoed directly behind her, and she tried to scramble away.

Too late.

Hard, meaty hands came down on her shoulders, wrenching her backward with painful force. Once more she tried to cry out, but she choked on the desperate plea for help, as if those powerful hands squeezed her throat. Rough fingers pulled at her with such violence she lost her balance. She fell against the clay floor, striking the back of her head.

She felt no pain.

He hovered over her, his breath coming in ragged rasps through the black silk of the cavern. She kicked up with her right foot and made contact. He bellowed as she rolled aside and scrambled to her feet, coming too close to the burbling water.

A vicious hand shoved her forward.

Again, she tried to scream as she lunged away from the whirling, icy pool.

No voice!

A heavy work boot rammed her in the back, breaking her balance. She felt herself slip down an incline of gravel, heard the small stones splash into the bubbling water, felt the startling coldness as her left leg thrust beneath the surface, and then she fell, headlong, into the storm of the whirlpool.

The vortex claimed her, draining the oxygen from her body. Her chest begged for air, and her body grew numb.

The blackness disappeared as Sable awoke, gasping for breath, fighting the blankets that twisted around her. For a few seconds, she couldn't move.

Dream. It was a dream.

The nightmare.

She gripped the comforter to her chest and waited while her heart slowed its beating and the terrifying images slithered back into the netherworld of darkness.

They would find her again. They always did.

In spite of the cold air in the room, perspiration dripped from her face and neck in tiny rivulets that had become so commonplace in the past six months that she barely noticed. She took another cleansing, calming breath, and looked around the room. Brilliant light filtered in from the window, highlighting the pile of discarded clothes she had worn last night. From the front pocket of her slacks, a corner of the folded letters peeped out at her. Grandpa's letters.

Her thoughts had often lingered on Grandpa in the few days since his death, and now her mind wrestled with the words he had written to Mom in December. What was the surprise he had hinted about? Why did he have to be so obscure?

The frustration nipped at her like the freezing raindrops that had trapped them here last night. She was no closer to answers, and she needed them fast.

She glanced out the window beside her bed and saw a bright sky punctured by the bare, frozen branches of the old maple tree that grew beside the house. To her dismay, a bank of clouds formed a dark wall on the western horizon, and even as she watched they crept closer. She checked her watch. It was nearly noon. From past experience she knew that, far from aiding their cause at the moment — their need to see the bus passengers on their way — the sun's rays would melt the ice just enough to make travel impossible for the next few hours.

Maybe the temperature would rise above thirty-two and stay there. They needed a quick thaw.

Her bruised flesh protested when she climbed from bed, and memories of last night surged into reality once more. She couldn't dismiss the past eighteen hours as a nightmare that could be discounted with the morning light. This nightmare had followed her.

"Oh, Lord, protect me," she whispered into the silence of the room on her way to the window. "Protect all of us here. Give me Your wisdom and strength, and give me faith. I'm so scared, God. If that's a sin, please forgive me, and give me Your peace."

She was new to the habit of prayer, but she had a feeling that she was about to get very accustomed to the concept in the days to come — she had to depend on God, because she'd never felt so helpless and lost in her life.

As she stepped between the filmy blue curtains at the window, the frozen, ice-white landscape that greeted her from below brought a gasp of amazement. Sparkling crystals coated even the slenderest of branches, making the trees look like those blown-glass figurines she had always admired in the gift shops in Branson.

She studied the trees more closely and remembered the sound that had echoed through her dreams earlier — the crack of gunfire, the crashing of glass, like the impact of a war zone. Now she realized that it hadn't just been in her dreams. Even the strongest oaks hadn't escaped the destruction from the weight of accumulated ice. Branches of all sizes littered the forest floor — this would prove to be another danger if they ventured outside.

As she gazed in wonder at the side-by-side beauty and destruction, a board creaked somewhere in the hallway. She stiffened and turned from the window and heard another creak, which she recognized. The sound came from the attic steps. This old house and its squeaky floorboards and settling timber . . . over the years she had learned the distinctive sound of each one.

She pulled on a worn terry robe and rushed to the door. When she turned the knob, the lock clicked, and she grimaced. By the time she stepped out into the hallway, all she saw was a slender, gray-haired female form disappear around the corner. Audry.

Something soft and fuzzy brushed

against her leg, and she bit back a cry of alarm. A cold nose pressed against her hand. Dillon.

She knelt and hugged him, accepting a kiss from his wet tongue. She pressed her forehead against his for a few seconds. "So you and Audry are friends, huh? I hope you didn't allow anybody else past this door."

Dillon whined and tried to lick her face again.

"No, go on downstairs. I'm up and on the alert again."

Closing the door again, Sable frowned, trying to convince herself that the older woman was most likely in search of another change of clothing.

After dressing in old faded jeans and a warm, sky blue turtleneck that fit a little too snugly after eight years, Sable drew the blankets and the pink rosebud comforter over her pillows. She resisted a twinge of guilt about the luxury that surrounded her in this bedroom. She'd slept in her comfortable, polished oak four poster, while Murph and Simmons were squeezed into bunks. Poor Murph probably had a crick in his neck and cramps in his legs this morning. And Perry Chadwick had drawn the rickety, uncomfortable cot in the sewing room. She hadn't heard a crash in the middle of the night, so maybe the cot was sturdier than it looked.

She surveyed the room she had decorated last summer. The pale pink walls and silver-gray Berber carpeting were a perfect setting for the carved bureau, the antique lantern, and the washstand. Grandpa had laughed at her when she purchased the washstand at an antique sale, but a few weeks later, after she'd stripped and stained the wood, she had seen the admiration in his eyes. She would probably be using it today. With no electricity, their only source of water was the hand pump downstairs in the kitchen. She didn't relish breaking that news to her guests. Someone would be kept busy carrying water upstairs.

She also needed to inform them as soon as possible about the outdoor privy. Although the indoor toilets were custom designed to hold water for extra flushes in case of temporary power outages, the water wouldn't last long. That would be an enticement for the "guests" to leave at the earliest opportunity.

She went downstairs and spotted Dillon lying in front of the fire with his head up, ears perked forward on alert, a self-appointed sentinel. As soon as he caught sight of Sable, he leapt up to greet her once more. She sank down onto the bottom step and wrapped her arms around him, burying her hands in his warm fur while deftly avoiding his tongue.

"I'm glad you're on patrol," she murmured against his neck. "Keep a close eye on this group, okay? You're my best protector."

She glanced across the room at the fire that glowed in the hearth and stood up to move closer to its warmth when she heard muffled footsteps from the open basement door.

She stiffened, and her fingers dug more deeply into Dillon's ruff. She hated the fear that made her heart beat faster and her muscles tense as the steps drew closer. But Dillon didn't bark. He didn't even react to the sound. He must have recognized the footsteps, or he had seen who went down.

Craig Holt came through the threshold, his thick, black hair tousled, a streak of black soot on his chin, apparently from stoking the wood furnace downstairs. Sable untangled her hand from Dillon's fur and allowed herself an audible sigh.

Craig tensed visibly at the sound. His

shoulders relaxed when he saw her. "What's the matter, sleepyhead? You look like you should've stayed in bed a couple more hours."

"And good morning to you," she said with a hint of the sarcasm that was traditional between them when they were growing up.

He grinned. "Yeah, sure, morning. It's almost noon, though." He waved his arm to indicate the empty room. "Didn't you bring anybody else down with you?"

"Not yet."

"Looks like we've got a bunch of lazybones on our hands. Who's fixing breakfast? I'm starved."

Sable shook her head sadly. "Almost thirty and still looking for someone else to fix your breakfast."

"Don't tell me your cooking hasn't improved," Craig teased.

"Not much. Is there any food left in the freezer from the funeral dinner?"

"Some. Your mom took a couple of casseroles with her to Randy's, and she sent the fried chicken home with Peter. She gave me the roast."

"It's at your house, I guess," she said.

He shrugged. "I didn't plan to move in down here."

"Great. What are we going to feed everybody?"

He shook his head and stuffed his hands into his pockets. "Well, if we're desperate, I guess I could try —"

"No, that's okay," she said a little too sharply. "I'll go in and figure something out. The last time you tried to cook you started a grease fire."

He shrugged. "Sorry, I was just trying to help. You're a little cranky today. Didn't you sleep well? I thought I heard someone bumping around up there earlier this morning."

"I didn't do any bumping around. I tried to be as quiet as possible so I wouldn't disturb everyone. What did you hear?"

"Oh, don't worry, it didn't disturb me, I just recognized the squeaky attic floorboards."

"Attic?"

He reached down and gave Dillon a quick scratch on the ears as he passed. "Yeah, I thought you were going to wait until later to dig out more clothes."

"But I didn't go to the —"

"By the way, I fired up the wood furnace in the basement. It'll be warmer now, but we'll run out of fuel faster. Fortunately, there are plenty of limbs for the choosing outside. I'm going to draft some help chopping after breakfast — if we get any breakfast." He gave her a sidelong glance, then stepped into his room and closed the door before she could reply.

Typical.

Before she could follow him and ask about the noises in the attic, the sound of footsteps on the basement stairs startled her once more. She turned back to find Paul Murphy wiping his feet on the mat at the threshold — his bare feet. She couldn't help staring.

"Size twelve," he said, grinning at her. "Good morning."

"Craig has reminded me it's almost noon. I think he's expecting someone to fix breakfast."

"Can't he cook?"

"Not if I can catch him at it before he does any damage."

Murph gestured toward a pair of socks spread out on the hearth, with his shoes beside them. "Sorry about the laundry in the middle of the living room. They didn't dry overnight." He finished wiping his feet and stepped across the threshold.

Sable still hadn't become accustomed to seeing this attractive man dressed in anything other than scrubs. She also hadn't grown accustomed to her own instinctive response, the quickened pulse, the warmth of attraction — and the concern that she looked like an unmade bed.

"Is something wrong?" he asked.

She realized, with a flush of embarrassment, that she was staring. "No. I'm fine. Really." She gestured toward his bare feet. "We need to find you some dry socks."

"Maybe after breakfast."

Oh, yeah. Breakfast. Maybe she could put off the moment of truth a little longer. "Does it take two men to tend the furnace?"

"Craig found me in the cave, so I decided to learn how the furnace worked while I was down there."

"You went spelunking with bare feet?" Sable exclaimed dryly. "Now that's what I call macho. No compliment intended."

He nodded, and his grin widened, revealing white, even teeth. "None taken. I found the cave door open this morning, and since Dillon dragged me down there, I went in to see what was going on."

Sable gave Dillon a final pat and turned reluctantly toward the kitchen. "I'm surprised Craig didn't take Dillon down with him when he went."

"Craig wasn't down there when we first

entered the cave. Simmons was."

Sable stopped abruptly and turned. "Simmons was down there?"

"Yes. In the dark."

She looked up the stairs, lowered her voice, and leaned closer to Murph. "Why?"

"My guess was he didn't want to be seen."

"By whom?"

Murph spread his arms. "Good question. I'm surprised Dillon didn't awaken the entire household with his commotion."

"Sound doesn't carry well from the cave into the house. Murph, I didn't give anyone permission to go wandering around in the cave."

"You didn't give me permission, either, but I agree it feels uncomfortable."

"I'll be glad when the weather clears," she grumbled.

"If Simmons is telling the truth, I imagine he'll be glad, as well. His mother is near death in Fayetteville."

"Oh." Sable felt a sudden pang of conscience. She needed to have more compassion. "That would be hard."

"Yes," Murph said slowly, "especially when he got on the wrong bus."

Sable stared into his suddenly somber green eyes. "Our bus wasn't going to Fayetteville."

Murph glanced in the direction of the kitchen. "You said something about breakfast?"

"Yes . . . breakfast." She turned once again toward the kitchen. "You think Simmons lied?"

"I'm not sure what I think right now. But you may want to avoid being alone with him."

"What about you? You're staying in the same room with him."

Murph followed Sable into the kitchen, the tread of his bare feet silent on the brick floor. "I'm bigger than you." He nodded toward the woodstove. "Do you know how to cook on that thing?"

"That depends on what you call cooking. If you mean the act of placing different foods together in a palatable form, all of us could starve while we're waiting for the weather to clear. For breakfast, I'm good at cereal and milk, and I can scramble eggs, although half the time I end up throwing them out. Cooking's never been my favorite subject. I nearly flunked home economics in high school."

"That's okay, as long as you passed your science and math classes."

"Now math and science I can handle," she said. Her eyes were drawn once again

184

to Murph's bare feet. Now that she was standing closer to him, she could see a few smudges of dirt on the tops and sides. "How far back in the cave did you go?"

"Not too far," Murph replied, following her gaze down to his feet. "Just back to the first ledge, where that pit is. I'd imagine you know that cave pretty well."

"Yeah, I've logged a lot of hours down there, exploring passages."

To her surprise, Murph gave her a quizzical look. "Spent much time down there in the past year or so?"

Why was he looking at her like that? "Some."

"Craig hinted about something that happened to you last summer."

"Craig has a big mouth. He told you about Jim?"

"No, he hinted. He said he would let you tell me about it if you wanted to."

She heard the question in Murph's voice. "He had no right to say anything about it at all." She marched to the kitchen sink.

"So Jim was the name of the crazy guy who attacked you?"

"I thought you said Craig didn't tell you about it."

"He didn't. I heard a few things in

Freemont, but not much. Noah told me what he knew, but apparently you and your grandpa weren't too forthcoming about that incident."

"Never mind." She wasn't in the mood to dredge up old, painful history on top of everything else that was happening. "Maybe I'll tell you more sometime. Have you been outside this morning?"

"Not yet, and I don't plan to spend a lot of time out there. I heard several crashes after I got up."

His willingness to change the subject impressed her. "So did I. I bet the ice is two inches thick on the ground." She took a clean pitcher from a cabinet above the sink and placed it beneath the spout of the manual water pump.

"The icicles on the eaves of the house could pass for javelins." Murph grasped the wooden handle and pumped it up and down. When water trickled from the spout, his eyes widened like those of a child with a new toy. "Hey, this thing really works, doesn't it?"

"Yes, and it's a good thing, because otherwise we'd have to carry water up from the creek. On that ice, it would be dangerous. There's also plenty of food. Enough to last us at least two weeks — it just needs to be cooked. And do you feel the warmth of the bricks?" She pointed down at the floor. "The furnace is directly below the kitchen."

He gave a low whistle of admiration. "Josiah knew how to prepare for the worst."

Sable opened the side door of the heavy, cast-iron stove. She struck a match and held it to the papers and kindling wood inside. Flames flickered and spread through the compartment. She tossed the match in and closed the door with a thump.

She opened the refrigerator and took out eggs, sausage, and milk. The contents of the fridge would need a new home after they ate — someplace cool which wouldn't be dependent on electricity to keep it that way. "What did you find down in the cave?"

"Some great formations and that nasty pit. Craig said the water level has dropped, and some of the pools have gone dry." He picked up a package of sausage and handed it to Sable. "Here, see if you can form this into patties while I mix up a batch of biscuits. Where are the flour and baking things?"

Sable pointed to the proper cupboards, then took the sausage from him with a wry

187

grimace. "Don't tell me you're a chef."

"Nope, but I like to cook."

"And you make biscuits from scratch?"

"My mother taught me. She was an army cook. You did say there was enough food to feed everyone."

"There's plenty, believe me. There are always rows of canned goods in the basement. Mom grows a huge garden every year and cans food until it's coming out the eaves of the house. There's flour, meal, and powdered milk and eggs in the pantry, and chicken, beef, and fish in the freezer. The freezer will keep the meat for several days, and if necessary we can put the frozen foods outside." Sable formed the first patty and placed it in the hot skillet. The meat sizzled and spattered, scattering the smoky aroma through the kitchen.

Their first guest arrived soon afterward. It was Audry, her short gray hair combed back from her face in a casual style. She wore a white turtleneck and brown slacks that belonged to Sable's mother.

"They look great on you, Audry," Sable said.

Audry snorted, dispelling the ladylike impression. "Honey, beneath this glamorous exterior lurks the body of a prune. I

188

have to confess I snooped in your attic this morning."

"That was you?" Sable knew it was, but at least Audry admitted it.

"Yes, I'm a sneak and an antique freak. Mind if I take another look around later?"

Sable couldn't prevent the slight hesitation before she said, "Of course not. I'm sure the others would like to look for more clothes." As long as they didn't spend a lot of time up there. Sable had a search to conduct, and she couldn't do that with an audience.

Murph sat with his back to the wall, at the end of the long, beautifully carved dining room table. As he handed out plates, passed the gravy boat, and poured milk for the others, he watched them, trying hard not to be obvious. But he wasn't sure if his ruse was working. After all, he wasn't an undercover cop or a spy, he was a paramedic. He didn't normally deal in subterfuge, but in the past month and a half he had attempted to teach himself a little finesse. He'd learned to watch people from the periphery of his vision instead of staring straight at them. He'd also learned to tune out chatter to focus on one conversation or one voice at a time.

That was how he overheard Craig telling fifteen-year-old Bryce about all the neat things in the attic, and it was how he overheard Audry remark to Jerri that the biscuits could have used a little more baking soda.

Tomorrow they could let her cook breakfast . . . if she was still here. Hopefully, she would be gone with the rest of the passengers.

"Delicious biscuits and gravy, Sable," Perry remarked as he selected two more biscuits from the platter.

Sable wrinkled her nose at Murph. "Okay, okay, I'll tell everybody you're the cook, and I'm the flunky. Satisfied?"

"Many men can cook better than women," Perry said, splitting open a biscuit. "Look at the great chefs on the cooking channel. They're mainly men. Emeril is my favorite." He raised his fork in the air like a baton. " 'Pork fat rules!' " he quoted the famous cooking show star.

Audry raised a brow at the chubby man. "I beg your pardon, but fat does not rule. Fat kills, especially animal fat."

"But you must admit, fat adds flavor," Perry argued. "Fat-free cooking just hasn't caught on in America."

"Obviously not for some of us," she chided.

Simmons nearly choked on his scrambled eggs but didn't say anything.

"That's right," Perry said. "Take it from me, the lard expert. Gaining weight is America's most popular pastime."

Red-headed Jerri sat down at the other end of the table. "So is that what you packed in that suitcase of yours?" she asked Perry. "That thing had to weigh at least forty pounds."

"Forty-five," Perry said matter-of-factly. "And the contents of my personal luggage are my business." His attention suddenly focused on something obviously more important to him than the conversation. He split two of Murph's biscuits in half and spread scrambled eggs over them. He broke up a sausage patty and crumbled it on top, then spooned a generous dollop of gravy on top of that. He looked up, beaming with anticipation. "Pork fat does rule."

Simmons pushed his plate away, as if he'd just lost his appetite.

Perry picked up his fork and scooped some of the gravy onto the tines. Like a connoisseur he touched the gravy to his tongue and smacked his lips, inhaling the fragrant steam rising from his plate. "Mr. Murphy, my compliments. I must get your recipe before we leave here."

"We'll have time for that," Murph assured him. "Unless we have a sudden thaw, we'll probably be stuck here for awhile."

Perry swallowed audibly. "Could be I need to check out that attic myself. I only brought one change of clothing with me."

Jerri choked on her coffee. "Just one change of clothes in that case?"

"It's nothing you need to be concerned about." Perry relished another bite.

They ate in silence for a moment, then Simmons pushed away from the table and picked up his plate.

"Before anyone else gets away," Sable said, "I need to warn you that it will be necessary for us to go outside. We'll need to use the outdoor privy."

Perry's slightly protruding eyes widened. "An outdoor privy? How far is it from the house?"

"Only about a hundred feet," Sable said.

"In case you hadn't noticed," Perry said, "I'm not at my most elegant on ice."

Simmons snickered. "You're not the one who went over the cliff edge last night."

The others fell silent. Craig's fork clattered to his plate.

"That's true," Sable said. "So if I can make it out to the privy and back without breaking my neck, probably anybody —"

"What are you talking about?" Craig asked.

"Sable went over the side last night," Jerri told him. "Up on the cliffs, while we were walking here from the bus. She lost her footing on the ice and just kept on going."

"Forgive me for pointing out that if not for the admirable length of my very own belt," Perry said, "we might not have rescued her."

"Well, hooray for you," Simmons muttered.

"Is there another way out of here, in case of emergency?" Jerri asked.

"There's another way out," Craig said, "but it's still uphill, and once you get to the road there's still a coating of ice."

"Everything is uphill from here," Audry muttered.

Murph studied Audry more closely from the corner of his eye.

"I wouldn't risk it right now," Craig said. "Not even with chains on my Jeep. Sable, you're okay now?"

"I'm fine."

He shook his head and leaned back in his chair. "If I was you, after all you've been through, I'd leave this place and never look back."

Sable took her plate and stood. "I notice you haven't left." There was an edge to her voice, and Craig didn't reply.

Simmons carried his plate to the sink and walked out without saying anything more.

Murph got up to help Sable with the dishes, needing activity to keep his worry at bay. *Lord, protect us. Especially protect Sable. Keep me on my toes . . . and help me have a little faith. You know I'm still having some trouble in that area, even after all these years.*

Craig walked to the door. "I need some help chopping wood for the furnace. Anyone want to join me?"

"I'll be out in a few minutes," Murph told him.

Perry Chadwick picked up his plate and carried it to the sink. "I would be glad to help with any of the indoor chores. Sable, would you like me to carry water upstairs for washing?"

"I was hoping someone would offer. Thanks, Perry, I'd appreciate that."

Perry and the others left, one by one, until only Murph and Sable remained. They worked for a few moments in silence. Murph had discovered over the past few weeks that he enjoyed working close to Sable, enjoyed being near her.

"Nice little family atmosphere we have, isn't it?" he remarked as peaceful silence enveloped the kitchen.

"Cozy," she drawled. "I'm glad this house is so —"

An angry shout interrupted her. A moment later Perry burst back through the kitchen door. "Where is everybody? Where'd they go? I can take the insults and the snide remarks about my weight and my luggage, but someone has pushed the limit."

"What happened?" Sable asked.

"They went through my things — riffled through my suitcase!"

Chapter 11

"Perry, are you sure?" Sable heard her own voice tighten with fear. "Was anything missing?"

Perry's pale eyebrows drew together in a worried frown, his high forehead grooved with anxiety as he paced to the table and back. "Nothing was missing, but it was searched, of that I have no doubt." He swallowed and took a deep breath, his gaze narrowing at Murph and Sable.

"Do you think they might have just been curious?" Sable tried to think who might have been upstairs when the rest of them were eating.

"Does it matter? No one had a right!"

"Do you have any idea who it might have been?" Murph asked.

"Simmons," Perry muttered. "He left before the rest of us, remember? After all that talk about my heavy suitcase and my . . . sizable presence, the man decided he could get away with invading my private space. I despise a snoop!"

Simmons came bursting into the kitchen,

his pale amber eyes intense with apparent apprehension. "What's happened now?"

Perry rounded on him. "If you've harmed anything in that suitcase, I promise I'll sue you for every —"

"What?" Simmons snapped. "What suitcase? What are you talking about? I haven't been near that monstrosity." He shook his head with apparent disgust and turned to leave.

"Don't you walk away from this." Perry grabbed Simmons by the arm.

Simmons swung around and knocked Perry away with lightning speed, shoving him against the counter.

Murph grabbed Simmons by the arm. "Enough, both of you."

Audry came rushing into the room, tendrils of gray hair falling across her forehead, face flushed. "What's all the yelling about? What's going on here, Perry? I nearly fell down the stairs, you startled me so badly, hollering and shouting like a house afire."

Simmons wrenched from Murph's grip, shot Perry a venomous glare, and shoved his way past the others.

"What did he do?" Audry demanded.

"He went through my suitcase."

"How do you know?" Murph asked.

"It was a mess. Nothing was in place."

"So?" Audry said. "My stuff was a mess, too. Even my purse. We were all over that road this morning."

"Yes, but —"

"Admit it," Audry interrupted, "you're just mad because we poked fun at you, and you've decided to blame Simmons."

"That isn't —"

Audry placed a hand on his arm. "I should never have made those comments about your weight, and I apologize. There. I'll take the blame for everything, okay? It's bad enough we're going to be stuck here together for who knows how long; we need to try to cooperate. Come on upstairs and leave poor Sable alone. She's had a rough time of it."

Perry hesitated. He took a deep breath, as if attempting a swift attitude adjustment. He forced a smile that didn't go past the tight corners of his mouth. "Of course you could be right, Audry. I'm sorry I've upset everyone. I suppose I could have jumped to the wrong conclusion about Simmons. I'm just ill at ease here because of the ice storm." He paused, then as if he couldn't help himself, muttered, "And Simmons is an obnoxious, big-mouthed —"

"Watch it," Audry warned.

"We're all uncomfortable," Sable said. "Believe me, if I knew of any safe way out of here, we would have taken it." And she would feel much safer in the house without these bickering strangers.

"I'm sorry." Perry really did look contrite. He dabbed beads of moisture from his forehead with the back of his hand. "I'm not accustomed to staying in a room with no locks." He paused, then brightened. "I don't suppose it would be possible for me to move into another room . . . the attic, perhaps, if there's a lock on the door."

"There isn't, but you can have my room," Sable said. "I'll move a cot —"

"Forget it," Murph said.

"That's right." Audry rested her stern gaze on Perry for a long moment. "I'd be ashamed, asking a young woman to give up her room like that."

"But that isn't what —"

"Give it up," Audry insisted. "You're more of a man than that. If you want, you can barricade your door with a chair. I've found that works as well as anything."

Perry shook his head with helpless frustration. He shrugged and spread his hands in surrender. "Of course you're right, Audry. How could I be so insensitive?" His voice held a heavy thread of dry sarcasm. "Sorry, Sable. I was a bit overwrought." He hoisted the band of his pants higher over his portly belly, then turned and left the room, with Audry right behind him.

Sable reached for the kitchen door and closed it firmly behind them. If there had been a lock, she would have used it. She leaned against the doorjamb. The silent questions haunted her, and she turned to find her own tension reflected in Murph's eyes.

"Do you think Perry imagined that?" she asked.

"It's possible." He didn't sound convinced.

"I didn't imagine being pushed into that ravine."

"I know."

"But I can't be sure it was intentional." She reached out and touched his arm. He took her hand in both of his. "Murph, what are we going to do? We can't call for help. We're stuck here with these people."

"For now, I think we should continue as we are. Maybe that will lure someone into a sense of security. When you're alone in your room, keep the door locked. If we tell the others about what's going on, it'll terrify them and possibly force someone —

whoever it is — to make another move on you."

"Or you, Murph. I was standing right beside you last night. What if they intended —"

"You're Josiah Kessinger's granddaughter. What would they want with me?"

"Maybe someone wants to narrow the playing field. I'm perceived as a helpless target, and if they get you out of the way . . ."

Reluctantly, she withdrew her hand from his and paced across the floor to the window to stare out at the frozen landscape.

He stepped up behind her. "You're not helpless, Sable. Never forget who is on your side."

She closed her eyes and nodded. "I know. It's just . . . sometimes I can't feel His presence. Sometimes I wonder if I've suddenly been abandoned."

"That's one of the things God can't do. You belong to Him." He stared with her out the window for a moment. "Maybe that's a lesson we both need to learn a little better."

The powerful beam of Sable's flashlight flickered against cobwebs that draped across the corners of the cavernous attic as feminine laughter drifted up to her from the hallway below. Audry and Jerri sat comfortably ensconced in Jerri's bedroom with the door open, serving as unintentional lookouts as they chattered about the places they had traveled and the books they had read. Sable felt reasonably safe — surely no one would attempt to hurt her with the women nearby.

She gave her whole attention to the memories that drifted over her — long-ago memories that caused no pain. Tall bureaus, fashionable when Grandpa and Grandma had first bought this place, loomed toward the high ceiling, their square corners jutting out, sentinels over endless boxes of old clothes and furniture.

She remembered being afraid of this place when she was a child. With its shadowy recesses near the dormer windows and the deep silence except for an occasional squeaking floorboard, it seemed to have eyes that watched every move she made. Now fear came at her from a different direction, but it was no less menacing. If anything, it was more real, more frightening because now she couldn't chide herself for being a baby or for being scared of the dark. And she couldn't tell herself there was nothing to be afraid of.

Two very dear people were already dead, and the reason behind their deaths lay somewhere in this house, or at least on this property.

Intrigued by the direction her thoughts kept taking her, she studied the shadows of the huge room more closely. She had no idea where she should look first or what she should look for.

"Grandpa, why didn't you talk to me about this?" Tears stung her eyes as she gazed around the attic at what was left of the things Grandpa had valued most — boxes and boxes of family treasures, pictures, albums, old letters — worthless things to anyone but family.

She suspected now why he hadn't told her anything. Aside from the fact that he had always tried to treat her like a "fragile female," he couldn't very well explain to her all the illegal ramifications of his activities.

She knelt beside the nearest wax-coated box and raised the lid. Old tax records. The next box she came to contained pictures and two broken clocks. The next was clothes. It wasn't until she opened the fourth box that she found something that caught her interest — letters from

Grandpa to Mom dated last December. Sable took out the contents of one envelope and scanned the pages.

There was nothing in it she didn't already know. He mentioned the buck Boswell had shot on their hunting trip here in November and how Boswell was still gloating about the fact that Grandpa had fallen into a sinkhole and broken his ankle. He complained again about Boswell nagging him to sell the place. For as long as Sable could remember, Boswell had wanted to buy this place, so that was nothing new, although he seemed to have increased the pressure since November, according to Grandpa.

She folded the letter and returned it to its envelope, then checked the dates on the other letters. She was reaching for another packet of papers when the bottom step creaked on the attic stairs.

She froze for a second and realized belatedly that Audry and Jerri had fallen silent. When had they stopped their chatter? Did they leave the bedroom? Why had she become so engrossed in Grandpa's letters that she'd lost track of time and dropped her guard?

She turned off her flashlight and stepped behind a bureau, fighting the sudden panic that throbbed through her. Someone came slowly — stealthily? — up the staircase. Without daring to breathe, she edged around the bulk of the bureau in the shadow and glanced toward the attic steps. They were dark. The intruder wasn't using a flashlight. Why not?

As the form came closer, Sable took an automatic step backward. Her foot caught on the clawed foot of the bureau. She lost her footing and stumbled against the wall.

"Who's there?" demanded a familiar male voice. It was Craig.

Sable managed to start breathing again as she righted herself and stepped out from behind the bureau. "Just me. I wish you wouldn't sneak up on people like that." She turned on her flashlight and caught the flash of startled confusion on Craig's face, as if he hadn't expected to find her.

"Sorry," he muttered. "Man, you're touchy."

"Looking for something?" She could hear her voice shaking, and she clenched her teeth. No reason to be afraid of Craig. She needed to stop overreacting to every little thing.

For a brief moment he stood frowning at her, then he relaxed and smiled. Sable noticed the smile didn't carry through in his expression. His eyes held a wary watchfulness.

"I thought I heard someone up here." He came up the last step and ambled toward her, the light from the gable windows placing the dark line of his eyebrows and hair in sharp relief against the winter paleness of his skin.

"I wasn't making any noise."

"What're you doing up here in the dark?" he asked.

She replaced the box lid she held. "I turned off my light when I heard you. I didn't know who it was. Instinctive reaction. I always was a little nervous up here alone."

"Yeah, I remember. So why come up here at all if you're still nervous?"

The question irritated her. Why should she have to answer to him? It was her home. "I guess I just miss Grandpa."

"So do I. It's hard to believe he's dead." Craig paced along a row of boxes, casually inspecting the contents of several boxes. He picked up the bowl of an old-fashioned butter churn. "Your company isn't the most congenial group, is it? Bryce told me about Perry Chadwick and that Simmons guy getting into it after breakfast. He said he heard Audry and Perry arguing about it in the hallway when he came in from helping me with the wood."

"Bryce was outside? Aren't the limbs still falling?"

"Not as badly as they were. I didn't let the kid stay out long, but Murph's out doing some chopping now."

"Where are the others?"

Craig shrugged as he replaced the churn. "I just saw Bryce lying in front of the fire with the dog. I think I saw Audry examining the antiques in the family room. No telling where Simmons is. Probably roaming around down in the cave again or searching through someone else's things."

Sable glanced up sharply. "Do you think he really searched Perry's case? I'd hoped he was just imagining it."

"Could be, but I have to admit I was curious, too. I mean, you should have felt that case last night; it must have weighed a good forty pounds."

"Forty-five," Sable corrected.

"Anyway, I picked it up once to put it out of the way, and Perry kept a close watch, like a mother watching a stranger hold her baby. What do you think he could've been carrying?"

"It's really none of our business," Sable said. Or was it? "Maybe he's carrying a laptop and doesn't want it stolen."

"A forty-five-pound laptop? Get real, Sable." Craig's eyes flashed with curiosity and a hint of suspicion. "It's your home, Sable. These people are strangers. I'd watch them a little closer if it was my house."

Sable dusted her hands together and bent over another box. "Sounds like you're doing enough worrying for both of us." She picked up another packet of letters and checked the names, then dropped them again. They were from relatives out of state.

"Sable?" Craig's quiet voice was suddenly filled with concern.

She straightened and glanced at him over her shoulder.

"Is something wrong?" he asked.

"What do you mean?"

He stepped around the box. His candid brown eyes met hers squarely. "Why did you turn around and come straight back here? You've had a wreck, you nearly died on the cliff this morning, and you've been awfully prickly today."

"I'm not prickly."

"You've been as jumpy as a buck during hunting season. Is it money?"

"Money?"

"Look, I know this place has been costing the family a lot of money to fix it up, and it's not doing you any good since you aren't farming it any more." He hesitated, glancing around the attic. "I wasn't going to bring this up yet, but . . . well . . . when your family decides to sell this place, I want to be first on the list."

"Sell?"

Craig cleared his throat. "Now don't turn me down just like that. I have more money than you think. The boat dock brings in enough. I wouldn't even have to work through the winter if I didn't want to. Besides, my expenses aren't that much, and I've stuck a lot in the bank. Enough to pay half down on the asking price."

"Asking price? I didn't know we had one."

"Your mother said something about it before your grandpa died. After all, you and Pete and Randy don't live here anymore, and your mom's all alone." He shrugged and fell silent beneath Sable's stare.

"Not for sale," she said quietly.

"But don't you have to ask the rest of your family?"

"Back off, Craig. Grandpa's not even cold in the grave yet, and you're already after this property. You could at least wait awhile." She shoved the lid back on the box, then pushed the box out of her way with her foot. Maybe he was right. She was prickly.

"Oh, come on, Sable, don't get mad. I just offered to buy the place, not burn it down."

"Sorry. I guess you could say I'm a little on edge." She bent down and lifted the lid from another box. "I'm just curious why you want to buy the family home all of a sudden."

"Sudden? This isn't sudden. My parents have left the county, and I need to find a home of my own. I can't farm their place — it's four hundred acres. They've had an offer for their property; they need the money to help fund Dad's campaign. I've always liked this place, you know that."

She replaced the lid to a box of clothing and straightened to scan the rear wall with her flashlight beam. "You sound like Otis Boswell — or didn't you know he was trying to buy Grandpa out, too?"

There was a long silence, and she turned to look at Craig, whose heavy, dark brows had drawn together in a scowl. "Josiah didn't sell, did he? Not to that goon."

"No, but do you have any good reasons why we shouldn't? He's got the funds."

"Filthy money."

"I know you have personal prejudices against Boswell," she said. "I've just never known why you don't like him."

Craig studied her face for a moment in the dim light, then sighed and stepped slowly to the shaded dormer window. He stood looking outside for a long moment. Sable had almost decided the conversation had ended when he turned around.

"Dad's running for state senator, you know."

"What does he have to do with Otis Boswell?"

Craig shoved his hands into the pockets of his jeans and turned to stare out the window again. "Dad's a good man."

She softened her voice. "I know he is. He's always been a good neighbor, and he'll be a great senator."

Craig hesitated again. "How . . . how loyal are you to Otis Boswell?"

"Apparently not too loyal. I don't plan to return to work in Freemont." And how loyal had Otis been to Grandpa?

"You don't?"

She relented slightly. "No, Craig. I want to come back here to live. With Grandpa

gone, there's nothing for me in Freemont."
Except arrest, perhaps.

Craig leaned closer to her, looked over his shoulder toward the stairs, and lowered his voice. "We've been friends a long time, right?" There was a vulnerability in his deep voice that touched her.

"Of course."

He paused and took a breath, as if for strength. "Remember when Jimmy Ray and I were in the wreck that killed Tom Hall?"

"How could I forget something like that? You were a senior in high school. I was in my first year at Columbia."

He closed his eyes and looked at the floor. For a moment she wondered if he had decided not to say more. "My blood alcohol was over .08."

Sable stiffened and drew back. "You were drunk?"

"Yes, but Tom swerved into my lane — all the way over. I didn't want to hit him head-on, and I couldn't pull off the road because it was on the bridge at Eagle Rock, remember?"

"So you traded lanes with him. I know all this. But, Craig, you were drunk?"

"He swerved back at the last minute. That's really what happened, Sable. It wasn't my fault, but nobody cared. All they saw was the alcohol. I was eighteen and could have been tried as an adult for manslaughter."

"Maybe I don't want to hear more."

He ignored her. "Dad was judge then. He pulled a lot of strings with his friends to keep me out of big trouble."

"So you're saying your father used his political influence to prevent you from being prosecuted?" She heard harshness in her words and voice, felt the hard knot that tightened in her stomach.

"I'm sorry," he said. "You can't imagine how sorry. I shouldn't have been drinking, I know that. I'll live with it the rest of my life, and believe me, it isn't easy. But I do remember the wreck, and I didn't cause it. You have to understand Dad."

"I understand he didn't trust the judicial system he'd sworn to uphold." She hated the sound of judgment in her voice, hated the fact that she was taking her pent-up bitterness out on Craig because Grandpa wasn't available to take her blame.

"He didn't want his son to go to prison."

"So that makes it right?" *Stop it, Sable! Stop it.*

"Dad doesn't make a habit of doing things like that. He's not that kind of man.

If I'd just been caught joyriding in a stolen car or shoplifting or driving under the influence, he'd have let me take my knocks, but this was different. You can see that, can't you?"

What she saw was that if it had happened to one of her brothers, no one would have pulled any strings for them. But what she also saw was Craig's anguish, even after all these years.

"Dad stuck his neck out," Craig said. "He laid his whole career on the line for me. He almost lost it, thanks to Otis Boswell."

"What happened?" She resigned herself to hear the dirty details.

"Jimmy Ray's father couldn't keep his mouth shut. He went fishing with Otis one day and told Otis what Dad did. A couple of years later, Otis had a chance to buy some private property in the middle of the Mark Twain National Forest. He petitioned for some zoning changes so he could set up a galena mine on the property, but his petition was blocked. He went to Dad and threatened to expose me if Dad didn't pull some strings."

"And Reuben gave in?"

Craig closed his eyes and nodded. "He didn't think he had any other choice. It didn't work, anyway. The land Otis wanted to buy suddenly went off the market. Otis went to Oklahoma soon afterward."

Sable leaned against the window frame as she digested this piece of information. "You mean Otis had reason to believe there was galena around here?"

"That's right." He turned and started for the stairs. "I've got wood to chop. If you change your mind about things, let me know."

Sable listened to the sound of his footsteps as he descended the attic stairs.

The silence of the cavernous room made her uncomfortable. She made *herself* uncomfortable. When had she suddenly become so angry with the world? Why couldn't she have just listened to Craig's story without hurling blame at him? He was baring his soul — risking his reputation and his father's — to warn her about Otis Boswell. Maybe she should pay more attention to the warning and lighten up on the guilt trip.

She leaned forward and pressed her forehead against the cold glass of the dormer window. "Oh, Grandpa, why?"

A movement outside caught her attention, and she saw someone several hundred feet away, splitting wood beside the creek.

As he moved, his shadow mingled in and out of the trees, but from his size and the breadth of his shoulders, Sable could tell it was Murph. He raised the ax high into the air and plunged it into a log in a perfect split. Two more strikes, and he moved to the next log.

She enjoyed watching him work. She was so grateful for his presence here — so glad he'd insisted on coming with her. He didn't seem to mind her company, either.

Now if they could just get through these next few days . . .

As she gazed down on the sharp, strangely threatening limbs that jabbed into the lurking sky, she felt the oppressive weight of the day's gloom. The browns and grays of winter had always depressed her. Until the sun broke through, or until the temperature warmed, the ground would remain encrusted with ice. She and Paul Murphy would remain stranded here with the others.

Impatient with her own thoughts, she studied the thick barrier of clouds that had invaded them this afternoon. The atmosphere in the house seemed to reflect the sky.

When she looked back down into the woods, she was surprised to see another figure moving through the woods above the place where Murph worked.

Murph still handled the ax as if it were a lightweight toy, breaking away ice with a flick of his arm. The newcomer balanced on a cleft above Murph, in a thicket of tangled brush so close she could barely make out the human form. At times the person was barely visible, at times merely a part of the dark green line of cedar trees near the ledge — except for a bright, red-orange halo that seemed to bob with the person's movements. A knit cap?

Something about this second figure grabbed Sable's attention, something stealthy, as if . . .

Sable gasped. "No!"

The newcomer raised a branch the size of a man's leg, moving into a line above Murph.

Sable unlocked the window and shoved it up. She fumbled with the lever of the storm window, trying to open it. The thing wouldn't move. The window was stuck. Why hadn't she fixed this last summer?

She pounded on the window. "Murph!" She looked around for something to hurl through the glass, fumbled once more at the window frame, and felt it give. She shoved it hard, and as the pane flew up she cried, "Murph! Watch out!"

The intruder heaved the branch at Murph.

At the sound of her voice, Murph straightened and looked around. The branch hit the side of his head lengthwise, then crashed to the ground with a sound like shattering glass. Murph plunged face first across a half-cut log.

Chapter 12

Sable raced downstairs from the attic to the living room two steps at a time. She flung open the front door and rushed out into the icy air, stopping only when she reached the slick steps that led down from the front porch to the yard. She grabbed the pickax someone had leaned against the steps and used it to balance herself across the frozen slope of winter brown.

There was no longer any doubt, no grasping for excuses in her mind; someone had tried to kill Murph — and may have succeeded! Someone had come after them, and he or she was in these woods, right now.

A trail climbed a forested hill a couple hundred feet from the house, and Sable followed it to a sharp incline. She raised the pickax over her head and swung with the strength of her fear, plunging the tip through the thick ice crust, and pulling herself up a few feet at a time, frustrated by the slow progress. When she reached level ground again, she scrambled through the trees toward the place where she had seen Murph fall.

"Murph!" She grabbed at the slender trunk of a dogwood to keep her balance. "Murph, answer me!"

A crash reached her from the depths of a stand of cedars, then a crackle of brush and the tinkle of ice — the attacker was getting away. She couldn't take time to follow.

At last, up ahead, just past a huge, bare-branched oak, she caught a glimpse of Murph's heavy tan coat. His limp body lay prone over the log where he had fallen, and the ax lay beside him in the ice.

Sable stumbled to a halt at the foot of a sharp incline. "Murph, please answer me!" Using the pickax again, she slammed the point of it into the ice and balanced against it to step forward. Sharp spines of a cedar branch slapped her face.

Murph groaned. Sable dragged herself up and skated awkwardly the final few feet to him. She grasped the material of his coat and heaved him over onto his side. "Paul Murphy! Listen to me! Please wake up!"

He moaned again, reaching out as if to catch himself. She grabbed his hand and helped stabilize him.

An ugly red welt followed the line of his right cheek and the right side of his neck. Several small cuts wept blood. He opened his eyes and winced.

From what Sable could see, his pupils were equal and reactive. She slumped against him with relief. "You're alive," she breathed. "Thank God, you're alive."

"I'm not sure I'm ready to be thankful for that yet," he muttered under his breath.

She smiled grimly. His speech wasn't slurred. "Well, I am. Tell me what day of the week it is."

"Saturday afternoon, we arrived earlier this morning in the middle of an ice storm, your birthday is next week, and you'll be thirty-one. Satisfied?"

"You can sit up. Slowly."

He blinked and raised his head. "Man, I didn't hear that coming." He sat up, grimacing. "Should've waited for Craig to help. Dangerous under these trees."

Sable darted a glance up the cliff, where she had seen the other figure. "That branch didn't fall."

Murph paused in his effort to pull himself up. His gaze focused on her. "What?"

"Come on, get up, I can't carry you to the house."

He moved cautiously, as if a bomb might

explode in his head if he rushed. He allowed her to help him to his feet. "If that wasn't a limb —"

"Somebody threw that limb at you from the top of that cliff." She gestured upward, where crevassed rocks loomed overhead, then pointed toward the log that had bounced a few feet away. "If you hadn't moved when you did, you'd have a crushed skull."

His face gradually lost its color, and Sable braced herself against him. "Murph, rest for a moment. I can't hold you, and you can't afford another fall."

He touched the side of his face, then turned his head from side to side, as if testing to see if anything was badly damaged. "I'll be okay. Did you see who it was?"

"All I saw was a shadow of green topped by red. Most likely a stocking cap. Did you hear me shout from the window?"

"Yes. That's why I turned." His gaze once more focused on Sable. He took her hand. "That was a close one. If you hadn't called to me . . ." His hand tightened gently around hers. "Did you see who was in the house as you left?"

"No. I'm sorry, but I was so panicked when I ran out of the house, I didn't think to pay any attention. I didn't tell anybody, I just ran." She shivered. "Oh, Murph, I was so scared. All I could think about was reaching you. I —"

He placed his fingers gently on her lips. "Shh, it's okay. You did fine." His voice and his eyes were filled with comfort.

Sable shivered again.

"You're terrified." His fingers trailed across her face, and he cupped her chin. Then he looked down at her turtleneck sweater. "You didn't even stop to get a coat." He undid the buttons of his thick, quilted jacket.

"I'll be okay. Let's get back to the house."

"We will, but first —" He pulled the jacket from his shoulders and placed it around hers. The lingering warmth from his body encompassed her. "If you have to rescue me, at least allow me to salvage some of my macho pride with a gesture of chivalry."

She accepted the coat. "I'll be glad to help. But let me complete my mission. You need some medical attention, and that's back at the house."

"Agreed. And now I'm cold." He bent over to pick up his ax, and he stumbled.

She grabbed his arm. "Are you okay?"

He retrieved the ax and straightened. "I'll be fine; I'm just a little dizzy when I bend over."

"Then don't bend over."

The fine lines around his eyes deepened with humor. He looked down at her as he put an arm across her shoulders. "It's nice to know you're so concerned. Think we can get back to the house without another fall?"

"If we walk in the brush and dried grass to the side of the trail, it isn't quite as bad."

"Good observation." He stepped into the patches of broken ice where Sable had used her pickax, and together they made their way back toward the house. Slowly.

"Murph, you know we've been wondering about Boswell?" she said when they reached a level spot. "I think he's the one."

"What do you mean?"

"I've been talking with Craig, and a lot of things have fallen into place. Boswell tried to buy some land and force a zoning change so he could mine it. He used blackmail."

"How does Craig know about it?"

Sable hesitated. She didn't want to break Craig's confidence. "His dad was active in local politics."

They walked a few more seconds in silence, then Murph said, "You're breathing heavily."

"I was scared. Terrified. I felt so helpless."

"Now maybe you have an idea how your grandfather must have felt when you were attacked last fall."

She groaned. "Have I mentioned that Craig has a big mouth?"

"He didn't tell me what happened."

"Of course not," she muttered. "He just dropped enough information to make you curious, so you'd harass me to death until I told you all about it."

Murph's arm tightened around her shoulders. "You're right, I'll probably drive you nuts until you tell me. So why don't you just tell me now? Haven't I proven I can be trusted?"

"It isn't a matter of trust, Paul." She stepped over a log and slowed her steps. The ice formed a more solid crust over the flat ground than on the hillside.

Murph walked in silence for a moment, then he said, "I'm sorry. I have no right to force a confidence from you. Talking about it must bring back bad memories . . . whatever those memories may be."

"Oh, for crying out loud, I'll tell you,"

she said. "The guy tried to drown me in a pool of water. You know that pit near the mouth of the cave? It was flooded after some heavy rain we had last summer."

"But why was he here? Why did he —"

She raised her hand to cut off his question. "Just let me tell this and get it over with. Last summer, when I first went to work at the clinic, I used some bad judgment and dated the wrong man. Otis Boswell introduced me to this guy named Jim at a company banquet, and we were seated next to each other during dinner, so we became acquainted. He asked me out, and I thought —"

"Otis Boswell introduced —"

"Yes. Now let me finish."

"Sorry."

"I went out with Jim for about three weeks, and I realized from the outset that Grandpa didn't like it. It didn't take long for me to figure out why. After a few dates, I'd had enough. Jim wasn't as nice as he'd seemed at first. He had a mean streak."

"Mean streak?"

"Oh, nothing I could put my finger on at first, but when we went to a restaurant, he'd treat the waitress poorly, complain about the slightest problem with the meal — and he had a temper if anyone argued

226

with him. He also liked to play 'chicken' when he was driving, he was rude to strangers, that kind of thing. Like I said, little things, but it got old in a hurry."

"I don't consider playing 'chicken' a little thing."

"The problem was, when I told him I didn't want to see him again, he went on a rampage. He called me several times at the clinic; he made three appointments to see me and threatened to sue me for malpractice when I canceled the appointments."

"Obviously, he didn't follow through."

"He couldn't. He was never a patient of mine in the first place, and when I saw his name on the appointment book, I reassigned him to Dr. Harvey, who was another physician in the group at that time. Anyway, Grandpa found out about the problem and insisted I take a week off and come home to get away from the guy. The other doctors weren't happy about it, but I did it because Grandpa threatened to kick up a fuss if I didn't."

"And the crazy guy followed you here?"

"All the way down to the cave. If Peter and Craig hadn't heard me screaming, Jim would have drowned me in that pool, or we'd have drowned each other. I put up a pretty decent fight."

"I believe you. What did they do to this guy?"

"Our county has a good prosecuting attorney, and Jim went to jail. The court process is slow, though. I have no idea how it'll turn out."

"Think he'll win?"

"The idea has kept me awake sometimes at night. You know what I think?"

"That Boswell introduced you to him for a reason?"

"It seems logical."

"But what would that reason be?" Murph asked.

"Good question. All I know is that Grandpa and Boswell nearly broke up their partnership over it. And Grandpa seemed just a little . . . oh, I don't know . . . unsettled around Boswell from then on. He was quieter, didn't get around as much. And he came back home more often."

They stepped out of the woods and across the frozen yard toward the house. The house was constructed of used brick, with white columns supporting the front porch, and black shutters at each window. Today, all the shutters were folded back, and the blinds were raised to let in as much light as possible. This gave the unfortunate impression of eyes open wide, watching every move Sable and Murph made.

"Maybe we should get out of here while we can," Sable said.

"We've already decided it's too dangerous, even with the chains on Craig's Jeep."

Sable knew this was true. The concrete bridge, just below the incline from the house, was covered with ice, and it slanted sharply. If they were to slide from it into the creek below, they were sure to be injured, even drowned in the swiftly flowing water that rushed between twin crusts of ice. Past that the drive to the road was a mere ledge that skirted a mountain, with a drop of at least two hundred feet. She'd already had a taste of what it would be like to fall from that. As Audry had said earlier, everything was uphill from here.

But Sable hadn't been talking about using the Jeep. Shame prevented her from explaining what she'd meant. She and Murph couldn't just slip away on foot and leave the others here with someone who had attempted murder twice already. They couldn't run now. But they needed to discover the culprit before anything else happened.

★ ★ ★

Murph had trouble concentrating as he stepped onto the front porch beside Sable — partly because his brain had a tendency to scramble lately when he was near her, but mostly because of the pain that shot through his head and down his neck with devilish insistence.

He decided he had a great deal in common with Josiah Kessinger — he felt an instinctive need to protect Sable, and in doing so he had downplayed his fear. Whoever had tried to kill him may be — probably was — planning to kill Sable after she led them to the object, or objects, of their search. If she didn't realize this yet, she would soon. They needed to protect themselves.

Sable had told him the living room was unoccupied when she rushed out, but when they stepped through the front door, Audry greeted them from the sofa.

"At last," she said, getting up. "For awhile I thought I'd been deserted. Where is everyone?"

"I don't know about the others," Murph said, "but we were out in the —"

"Murph!" The older woman rushed toward him, reaching up to touch the side of his face. "What on earth happened to you?"

Murph winced and stepped back. "A limb hit me. I'll live."

"A limb? I knew it would happen. These storms are deadly. We need to get some ice on that right away. I'll get a dish towel and step out the back — won't have any trouble finding enough ice. I'll be right back —"

"Audry," Sable interrupted, "do you know if anyone else went outside recently? We wouldn't want anyone else to be in danger."

"Nobody I know of," Audry said. "It's a pretty sure bet Perry wouldn't try it. He barely made it to the outdoor privy this afternoon. Took him thirty minutes to get there and back, and I saw him fall twice. I think he's taking a nap now. He has decided to haul water for the indoor facilities."

"And Simmons?" Murph asked.

Audry shrugged. "Haven't seen him, and I don't want to."

Before Murph could ask about Craig, the basement door opened and Craig stepped through it. He switched off his flashlight and set it on the shelf behind the door. "The wood furnace is filled," he said. "To capacity. How'd you do out there, Murph? Do we have enough wood to last us a few days?"

Murph paused. "Not as much —"

"Man, can't you see he's wounded?" Audry exclaimed. "Anybody who goes outside ought to wear a helmet. Surely you can make what we have last until the ice stops breaking the branches."

Craig's surprise and concern appeared genuine to Murph, but there was no time to think about it before the door to the family room opened across the hallway from the kitchen.

Bryce ambled out with a book in his hand. "Hey, Sable, can I borrow this? There's no electricity for a TV or computer, and I'm getting bored."

Sable stopped to talk to him, and Murph followed Audry into the kitchen before anyone else could ask questions about his accident. He needed to be the one asking questions. He needed to know where the others had been while he was being bashed in the head.

Chapter 13

Light from the fire in the living room hearth flickered against the paneled walls with a muted glow. Usually at this time of the afternoon the sun filtered in through the long bay window, highlighting the blues and earth tones Sable had chosen so carefully last summer. By early afternoon, however, the sun had been dimmed by a wind-whipped covering of low clouds that only occasionally broke away to reveal a faded patch of sky.

Sable turned from the window to the fire. The sounds of chatter and laughter drifted from the family room where Audry, Jerri, and Bryce had congregated. Murph was upstairs lying down.

She knew he was as frustrated as she was. Someone had tried to kill each of them, had nearly succeeded, and apparently had left no trail to follow. This morning in the darkness, no one had seen who pushed her from the road. This afternoon, anyone could have hefted that log at Murph. The guests had been scattered throughout the house when Murph was attacked; consequently, no one had an alibi that could be independently verified.

Even the colors worn by Murph's attacker gave her no good clues — there were always two or three green coveralls and a couple of red knit caps in the mud room, used often by the family in the wintertime. Murph's assailant had obviously found the mud room.

Murph had left firm orders for Sable to stay near the others, and when she couldn't do that, to keep Dillon with her. Sable, in turn, had given firm orders for him to rest and to let her know immediately if he noticed any changes in his vision, any dizziness, or worsening of pain. He knew the routine. She had checked on him twenty minutes ago and would continue to check him.

Simmons was in the dining room with a cup of coffee and a back copy of *Field & Stream.* Craig had gone back outside to round up more wood, in spite of Audry's multiple warnings to stay indoors and out of trouble. Perry was carrying water upstairs.

Dillon lay at the hearth and kept watch, obviously on heightened alert. His ears perked forward every time someone stepped through the living room.

Sable paced in front of the fireplace. The lack of light added to her paranoia and the isolation she felt being so far from any neighbors, from dependable help, should it be needed. And she was terribly afraid it would be needed before this nightmare ended. She paused at the old rock collection on a low shelf beside the staircase.

Before marrying Grandma, Grandpa had traveled extensively throughout the United States, hitching rides on boxcars. His stories about the places he visited and this small display of stones were the only things remaining from his travels.

Sable knew the shape and color of every mineral specimen and the story that went with each. By the time she was ten, she had known more about Grandpa's collection than he knew himself. Something had seemed odd to her last night when she glanced at the shelf, and now she knew why. As she studied the collection, she realized that some of the mineral chunks had been switched around.

She picked up a lump of coal Grandpa had carried from Pennsylvania and studied the position of the rose quartz. Hadn't there been a chunk of galena between them? The galena was now at the far corner where the sphalerite used to be. Sable had never labeled them because she had known them by heart. But now . . .

"That dog seems to like you," Audry's voice drifted quietly from the hallway.

Sable stiffened, then took a breath and willed her shoulders to go slack. She was going to have to stop tensing up every time someone approached her.

"I like him, too," she said, turning from the display case.

The older woman's sherry brown eyes filled with sympathy as she ambled toward the sofa. "Sable, I was so sorry to hear about your grandfather. We haven't had much time alone to talk. Would it be too intrusive to ask what caused his death?"

Sable walked over to the bay window and stared out across the frozen lawn. "Automobile accident."

"I'm so sorry." Audry placed a hand on Sable's shoulder.

Tears sprang to Sable's eyes without warning. Not now. She couldn't allow the grief to cloud her judgment, giving in to the emotional quicksand that had dogged every moment since she'd received the news. She missed Grandpa so much. . . .

"What's wrong?" came a voice from the staircase.

Both women turned as Perry Chadwick thumped heavily down the steps. "Please don't tell me something else has happened." He shuffled into the living room and perched on the arm of the sofa. He wore a tan dress shirt and a pair of slightly wrinkled brown slacks. His thin, sandy hair hugged damply to his scalp, and the scant light from the window revealed a red blotch on the second fold of his triple chin.

"We were just . . . talking," Audry said. "You know, woman talk. You're going to have a nasty bruise there. You should have let me put a vinegar poultice on that place."

"What happened?" Sable asked.

"He can't stay on his feet long enough to get wood from the porch into the house," Audry said. "Perry, you're just not coordinated. If you'd gone to help chop in the forest, they'd have had to carry you back in a stretcher."

Perry nodded. "It's the feet, you know. They aren't big enough to balance the weight of my body."

"Then maybe you'd better whittle that body of yours back down to the right size," Audry suggested dryly.

"I may just have that chance if we're

stranded here long enough. I've been looking over the food supplies."

"Naturally," Audry said.

"Lots of good canned stuff, lots of meat." Perry shook his head. "But there are quite a few people in this house, and we don't know how long we'll be here."

"This is the Ozarks," Audry reminded him, "not the North Pole. We aren't going to starve."

"Speak for yourself," Perry protested. "You don't need as much fuel to keep you alive."

While the two exchanged mild barbs, Sable thought again about the case that Perry had guarded with such fierceness and the mystery of what might be inside.

With a shake of his head, Perry gave up the argument and strolled toward the kitchen. "You just might get your wish, Audry. This may be the diet of all diets."

Audry chuckled as he disappeared. "He reminds me of my grandson, the rascal. Always hanging around the kitchen underfoot." She glanced at Sable. "I took the liberty of preparing some stew this afternoon, and every time Perry returned for more water, he had to sample the food, offer suggestions for seasoning, make a nuisance of himself. He can be amusing when he isn't busy worrying about that silly suitcase of his."

"I'm glad somebody has a good attitude about all this," Sable said. "I'm also glad he's carrying the water. That's quite a job. I wouldn't want it."

"You're in good physical condition; you don't need help getting into shape. Perry does. I'm going to jump-start his exercise program and show him how much fun it can be."

"What are you, a personal trainer?" Sable asked.

"I was a girls' basketball coach. Had a winning team before I retired."

Sable considered the older woman's slender, wiry form. "You don't act retired, the way you tackled that road last night."

"I try to keep in shape. Time to check up on Perry. Can't let him ruin dinner — or eat it all up."

Sable waited until she heard Audry and Perry arguing in the kitchen, then glanced up the stairs. If Murph didn't come down soon, she would check on him again.

Meanwhile she had a crazy thought that wouldn't go away: What had the snoop found in Perry's suitcase?

It was none of her business, and Perry

was barely able to navigate outside, much less possess the nimble precision it would take to hover over a cliff edge and target Murph's head with a limb. If he had been the one to push her last night, he would most likely have fallen with her.

But what if he was faking? She couldn't avoid the questions. What could be so important to Perry that he would lug a heavy suitcase all the way here last night and protect it as if it were precious cargo? He'd had other luggage on the bus, and yet he had chosen the one piece, and it had contained only one change of clothes.

She glanced toward the kitchen door to assure herself that Audry and Perry were busy. The rise and fall of their voices told her they were still embroiled in their good-natured argument. The others, except for Murph, were either downstairs or outside. If she wanted to snoop, this was the time. She gestured silently for Dillon to follow her.

The sewing room that Perry occupied was down the hall to the right of the staircase. Directly across from that was the room that Murph and Simmons were sharing. The sewing room had two tall, wide windows that allowed a surprising amount of light through, considering that the window at the far end of the room faced the mountainside.

Sable opened the door and glanced into the room. She hesitated. Why was she even bothering? The case was surely locked, especially since Perry was convinced someone had broken into it this morning. Still . . . She took a step forward.

The door across the hallway opened suddenly. She stiffened as icy needles of tension shot beneath her skin. Her heartbeat pounded in her ears.

"Doing some dusting?" came Paul Murphy's dry voice behind her.

She sagged against the doorjamb with relief. "It's no use; I can't do this. It's crazy."

"Dusting is crazy?" He came closer.

"I was going to find out what's in Perry's overnight case," she whispered, automatically turning to check the injury on his face. For the amount of abuse his face and neck had sustained since last night, he looked surprisingly good.

"That isn't an overnight case; it's a steamer trunk," Murph said. "Don't let me stop you. I'd like to see for myself what's inside."

"Then feel free to go on in. I was just chickening out. Remember how Perry said he hates snoops?"

Murph pushed the door open wider, coming so close she could feel the tingle of his breath against her forehead. "We're both in on this one," he said. "After you."

Sable hesitated. Much as she hated to admit it, she didn't feel quite so nervous about doing this with Murph along. "But should we be doing this?" she asked.

His chuckle echoed softly as he urged her forward. "We're not stealing anything; we're trying to protect ourselves from being murdered. I don't think God minds." He turned to Dillon. "Stay and watch, boy. Warn us if anyone starts up the stairs."

The German shepherd sat, ears perked forward, on alert.

Sable checked the upstairs landing once more, then quickly stepped into the room. "Perry will have a seizure if he catches us. You saw how angry he was earlier."

"That's why this is a good idea. What's so important about that suitcase? Why was he so concerned about its contents? When I borrowed some toiletry supplies from Craig, he told me Perry had asked to use them, too. So what's in the case?"

They saw a laptop on the cot. That would count for five or six pounds. Sable found the suitcase beneath the cot. She tugged at the handle to pull it out and lost her grip. "Wow. That thing is heavy."

Murph reached down, pulled out the oblong, hard-sided black case, and set it on the thin mattress beside the laptop.

"Can you pick locks?" Sable asked.

"Yes, but first let's try the old fashioned approach." He pushed against the metal latches, and they snapped open.

Sable stared at it.

"Now who's the pessimist?" Murph teased. "Obviously he wasn't expecting company." He lifted the lid of the case to reveal the colorful — and heavy — contents.

For a moment, they were both too surprised to react. Nestled in the old, worn suitcase that Perry Chadwick had carried so protectively in the ice storm were several volumes of books with pictures of food on their covers.

"Cookbooks?" Sable exclaimed.

Slowly, as if not believing what he saw, Murph pulled out a large hardback. "Betty Crocker." His deep voice was hushed with wonder. "Master Chefs."

"Cookbooks," Sable said.

Murph chuckled.

"Shh!" She picked up another heavy tome. "All cookbooks. At least we know Audry wasn't the one who snooped earlier. She won't let Perry near the food."

"Maybe that's a ruse to deflect suspicion."

Anxious to retreat quickly, Sable replaced everything as she had found it and closed the case.

Murph lifted it and placed it back beneath the cot. "Nothing interesting. Let's get out of here."

Sable hurried out into the hallway with Murph. She walked toward the window at the end of the hallway while Murph closed the door behind them. She watched him as he came toward her, with Dillon at his side. Even in the dim light she could see the deep red mark at the side of his face.

Without thinking she reached up and gently touched the swollen welt. "How do you feel?"

His jaw tensed.

"I'm sorry. I know it hurts."

A comfortable smile spread across his face. "You've got the healing touch, Doc. It doesn't throb the way it did. I think I'm going to live."

"If I thought otherwise I wouldn't have let you out of my sight."

His smile widened. "Speaking of which, I don't think I've thanked you for saving my life."

"You're welcome, but you're still one up on me. You've rescued me twice now." The impact of her words registered, and she suppressed a shudder. "Have I told you I'm scared?"

He gently placed his hands on her shoulders. "So am I. Of course we're afraid. It means we're normal." He moved his hands to the base of her neck and massaged it in slow, easy movements. "Very normal. I don't see anything wrong with fearing for our lives."

Instead of relaxing her, his touch sent automatic warning signals to every nerve in her body. A different kind of danger. She stepped aside.

Reluctantly, he released her. "Don't trust me, either?"

"I don't want to complicate an already complicated mess."

"Who's complicating things? Your neck muscles are really —"

"Would you stop it?" In spite of her tension, she couldn't prevent a smile. Paul Murphy was an easy man to like. "I'm sorry, Murph."

"Sorry about what?" He didn't move away, and he silently drew her gaze, though he didn't touch her again.

"I'm sorry that I'm not eager to become involved in a situation that from past experience I find dangerous."

"Excuse me, but those few dates with a homicidal maniac have nothing to do with a true, loving relationship between a man and a woman, not in any way. That's like comparing fertilizer to precious jewels."

Loving relationship? "A relationship is the last thing we should be discussing right now. What we should be discussing is a way out of this mess."

"So you're saying that danger and romance don't mix."

"Fear can do strange things to a person. It can trigger emotional decisions they wouldn't ordinarily make, and those can be the wrong decisions."

"So if I understand what you're saying," Murph said, "you're afraid that if our friendship were to grow into something that resembled a relationship, that I would suddenly become a different person from the one I am now, and I might try to hurt you in the future?"

"You're twisting my words. I just think we need to get through this situation alive before we allow our emotions to cloud the issue."

He inclined his head in agreement. "That makes sense. We'll get through this situation first, taking every possible step we can to protect ourselves."

"Exactly." Sable turned and walked toward the stairs.

"Afterwards, we can concentrate on the romance," he added.

"That isn't what I meant."

Murph caught up with her. "So what did you mean?"

She turned to look up at him and felt her pulse quicken at the serious expression in his eyes. This was no flirtation; he meant business. But so did she.

"I don't even want to think about romance or about trust or about all the confusion that goes with a romantic relationship. I'm not interested, I don't want it, and I don't plan to fall victim to it. I love my career and my independence. I'm sorry, but I have to make this clear."

"But you're lying," he said softly, "and I didn't take you for a liar."

That smarted. "You have no right to make a judgment about my character when you've known me little more than six weeks."

"Sorry, I should have worded that differently." The tone of Murph's voice grew silky. "I should have said — macho horse manure and trite as it may sound — that your actions speak a different language."

She scowled. "You could be reading my actions in the wrong way." He wasn't. "I'm a doctor. If you're referring to my so-called healing touch, I try to do that with all my patients."

"Seems to me I've picked up on a little more than professional interest," he said.

"You don't have a problem with self-confidence, do you?"

"Actually," he said, then paused thoughtfully. "When it comes to you, I feel extremely insecure, but with something that could become very important to both of us, I think it would be a mistake to turn tail and run."

She blinked in surprise. Transparent honesty? In a man? Wow.

"Besides which," he continued, "come to think of it, you did tell me, in so many words, how concerned you were about my welfare. Remember? Up on the hill?" He gingerly touched the welt on his cheek. "I think I can take that personally."

"You're too pushy, Paul Murphy. It could land you in trouble someday."

To her surprise, she caught a glint of humor in his expression. Feeling a sudden, inexplicable smile attempting to take over her face, she swung back toward the staircase.

"Wait a minute, where are you going?" he asked.

"Downstairs to warm up and check on the food. I'm cold and hungry, and arguing with you isn't helping."

"If it's okay with you, I'd like to look around the attic. I know you said your grandfather put all his important things in an impossibly locked safe, but it doesn't hurt to keep trying. Maybe I can even figure out the combination."

Sable hesitated.

"Do you need me to come downstairs with you for some reason?" he asked.

"No, I just . . ."

His expression changed, and all the teasing lightness in his eyes vanished. "You don't trust me alone in the attic." There was a hint of vulnerability in his voice.

"I trust you, but you could be attacked up there as easily as you were attacked outside."

"Oh." Some of the lightness returned. "Then keep watch. Everyone is downstairs, right? Make sure they stay there. And keep Dillon with you." He gave her a reassuring smile. "I'll see you later."

She watched as he padded up the attic steps in his stockinged feet, then she turned and went downstairs. Every time she was with Murph she felt as if tiny fibers of friendship, of mutual support, of attraction, joined them together, drawing them closer.

She had been attracted to Jim last summer, and that attraction had prevented her from breaking off the relationship sooner, when she picked up on those first few hints that his character did not match the outward charm of his personality. She had made faulty decisions based on loneliness and on a desire that he would be the "man of her dreams."

When she reached the display case with the rock collection downstairs, she studied the specimens again. Nothing was missing, just rearranged. The chunks of galena and sphalerite — the only specimens Grandpa had collected from his own cave — were still there.

She turned from the shelf and glanced up the stairs. She wanted to join Murph, lock the attic to all the guests, and search every box, every envelope, every drawer. But that would take days. At this point, whoever had followed them had no reason to suspect the attic might hold any more evidence than the rest of the house. For that matter, she couldn't be sure, herself, where —

"I've been meaning to ask you about that stuff," a voice came from behind.

Sable started and swung around to see Jerri coming toward her from the direction of the family room. Jerri had short, curly hair the color of sweet potatoes, streaked with blonde at the temples. She was slightly shorter than Sable's 5'6", and weighed about forty pounds more — much of that in muscle.

"Sorry, I didn't mean to sneak up on you." Jerri's voice was low and melodious. "You're not thinking about the ghosts, are you?"

"Ghosts?"

"You know, the ones Craig was talking about last night." Jerri wandered over to the collection shelf. "Just kidding. I was looking at this stuff after breakfast today. Craig told me a little about how your grandfather went around collecting all of it. Sounds like an interesting man."

"He was."

"Craig sure has a thing for all this stuff. He told me about the different stones and the minerals they had in them."

"Craig's a spelunker and amateur rock hound from childhood. He knows these hills better than I do."

"He's smart, all right," Jerri said. "Never thought a plain old rock could be so interesting." She paused and winked. "Of course that might have something to do with who's talking. But really, Sable, are any of these pieces worth anything?"

"Only memories." Sable picked up a geode and watched the sparkles inside the hollow rock reflect light from the room.

"So that story about the history of this place was just a story?"

"No, it was true enough. I mean, those two partners actually did own this place, and they did disappear. But as for the silver, you know how rumors get started. Someone probably found a piece of galena down in the cave and jumped to conclusions."

"Must've been somebody who didn't know much about minerals. Even I know what galena looks like, all boxy, straight sides." She indicated the piece of galena on the shelf.

"Really?" Sable said. "Not a lot of people know the difference. Are you interested in geology?"

"I'm interested in a little of everything, especially when Craig Holt is doing the talking." She grinned. "He explained these stones to me earlier. Maybe those guys started the rumor about silver so they could sell the cave for a profit."

Sable winced at the words. Was that really

what Grandpa had done with the Seitz mine? "That's a thought."

"Good as any, huh? Wonder how dinner's coming. I'm getting hungry. Think I'll go take a look."

Sable watched Jerri leave, then turned back to the case, hating the suspicions that persisted in her mind, hating her jumpy nerves every time someone spoke to her. Was Jerri only casually interested in this place, or was there something else on her mind?

Audry poked her head out of the kitchen door. "Food's ready as soon as Murph and Craig and Simmons come in."

"Simmons? I thought he was in the dining room."

"Are you kidding? He's still sulking. When Perry and I came into the kitchen earlier, Simmons left. When Perry went to find him and apologize, his jacket wasn't on the hall tree. He must have gone outside."

"Okay, Audry. I'll wash, then go find them if I can." She called Dillon to follow her upstairs.

The moment she stepped into her bedroom, Dillon growled behind her.

She froze in the threshold. "What?"

He brushed past her, obviously on alert,

his legs stiff, the fur of his ruff prickling upward with obvious alarm. He growled as he sniffed the comforter.

"No, wait. Dillon, get back." What if someone was in here? They could be under the bed or in the closet. They might even be hiding in the cedar chest. "Dillon, come on, let's get out of here."

Chapter 14

Murph was brushing cobwebs from his arms and shoulders when he descended the last of the squeaky attic steps. A rushing whisper of sound startled him, and he looked up to find Sable racing toward him down the hallway. Dillon quick-stepped beside her, a low, suspicious growl emanating from his throat as he cast glances back along the hallway.

Sable's frightened blue eyes brought out Murph's protective instincts. "What's wrong?" He caught her by the shoulders. "What happened?"

"My room . . . I think someone's been in there, or maybe still is." Her voice rose on a note of panic. "I took Dillon in with me, and he started growling — you know how he acts."

"I'll check it out. You stay here." Instinctively, Murph reached beneath his shirt and freed the Detonics from its holster, wishing he had warned her earlier about the loaded weapon he carried. Now there was no time. He pulled the gun out.

She gasped when she caught sight of the gun metal. "What's that for?"

"Stay here." He gripped the gun in both hands and crept down the hallway. Dillon followed, his growls still rumbling in a nervous tremor. When they reached the open door, Murph paused at the entrance and listened.

All he heard was the chatter of voices downstairs, and Sable's frightened breathing behind him . . . directly behind him.

"I thought I told you to stay put," he muttered.

"Is anyone in the room?"

"I don't know yet." He allowed Dillon in first.

The dog growled softly as he approached the cedar chest. He sniffed it thoroughly, then followed some invisible scent to the straight-backed chair beside the antique chest of drawers. He didn't growl this time but sniffed at the drawer handles.

"I don't think anyone's here now." Still, Murph entered carefully, arms braced. He crept to the closet and opened the door.

No one.

He stepped over to the cedar chest and lifted the lid. Nothing. With one foot, he raised the dust ruffle of the bed and peered underneath. "I think it's clear."

Sable came in behind him. "But someone's been here, I can tell." She gestured toward the cedar chest. "This has been moved away from the bed. I know, because I tried to pull the comforter up last night and it was stuck between the chest and the bed frame." She walked to the closet and peered inside, then opened the top drawer of the bureau.

"Is anything missing?" Murph asked.

She shuffled through a stack of folded underwear. "The letter is missing." She looked up at him. "The one he wrote to Mom that we read last night."

"Not the confession note?" Murph asked.

She patted her pocket. "I have it here. But I put the other letter in this drawer this morning when I dressed, and it's gone. Obviously, Perry wasn't imagining things. I wonder if the other rooms have been searched."

Murph engaged the safety of his pistol.

"Paul, where did you get that gun?"

"I've carried it with me since I arrived in Freemont."

She sank onto the bed. "It's yours?"

"Of course it's mine."

"I don't understand."

"I'll explain it later. Right now we have more important things to discuss." He reached into the pocket of his jeans and pulled out a 3" x 4" photograph. He held it to the light from the window. "Recognize any of these people?"

"Murph, this isn't exactly the time . . ."

She looked at the picture. Her interest focused. "That looks like a really old picture of Grandpa and Otis Boswell, and . . . the woman looks familiar."

"I thought so, too."

She took the picture from him and carried it to the window, holding it to the light. "That's . . ." She looked up at him, obviously mystified. "Who . . . does it look like to you?"

"I've already jumped to my conclusion. Your turn."

The woman's hair was dark, cut in a pageboy, and a few tendrils of it fanned across a very attractive face. "Is it . . . Audry?"

"That's what I thought."

"But this had to be taken thirty-five or forty years ago," she said. "Impossible."

"Why? She told us herself she once lived in Eagle Rock and that she knows this area. Remember?"

"But why didn't she say anything about knowing my grandfather?"

"There could be any number of reasons."

"What's your first guess?" Sable asked.

"Obviously I'm suspicious. It could be she either knows something she doesn't want to talk about, or she's still connected to Boswell in some way."

Sable paced away from the window. Dillon paced along beside her, like a loving, protective shadow.

She stopped in front of Murph and looked up at him. "I think I'd better have a talk with her."

"Are you sure that's wise? What if the outrageous is true and she's our stalker? Shouldn't we treat this as just more evidence and keep our mouths shut for now?"

Sable studied the photograph a moment longer, then handed it back to Murph, pointing at the proprietary hand Audry had on Grandpa's arm. "What does that look like to you?"

"Don't jump to conclusions, Sable," he said gently.

She turned away, and her hand reached up and grasped the old pocket watch that hung from a chain around her neck. Her fingers rubbed across the smooth metal, as if it had the power to keep her safe.

"You do that a lot, don't you?" Murph said.

"Do what?"

He gestured to her hand. "You love that watch. You're always touching it, always reaching up for it, as if something about it reassures you. I'm curious why Josiah would give you a watch that didn't work. I know it's a keepsake, but surely it wouldn't be too expensive to replace the mechanism inside."

"I think *that's* looking a gift horse in the mouth."

"I'm not complaining, Sable." Murph reached out and fingered the delicate design of the watch, then took it in his hand and tested the weight. "I'm wondering . . ."

She frowned. "Wondering?"

"In spite of his apparent weak spots, your grandfather was a generous person."

"He could afford to be, couldn't he?" she said, and there was a strong hint of bitterness in her voice. "He was using someone else's —"

"Stop it."

She blinked up at him. He hated the disillusionment that shadowed her eyes.

"I'm sorry," she whispered. "I really am so very sorry about everything. If not for Grandpa, Noah might still be —"

"I said stop it." He regretted his sharp tone, but it had the desired effect. "I've already warned you not to take on the guilt of the whole world. What I started to say was that I'd have expected Josiah Kessinger to have this watch repaired before he gave it to you, unless there was some reason to do otherwise."

She turned the watch over. "He had it engraved."

Murph read the words on the smooth metal. " 'To Sable with love. A treasure for a treasure.' " He smiled at the sentiment. "Maybe I'm just grasping at straws right now. Maybe that bump on the head affected me worse than I thought, but have you checked the inner workings?"

"No. I never thought —"

"Now might be a good time to look."

She slipped the chain over her head. "I just took it for granted Grandpa was giving this to me because it had been so much a part of him, and he knew I loved it."

"But it wasn't working when he gave it to you."

"No, and it had always worked before. I remember what he said when he gave it to me, too, because at the time it sounded kind of strange. He said, 'You may need it someday, punkin'. I know all I have to.' But I wondered what he meant." She tried to twist the back plate without result. "Do you have a pocketknife?"

Murph pulled one out, opened it, and handed it to her. "Wouldn't hurt to check."

She slipped the point of the blade into the tiny groove between the back plate and the body of the watch. With care, she pried at the plate until it slipped into her hand.

A square of thin, white paper was stuffed into the casing where the inner workings of the watch should have been. Sable used the knife to pry this out, as well.

Murph barely caught the small, shiny nugget that fell from the folds of paper.

"Galena?" Sable asked, reaching for the nugget. She caught her breath when he dropped it into her hand. "That isn't galena. That's . . . that looks more like . . ."

She grabbed the paper from Murph and unfolded it quickly, tearing off a corner in her haste. She scanned the page quickly. "Murph, this is a metallurgists' assay sheet. According to this report, this metal is silver."

He took the paper and read it. "From where?"

"I don't know."

"You sure Josiah never said a word about this?"

"Don't you think I'd remember something like that?" She held the nugget to the murky light from the window.

"Could it be on this place somewhere?" Murph asked.

Sable looked up at him. "You ask a lot of questions. As far as I know, there's never been silver found in this part of Missouri before, especially not a vein of high-grade silver like this."

"Could that story about the cave be true?" Murph asked.

"I don't know."

"Could it have something to do with your grandfather's death?"

The words fell between them like chips of ice, solid with frightening possibilities.

Sable's face grew vulnerable with pain. "I don't know what to think right now," she whispered.

Murph refolded the analysis sheet with the silver and stuffed it back inside the watch. He took the back plate and snapped it on. "There's still not enough evidence to do more than guess. The best place for this is where it's always been." He slipped the chain over her head, then smoothed a tendril of soft black hair from her face. He wished he could smooth all her heartache away, protect her from all harm, and prove to her that the world wasn't really as frightening as it looked right now.

He could do none of that. He could only pray that God would. "Meanwhile, stay close to me," he told her. "If you find something even remotely questionable, tell me immediately." His fingers caressed her soft cheek, and then, as if he couldn't help himself, he allowed a feather-light touch along her neck to rest lightly against the beating pulse at her throat. "Your heart's racing."

"Of course it's racing. I'm scared."

"Me, too."

"Murph, if you can have a gun, I want to carry one, too. There's an old .22 pistol down the hall in the closet. My brothers and I used it for target practice. I'm going to —"

"I don't think that's a good idea."

"Why not? You're carrying one, and you've obviously been carrying it for some time. If you can carry a concealed weapon, why can't I?"

"You don't have a license. I do."

This bit of news surprised her, but she recovered quickly. "Are you a policeman or something?"

"No. I had to work a job out of the country for awhile, and I was required to carry this for protection."

She crossed her arms over her chest. "You know, Murph, your macho attitude is getting on my nerves just a little. Grandpa would have been proud, but I'm not impressed."

In spite of the serious circumstances, Murph felt a grin spread across his face, and he couldn't stop it. He saw Sable's eyes narrow, and he braced himself for an onslaught. It didn't come. Instead, she pivoted away from him suddenly, reached for a flashlight that lay on the bureau, and stalked out of the room. Dillon followed at her heels.

Murph had no choice. He had to go with her. "Sable, are you willing to shoot someone, to take a life? Do you even remember how to use the gun?"

"It's been awhile, but I know how." Her footsteps didn't falter as she led the way down to the other end of the hallway, past the staircase, and opened the door to a walk-in closet. "This is where Grandpa stored his hunting gear."

The heavy smell of gun oil mingled with rancid doe scent that hunters use to attract bucks during hunting season. Sable didn't even pause to catch her breath. "Awful stink. I hated hunting season." She opened the lid of a long, metal gun chest and pulled out a black .22 pistol that fit perfectly in her hands.

"You did say you know how to use that," Murph said.

"Would you quit worrying? It's simple. Let's see . . . there are some bullets here somewhere." She searched all the junk in the chest, which was filled with gun cloths, hunting caps, vests, everything but bullets. "There have to be some in here." She dug more deeply. Cleaning wires and three half-used cans of gun oil tumbled onto the floor. Beneath it all lay a cardboard box. She opened the lid, and the flashlight beam fell on shotgun shells — and cubed chunks of silvery ore.

Murph heard her swift intake of breath. "Galena," she whispered.

Murph picked up a broken shotgun shell. Galena spilled from it.

"No." Sable's voice caught, and the beam from the flashlight faltered, shooting shadows across the walls of the closet.

Murph replaced the shell and reached out to hold the flashlight steady. "Sable, I've already warned you not to jump to conclusions." He lay a hand on her shoulder.

She shrugged him away and slumped against the wall, squeezing her eyes shut.

266

"Oh, Grandpa, how could you?"

"Sable."

"Don't say it. Just don't say anything right now. It's all true." She reached over to a glassed gun case and swung the door open. The case was empty except for one short-barrel shotgun. She pulled it out. "He salted the mine. What else could it have been? He used this gun to shoot the ore into the soft sides of the Seitz mine."

"You can't be sure."

"See that reloader over there in the corner? He used it to fill these shells with ore, then he —" Her voice caught. "He tried to sell the Seitz place by salting a barren hole in the ground."

Murph took her arm. "What are the gun and reloader doing here if he used it in Oklahoma?"

"He brought it back here. He came home often, and he certainly wouldn't want to leave evidence lying around Freemont."

"I'm sorry, Sable. I know you feel awful. I know how I would feel if —"

"Do you?" She shoved the shotgun back onto a shelf and closed the door. "Did you ever have to live with the humiliation of knowing a close family member cheated people out of their money?" Tears sparkled from her eyes in the dim light. She slumped down onto a rickety chair.

He knelt beside her and took her hands in his. "Wait until all this is over before you draw your conclusions. We don't know all the facts yet, and we definitely need to keep digging to find them. It could be —"

A faint, panicked female voice reached them suddenly from somewhere outside. "Help! Somebody come quickly! There's been an accident!"

Chapter 15

Murph and Sable rushed down the stairs to find Jerri and Bryce scrambling into the hallway from the family room. Perry burst through the kitchen door, his shirttail half out of his slacks, wiping his hands on a dish towel.

"What happened?" he cried. "Was that Audry? She was screaming like a banshee. I nearly caught the kitchen on fire."

"Someone hurt?" Jerri said. "Again?"

Murph shoved on his boots. He was tying his laces when the back door flew open and Audry stumbled inside. She wore an orange-red knit cap and her thick, green wool coat.

"I found Simmons in the creek," she said breathlessly. "I've tried to get him up, but he's too heavy. The guy's freezing to a chunk of ice. Come and help me get him inside."

"Is he breathing?" Murph asked as he followed her out ahead of the others.

"He was when I first grabbed him, because he fought me. I had to wrangle him out of the creek, and he passed out on me."

Murph caught up with Audry halfway across the backyard. "Where is —"

"Look." She pointed toward the creek a couple of hundred feet away. "I saw him from the kitchen window, floating face-down in the water, looked like to me. When I got there all I could do was grab him by the sleeve and drag him to the bank. I couldn't get him all the way out of the water. Don't have the strength I used to, and it's impossible to get any traction on that ice. I can't imagine what he was doing out there, the silly thing."

Murph recognized the muscular, broad-shouldered form of Simmons lying faceup, half out of the frigid, rushing water of the creek.

He scrambled over the treacherous ice to the man's side, sank to his knees, and grabbed him by the shoulders. "Simmons!" he shouted, shaking him vigorously.

No response. Murph leaned close and felt no warmth of exhalation and heard no sound. He gently tipped the man's head back and lifted his chin to establish an airway.

Still no breath, no movement.

"What's going on?" Audry demanded behind him.

"He isn't breathing." Still holding Simmons's face tilted slightly upward, Murph managed to pinch the nostrils shut. He covered the man's mouth with his own and exhaled twice, deeply, slowly.

Still no response.

Murph slid the first two fingers of his right hand down into the hollow of the victim's neck, feeling for the carotid pulse. He couldn't tell, for sure, if what he was feeling was Simmons's pulse or his own. If it was Simmons's, it was very weak.

"I've got to start CPR," he told Audry. "Get Sable —"

"I'm here," came a very welcome voice behind him.

"Take his head; I'll do compressions." He scooted aside and unzipped Simmons's jacket while Sable slid into position at the man's head.

Murph had just found his anatomical landmarks and was on his knees beside Simmons, in position to begin the first compression, when he saw Sable give another rescue breath.

With the fingers of both hands locked together over the lower third of Simmons's breastbone, Murph gave five compressions.

Sable was just leaning forward to breathe for the patient again, when Simmons choked, gasped, sat up suddenly, and coughed violently, spewing creek water.

Murph held him steady until he stopped coughing.

Simmons jerked around, eyes wild, shivering. "What hap—"

"It's okay," Murph said. "We've got to get you inside. Let us help you up —"

"No!" Simmons cried. He choked again, a loud, rasping sound that brought up more of the creek water.

"Mr. Simmons," Sable said, leaning on Murph's shoulders to lever herself up to her feet, "you fell into freezing water. We've got to get you inside and warm you up. Can you walk?"

Simmons crabbed sideways in the water, his legs pumping ineffectively. "Can't feel them . . . can't feel my feet!"

Murph nodded to Sable, and together they helped the man up. "Hang on," he said, grasping Simmons around the waist and lifting him over his shoulder.

The drenching chill of water soaked through his shirt. Immediately, his feet slipped and he stumbled forward. "I need help. Is Craig —"

"*I'm* here," Bryce said, scrambling down to them. "Here, let me."

With Bryce's help, Murph and Sable

manhandled Simmons up the treacherous ice to the house, where Audry, Perry, and Jerri waited.

Simmons choked again.

"Is he okay?" Jerri asked.

"What was he doing all the way down there, anyway?" Perry held the door open for them. "The outdoor privy is way back up here on the hill. He couldn't have slipped and fallen all the way down there, could he? He's soaking wet! Did he fall into the creek?"

"Of course he fell into the creek," Audry snapped. "What does it look like? He went swimming?"

Murph carried Simmons into the house and lowered him onto the hearth in front of the fire.

Sable rushed to take the wet clothes Murph peeled from Simmons's near-frozen body. "Perry, would you pump a pot of water and start it boiling?" she asked. "We'll need as much warm water as we can get. Bryce, he'll need something warm to drink. Audry —"

"Right, warm blankets and lots of them." The older lady pivoted and ran up the stairs.

"Good. We need more heat in the house. Craig, would you —" Sable turned around, surprised, as if she had just realized Craig wasn't there.

"I'll stoke the fire," Jerri said. "Craig's probably out still hauling wood. It was pretty scarce down in the basement when I checked last." She disappeared down the basement steps.

Murph rubbed Simmons's hands. "Just relax. We'll get you warm."

"Just keep away from me!" the man said through chattering teeth. "Stay away from me. I couldn't get out, nobody'd help me out of the water! You were all just gonna stand there —" He coughed again, gasped for air, and shook his head. He peered around the room, checked over each shoulder, then narrowed his eyes at Murph. "You'd've let me drown."

"We didn't let you drown, obviously." Murph eased Simmons backward and removed his shoes and socks. His feet looked pale and were icy cold to the touch. "You're safe now. You're here in the house by the fire. What happened?"

The sound of brisk steps echoed from the staircase. Simmons swung around and glared over the top of the sofa.

Audry came toward them with an armload of blankets, still in her stocking cap and coat. She dropped the blankets onto the sofa, then unfolded one. "Here, wrap this around him."

Simmons stiffened. "Keep her away from me," he told Murph through gritted teeth.

"Nonsense, you're delirious." Audry spread out another blanket.

Simmons cringed against the stone hearth. "Get back!"

Audry frowned. "All right, what is it? What's going on here?"

"You wouldn't let me out of that creek."

"You really are imagining things," she snapped. "You lost your footing and fell into the creek, then couldn't climb out onto the slick ice. I'm the one who dragged you out of there, so don't go blaming me for your clumsiness. What were you doing out there, anyway?"

He raised a trembling hand and pointed at the knit cap on Audry's head. "I didn't imagine the orange head when you pushed me back into the water. I didn't imagine the green shoulders."

"I did not push you into the water."

"Out of the way," came Perry's voice as he carried a mug from the kitchen. "I've got a nice, warm cup of soup broth here. It's our dinner. Come on, Simmons, drink up. This will warm you faster than —"

There was a thump from the front porch, and Dillon barked. Perry sloshed broth over his shirt. The front door flew open, and Craig entered noisily, stomping his feet on the welcome mat, unzipping the front of the coveralls he wore. His movements gradually slowed, as if he realized he'd become the focus of attention.

"Where'd you get those clothes?" Audry demanded.

Craig pulled off his orange-red stocking cap and shrugged out of the dark green coveralls. "From the mud room. Sorry I didn't mention it earlier, but there are a couple more coveralls and caps out there, in case anyone wants to go for a walk. Not that I'd recommend it." He tossed the outer clothing over the hearth, then looked over at the silent group with a frown. "What happened? What's wrong with Simmons?"

"He fell into the creek," Audry said.

"Someone tried to drown me," Simmons snapped. "Someone in an orange cap and green coat. I remember that."

"Well, it wasn't me," Audry scoffed. "What I want to know is what you were doing down at the creek." She pulled the knit cap from her head, and her short, gray hair tried to cling to the material with static electricity.

"I wanted to see if there was a way out of here." Simmons shivered. "I checked the bridge, then started back to the house when I . . . when I lost my footing."

"Meaning you fell into the water all by yourself," Audry said. "You didn't need pushing. Just as I thought."

Simmons jerked the blanket more tightly around the thick expanse of his shoulders. He coughed and didn't argue any further.

"Seems they were wearing clothes like that." Audry pointed toward Craig's discarded clothing.

"But why would anybody —" Craig began, then stopped. His dark brows lowered. "What's going on here? This is too much. There've been too many —"

"We'll discuss it later," Sable said. She slipped past Murph toward the stairs. "I need to get my medical bag and check our patient."

After dinner, Sable left Murph and Craig sitting with Simmons by the fire while she escorted Bryce, Perry, Audry, and Jerri up to the attic to see if they could find more clothes. The sky continued to thicken with clouds as the sun went down. The temperature hovered in the mid-twenties. They were making plans for a longer imprison-

277

ment unless the weather improved.

"I still think Simmons was hallucinating," Audry muttered as she searched through a huge old cedar chest in the light from Sable's powerful battery lantern. "Did you see how fast he recovered during dinner?"

"Yeah." Jerri lifted an old sweater and held it to the light. "But he wasn't quite as gruff. I think I like his post-accident personality. Maybe someone should've done that earlier."

"No one did anything." Audry pulled out a blue suit that Sable remembered seeing Grandpa wear to special functions when she was a little girl. "I remember this," the older woman said.

"You do?" Sable asked.

Audry didn't meet her gaze. "I mean this style. It's back in fashion now, did you know? Too bad all the rest of us old things can't be back in fashion."

Jerri laughed from across the room. "I think you have to be dead first."

"Audry doesn't plan to die for a long, long time," Perry said. "She can't boss people around from the grave."

"Watch your mouth." Audry patted Perry's tummy. "I've been good for you. We've probably run two pounds off that portly paunch already today. You need it. I heard the way you were panting when you carried water upstairs this afternoon."

"I was not panting," Perry retorted. "When I offered to help out in the kitchen during our stay here, I wasn't giving you the right to make a track star out of me in two or three days. You've had me running up and down stairs all day, carrying water for baths and flushes. I can do other things beside run steps, you know."

"Of course you can." Audry turned and appraised the rest of the attic. "Beautiful. This is almost like an antique store." She closed the lid of the chest and stepped around a box to get a closer look at an old pitcher and bowl set. "I love to look at old things and dream about who used them and imagine what kinds of lives they must have lived. This place is wonderful, and it's so huge."

Sable itched to ask Audry if Josiah Kessinger had ever been a part of those dreams. The only thing that kept her silent was Murph's warning not to broadcast their circumstances to the guests.

"Audry, look," Jerri said. "We could decorate a whole house with these things." She skirted more pieces of antique furniture and rows of labeled boxes. "Well, maybe a small cabin. Is that what you did, Sable? Audry, your room is furnished with antiques, isn't it?"

"Yes, I think most of them are." Audry picked up one of a set of ruby glass vases and held them to the light, for a moment unaware of Sable's sudden, intent interest.

"Did Craig give you the grand tour?" Sable asked.

"No, and I wish he had," Audry said. "Jerri and I took one ourselves while the others were preparing for sleep. Simmons complained about the noise we were making. Properly chastised, we went to bed."

"Leave it to Simmons," Perry remarked from the far corner of the attic, where he leaned against an old chest, examining a stack of pictures. "He seems to enjoy ruining a good time."

"That's okay," Jerri said. "Because the lights went out soon after, and I wouldn't've wanted to be up here then. Call me a coward, but even on the most fundamental level, this place could be dangerous. Look at all the things a person could fall over." She reached down and raised the lid from a box of clothes. "You could trip on this and hit your head on that old sewing machine hard enough to crack a skull."

"Is it necessary to be so morbid?" Perry complained. "I came up here to find clothes, not to hear scary stories. I think we're all frightened enough as it is."

"It would be easy to believe those ghost stories about this place," Jerri said. "And I'm superstitious, anyway. There've been too many accidents — what with Sable almost falling into the ravine and Murph getting conked on the head this afternoon and now poor Simmons."

"If you're being superstitious, we have nothing further to worry about," Audry said. "They say accidents come in threes, and Simmons makes number three."

"For me, it makes four." Jerri swept through a curtain of cobwebs and peered at an antique pie safe in the corner. "I wasn't even supposed to be driving this route. I drove up from Oklahoma City and got stuck in Joplin because my replacement was stuck somewhere on a road in Kansas. I shouldn't even be here."

Allowing the conversation to go on without her, Sable examined a pile of boxes along the back wall. "There's clothing over here. Why don't you three go through some of it while I show Bryce some of the clothes my brothers used to wear." She hoped they would take the polite hint. She had brought them up here to find clothing, not antiques. She didn't want them rummaging around in any of the unopened boxes before she had a chance to search, and she didn't need any dire predictions about impending accidents. She'd had enough of those.

To her relief, the attention of the others finally focused on the boxes of clothing, and she was free to concentrate on Bryce.

Many of Randy's old jeans looked as if they would fit the fifteen year old, so he stepped behind a huge wooden wardrobe to try them on. While Sable waited, she gazed around the attic. With studied nonchalance, she strolled over to a cardboard file box but was disappointed to find that all it contained were pictures.

Mom was an avid photographer, and her interest had infected Sable at an early age. Sable had taken some good pictures of her favorite haunts down in the cave. She hadn't visited those places in months. But Jim was gone. Judging by recent events, she would probably be safer beneath the ground than she was inside the house. Besides, she needed to do some exploring, and she desperately needed to get away by herself for awhile.

But would the cave be safe now? Anyone

could follow her down — not that anyone knew the cave as well as she did. Except maybe Craig.

She raised the lid from a box of pictures and sorted through them idly. Several were of the cave, many of which she had taken when she was a twelve year old. There'd been a drought here when she was twelve, and she found a picture that showed the crystal cavern empty of water. The walls of the cavern held the silvery cubes of galena and the rough sphalerite chunks — ore that hadn't come from the cave. Those poor men who had been fooled into buying this place must have been bitterly disappointed.

Disappointed enough, perhaps, to have started the rumor about finding silver so they could unload the property on some other unsuspecting buyer? If that was so, where did the silver in her watch fit into the story?

Despite all the photographs she had taken over the years, her favorite rendition of the cave was a hand-drawn map Grandpa had been working on for years. He'd kept it as complete as possible, including every cavern, every passage, almost every formation.

"These don't fit." Bryce broke her train

of thought as he stepped from behind the wardrobe, holding a pair of jeans up for Sable to see.

"Oh, well, there's plenty more where those came from. Just keep digging." Sable motioned with her hand toward the open box resting on the floor.

As Bryce moved past her, she walked over to that map, which hung on the wall between two windows. Once upon a time it had held a place of honor in the family room downstairs, but when they redecorated last year, Mom had taken it down. Ordinarily, when the power was on, an overhead spotlight could be turned on to illuminate the map like a museum exhibit, but now in the half light offered by the oil lamps they had brought with them to the attic, Grandpa's intricate drawing looked like hen scratchings on the wall.

While Bryce continued trying on clothes, Sable leaned closer to the map. A smudge of red ink caught her attention from the far right, at the end of one of the smaller passages. She held her light closer. The new drawing was in the shape of a funnel, and below it was a circle with markings . . . it looked like the face of a clock.

Her hand went up to the watch hanging from the silver chain around her neck.

Bryce came over wearing a pair of jeans Randy had outgrown many years ago. "These'll work."

Sable lowered her light and inspected the fit. They were a little loose on him, but they would work. "Are there any more? You may be here awhile."

"There's a couple more, and . . . hey, is that a map of the cave?" Bryce stepped closer and peered at the wall. "Wow! That's great."

"My grandpa drew it, and he had to keep updating it as we explored and found more passages." As she talked, her mind continued to search for pieces of the puzzle. *The funnel . . . could that be . . . ?*

"Can we go down?" Bryce moved closer to examine the map. "At least a little way?" He turned to Sable beseechingly. "I found a pair of old jeans I could wear down there."

"Oh? When did you plan to do that?" Sable asked. *A sinkhole? Could the funnel be a sinkhole?*

"Whenever you're free," Bryce said.

"Craig makes a good guide," Sable said, turning her attention back to the teenager.

"But it was your grandpa who owned the cave, right? And he's almost like a legend, hearing Craig talk about him."

"Yes, but Craig —"

"Come on, Sable." Bryce leaned forward and gave her a dimpled, entreating smile. "Why can't you take me?"

Sable hesitated a moment more. She could imagine him charming his mother with that smile . . . or girls at school. She glanced back at the map. "We'll see."

"All right! When do we go?"

She hadn't said for sure they would, but the more she thought about it, the more eager she became to get out of the house for awhile. "I'd like to wait until morning."

He looked at the pictures Sable held in her hand. "Are those of the cave?"

She held them up in the glow of the lantern for him to see more clearly. "Yes, I took them myself. Do those other jeans fit?"

"They're okay. I thought Craig said something about a collapse in the cave."

"A very minor one, and nowhere near where we'd be going." Sable pushed all the old pictures back into the box, thinking about the sinkhole Grandpa had stepped into last November. Could that be what he'd drawn? "There's usually no danger of a collapse in a natural cave."

Jerri joined them to inspect a box of clothes and shoes and insinuated herself into the conversation. "I'm afraid of caves. What about snakes?"

"Would you want to live in the dark?" Bryce asked.

"No way."

"Neither do snakes. Besides, the caves in Missouri are too cold for snakes." He sounded like a tour guide. "The average temperature down there stays around fifty-four degrees, and snakes are cold blooded; they don't like it. Of course, if you don't want to come with us . . ."

"I don't." Jerri grinned. "I'll stay up here and stay warm."

Audry joined them. "I don't like caves, either, so I'll stay behind with you. Sable, would you mind if I borrowed this?" She held up a ruffled mauve blouse.

Sable stood up, searching for a box of her mother's clothes. "Of course not. Why don't you take that box down to your room? Then you can pick and choose at your leisure."

As the others continued looking through clothes, Sable wandered to the far corner of the attic, where the door of Grandpa's safe was camouflaged by a rack of clothing. Beside it was an old metal file box. Sable didn't expect to find anything special in it, but curiosity prodded her to open the rusted latch and pull the lid back. There was a manila envelope at the top, with the return address of Tri-County Labs in Freemont, the same firm that had analyzed the silver inside the watch casing.

This could be something. Sable placed the tray into a box of clothing and covered it with an old blouse. She would carry it to the safety of her room and close the door, to hide from prying eyes.

Chapter 16

The attic door squeaked softly when Sable pulled it shut behind her. She made sure the latch had caught before turning away and picking up her box from the floor.

Jerri's voice drifted along the hall. "Probably can't fit into any of these, but I'll give it a try. Too bad Sable didn't have any fat family members."

"Perry's the one who needs to worry," Audry said.

"I heard that!" came Perry's voice from behind the closed door of the sewing room.

Sable carried the box to her room and placed it on the bed. She took the blouse from atop the metal tray, then turned back to close the door.

Audry stood in the doorway, hands on hips as she focused her glare on Sable.

"Did you think of something else you needed, Audry?"

Audry's gaze flicked across the contents of the box, but she didn't comment on it. "Sable, you've got Bryce all excited now about going down in that cave. Are you sure it's safe? You said yourself this drought has changed things. I've heard of all kinds of accidents killing people in those places."

Sable resisted the urge to toss the blouse back on top of the tray. "Mines. You're thinking of mines, Audry. This cave was formed naturally, just another part of the earth. Outside, under the trees, is where it's dangerous right now."

A deep voice reached them from the hallway behind Audry. "You can say that again." Murph's dark auburn hair shone in the glow from his flashlight as he joined her in the threshold. The truth of his statement was etched plainly on the side of his face. "What's this about caves?"

"Sable is taking Bryce down in the morning," Audry said. "I just don't think it's a good idea for her to be down there alone with nobody but a fifteen year old for company."

"Hey!" Bryce shouted from down the hall. "I heard that!"

"I'm sorry, but facts are facts."

Sable fidgeted. Her room had suddenly become a little too high-profile. "We'll be perfectly safe, Audry." Honestly, the woman had an irritating inquisitiveness.

"She grew up here, Audry," Murph assured the older lady. "She knows that cave pretty well."

"But Murph, I would feel so much better if you would go with them."

Sable's suspicions were aroused. Why, all of a sudden, did Audry want Murph out of the house?

"I'll be with them," he said. "I wouldn't mind doing a little spelunking myself while I have the chance."

"That isn't necessary," Sable told him.

Audry smiled and spread her hands apologetically. "Forgive an old lady for being so anxious, but what would happen if we had an accident we couldn't handle? We can't get out."

"How is Murph going to keep us from having an accident in the cave?" Sable heard the sharpness of her own voice, and she tried to soften it. "I know that cave, and I'm not going to do anything stupid. We'll probably only be gone a couple of hours, maybe longer if there's water. The pools and streams would slow us down."

"But you'd be back in time for lunch?"

"I'm not sure. If we're not, we'll eat when we return. I don't think it's something you need to worry about. We'll eat whatever we can find to eat." For Pete's sake, it wasn't as if they were expected to have a family-style, sit-down dinner every morning, noon, and night. Sable reached for the door in an obvious hint that she wanted to be alone. She barely resisted the urge to remind Audry that she wasn't anybody's mother here, and she had no authority in this house.

Finally, Murph caught her message. "Audry, why don't you show me some of the treasures you found in the attic? I may have to look for something myself." The two of them sauntered down the hallway, and Sable closed the door behind them.

"Calm down," Sable muttered to herself. "Don't let the tension get to you. Audry's only being her bossy self . . . probably. Her bossy, manipulative self . . . her bossy, nosy, annoying . . . self."

Probably.

Rubbing her neck to relieve some of the stress, Sable turned once more to the box on her bed. She raised the lid of the tray and pulled out the large manila envelope. Inside were several stapled pages under a cover letter to Grandpa announcing the enclosed three analysis reports. The next page was smaller than letter size, a thin sheet of paper that was a report on the galena, with a high content of lead.

So that could be why the specimen collection downstairs was rearranged. Maybe Grandpa had taken the galena and sphalerite to Tri-County Labs to be analyzed.

She turned the page to find the sphalerite wet chemical analysis. It was rich with zinc, but so what? Why even bother to have it analyzed? Grandpa knew it wasn't native ore. Or maybe he'd requested the analysis for another reason, like maybe it was connected to the ore-filled shotgun shells in the gun closet. But how?

She flipped back the sphalerite analysis sheet, but there was no third sheet. She looked at the cover letter again, which specifically mentioned three analysis reports.

She knew where the third one was. She fingered the watch that dangled around her neck, wondering what it could all mean. Grandpa had been up to something. What could all of this have to do with his death? Or Noah's?

She slid the sheets back into their envelope and searched the rest of the tray, which was approximately four inches in depth. She found a couple of letters from Grandpa, which she opened and scanned.

They were old letters, written in November, when Grandpa had fallen in a sinkhole down by the creek and broken his ankle. In one letter he praised Mom for caring for him while he was incapacitated, then went on and on about what a good thing it was he fell. He'd found another opening to the cave, a sinkhole which was ordinarily underwater.

That was it — the fresh markings on the map upstairs. The "funnel" shape was a sinkhole. He'd already drawn it in.

In the second letter he told about buying the Seitz property, with Noah and Otis as partners. He didn't sound enthusiastic about it — an unusual thing for Grandpa. Ordinarily, if Grandpa didn't feel passionate about something, he took that as a cue that he should not be involved.

But then, what made her think she knew Grandpa at all? He'd managed to trick her — trick everybody — hadn't he?

Hadn't he?

Nothing else in the letter seemed significant. She folded the pages, replaced them in the tray, and sifted through the remaining contents. Near the bottom she found an open envelope, again with Grandpa's handwriting. It was dated three days before Christmas. She pulled the pages out quickly.

I should never have signed my name to that contract, but now that I have, I'm as guilty as anyone else. I was so close I could have smelled the money — I thought this would be the best chance to get out of debt and get on top of things. What would it be like to be debt free? Even better, we would never have to worry about mortgages or bill collectors again. Now I'm not sure. I need to talk to you and the kids about some things. Maybe even the police. There may still be a chance. I just want Sable out of this stinking town.

The police. Which police had he talked to?

She flipped the page and gasped. There were copies of a note and a deed of trust. To this place.

Otis Boswell held the mortgage. At the top of the first page was a handwritten note in blue ink: "Just thought you'd appreciate a reminder."

The papers seemed to burn her fingertips, and the letter fell to the floor. Grandpa had borrowed the money from Boswell to buy that mine, using this place as collateral. That blue-inked note wasn't in his handwriting.

Was it Boswell's, perhaps?

Sable slumped against the dresser. Boswell again. It always came back to him. What if he suddenly called in the loan? How deeply was he involved in this thing? He always seemed to be breathing down their necks. . . .

Breathing . . . was that breathing she heard? No, wait, it was squeaking. She heard squeaks coming from . . . from somewhere nearby.

Footsteps echoed gently along the hallway. There was a familiar creak, and then the footsteps receded in the direction from which they had come.

Okay, good. Probably Audry had come to pester her again about taking Murph with her, had seen the closed door, and had taken the hint.

Sable shoved the metal tray beneath her bed, then picked up the box. She would carry it upstairs to the attic and see if she could find more records or files that might be helpful. She desperately wished she knew the combination to that safe. And she needed a better look at that map. The funnel-sinkhole had been at the end of one of the passages, but she'd been too distracted by Bryce and the others to study it closely.

She stepped back into the hall and crept to the attic door. She opened the door as quietly as possible and closed it behind her tightly enough that she would hear the latch if anyone else tried to open it. She slipped up the steps and managed to reach the upper floor with only two telltale squeaks.

For some reason, the huge old room seemed darker than it had just a few minutes ago. And colder. Sable shook her head. It was just her imagination. She had seen everyone leave, and she knew she was alone. She would have heard anyone who might have come up here. She was safe. The others were on the floor below, and if someone tried to come upstairs on her, she only had to scream to bring everyone running.

But no one was up here. She knew that.

Dark shapes of heavy furniture loomed around and over her, and for no good reason she developed an acute case of goose pimples. She raised her lantern high, dispelling a few of the shadows. Amazing how much more frightening things could be when you were alone, and when you feared someone might be watching . . . and when you didn't know who that someone might be.

A small squeak echoed from the darkness, and she paused to listen. A mouse, probably, but she shivered. It felt colder up here without the others.

Jerri's laughter rang out from below, and Sable relaxed. She had never been afraid of mice before, no reason to start now.

The tall, mirrored bureau stood at the edge of the very top step. She turned, caught the reflection of her movement in the mirror, and jumped.

"Stupid," she told herself impatiently. The fear in her eyes reflected back at her in the glow from her flashlight. Did she appear this obviously spooked to the others?

She couldn't help recalling those hours after she'd found Noah's body lying in the doorway. A shudder passed through her every time the memory replayed in her mind. Now, every time she was alone, she had to fight that creeping feeling of danger and remind herself that her safety and Murph's depended on how well she kept her fear in check — how well she remained prepared for attack from any side.

Floorboards creaked beneath her feet as she stepped past the looming furniture. Many pieces had been covered with sheets to protect them from dust; someone might even be tempted to hide beneath one of those sheets.

Though annoyed by her own fears, she made as little noise as possible as she crept toward the file box at the far end of the cavernous room. She stopped between the dormer windows and looked at the boxes and chests stacked in rows. Somehow, it looked different. Of course, they had taken several of the smaller clothing boxes downstairs, but there was something else. . . .

She inspected the rack of clothes in front of the safe. Had it been disturbed? She stepped closer and pushed the garments aside, holding the lantern up high. The door was tightly closed with the lock in place. But something . . . She glanced over her shoulder with a frown and saw an empty spot between the two windows.

The map was missing.

But how could that be? She'd been the last one to walk out of here just a few moments ago. She'd seen what the others had carried, and no one had the map — no one had taken it from the wall.

Feeling less and less comfortable, she went to the file cabinet. What else was missing? What if there had been someone up here besides Bryce, Audry, Perry, and Jerri? There were places they might hide. . . .

"Stop being ridiculous," she whispered to herself. She needed to trust her own sense of hearing. She'd just left here a few minutes ago. Anyone would have had to pass her door. She would have heard them.

So who took the map?

There was another rustle somewhere in the darkness — the skittering feet of a tiny mouse. Big deal.

But it sounded strangely like breathing. She *heard* breathing.

She tensed and straightened to scan the shadowed attic. She *had* heard the breathing.

Someone was in the attic with her. She tried to tell herself it was just more paranoia, but her gaze stopped at the bulk of a tall pie safe covered by a paisley print sheet. The sheet wasn't hanging right. The noises she'd heard earlier had come from that direction.

It's only my imagination. She couldn't let herself get carried away.

She crept quietly across the floor, the hairs at the back of her neck prickling with sensitivity. When she drew close enough to reach out and touch the sheet, a board squeaked beneath her foot.

The sheet moved with a jerk, lifted, came toward her and down over her head. She opened her mouth to cry out, and a rough hand shoved a wad of the sheet into her mouth. With skill and speed, her attacker pulled the material tightly around her body and shoved her to the floor. She whacked her elbow on the hardwood as she rolled over, kicking the air, struggling frantically with the binding material as someone raced across the attic and down the steps.

She rolled the other way, kicked out at the bottom of the sheet, and gripped a loose end. By the time she was free of the sheet, it was too late to pursue her attacker.

Chapter 17

Murph tossed another log into the furnace in the basement and closed the heavy iron door with a solid *clonk.* If the weather didn't break before long, he would go out and chop more wood, but not alone. He desperately hoped the weather would break.

He checked the latch on the furnace door one more time, then pulled off the gloves and placed them on a shelf. He closed the door that led into the cave, resisting the urge to do a little spelunking tonight. He would go with Sable and Bryce in the morning, if Sable didn't pull rank on him and bar the door. If she did, he would remind her that she was no longer the doctor in charge, they no longer worked at the clinic, and he didn't have to take orders from her.

He smiled at the thought of her. She had permeated his dreams lately, as well as his heart. The problem was, he didn't trust the instincts that told him she felt the same kind of attraction. She was suffering too much heartache right now, and she was vulnerable.

His self-control was definitely waning where she was concerned. Every time he looked at her, she was more beautiful to him, but in the past week he'd seen a darkness there — deep grief. He only wished he possessed the power — or at least the knowledge — to ease her pain.

"Lord, protect us," he whispered. "Strengthen my faith in You, because right now I'm really struggling with it. And Sable . . . Lord, You're so new to her. Let this draw her closer to You instead of damaging her fresh faith." He paused. "I could use some help about how to talk to her and how to protect her." Here he was, supposedly a strong man, and he felt so helpless. As Noah used to say, it was especially good for a man to be forced to depend on the strength of Jesus Christ alone. That was where a man really found his power . . . and his humility.

"Okay, so I need more humility, Lord," he murmured. "Let Your will be done. Just protect us. Especially, protect . . ." He heard a scatter of footsteps overhead.

As if his prayer had conjured the reality, he looked up the basement stairs to find Sable racing down them. Her face was flushed, and she rubbed her elbow as if in pain. Her wide blue eyes held a confusing combination of anger and fear as she scanned the basement.

His body went cold. Something else had happened. "Sable? What —"

"Did anyone go through the living room just a minute ago?" Her voice quavered.

"I don't know; I've been down here. I didn't hear anyone. What's wrong?"

"I was attacked in the attic."

"Attacked?" He rushed to her side. "Who? Did you see them? Are you hurt?"

"I didn't see who it was. I'm not hurt; I just bumped my elbow."

"You went up there alone?" She exasperated him.

"It should have been safe. Murph, I could have sworn no one came past my door. You know how the stairs creak."

"And so does everyone else by now," he grumbled. "Any intelligent person would have little difficulty finding ways around that."

"Still, I apparently surprised someone, and they hid. When I got too close, they shoved me to get away. If they'd meant to hurt me —"

"I can't believe you're trying to excuse them for —"

"I'm not trying to excuse anyone."

"Where's Dillon? Why wasn't he with you?"

"I saw him in the kitchen, eating from his dish." She sounded defensive. "Even a watchdog has to eat."

"Come upstairs with me." Murph took her hand. "Where is everybody? Did you see them when you came through?"

"Most of the doors are closed — they're either trying on clothes or resting. Bryce was reading in the family room by candle-light."

Murph led the way cautiously up the steps to the living room. "Dillon," he called. "Here, boy."

They heard the click of canine toenails and saw the German shepherd trot through the open kitchen door, ears perked forward, water dripping from his chin.

"Come, Dillon." Then, dropping his voice to a whisper as they climbed the staircase to the second floor, he said, "Sable, I don't suppose you would agree to stay in your room while I check this out."

"If you're going to the attic, so am I," she said.

Murph reached for the gun beneath his

shirt as they walked down the hallway and approached the attic entrance. "You could at least stay behind me."

"Fine."

Dillon whined beside her. Some brave watchdog he was turning out to be.

When they passed Audry's closed door, Murph heard feminine laughter. Jerri and Audry. That eliminated the suspect list by two.

Maybe.

He felt the rush of cold air when he opened the attic door. He barged up the steps into the huge, cavernous room, gun at the ready.

Nothing, of course. The attic was deserted. Dillon snuffled around some boxes, and Sable picked up a colorful sheet that had been tossed in a heap beside the antique pie safe.

"Somebody must have sneaked past my bedroom door," she said. "Whoever it was hid under this sheet, then threw it over my head, knocked me down, and ran."

He checked the shadows and peered into corners, aiming his flashlight into every cranny where an intruder might have hidden. He found nothing.

He returned to Sable's side and placed a protective arm around her. She rested her forehead against his chest. It fit so naturally there.

"Did you get any sense of who your attacker might have been?" he asked. "Size? Did they say anything?"

"Nothing. I was too startled." She raised her head and looked up at him. The lines of tension tightened around her mouth.

He pushed up the sleeve of her sweater and examined the small red welt near her elbow. "Please tell me you didn't try to give chase."

"I didn't have a chance. By the time I got untangled from that mess, they were gone. But I would have."

"Sable, they could have —"

"I know, they could have killed me."

Murph groaned, frustrated with her and with himself, feeling more and more helpless every moment.

"They could have, yes," he said at last. "They didn't. Thank God."

She looked up at him. "Speaking of God, if we belong to Him, why is this happening to us? Why aren't we being protected?"

"What makes you think we aren't? Look at all that's already happened, and we're still here." In spite of the lack of value she seemed to be placing on her life right now.

"But for how long?" she whispered.

"I don't have any idea," he said, drawing her closer, wishing he could take all of her fears away. But he couldn't. And he knew God didn't want him to. It was a failing of his, trying to take on the worries of the world, especially of those he cared about.

He was beginning to care about Sable very much.

"Someone's stalking us," she said, "just to find out what we have and what we know." She drew back and looked up at him. "I might have just found a big clue."

"What kind of clue?"

"Boswell holds a mortgage on this place."

"How? Why would he —"

"Grandpa apparently borrowed money against this place when they purchased the Seitz mine. Along with the deed of trust, I found two analysis sheets. The letter attached said there were three, but I only found two. One for galena and one for sphalerite. The other must have been for the silver. I'm not sure why he would have had them analyzed."

"Unless he suspected they really were native to the mine."

Sable turned away. "Or unless Grandpa planned to use them to dupe —"

"No, Sable, don't say it. You've got to stop allowing your anger and disappointment with Josiah to cloud your deductive reasoning. He was human and he made mistakes, but I can't help feeling there are a lot of pieces to this puzzle that we haven't even seen yet."

She was silent for a moment, then she nodded. "I know. You're right. It's just that I thought I could depend on my knowledge of my grandfather, and I discovered I was apparently wrong."

"But remember that I warned you not to jump to conclusions. We need to keep collecting pieces. I wonder if Boswell knows the results of the analyses?"

"I believe he had his ways of finding out. For all I know, Grandpa had the ore analyzed just for that reason, so Boswell would think this place was worth more than it is and would loan the required amount of money." Her voice wobbled. "And I'm not jumping to conclusions now, I'm just trying to make the pieces fit."

"But he didn't confess to doing that, did he? It seems to me, if he confessed one thing, he would confess everything."

She stepped to the window where she'd been when Murph was attacked that afternoon. "Okay, so you're saying Boswell might have known about the silver analysis and was willing to do anything to get it away from Grandpa. Now he could call in the loan, and we can't pay it." She continued to stare out the window. "Otis Boswell could have controlled Grandpa, holding that mortgage over his head." She glanced over her shoulder at Murph. "The copy I saw of the mortgage contract had a note jotted atop it — almost a taunt. Or a reminder. And it wasn't in Grandpa's writing."

"A reminder?"

"I'm not trying to excuse Grandpa for what he did, but is it possible Boswell coerced him into it?" Sable asked.

"It's possible *if* Josiah even did anything wrong in the first place. You told me he never wanted you in Freemont."

"That's right."

He joined her at the window. "Tell me, do you recall how many accident patients you've seen from the mines since you went to work at the clinic?"

She shrugged. "A few. The other docs see more, because they have more patients. I'm still considered new, inexperienced, and I'm a woman. I see more of the miners' wives and children. Why do you ask?"

"Because one of the reasons Noah suggested I go to work at the clinic in Freemont was because he thought there might be some safety issues in the mines."

"Safety issues?"

"He thought they might cut a few corners to save money. It does seem to me that we received more accident victims at the clinic than I would have expected in the six weeks I worked there."

"I saw some results of stupid actions," Sable told him, "but I always reported them properly. I'm sure the other docs did, too. We could get into too much trouble if we didn't. Not to mention it's unethical."

"Of course you would do the right thing," he said.

Sable looked up at him, her gaze flitting across his features searchingly.

Murph had never realized the sensuality a woman could bring to a single glance, nor the guilt he could feel over such overwhelming attraction at a time like this. "Are you going to look for anything more tonight?" he asked. "Because if you are, I'm sticking to you like Dermabond adhesive."

"I'd like to try to make some sense out of what we already have." She spread her hands in a gesture of frustration. "This is all such a shock. Why did Grandpa sign those mortgage papers? Why didn't he talk to us about it first? We might have been able to figure something else out."

"Judging by what Craig said about your grandpa, he was kind of an impulsive man. Maybe he didn't want you to try to talk him out of doing what he wanted to do."

She turned away from the window. "We're missing something."

"Isn't that what I've been saying? It looks like we're missing a lot. If you insist on going down into the cave in the morning, I'm going with you."

Her chin came up. "Why? Just because Audry told you to? She doesn't have any right to go bossing people around in this home."

"Audry has nothing to do with it."

"Maybe you should stay here to keep an eye on things. Bryce will be with me in the cave."

"I'm going with you," he said. "Your safety is more important than anything happening in the house or any amount of evidence. The only way you'll get me to stay here is if you're here."

"I want to check on some things down there."

"Is it important?"

"It could be," she said. "I'd like to see the crystal cavern again, and I want to look for a sinkhole. Grandpa mentioned it. The map had some new markings on it, and I think it had the outline of a clock face."

"A clock?"

"Or a watch." She touched the pocket watch, then turned to the window again, where the moon peeped out from between the clouds, glistening on the frozen landscape. "The problem is, our intruder took the map, and I'm not sure about the location."

"Then we'll look for it together. I want you safe."

"You just want to play bodyguard."

"You have a problem with that?"

Sable gave him a grin over her shoulder. "Just like Grandpa. You're probably one of those guys who think it hurts their male image to work for a female boss."

He could tell she was teasing, but he needed to make a point before she put herself in jeopardy again. "No, but I do realize my own strengths and weaknesses. I don't think you quite have a grasp on yours."

"Meaning?"

"Meaning sometimes you try to play gladiator, taking on all comers with no help from anyone. Your strength and independence are admirable. In fact, they are two of the many things that attract me to you." He lowered his head and kissed her quickly, before she could stop him — be-

313

fore he could stop himself. The touch of her soft lips on his were almost his undoing. The big shock came when he felt her response. He pulled back, overwhelmed by what he'd done.

"But in this case it's just plain stupid," he said, trying to keep his voice under control. "Accept help where you can get it, Sable. You've got it from me, and we don't know who else we can trust. I would appreciate it if you would ask for my help before you get into more trouble."

He saw the shock in her eyes and was even more amazed by what he had just done, kissing her like the insufferable, macho man he was. But he also saw an amazing vulnerability.

In the fleeting expressions that washed across her face, he saw something else, too, something he knew she wouldn't want him to see. He saw the attraction flash alive in her eyes. He couldn't stop the grin that spread across his face in spite of the darkness and danger that hovered over them.

Sable pulled from his grasp and spun away from him without a word. He watched her bulldoze past a stack of boxes, a dresser, and a washstand. He followed meekly behind her. Time to play it cool for a while.

This time, Sable couldn't hear the squeak of the attic floor over the roaring in her own ears as she rushed through the huge, shadowed room. She was no longer afraid of the shadows around her — Murph was with her. She knew that wasn't fair to him, and it wasn't realistic. He was as physically vulnerable as she was. Almost.

Was his heart as vulnerable as hers, as well?

Instinctively, she raised a hand to her lips, vitally aware of his nearness and desperate to concentrate on the danger — and the puzzle — at hand.

"If you ask me, my attacker could have been a little more original."

"He got what he wanted, didn't he?" Murph turned and glanced around the room. "Okay, you've told me about some of the records you found up here. What about the confession note? Where is it now?"

Sable reached into the front pocket of her slacks. "I've kept it on me. I'm not sure why." She spread it open in the glow from Murph's flashlight. Together, they read it again:

My Dear Family,

I'm not sure what words to use that will explain what I'm doing. I only hope that someday you will forgive and accept. It's been more than eleven years since Grandma died, and I've never looked back, never considered anything like this before.

By the time you get this letter, you will have heard the story. I'm sorry for the trouble this will cause you. I'm sorry I'll miss Sable's birthday party this year, because I know how she loves them. You'll have to combine the watch I gave you for Christmas as a birthday gift, as well, Sable. Don't try to take on my own guilt. I'm no longer afraid of the truth. Don't worry, I'm safe in the afterlife.

I now ask my partners to forgive me for the fraud connected with our purchase and attempted resale of the mine back on the old Seitz place. To our misfortune, the buyer checked the mine more thoroughly than I had anticipated and discovered what others had overlooked. The walls were salted with sphalerite and galena from elsewhere. I must confess, and I leave my guilt in the hands of Christ.

But still, there is so much more involved here.

May God Help Me,
Josiah D. Kessinger

Sable looked up at Murph, struggling to bank down the sudden hope that flared as she considered Grandpa's written words more carefully. "I don't think this is a confession," she whispered, amazed.

"What do you mean?"

She held the note closer. "Why didn't I realize this sooner?" *Oh, Grandpa, if I'm right, I'm so sorry for doubting you.*

"Tell me what you're thinking," Murph said.

She pointed to the second paragraph. "I was already suspicious about this word 'story.' He always used that when he was telling a tale. A fictional tale. He would trick us that way, tell us a long, wild story about somebody he used to know, have us believing him, then explain that it was just a story. Fiction."

"But why write it at all?" Murph asked. "Why not just tell you in person?"

"Maybe he didn't have time. Maybe he tried to call me and talk to me and I wasn't home. If he was afraid of something or someone in Freemont, he would have mailed this note home, as he did. What if he was coerced?" Her voice trembled with the heaviness of her words.

"Or what if he was afraid the note might be intercepted?" Murph asked.

"Oh, Grandpa," she whispered. "How could I have doubted you?"

Murph placed a hand over hers. "We need to concentrate on this letter and see if he managed to get any kind of message to you."

They read the note again.

"Why didn't I notice all these things before?" Sable asked.

"What are you noticing now?"

"Grandma died twenty years ago. That's quite a bit more than eleven. I didn't pay any attention to the specific numbers."

"What could it mean?"

"I'm not sure," she said. "The very first sentence hints for us to look closely at the words he used. He also says we'll know the story. As I said, whenever Grandpa stretched the truth, he cleared himself by telling us it was a story. And nobody was planning a birthday party for me this year. Everyone knows I hate birthday parties."

"So why mention your birthday? And why use the number eleven when it should have been twenty? He also mentions the watch as a combination of Christmas and birthday —"

"Combination!"

"What?"

She studied the note again. "He's giving us numbers — the day, month, and year of my birth, plus the number eleven. Look, it says, 'Don't worry, I'm *safe* in the afterlife.'" She looked up at Murph, eyes widening.

"Safe!" he said. "Where is the safe?"

She refolded the note and slid it back into her pocket as she led him through the shadows to the far wall. Hurriedly, she shoved the clothing rack aside to reveal the dark gray shape of the old safe.

"Does anybody besides family know about this?" Murph asked.

"I don't think so, except maybe for Craig."

Murph raised his flashlight to show the numbers on the dial next to the handle. "We obviously have numbers. Show me the note again."

She pulled it out of her pocket once more and spread it in the light.

Murph studied it. "Which way do we turn? How many times?"

Sable sat on a wooden box behind her, focused on keeping her hands steady. She studied the page a moment, then looked up. "Try turning it clockwise to eleven." She held the paper out for him. "See the word 'forgive'? That could mean forward. Then turn it back, counterclockwise to two, because he uses the word 'back.' Then clockwise to fifteen. Do that twice, because he has two 'for's before he has another 'back.' Then go to seventy-two."

"Got it."

"Did it click?"

He shook his head, tried the handle, pushed the door in and tried it again.

She watched, excitement and tension drawn so tightly across her chest she was afraid to breathe. "Did it work?"

Murph tried one more time to turn the heavy metal handle. "Nope. Nothing."

There was a squeak of floorboards on the stairs coming into the attic.

"Sable? You up here?" Audry called. "It's Jerri and me. Think we could look through some more clothes? Jerri needs —"

"I need fat lady clothes," Jerri called out with a chuckle as the stairs continued to squeak with approaching footsteps.

Murph shoved the clothing back into place while Sable stuffed the note into her pocket once more. She was disappointed, yet at the same time so vastly, infinitely relieved.

Fiction. It was all fiction. Maybe Grandpa wasn't guilty after all.

So much for clue-finding tonight. Soon it would be time for bed, and first thing in the morning they'd be searching the cave for more clues.

Chapter 18

Sable scrambled over a threshold of limestone and stood to her feet just inside the low entrance to the cave. She aimed the beam of her light along the passage, toward the place she had visited often in her most recent nightmares. There was no water there now, just a black, gaping pit with rocky, jutting edges that would look like giant fangs if she allowed her imagination to take it too far.

That pit was always the last one to fill with water when the rest of the cave flooded, and the first to go dry when a drought hit the Ozarks. As of yet, it hadn't filled with water — all the recent rains were frozen in an icy trap above them.

She stepped forward so the others could come through, and as she waited for them, she reacquainted herself with the dark secrecy of the cavern. She had expected to be haunted by memories of terror and evil and shouted anger. She'd expected to feel a sense of betrayal, because the last time

322

she came down here, her hiding place betrayed her.

All she felt now was a waiting peacefulness, good memories of when she and Peter and Randy — and many times Craig and his sister, Candace — had explored and played and shared the wonder of this special playground. She wished she could believe Noah's assurances that she would heal from the horror of that one bad experience. But there were too many more horrors piling up after it. Would it ever end?

But she didn't want to think about that right now. She wanted to reach past those frightening memories and find a place of peace. She also wanted to check the crystal cavern and search for the sinkhole.

She turned to the others as she took a breath of the clean air. "I always love the way it smells down here." She relished the feel of the comfortably humid atmosphere after the dry heat of the house.

Bryce joined her in the dripping silence. Murph and Craig followed as they walked single file, more deeply into the hovering darkness. For Sable, it felt like a warm homecoming.

"I can't believe Jerri worried about snakes," Bryce said. "A lot of people think caves are dangerous."

"I've been exploring Missouri caves since I was much younger than you," Sable said. "I've never found anything dangerous in them yet, except carelessness." She slowed her steps and gestured toward the pit. "That hole is perfectly safe if we stay away from it." She suppressed a sudden impulse to go and check it out — the place where her life might have ended last year.

Bryce aimed the beam of his flashlight toward the pit. "Look at all those rocks. A guy could fall into that and never make it out." He walked over to the edge of the gaping hole and whistled through his teeth. "Dangerous."

"Exactly," Sable said. "That fills with water just like a dry creek whenever it rains, and it goes down just as quickly." She turned around to the men a short way behind. "Remember, Craig? We used to float our homemade toy boats on it."

"The drought dried up a lot of pools in this cave," he said, "but I don't know how many. I haven't had time to look at them yet."

Murph played the beam of his flashlight over every inch of the cave with methodical thoroughness. The light paused at a cluster of quartz crystals in the cave, then moved back to the pit for a final moment.

A quick glance at his shadowed face told Sable what he was thinking, and she felt a comforting connection to him. It helped ease some of the painful memories, as if he was returning with her to the time of her attack, and he was taking some of the blows for her.

She knew that as the victim of that attack, she should talk about it more, get it out of her system, dislodge the nightmares that looped through her sleep. She also knew, from talking with Noah, that in order to heal properly, she needed to learn to forgive.

It was an outrageous concept to her — to forgive someone who had tried to kill her. When she'd demanded to know how she was supposed to do that, he'd said, "You've got to learn how to bless your persecutor, Sable. You pray for him." She could hear his cracking, earnest voice even now. "You don't have to feel all warm and fuzzy, and you don't have to talk to him about it, just pray for him. Put it in God's hands."

At her expression of outrage, he'd said, "The Bible says to do it. I don't think it means you have to wish him well; it means you pray for God's power to overcome the power the devil has on him. While you're praying, you're putting yourself in God's realm. You let me know when you want to get together and pray for him, and I'll be there for you." She hadn't been able to do it while he was alive. She didn't think she could tackle such a chore on her own.

She glanced at Murph and then quickly away. Would it be possible? After all, he was Noah's nephew. He had obviously been acquainted with all this God stuff much longer than she had.

When they climbed downhill to the next cavern, Bryce stopped and gazed in awe at a room of rust-colored formations. "This is great." He ambled forward, his dark eyes huge with admiration. He reached out to touch a tall column, its sides glistening with moisture. "Oops." He jerked his hand back. "I almost forgot. I learned in science class that you aren't supposed to disturb a living cave. Even our walking here changes its growing patterns just a little." He gestured around them, to the multitude of stalactites and rising stalagmites colored by iron deposits.

"There were once several pools of water in this large cavern," Craig said. "Most of them were placid, but two of them swirled constantly."

"Whirlpools?" Bryce asked. "Were they dangerous?"

"Let's just say we had a healthy respect for them," Craig said. He shone his light down into one of the empty hollows where a whirlpool had once splashed and bubbled. "Water level's way down. I'm not even sure I've ever seen the bottom of this one before. I knew it had been dry, but not this dry."

"Give us a good, sunny day up above," Sable said, "and the water level will fill up down here in a hurry. Remember, we're already at the bottom of a hollow. When the ice melts from the hillsides, the streams will fill up, and the streams in this cave are the lowest ones around. That's when it can get scary down here."

"We've picked a good time to come down," Craig said. "We're setting a fast pace because there's no water to slow us down, no streams to ford, no pools to skirt around."

"A cave is a living thing," Sable told Bryce. "It's a world all its own. It even breathes with the rise and fall of the barometer; that's why the air is so fresh, instead of musty, like you would expect." She stepped over to an empty hollow where a whirlpool once flowed. "This is where my older brother, Peter, tried to skin-dive and nearly drowned."

Craig laughed. "I remember that. He almost drowned me when I tried to get him out."

"Serves you right," Sable said. "You helped him and Randy play tricks on me all the time. Remember when Randy dressed up in that sheet like a ghost and jumped out in front of me down at the end of the soda straw passage?"

"I remember he dropped his flashlight and broke it."

"What happened then?" Bryce asked.

Sable grinned at Craig. "I turned off my flashlight and found my way home in the dark."

"And just left him down here?" Bryce asked.

"Yes, and I got into big trouble, especially when I told Grandpa I wasn't sorry because they'd been picking on me all summer."

Craig laughed. "You were spoiled, admit it."

"I was not spoiled. Grandpa appreciated my honesty."

"The rest of us would've had our hides tanned. When you complained about the way we picked on you, he gave you lessons in street fighting."

"I never misused that knowledge," Sable said.

Murph turned to her with a grin. "Oh, really?"

Sable smiled back. "That's right, I only use it when pestered, provoked, or detained in a dangerous situation."

"Happens to you a lot, huh?" Craig said.

"Not so much now that you and my brothers are out of my hair most of the time."

"Did your brother get lost when you left him down here?" Bryce asked.

"Yes," Craig answered for her. "He wouldn't admit he was lost, but it took me and Pete and Josiah three hours to find him. We all got a good talking-to about the dangers of falling or getting lost or otherwise suffering harm down here. Our parents wouldn't let us come exploring alone for a long time afterward."

"Something good came of that incident, though," Sable said. "They found another passage while they searched. Grandpa was ecstatic. He loved this cave. He was always finding new passages and interesting formations." *And sinkholes. And . . . silver?*

"Where's the crystal room?" Bryce asked. "Audry said there was a crystal room down here somewhere."

Sable stumbled to a stop. She turned to look at Bryce. "Audry said that?"

"Yeah, she told me about it yesterday when we were looking at the rock collection in the living room."

Sable caught Murph's gaze, remembering the picture he had found of a younger Audry with Grandpa and Boswell. Just how well did Audry know them? And why hadn't she said something about it?

"What else did Audry tell you?" Murph asked the teenager.

"She said to be careful down here," Bryce muttered. "She said that probably ten times or more."

"She's right," Murph told him.

Sable scowled. "It isn't dangerous as long as we're careful."

"Want to check out the crystal room?" Murph asked.

"That was where I'd planned to go," she said. She wished she had that map — and that she'd paid more attention when she saw the new marks on it. Unfortunately, it might now be showing someone else where to look. If they knew what they were looking at.

But how could they know? She and Murph were the only ones who were aware of the contents of her watch case.

They entered the next cavern, and Sable was entranced anew by the sight of huge boulders piled on top of each other, reaching to the ceiling of the room. The limestone ceiling had buckled, which caused a gaping blackness above it.

"What's this?" Bryce asked.

Sable pointed upward with her large flashlight, glad it was powerful enough to penetrate the gloom. The high, domed ceiling was dry, unlike those in the other rooms. "This is a breakdown cavern, and it's no longer growing formations."

"What's a breakdown cavern?" Bryce asked.

"Exactly what it says." Sable stopped to peer at twin stalactites of milky crystal. "It's a limestone cave where the ceiling grew so heavy in the past that it collapsed. And see the crack that runs between those slabs forming the ceiling? It's a fault line."

Bryce whistled through his teeth. "You mean like the San Andreas fault on the West Coast?"

"Only much smaller, of course," Sable replied.

"Don't worry," Craig said, "this breakdown occurred maybe sixty or seventy years ago, and it's a rarity. We're safe." He shot a look at Sable. "Of course, your grandpa did discover that new sinkhole last fall."

Sable stepped over a boulder and passed a small, raised ledge where she and her brothers had hidden from one another many times. "What did he say about the sinkhole?" Sable kept her voice casual.

"Not much. I think it was nearby, though. He and Boswell had just left the house not long before. I remember your mom telling everybody it was a good thing, because they would have had a lot of trouble getting him out of the woods if he'd been too far away."

"Did he think it was part of this cave system?" Sable asked.

"He didn't say, but it sure sounds like it to me," Craig said. "Your mom said he spent a lot more time down in the cave afterward. I wonder if he ever found it."

The passage split, and a dry streambed angled downhill from the familiar limestone path.

Craig stopped and shone his light along the declining rocky bed into the darkness beneath a low ledge. "Now that looks like a new passage." His baritone voice quickened with excitement. He turned to Sable. "Why don't you let me check it out? May not go anywhere, and if it doesn't I'll catch up with the rest of you."

"You'd miss a trip to the crystal cavern just to crawl on your stomach over a bunch of rocks?" she asked.

"Radical idea, I know." He grinned at her.

She remembered how Craig and her brothers had competed with her, and with each other, trying to be the first to explore a new passage or to scale a formerly unscalable wall.

"Go ahead," she said. "It could dead-end ten feet down. If it goes anywhere, maybe you can show us later."

"Or it could lead us into a whole new area," Craig said.

"Let me go with you, Craig," Bryce said with teenage exuberance. "Please?"

"I thought you wanted to see the crystals," Sable reminded him.

"Couldn't we see both?" Bryce asked.

"And worry Audry?" Sable teased. "If we're late for lunch —"

"I'm just going to check it out, Sable," Craig said. "I'll catch up with the rest of you."

"And me. I'm going with Craig," Bryce said.

"You may have to do a lot of crawling and scooting on the ground," Sable warned Bryce. "You could get filthy."

"I'll wash my clothes myself when I get back to the house, okay?" Bryce pleaded.

"Sounds fine with me," Craig said. "We can let Sable and Murph go on ahead, then we'll catch up with them if we can. If it gets too late — let's say, after eleven — we'll automatically head back toward the house. Sable, what time do you have?" He gestured to the pocket watch that hung around her neck.

"I don't know; this doesn't keep time. Murph will have to —"

"What do you mean it doesn't keep time? That thing's always kept good time." Craig raised his flashlight to peer at the antique. He reached toward it, and Sable eluded him.

"Take my word for it, Craig," she said dryly.

He shrugged. "Anyway, I'm going to check this out."

She noticed Murph peering back the way they had come, the beam of his light poking into the shadows.

Craig followed Sable's gaze. "Lose something?"

Murph inspected three more dark corners, then shrugged and joined them. "No, I thought I heard something."

"Like what?" Craig asked.

"Probably nothing. I'm just a little edgy." He glanced at Sable. "Simmons got up when I did this morning. I haven't seen him since."

"He was in the family room just before we came down," Bryce said. "He played a game of checkers with me."

"He was still there when we came down here?"

"Nope, he left when I went to put my shoes on."

"I'm heading down," Craig called over his shoulder as he dropped to his knees and crawled beneath the rocky ledge. Bryce followed him.

Sable watched them disappear into the narrow tunnel, listening to Bryce's eager questions and to Craig's equally eager replies. *Like a couple of kids.* She had to remind herself that Craig was a grown man who could take care of himself. She just hoped he also extended that care to Bryce.

"So tell me where we're going here," Murph said.

She aimed the beam of her light down the passage to their right. "This path wanders back for about half a mile before it reaches the white room and the crystal cavern."

"The place Audry mentioned to Bryce."

"Right."

"And you're wondering why," Murph guessed.

"Aren't you?"

"You better believe it. Maybe you should have that talk with her after all."

"You thought it would be dangerous when I mentioned it yesterday."

"I don't think it would hurt to drop some broad hints. Maybe she'll be forthcoming, and we won't have to pry too much."

"Agreed. Meanwhile, let's check out the crystal cavern."

As Sable led the way, Murph took slow, thoughtful steps, studying every shadow with deep concentration.

After about fifteen minutes of turtle-walking, Sable glared at him over her shoulder. "Murph, are you sure you want to go on?" she asked. "You don't seem —"

"Come here and look at this." He aimed his light on the clay trail. "Footprints."

"Of course. You heard us talk about the times we came down here."

"But look where they lead." He followed them with the light around a rust-colored column and back out to the trail. "I know this sounds strange, but I think they're fresh."

"How can you tell?"

Murph inhaled. "Take a whiff. Smell anything that doesn't belong in a cave?"

Sable sniffed the air, watching Murph quizzically. "I'm not exactly a bloodhound. What are you trying to tell me?"

"Cologne. I guess I recognize it because Simmons reeks of it every morning."

"You already know Simmons has been down here — you saw him here yesterday."

"But I don't think the scent would linger that long."

"So maybe he came back down this morning," Sable said. "Do you think someone really tried to attack him yesterday?"

"No, I think he fell in and his macho pride was hurt when a woman old enough to be his grandmother had to pull him out."

"What if it happened when he was on his way back from an attack on you?"

"Could be."

"Except he really did seem scared."

"I would be, too, if I'd almost drowned," Murph said. "And he didn't convince Audry."

"Speaking of whom, I have some questions about her, too. Anyway, somebody has that map from the attic wall. I don't know what they think they're going to find with it." She stepped ahead of Murph. "Let's go check out the crystal cavern before Craig and Bryce catch up with us."

"That's the place that was salted back in the forties, right?" Murph asked.

"Yes."

"I'd like to see it."

Sable led the way through a long, narrow passage, the powerful glow of her light illuminating more formations, alien sights to most people, but familiar to her. There was no path here, but they traveled easily, except in a few places where the clay was wet and sticky or where they had to climb over a pile of rocks. Occasionally, the passage split, and Sable indicated the markers she used to find her way. At one intersection she showed Murph a whirlpool dome, and at another she pointed to a unique helictite formation.

The passage widened at last, and they stepped into a broad cavern with a low ceiling and walls of uninterrupted white. The beams from their flashlights reflected from the smoothly undulating surfaces with a supernatural incandescence.

Sable heard Murph catch his breath and emit a low whistle. "This is beautiful." He strolled over beside Sable. "No wonder you love this cave."

"This and the crystal cavern are my favorites." She aimed her light to the left. "The crystal cavern — or room, as some like to call it — is there. See that ledge of rock above it? It's a natural bridge, leading from nowhere to nowhere. I used to hide there and jump down in front of my brothers to frighten them."

Murph chuckled. "You gave as good as you got."

"You'd better believe it."

"You still do."

She grinned. "You don't know the half of it."

"I'm learning quickly."

The white flowstone passage opened into a larger cavern that angled upward to their right. Murph entered the huge, domed room. Sable was about to follow when a soft sound arrested her attention — like the scuffing of a shoe on stone.

As Murph disappeared from sight, she turned and listened. Was that the trickle of a stream she heard, or something else? Was the crystal cavern still underwater? It shouldn't be.

She stepped along a dry streambed and around a curve in the passageway, then down a graduated shelf of solid rock that she remembered sculpted a beautiful waterfall after heavy rains. She circled another pure white column, then stopped and gazed down into a dark, trickling cavern where water had once splashed and swirled in wild agitation.

"Just as I thought," she said softly.

The cavern was almost dry. Stooping, she shone her light into its mysterious depths. Sphalerite and galena glittered, shattering the brilliance of Sable's light into thousands of pinpoints, illuminating the cavern with the glow of a beam through a prism.

She frowned. "Murph?"

"Yes?" he called from the white room.

"You might want to see this."

He rounded the corner quickly, his flashlight increasing the sparkle in the pit. "Did you find something?"

"Look at the ore. There wasn't this much the last time I was down here."

"How can you be sure? When was the last time you saw this place without water?"

"A long time ago, but yesterday I found a picture in the attic. I took it here when I was twelve. There wasn't this much ore."

"Maybe the water eroded the limestone away."

She shook her head. "Impossible. The water causes limestone buildup. The longer the water has to work over the ore, the thicker the limestone should be around it."

"Are you sure there wasn't this much ore last time?" Murph asked. "That was almost twenty years ago."

"Positive." She pointed to a chunk of galena, about one-quarter-inch wide. "Would you like to estimate about how long the water's been working over that ore?"

Murph bent down to get a better view. "I don't see any limestone over it."

"None," she said.

He looked up at her. "Meaning what? How long has it been this dry here?"

"What I'm saying is I think this is recent. Very recent. Within the past year — maybe even the past few months."

"Are you sure?"

"Why would anyone salt this place now? It isn't as if they're going to mine it. Who would do it?"

"Sable —"

"Whoever handled that shotgun we found in the gun room. I'd say, judging by what we've discovered so far, Grandpa had something to do with it."

"But I don't understand why." Murph studied the ore, then turned and shone his light on the quartz crystal along the sides of the limestone bridge above them. "Any theories?" His voice was gentle with sympathy, and she could read the direction of his thoughts.

"One." She studied the flicker of her light against a strangely shaped white protrusion at the bottom of the pit. The protrusion was just to the left of a stream of opaque buttermilk water. "Maybe that shotgun and ore shells we found upstairs in the house never left this place."

"What about the analysis sheets?" Murph asked. "Galena and sphalerite . . . what about the silver?"

She lay on her stomach at the edge of a limestone ledge and shone her light over the gleaming ore. "High-grade silver would be black. Do you see anything that looks like it might be tarnished silver? Maybe a fine thread of black?"

Murph knelt next to her, and together they aimed the beams of their lights over the vertical sides of the cavern walls, methodically examining every sparkle, every mark, every indentation in the limestone.

Sable's attention soon returned to the bottom of the cavern, where a set of matching indentations drew her attention a few feet from the stream. She aimed her beam directly on them and frowned.

"Footprints," she said.

Murph peered over her shoulder. "Someone's been down here since it dried up."

"But Craig said he hadn't come this far."

"Can you trust his word?"

"I always have before."

"What about your brothers?"

"No, I asked them about it at the funeral. Peter and Randy both told me they'd been too busy to explore lately. Maybe Grandpa —"

"Look, someone's been digging down there, too." The ray of Murph's light showed freshly disturbed earth and rocks.

"Do you think —"

The sound of scattering pebbles echoed from the darkness behind them.

Murph swung around. "What was that?"

There was scuffling and a movement of shadow from the natural bridge above and behind them. Rocks clattered down on them. Murph lunged forward to protect Sable from the rockslide, and something hit them from behind.

She shifted to retain her balance, and the ledge beneath her right foot crumbled. Her arms flew out automatically, and she lost her grip on her flashlight. It bounced with a clatter against rock and earth to land in the pit below.

"Murph!" She fell hard on the edge of the pit and clawed at the limestone floor, feeling herself slide.

Murph caught her by the back of her shirt. "Sable, grab me!"

She reached up and grasped his arm, arresting her slide for a brief moment. Then the ledge crumbled completely, and she cried out as wet earth and loose rocks fell beneath her. Murph reached for her other hand and missed.

She scrambled to step back onto solid ground, but the earth continued to fall away beneath her feet. Sharp rocks dug into her legs.

The ledge gave way beneath Murph. He jumped back, still holding Sable's shirt. The fabric ripped. Sable flung her free arm up to catch at Murph, but her blouse tore loose from his grip. She plunged down into the darkness, fighting the mud, until she landed, with a cry of pain, at the bottom.

Chapter 19

Murph lay panting at the edge of the pit, his eyes straining against the impenetrable darkness, his hands, arms, and shoulders flecked with drying mud. The distant echo of footsteps reached him; whoever had pushed them was running away, stumbling over rocks as they went.

"Sable! Sable, are you okay?" he shouted. "Sable, say something! Answer me!" Frantically, he felt around for his flashlight. "Sable!"

He heard a rustle of movement several yards below him. She groaned weakly.

"Sable? Wake up!" She didn't answer, and she didn't move again. Was she still breathing? He couldn't tell. He kept praying under his breath. "Please, Lord, please, Lord, help us. Please don't let Sable . . . please take care of her."

He dug through the damp earth until he felt the end of his flashlight and discovered that it hadn't gone out, it had only been caked with clay. When he wiped it off, the glow illumined the cave once again, and he pointed it at Sable. Her pale, still face frightened him.

"Sable!" he shouted. "You've got to wake up, sweetheart! You've got to hear me!"

He searched for a rope, for handholds or footholds on the face of the cliff that had just collapsed with her. Nothing. He studied the length of the ledge and beyond, to the bare rock face of the wall that circled the cavernous pit and rose above the ledge on which he stood. He saw nothing but slick limestone and fragments of the galena that had been scattered there.

The pit was at least fifteen feet deep; he couldn't climb into it and back out without a rope. If only he could take her in his arms, hold her, make sure she was still breathing . . . but if he did that, he couldn't get back out. Craig and Bryce might not even come this way if they found the other passage more interesting. He couldn't just sit and wait. But he couldn't leave Sable.

"Sable? It's Murph. Can you hear me?"

He waited endless seconds, his flashlight still illuminating Sable's deathly still features, her hair slithering like a living thing in the tiny stream of milky water beside her head. "Lord, please!" He couldn't tear his fearful gaze from her face.

She moved.

"Sable, wake up!"

Her dark lashes fluttered, and she winced.

"Thank You, God!" he shouted. "Sable, can you hear me? Look up at me!"

Sable's mind, foggy with pain, steadied at the sound of Murph's voice, concentrating hard on it, struggling against the dizziness that drew her down.

"Murph," she croaked, her head throbbing with the effort to form her words. "You okay?"

"Forget about me. Did you hit your head on something?"

Sable squinted up toward the sound of his voice, and her blurred sight caught the ghostly shape of his head above the beam of his flashlight. "Murph?" Her voice sounded louder to her as the pounding in her head receded. "You sure you're okay? Did you see the person who hit us?"

"See him? I felt him."

"Was it a him?" Her voice tapered, and her mind drifted. "Maybe it was a her . . . or maybe . . . Whatever it was, it sure hit hard. I don't believe in ghosts, but . . ."

"We'll deal with that later; I heard someone run away. It's you I'm worried about. Where are you hurt? Can you move?"

Sable became aware of the scratches on her arms, of the pain at the back of her head, of the water swirling close to her ears. Tentatively, she moved her legs and hips, then sighed with relief. "I don't think anything's broken, except maybe my skull." Her head throbbed. She wiped something sticky from her face. "That's . . . that's not blood, is it?"

"Can you get to your feet?"

She noticed he didn't reply directly to her question. "Blood, Murph. Is it blood?"

"I can't tell for sure, but from here it looks like mud. Can you stand up?"

Sable groaned. "Have a heart. I can't even see with you shining that stupid light in my eyes." The brightness eased. "Thanks." Afraid she might frighten him worse, she struggled to sit upright, but the pain shot through her head with an unrelenting stab when she moved. She slumped sideways into the sticky clay and relished the comforting coolness against the side of her face.

"Where are you hurt?" Murph demanded.

Sable struggled against the dizziness. "Really, it's noth—"

"Where are you hurt?" His voice grew rougher.

"My . . . my head seems to be coming apart in several places," she said, attempting a flippancy that failed. "I must've hit it on a rock in the water."

"Are you dizzy?"

Darkness converged on her again. The cave whirled around her, scattering the beams of Murph's flashlight.

"Sable, talk to me! Now!"

"Murph, I know the . . . the symptoms, I just can't seem to —"

"You've got to try to stay conscious. Concentrate. Are you dizzy?"

She raised her knees and leaned her forehead against them. "No, I'm not too dizzy." *Tell him the truth.* "At least, I think I'll be okay in a little while." *It could be true.* "I don't know where my flashlight went. Can you shine yours around and find it?"

She closed her eyes as he searched, allowing the pain to wash over her in a cacophonous roar in her ears. The sound resisted his voice when he spoke, and she had to ask him to repeat himself.

"I'm sorry, sweetheart, but I can't find it. I'm going to try to come down to you."

"No!" She sat up, wincing at the sudden movement. "You'll be stuck down here with me. We need help. Go get Craig and Bryce."

"And leave you here alone for the attacker to return?"

"We don't have any idea when Craig might decide to come and find us," she said. "We need help now."

"Could you climb out if I gave you a boost?"

"And leave you stuck down here? Please, Murph, I need . . . I need you to get the others."

"First you need to find your light. Dig through the mud, Sable."

Sable roused herself enough to search the area around her, and at last her fingers came into contact with a hard, oblong object in the water.

"I've found it. I think." Whatever it was. "Now will you please go?"

"Does it work?" Murph asked.

She grasped it more firmly and tried to pull it out of the water. It wouldn't budge. She moved her fingers farther down and jiggled, then dug around the end of the object. How could it have become so embedded? It finally loosened in her fingers, and she pulled it out. From the reflected glow of Murph's light against the crystals in the cave wall, she saw more than she wanted to see.

"It isn't . . . it's not the flashlight after

all," she said. Her fingers explored further.

Tingles of shock fled along her arm, setting off once more the pounding pain in her head. Now she knew what the white protrusion was in the water — what had dented her head.

"Sable," Murph said impatiently, "find the flashlight."

She released the object — the water-polished human leg bone — and scrambled away from it. A moment later she found her flashlight by the cave wall. The switch was still in the "on" position, but there was no light. She shook it and hit it, the throbs in her head keeping time. Nothing.

"I've found it," she said quietly, clamping down hard on the panic that threatened to spiral out of control. "It doesn't work."

"That means you'd have to sit here in the dark until I come back."

"Yes," she whispered. "Go now. Quickly. I learned a long time ago not to be afraid . . . afraid of the dark." But what was in the dark right now? Was the intruder still up there somewhere, waiting? Would she endanger Murph worse by insisting he go?

He stood. "I'll be back as soon as I can. Just stay calm."

"Do you remember how to . . . to get back?"

"I remember," he said softly. "You're a wonderful guide. You showed me every marker."

Sable heard him moving off, as if a great distance already separated them. Blackness covered her. She might die here. Or Murph might, if he wasn't careful. She couldn't stand the thought of that.

"Murph?"

He stopped. "Yes, what is it?"

"Please be careful. Don't let them get you."

"They won't." She heard him turn to walk on.

"Murph?"

He stopped again.

"I mean it. I . . . couldn't handle it if something happened to you."

"Really?"

"Really."

"I'll be careful. Stay awake, Sable. You can do it." He raced away, the slapping echo of his footsteps reaching her for several moments as she lay with her eyes closed in the heavy darkness.

It was a darkness suddenly crowded with ghosts from the past. Where else did ghosts come from but the past? But right now those ghosts didn't frighten her nearly as much as the living.

She opened her eyes and rubbed her neck. The pain in her head had receded to a dull throb, but her head still whirled, and nausea clenched her stomach. She didn't have the strength to claw her way out of here even if she had a light to show the way. She couldn't even keep her mind from going fuzzy on her.

She had been in complete darkness like this lots of times, but never when someone dangerous was possibly waiting for her above. She preferred the skeleton at the moment. But Murph had said he'd heard their attacker running away. Much as she wished Murph could have followed them, she was relieved that at least they had run. It meant they were afraid to be seen. Maybe they wouldn't be back this way.

Why hadn't she tried harder to get Craig and Bryce to come this way? If only . . . if only she could think. If only she could move without her head pounding. All she could do was sit and listen . . . and re-member.

She remembered Noah's kindness and strength one day when they were exploring the Seitz property, deep in the darkness of a tunnel. She could still close her eyes and almost see his craggy face and his green eyes — much like Murph's, now that she thought about it.

"Noah, I'm always afraid," she admitted at last, many weeks after the attack. It had been a painful admission for her. Like Grandpa, she always prided herself on an indomitable spirit and on putting on a brave front. "I can close my eyes and see Jim's face, and I can hear his voice."

Noah nodded, and his lined face twisted in sympathy. "Let me tell you the only way I know to overcome the fear," he said gently. "You know how much you like to explore caves?"

"Sure."

"It wouldn't be much fun if you didn't have a light, though, would it? You'd miss all those beautiful formations and crystals, and you'd stumble around and fall and probably get hurt, maybe even killed." He reached for her light, and she allowed him to take it. "This world's a lot like a cave, with all kinds of beauty around you." All at once, he switched off both their flash-lights. "That's what it's like without the Light of the world in your life. Dark and frightening."

She moved closer to him. "The light —"

"Jesus Christ. The Bible says He is the light and in Him is no darkness. With Him in your life, it's like having a good, strong lantern in a cave." He switched the lights back on and handed hers back. *"Follow Him, and you'll have enough light to see the world around you — not too far ahead, mind you, but enough to see which way to go. The more He shines in your life, the more you'll be able to see. You won't be stumbling around in the dark."*

His kind face and voice faded from her mind, and all she heard was the trickle and drip of water. But that memory was enough. "Thank You, God," she whispered. She had His light.

Shadows loomed huge as Murph raced from a narrow passageway into another shadowed cavern. He scrambled over a slippery rock, aimed his flashlight at the ceiling, then frowned at the forked section of passages.

Sable had told Bryce that a cave was a living, breathing world of its own. How true that was now. Never before had a cave seemed quite so alive. It throbbed with life. Murph could feel it pulsating all around him, and it seemed sinister, almost as if it were purposely trying to trap him — to keep him from reaching help for Sable.

He rushed headlong down the right fork, and almost immediately a filmy, white mist met him. The mist didn't thicken as he made his way along it. He wondered if Craig and Bryce had found a viable passage, or if he would have to follow them through this labyrinth to the end to get help. He might even be better off going back to the house.

He drew near to the sound of splashing water somewhere to his right, but his light didn't show any kind of pool. This cave was filled with tunnels, probably false passages. No wonder Sable's brother had gotten lost down here. He just hoped Craig and Bryce hadn't gone too far.

He ducked his head to go beneath a low rock, and as he did so he heard another sound over the splashing water. It was the definite sound of metal hitting rock.

He swung around and aimed his light back the way he had come. "Who's there?"

Nothing.

"Craig? Bryce? Where are you?"

Still no answer. No sound of retreating footsteps. He backtracked, listening through the silence for a telltale sign of life, but he heard no more.

Craig and Bryce couldn't have gotten far; he would catch up with them soon.

Sable splashed her face with some of the water in the small stream that trickled past her. She could only pray that their attacker hadn't followed Murph.

Carefully, she shifted positions.

Pain once again struck her, dissolving her concentration. Her head throbbed. But she could tell, even through the pain and nausea, it was getting better. She'd taken falls before, maybe not quite as painful as this one, but bad.

Again, she splashed water in her face. That helped the throbbing and helped her to think more clearly. It also served to push away some of the fear. She found herself wondering about the human bone.

Nobody in the family had ever taken seriously the story about the previous owners finding silver here, because silver didn't occur naturally in this part of Missouri. If they found it at all, it was only as a byproduct of another mineral — a very valuable by-product.

But even if they hadn't found silver, the two men had existed and had disappeared mysteriously. Had she just fallen on the remains of one of those partners? Dared she dig through the mud to see if she could find more of the skeleton?

Perhaps not now, but later. The men could have drowned in the flood that had taken place at the same time of their disappearance.

Another thought occurred to her: The breakdown in that one cavern had struck in relatively modern times — a rarity. Could there have been a small earthquake around the fault line? And if so, was it possible that the owners were in it at the time? This leg bone could have washed to this pit later, during another flood.

A sound reached her from far away — a rattle of rocks. She caught her breath and struggled to sit up. Her eyes opened wide, peering into the darkness. Did she detect a shade of light? A movement of shadow? It could be Murph coming back with Bryce and Craig. Or it could be their attacker. Wouldn't Murph have called out to her by now?

Sable scrambled backward and upward from the streambed. She was in a deep chasm, about fifteen feet from the ledge from which she fell and about twenty feet from that ledge to the other side, which formed the wall of the cave. Her right hand encountered some pebbles, scattering them down the gentle slope into the water. They splashed.

She heard a footfall, then another. Her heart rate soared. There was no light — none! How could someone be walking in the darkness?

The footsteps came closer, softly. She stared into the blackness. Had she lost her vision? Blindness?

Another footstep, directly above her on the ledge. She stared hard into the darkness and thought she detected a faint — very faint — green glow . . . like the glow of animal eyes reflected in the headlights of a car, only not nearly as bright.

Ghost eyes.

She blinked, rubbed her eyes, and looked back up at the ledge.

"Who is it?" she whispered.

No answer.

She cleared her throat. "Who's up there?"

The glow dipped and disappeared.

She waited.

She heard the clink of something metal and another scuffle of footsteps.

She scrambled backward in the mud, feeling for — and finding — the bone she had earlier thrust from her. If only she could keep her mind clear; if only the pain would stay away long enough for her to get her bearings.

"Who are you?" she asked, focusing to keep her voice steady.

No reply.

For the first time, she wondered if it was possible someone had found a way through these passages to the house from some other place . . . or was she hallucinating?

She couldn't be hallucinating. And she didn't believe in ghosts.

"What are you doing here?" she demanded. "Did Boswell send you?" Holding the bone, she crept backward, feeling her way through the mud until she found the limestone wall embedded with galena and sphalerite.

She could do this; she had done it before. There was a tiny crawl space about five feet to her right, if she remembered correctly. She had explored it once, barely fitting through. She could do it again if she had to.

She heard rustling. She turned back to look toward the ledge and saw the ghost eyes bobbing in the darkness once again. She stood to her feet, stepped backward, and stumbled on a rock. She bent down and picked it up. Still clutching the bone in her left hand, she drew back and flung the rock toward the ledge. It hit the ledge with a clatter and bounced back into the cavern.

The glow disappeared, and she heard more sounds of scuffling, the scattering of tiny rocks and dirt. For the first time, she heard the sound of heavy breathing.

He was climbing down the side of the ledge.

"I'm not dead yet," she said. "And you're not getting me without a fight." She bent down and felt for another rock. There were lots of rocks down here. "The others are on their way here, so if you want to escape, you'd better do it while there's still time." She grabbed another rock and threw toward the sound of breathing.

The glow reappeared for a few seconds, as if the ghost had turned to get its bearings again before continuing down.

She felt around her for another rock, scrambling sideways toward the tiny passage.

Murph scrambled beneath the rocky ledge, picking his way carefully but quickly along the dry streambed. He recognized this place now. It was the passage Craig and Bryce had taken, he was sure of it.

"Craig!" he called. "Bryce!"

He had to drop to his hands and knees

and crawl over a scattering of rocks for about twenty feet, and then suddenly the ceiling lifted and the passage broadened. The fog was thicker this time — so thick it reflected the beam of his flashlight back at him.

"Craig! Are you down here?"

He squeezed through another narrow passage thick with fog. "Craig!"

A distant voice echoed from the limestone wall.

"Here . . . we're here," came a faint voice.

They were perhaps a hundred feet away, maybe farther. He scrambled up a steep incline, and by now the fog was so thick he had to cup the beam of his flashlight with his hand to keep the glare from blinding him.

"Help! We need help!" He stepped out into another huge, columned room, and he stopped. "Sable fell! I need help getting her out."

"We're coming!" It was Craig.

Murph waited. Craig and Bryce came rushing through the fog a few moments later, breathless and dirty.

"What happened?" Craig asked.

"Sable fell in the crystal cavern. I can't get her out without help."

"Is she hurt?" Craig asked, leading the way back.

"She hit her head, but I couldn't get down to check her out without getting stuck with her. I didn't know if you would come that way, and I couldn't take the chance. She was conscious when I left her."

"No broken bones?" Craig asked. "Maybe we should go back to the house and get a rope."

"I don't want to take the time. The three of us can get her out without a rope."

"We could use our belts," Bryce said. "Like last time."

"Let's just hurry and get to her."

Sable threw another rock. "Trying to decide what to do about me? Are you going to try to kill me again? Murph's on his way back right now, and he's bringing help. You'd better get away while you still have time."

Her head throbbed with the exertion of shouting. She felt a break in the limestone wall, dropped to her knees, and tried to crawl sideways into a protective tunnel.

There was a sound of shoes scraping against rock. She turned. The ghost eyes hovered above her. Directly above her.

Murph wasn't going to return in time. She was going to die.

She screamed. Her head throbbed.

She tried to scoot farther back into the passage but the ghost grabbed her from behind. She felt the pressure of the watch chain tightening at her throat.

The chain broke, and she screamed, falling forward into darkness.

A cold knot of horror tightened Murph's stomach at the echo of Sable's scream. He pulled himself up from the low passage and raced toward the crystal cavern. "We're coming, Sable!"

She didn't answer. Panic spurred him through the last two caverns, along the rocky passage and out the other side.

They reached the pit and aimed their lights into the blackness.

"Sable!" Murph shouted. He aimed his light around the darkened crevices of the pit until he spied something blue — her nylon jacket. His eyes made out her prone form.

He turned to Craig. "Get me down there, fast." He handed his light to Bryce. "Hold this for me. I'm going down."

"Wait," Craig said. "You can't just jump down there. It's too dangerous with all those rocks. We need a rope."

"We don't have time to get a rope!" Murph rammed the toe of his boot into the packed mud below. He took a step down, then another.

Craig took off his jacket. "We can use this. It's denim; it'll hold. Here, take one end. Can't have you falling, too."

Murph grabbed the sleeve and allowed Craig to lower him as far as possible, then jumped the last few feet. He rushed to Sable's side just as she raised her head and began to stir.

"Sable, what happened? Are you okay? Why did you scream?"

She turned glazed eyes toward him. "Someone came after me," she whispered. "They got my watch." She winced and raised a hand to her head. "Jerked it off my neck."

"They came down here? Did you see who —"

"Couldn't see. It was like . . . ghost eyes."

Ghost eyes? That scared him. She wasn't making sense. "Okay, just hold on. I'm going to look you over." He checked her pupils and was relieved to find them equal and reactive. "You can see me now, can't you?"

She peered up at him. "I can see you. I can see fine."

He did the usual neurologic exam — as much as he could do quickly — and gave her a score of fifteen on the Glasgow scale. Whatever had happened to her a few minutes ago, she was stable now.

"Let's get you out of here," he said.

"Yeah, let's get out of here." She reached for him, looking askance into the water flowing lethargically past them a couple of feet away. "Maybe I was hallucinating. Or maybe we really do have a ghost," she mumbled as she leaned against him.

Murph helped her up to Craig and Bryce. "Let's get her to the house."

Chapter 20

By the time they reached the mouth of the cave leading into the basement, Sable dropped the pretense. That had been no hallucination. Although her head throbbed and her legs shook, she knew she hadn't been injured badly enough to hallucinate.

And she did not believe in ghosts.

She just couldn't think of any other explanation for what she had seen.

When they came to the basement steps, she stumbled and would have fallen if Murph hadn't caught her.

Without a word, he lifted her into his arms and carried her upstairs and through the door into the living room. Only once before had she been so glad to leave the cave behind. For the second time, its shadows mocked her as she left.

Outrage throbbed with the rhythm of her heart, pounding through her head. Once more an intruder had breached her own private sanctuary. She had fought back before and had won. She would find the strength to fight back this time, too, if only she could stay alive.

Later she would fight. Now she had no defense, only an ally, and Murph was reeling from the attacks, as well.

When Murph carried her through the basement door, Audry was sitting on the sofa. She looked up from her crossword puzzle and gasped.

"What on earth!" She tossed the book aside and jumped to her feet. "Sable! What happened?"

"I fell." She didn't have the energy to explain more.

"I knew it. I knew something would happen. Sable Chamberlin, you wouldn't listen to me, would you?"

"Careful, Audry," Craig warned. "She's not in the mood to get yelled at."

"I should say not. Here, Murph, sit her down on the sofa. I don't know what we're going to do with you, honey."

"You don't have to do anything with me," Sable snapped.

Audry ignored her. "Craig, bring me some towels. We'll need to clean her off before we can see where she's hurt."

"Murph has already checked me for injuries," Sable said, relenting enough to allow Audry to help her remove her mud-caked nylon jacket. "I hit my head. It'll be okay." She hoped. "Ice, though. I could use some ice."

"I'll get some," Bryce said and ran into the kitchen.

Audry bent down to pull off Sable's boots. "How did it happen?"

"I told you. I fell."

"Yes, after all that talk about caves being safe." Audry took the towels when Craig brought them to her. "Thanks, that'll be enough. Now, Sable, let's get you up to your room and get these filthy clothes off."

"First, tell me where everyone has been since we left."

Audry stopped bustling around Sable. "What do you mean? We've been right here, of course. Where did you expect us to go? Boys, if you're hungry, there's some lunch in the kitchen. Jerri had KP, but you'll have to serve yourselves now."

"Where is she?" Sable asked.

"I think she might have gone upstairs to the attic."

"And Perry and Simmons?" Murph asked.

"I'm not concerned about those two right now, I'm concerned about Sable."

"Just tell us where they are," Sable snapped, allowing her so-called bad mood to make itself known a little more force-fully.

Audry shook her head. "You people don't make any sense. I heard Dillon growling upstairs earlier and went up to find a face-off between him and Simmons in the hallway."

"When did this happen?" Murph asked.

"Oh, I'd say about twenty minutes ago. Couldn't tell you what it was about, but I let Simmons know right quick he'd better not be disturbing anybody's stuff. He's kept a low profile ever since. Long as he keeps the fire stoked, I'm happy."

"And Perry?" Sable asked.

"I saw him carrying water upstairs about thirty minutes ago. Now you men go on, shoo. I'm getting Sable upstairs. Honey, do you feel like you can walk?"

"Of course I can." Sable stood up. "Did you see either of the men before that? What have they been doing since we left?"

"Honey, I don't keep track of those two." Audry clicked her tongue and shook her head. "Simmons sure wasn't thrilled with your dog, though. Let's get you upstairs to bed, Sable."

"You're not really putting her to bed, are you?" Murph asked.

"I didn't say sleep, I said bed. We'll keep an eye on her."

"I'll help," Murph insisted.

"Not while I help her undress, you won't. Now give us some room to work, why don't you?"

"I don't need help undressing," Sable said.

"You don't need to be left alone, either."

Bryce returned with a plastic zipper bag filled with ice. Sable took it gratefully and held it against her skull.

Upstairs, Audry's hands were gentle as she washed away the top layer of drying mud from Sable's face and arms. "I don't see any blood."

"Just mud," Sable said. The ice felt wonderful, but her head still throbbed. "Audry, how much did you see of the others while we were gone?" She hesitated. "And what did you do?"

Audry shuffled through the top drawer of Sable's dresser, selected a T-shirt, and tossed it to Sable. "I can't help wondering why you want to know all this stuff right now, when your health is more important."

Sable changed quickly into the T-shirt. "If there were strangers in your home, wouldn't you want to know what they were doing with their time?"

Audry tucked the muddy blouse under her arm and searched through the dresser until she found an old pair of scrub pants.

She handed them to Sable. "I guess when you put it like that . . . Well, let me see . . . First of all, I think I was taking a bath before you left."

"I thought I heard water splashing in there. Did Perry tote the water for you?"

"Nope, I heated it myself. Mind you, it was a shallow bath, but it sure felt good."

"Okay, so you didn't see anyone for awhile. What else?"

"Jerri hollered at me through the door about finding some jeans she could wear, but she had to hem them. I think she was going to rummage through the sewing room for a needle and some thread."

"Yes, yes, I heard that. And then Perry accused her of snooping through his things."

"They had a few words about it, but she told me later she had no interest in his silly toys."

"Toys?"

Audry shrugged. "Seems he's a photographer. Can't believe he was idiot enough to haul his stuff down here with him."

"Okay then, what about Simmons?"

"He made himself scarce most of the morning, but he kept the fire going in the basement; that's all I cared about. It's a big house, Sable. Four people can avoid each other for a long time. Now . . ." She sat on the bed while Sable changed into the scrub pants. "Time for you to lay down and keep that ice on your head. We need to keep a close eye on you for the next few hours."

"I'm a doctor, Audry. I know the drill."

"*Now* are you going to tell me what happened down there?" Craig slid a plate across the dining table toward Murph and lifted the lid from the roasting pot, where the aroma of roast beef drifted through the room. "I heard you two talking."

Murph shoved the plate away. He wasn't hungry. "Someone attacked us."

The lid clattered to the table. "What!"

"I'd appreciate it if you didn't say anything about this to the others." Murph glanced toward the door. Bryce might come walking in at any time. "Someone must have followed us. We were looking at the crystal cavern when that natural bridge seemed to crumble on top of us. Apparently, someone was hiding there and lost footing."

"And you didn't see who?"

"It happened so fast I couldn't focus my light on them. Sable was in front of me, they shoved us, and I wasn't braced. She was so close to the edge that it didn't take more than a nudge for her to stumble forward. The ledge collapsed beneath her, and I couldn't hold onto her. Her shirt ripped out of my —"

"And you didn't even see who it was?" Craig demanded.

"If I knew who it was, do you think I'd be sitting here?"

"But that's crazy. You're saying somebody intentionally tried to shove you into the pit? Why'd *she* fall in if they pushed *you*?"

Murph leveled a cool look at him. "I just told you."

"But why would they do it?"

"Good question," Murph said. "We're still trying to find an answer to —"

"Wait a minute." Craig shoved the pot aside and leaned over the table. "This is too much." He held up his right forefinger. "First, Sable wrecks her car down in Oklahoma . . ."

"Keep your voice down."

Craig held up a second finger. "Next," he said more softly, "she nearly falls into the ravine." The volume rose again with every word. "Then someone tries to drown Simmons in the creek."

"Maybe," Murph said. "Maybe not. Please lower your voice."

"What other explanation is there?" Craig asked.

"He said he slipped and fell in. It wasn't until afterward he decided someone tried to drown him. What I want to know is what he was doing out there in the first place."

"What about Sable? Is Audry still upstairs with her?"

Murph nodded, frowning. He was becoming less and less comfortable about that. His suspect list had suddenly taken on a new dimension, and Audry was on it. She'd moved a couple of notches closer to the top, even though there were still one or two ahead of her.

If Boswell had wanted to fool everyone — if, indeed, Boswell was behind this — Audry would be a good choice. She may behave like a kind, talkative woman, mature in years, but she was in good physical condition, and she was sharp.

She also knew how to control people, as was obvious yesterday when she'd helped prevent a fight between Simmons and Chadwick, and when she'd convinced Murph to accompany Sable and Bryce down into the cave.

The door opened and Bryce entered the kitchen. "I tried to check on Sable, but

Audry was in there yammering at her and wouldn't let anybody else in. Got any food left?"

Murph slid his unused plate, fork, and knife across the table. "Plenty. Have some."

Bryce took a seat across from Murph and reached for the pot. "I'm starved. Who cooked this?"

"Jerri, I think," Murph said. "Tell me something, Craig, why did you go to the cave with us this morning?"

"What does that have to do with —"

"Who told you we were going down?" Murph asked.

"I did," Bryce said. "Soon as I told him, he wanted to go along."

"Is there a problem with that?" Craig demanded.

Bryce's movements slowed, apparently picking up on the tension in the room. "Is something wrong?"

"Everything's fine," Craig snapped.

"Audry didn't suggest that you accompany us?" Murph asked.

"No, and if you're implying that I had anything to do —"

"I'm not implying a thing," Murph said.

"I need to go talk to Sable." Craig dropped the oven mitt onto the table and stalked from the kitchen.

Murph propped his elbows on the table and rubbed his face wearily. He drew back when he saw flecks of drying mud scattering across the tabletop.

"I need to go clean up." He glanced at Bryce.

"Okay."

But they both sat there in silence. Bryce seemed to have lost his appetite.

There was an abrupt knock at the door, and it opened slightly. "Sable? You decent?"

It was Craig's voice. The sharp spikes of fear that shot through Sable eased once more.

"She isn't taking visitors right now," Audry said from her eagle-eyed position on the chest at the end of the bed.

"It's okay." Sable avoided Audry's warning scowl. "Come on in, Craig."

As soon as he stepped through the door she could tell he was upset. "How are you doing?" he asked.

"She'd be better if she had a chance to rest," Audry said pointedly.

"I'll be fine." It was true. Sable's head still hurt, but she felt no nausea, no dizziness — although it was difficult to tell, since Audry wouldn't let her out of bed.

"I need to talk to her alone for a minute," Craig told Audry, as if she had suddenly become Sable's guardian.

Sable nodded. "I'll be okay, Audry. I'd like to talk with him if you don't mind."

The woman's eyes narrowed. She crossed her arms over her chest.

"Please, Audry. I'm a big girl, I know how to take care of myself."

Audry raised one gray brow that spoke her thoughts without a word, then she stood slowly to her feet, burrowing a glare into Craig that would make a more observant man cringe. He didn't seem to notice. She walked stiffly from the room, leaving the door open.

Sable got up and closed it, then returned to her place on the bed. "Okay, tell me what's so important you had to disturb me from my deathbed," she drawled.

Craig took Audry's place on the chest at the end of the bed. He leaned toward her, keeping his voice low. "Someone tries to kill you what . . . twice? Three times? And you don't think it's important?"

Sable groaned and pressed the ice against her head once more. "What did Murph say?"

"I don't care what Murph has to say, I want to know what you say. What's happening here, Sable? You can't just leave everybody in the dark like this, not when you're in danger. I guess you realize that puts everyone in this house in danger right along with you."

"Okay, okay, relax. Slow down." Her head hurt worse. "I'm sorry. I know we probably should have told everyone about this sooner, but honestly, we thought it would cause more —"

"What's this 'we' business? You're talking about Murph, right?"

"That's right. Apparently, someone followed us from Freemont."

"And that's important because . . . ?"

She stifled a groan. She didn't have the energy for another explanation. "I'm not sure yet. It's what we're here to find out."

" 'We' again. Sable, has it ever occurred to you that Murph is the one who followed you? Doesn't it strike you as strange that —"

"Murph isn't the bad guy here."

"Forgive me if I don't automatically trust your judgment on that," Craig snapped. "It wasn't too long ago that you made another misjudgment of character, and it nearly got you killed."

"Thanks for that compassionate reminder."

"You *should* thank me. Somebody needs

to keep an eye on you now that —"

"Oh, relax, and keep your voice down."

"That's another thing. Why does everybody tell me to keep my —"

"Someone tried to kill Murph." Honestly, Craig Holt was the most irritating —

"What!"

"Keep your voice down! We're trying to keep this from making the papers this afternoon, if you don't mind. It happened right out there on the hillside while he was chopping wood yesterday. You saw his injury."

"He could have done that himself."

"Oh, come on! You think he's going to hit himself in the head? Someone threw a limb at him, and I saw it happen. If I hadn't warned him, it would have hit him dead-on. Now stop with the big brother act."

Craig spread his hands and stood up. "Fine." He paced to the window, arms folded across his chest. "What did the police tell you about Josiah's automobile accident?"

She hesitated at the abrupt change of subject. "They thought he might have fallen asleep at the wheel or swerved to miss an animal on the road, and his truck went off the road."

"And that killed him?"

"He hit a tree."

Craig was silent for a moment. "Sable, your grandpa didn't have any automobile accident down in Freemont — at least that wasn't what killed him."

"What are you talking about?"

"There's something else you need to know. Something only the mortician would see."

"A mortician? Are you talking about Bobby Ray?"

"Yes, but he could get into big trouble if anyone found out."

"You'd better tell me."

Bryce drained a glass of milk, carried it to the sink, and rinsed it out. "Murph, you know you asked Craig why he went into the cave with us this morning?"

"Yes."

"Why did you want to know?"

Don't scare the kid to death. "Because it's come to our attention that not everyone in this house right now is what he seems to be. We've found some things missing and some inconsistencies of behavior that have us a little concerned."

"Somebody's been stealing from you?"

Murph nodded, wondering how much

more he should tell Bryce — or anyone else, for that matter. Should he even have told Craig about their attack?

"We're just watching the guests a little more closely and keeping track of their activities," Murph said. "I want to know the motives behind those activities."

The youthful lines of Bryce's face looked drawn, his eyes shadowed. He returned to his seat and rested his elbows on the table. "Then I guess I better tell you something."

Murph waited.

"Craig took off and left me in that passage today," Bryce said.

"He left you?"

"He kept aiming his flashlight at the ceiling of the passage, like he was looking for something specific. You know where all that fog got so thick? We came to a little stream of water trickling from up above, and he got so excited he climbed the side and disappeared into that fog. After awhile I couldn't tell the difference between the scuffing sound of his shoes and the dripping of the water, and when I called to him he didn't answer. He'd just disappeared."

"He never told you what he was searching for?"

"Nope."

"How long was he gone?"

"I don't know, maybe ten or fifteen minutes."

Murph shoved his chair backward. "I need to check on Sable. Why don't you go find the others?"

Sable stared at the suddenly serious, almost frightening expression in Craig's eyes.

"You won't believe me," he said. "You won't want to."

"Why not?"

He looked at Sable for a long moment. "Better be sure you want to hear this, because you won't like it. I swear it's the truth, though. Bobby Ray wouldn't lie about this."

"Craig, tell me."

He took a deep breath and reached up to comb his fingers through his damp, black hair. "Bobby was supposed to keep the casket closed, right?"

"Yes. The body was prepared in Freemont. There wasn't any reason for Bobby to do anything."

"He always respects the family's wishes. He's a good mortician."

"Craig, what did Bobby Ray do?"

"The mortician in Freemont called him after the body was shipped, reminding him not to open the casket under any circumstances."

"And?"

"Why would he be so adamant about that?"

Sable glanced toward the closed door. "Craig, tone it down a little."

He turned from his vigil over the window and bent toward Sable. "What did they tell you about the body?" he asked softly.

"They didn't advise an open casket because of the damage," she said.

"There wasn't any damage. I didn't tell your family this, but there wasn't a mark on Josiah's body."

The ice bag fell from Sable's hands. "How would you know that?"

"I convinced Bobby Ray to open the casket."

"Against the wishes of the family? Craig, how could you —"

"Remember it was his son with me when . . . when I had that wreck that got me into such hot water. Bobby Ray knew what Boswell did to Dad afterward, and from that day on I never trusted him. Neither did Dad. I didn't think it would hurt anything to just check and see why they were so adamant about a closed casket."

"Why would you be so suspicious about something like that?"

"I knew from some of the remarks Josiah made the last time I saw him that he was unhappy about his job. He wanted to talk to Dad about contacting the legislators in Oklahoma about some mining discrepancies."

"Discrepancies?"

"Ground pollution. Contamination from the tailings from the mine. Right now there aren't a lot of laws to control the mining companies, and the unethical ones swoop in, tear up the land, and swoop back out, leaving millions of dollars worth of cleanup that they don't have to do anything about. You can bet Boswell would leave the mess if he could."

"And you're saying Grandpa was worried about this pollution?"

"That's what I'm saying, and you can bet if Boswell found out Josiah talked to Dad, he pitched a fit."

"Craig, are you suggesting he killed Grandpa to stop —"

"Josiah's body didn't have a mark on it — no bruises, no blood. Does that sound like he died in a car wreck?"

"So why did they tell us —"

"Exactly. Why force you to have a closed

casket when there was no reason for it? But Bobby Ray had his orders, and he could get into big trouble for what he did."

"And so he didn't say anything."

"Sable, a body doesn't bruise after it's dead, isn't that right?"

She nodded.

"And he was found in that wreckage. There was a wreck. The thing is, it sounds like he was already dead when the wreck happened."

"Which means —"

"Looks to me like the wreck was a cover-up. I think somebody killed Josiah, and you can bet the farm that Boswell was in on it. Josiah thought he'd gotten such a good deal when he and his buddy bought into the mine deal down in Freemont." Craig sat down beside her. "Now are you going to tell me what's really going on around —"

The door flew open and Murph strode into the room, eyes blazing fury. "Get away from her."

Chapter 21

It had been a long time since Murph had felt this nearly uncontrollable urge to punch someone. Apparently, his face reflected his feelings, because as he stepped across the room toward Craig, Sable scrambled from the bed.

"Murph, what are you doing? It's okay, he isn't —"

"I said get away from her." When Craig didn't move, Murph reached beneath his shirt.

"No!" Sable cried. "Murph, please, what are you doing?"

Murph didn't take his gaze from Craig. "Why did you leave Bryce alone in that passage?"

Craig groaned and rolled his eyes. "He told you about that? Look, it was no big deal, okay?"

"What did you do with the watch?"

"What are you talking about?" Sable asked.

"That's what I'd like to know," Craig said. "You're losing it, pal. I mean, you're really losing it here."

Murph continued to glare at Craig. "Our attacker took the watch and chain from Sable's neck."

Confusion did a relay across Craig's face. "That old thing? But why?"

"Good question," Murph said. "Sable told you just before we separated down in the cave that her watch didn't run."

"And that's supposed to make me want to steal it?"

"If you knew *why* it didn't work," Murph said.

"Like I should care? I knew it was a sentimental thing for her. It was Josiah's watch. Besides that, how was I supposed to have attacked you and taken Sable's watch when I was halfway on the other side of the whole cave system with Bryce? You're not making sense."

"You left Bryce alone in that passage," Murph said. "You know the cave as well as anyone. If there's a shortcut to the crystal cavern —"

"You're trying to say I'm the one who pushed you?" Craig asked. "Man, you're crazy."

"Who else? Bryce? We were the only four down there."

"I think this ice is getting to you," Craig said. "Why would I want a broken watch?

And there's no shortcut I know about."

"Why did you leave Bryce alone in that passage?" Murph asked again.

"Look, it's no big deal, okay? You're overreacting. We were looking for the sinkhole Josiah fell into last fall, right? Naturally, when the fog thickened, I thought for sure there was an opening nearby — you know, dry, cold air mingled with warmer, moist air from the cave. I found it, that's all."

"You found it?" Sable exclaimed. "The sinkhole?"

Craig shrugged. "Doesn't amount to much, and I had to climb. I couldn't get out because the hole was about four feet above my head." He looked back at Murph. "Are you satisfied?"

"Why couldn't you have told Bryce that?" Sable asked.

"Oh, come on, Sable, if I'd have told Bryce, he'd have blabbed it to you, and —"

"Stop with the kids' games," Murph said. "You scared Bryce, you left him alone in the cave —"

"So why is that such a horrible thing? Sable did it to us. Bryce laughed when we told him our stories. I thought he'd get a kick out of it, and then I'd get to tease Sable for months, because I knew something about the cave that she didn't know."

Murph leaned against the doorframe and crossed his arms over his chest. Craig Holt was a big kid. A goof.

Right now Murph was beginning to feel like a goof himself. *So much for logical conclusions.*

Sable sank back onto the bed and picked up the ice pack. "Craig, would you mind filling this with ice again?"

He responded with eagerness, obviously willing to escape the room before Murph could complete the interrogation.

Murph watched him closely as he walked away, then sat down on the chest. "Sorry. It was too great a coincidence to ignore." In his peripheral vision, he thought he saw Sable smile. He looked at her. She was smiling. Grinning, even.

"It isn't funny," he said.

She laughed out loud, then immediately groaned and reached for her head. "Remind me not to do that again."

"I wasn't exactly trying out a comedy routine on you."

She smiled again. "Paul Murphy, you are my hero. You're definitely my hero after that. You really had Craig going for a minute. I wish I'd had a camera. My brothers will love hearing about this."

He knew he shouldn't allow his masculine pride to be offended. "I nearly pulled my gun on him. I don't think it's funny."

"I'm sorry." She made an obvious effort to revamp her expression. "Okay, granted, you don't know him the way I do, but it's just like him to look for that sinkhole and then try to keep it a secret."

"And if he kept a shortcut to the cavern a secret, as well?"

"Extreme long shot." She got up from the bed and closed the door, then sat back down. "Murph, I don't believe in ghosts."

He blinked. Okay. He hadn't been expecting that. "You don't?"

"No, but I don't know how else to explain what happened down there. How does someone see without any kind of light?"

"Ah, the ghost eyes. When you mentioned that, it scared me. I thought you might be injured worse than I had first thought. They didn't say anything, and you didn't see anything else."

"I thought they were trying to strangle me, Murph, but the chain broke, and they took it and left. They just left."

Murph reached for the flashlight on her dresser. "Could it have been some kind of temporary blindness?"

"Could have been a reaction to the concussion, I suppose. I don't know any other way to explain it."

"I'm going to check you again. Are you having any trouble with your vision now?"

"None. I can't understand. Why would anyone take my watch?"

"I don't know. It doesn't make sense, unless they had reason to believe there was something important in it. The only person who knew it didn't work besides you and me was Craig."

"And Bryce. A couple of kids. But also, the map had a drawing of the watch face next to the etching of the sinkhole, and someone took that map. Maybe they made the connection somehow."

He shone a beam into her right eye, then her left. Pupils equal and reactive, as they had been the last time he'd checked them. "You know what day this is?"

"Sunday."

"Your age?"

"Thirty-one on Tuesday."

"Where are we?"

"Missouri Ozarks. Murph, this is silly. I'm fine, I know I am. I can see you, I'm alert and oriented."

He put the flashlight back on the dresser.

"Grandpa was murdered," Sable said quietly.

Murph frowned at her. "Well, we had considered that, of course, but what makes you think —"

"Craig told me."

"Craig? How would he know?"

"He saw Grandpa's body after they shipped it back here."

"And he saw something no one else did?"

"The casket was sealed," Sable explained. "The rest of us didn't even see Grandpa's body; we were advised not to because of the damage. Even I didn't see him. But Craig said there wasn't a mark on the body."

"He opened a sealed casket?"

"That isn't my point right now." She leaned forward. "Murph, he knows something's up, and he's trying to find out what it is. He wants to help us. I believe him."

There was a knock at the door. Murph stiffened. "Who is it?"

"Ice carrier."

Murph opened the door, and Craig brought in two plastic zipper bags filled with crushed ice. He presented them to Sable with a flourish.

"Thanks," she said, taking them.

"It's the least I could do, after ruining your day."

Sable nodded to Murph. "Close the door. He needs to know what's going on."

Murph agreed — reluctantly. "Have a seat, Craig. We need to talk."

Sable let Murph feed her neighbor information in gradual sound bites. For the most part, Craig took it without comment, his dark brows drawing closer together with each new revelation, until they formed a slash across his forehead.

"So you're wanted by the police," he said at last, when Murph had finished his story. "They're blaming you for the murder of your friend?"

"That's right," Sable said.

"Morons," he muttered. "Guess it's a good thing we had this ice storm, or you could be in jail right now. I think you need to tell the others."

"Craig," Sable said impatiently, "one of the others obviously followed us from Freemont."

"Right, but four of the others didn't. Shouldn't they be warned there's a killer in the house?"

"I don't think they're in danger."

"Oh, sure, not unless this bozo decides

394

to blow the place up or something. Maybe one of them has seen something that could tip you off."

"And then that would put them in danger," Murph argued.

"Look, all I'm saying is that I'm sure glad you told me, okay? Don't you think the others would appreciate it, too? They've got to know something's going on, anyway, with all the so-called accidents happening around here."

"Let's wait," Murph said.

Craig shrugged and stood. "Fine with me, but I think you need more people to watch your backside, if you know what I mean. I'm going downstairs to check the fire."

When he left, Murph reached for Sable's arm. "Do you feel well enough to come to the attic with me? We need to find out what's in that safe, and I think we must have missed something in that note from Josiah. I could try it myself, but I don't want to leave you alone right now."

Sable retrieved the note from the pocket of her discarded slacks and went with him to the attic. Dillon joined them in the hallway and accompanied them up the attic steps. When they reached the landing, they closed the attic door behind them, leaving Dillon to stand watch, and went to the safe.

"Read the note to me again," Murph said. "We're missing something, but I think we've got the right idea."

She read it aloud, slowly, more and more convinced, as she read, that the note referred to something far deeper and more sinister than his involvement with the Seitz mine — although that was bad enough.

Why would he have salted the crystal cavern? It didn't make sense. It wasn't as if he stood to gain anything by it. Why would he have had those chunks of galena, sphalerite, and silver analyzed? She didn't know.

"Okay," she said, watching Murph try the handle again to no avail. "Do the same thing, but this time only turn it once after fifteen. He probably didn't realize he was writing 'for' twice."

Murph followed her directions. This time the metal handle slid up stiffly.

"It worked!" He swung the thick door open, and they peered inside.

The shelves were crammed full of papers, birth certificates, marriage licenses, and titles.

Sable pulled out a folder marked "photographs." She thumbed through the first few, holding them up to the glow from Murph's flashlight.

"It looks just like the crystal cavern," Murph said. "Why would he take a picture of that?"

She turned the photograph over. Grandpa had written "Seitz mine" in his flamboyant script.

Murph gave a low whistle.

She held up the next photo. "This one is the crystal cavern."

"Then what's this one?" Murph asked, picking up the next one on the stack. He read it and whistled again. "That's Number Three, one of the working mines outside of Freemont. It almost looks as if he was comparing the appearance of each place."

"Maybe he was trying to figure it out for himself," Sable said.

"Possibly."

She held the three photos up together. "These were all dated in January of this year. What do you think about this, Murph? He checked the Seitz mine a little more closely and maybe had the ore analyzed. He compared it to an analysis of Number Three and found them surprisingly similar. Then he became more concerned and decided to try a little experiment. He came home and figured out how to salt the cavern below, just to see if it looked similar to the Seitz mine. That's something Grandpa would do."

"You knew your grandpa pretty well. I think that sounds like a feasible explanation."

"It's something he would have done. I can believe that a whole lot easier than —"

"I know."

They sorted through more papers, then pulled out a thick manila folder labeled "Boswell Enterprises, Inc."

Murph peered over her shoulder. "I didn't know Boswell had another corporation."

"Neither did I. And what's Grandpa doing with this?" She opened the folder and found a stack of photocopies.

"What the —"

"Workers' comp reports."

There was a sticky note at the bottom of each copy: "Not filed." She shuffled through the pages until she came to a sheet with her signature at the bottom.

"They didn't turn these in," Murph said.

"You asked me about that," Sable said. "You were right."

He had never been less pleased about being proved right. "Paid, it seems, or there would have been an outcry."

Sable thumbed through several of the other pages. All contained information on Boswell Enterprises, the corporation name written in Grandpa's hand. "It looks like a history," she said. "Boswell's history. Craig told me something yesterday about an incident that happened when he was a teenager. His father, Reuben, was a judge at the time, and he did something he wasn't proud of." She didn't go into details. "According to Craig, Boswell tried to blackmail Reuben. This looks like Grandpa was keeping a history on Boswell." She handed the copy to Murph and held the next page to the light. "Look at this."

"It's a list of people who died from accidents in the past six years."

"Mining accidents?" she asked.

"No. This one was an automobile accident; this one fell into a grain elevator."

"Here's the name of a friend of mine," Sable said. "She was supposed to have died in a car wreck."

Murph took the sheet, which was stapled to several others.

He put the copies down and looked at the next stack of stapled pages. The top copy was of a ledger sheet. Scrawled across the top in Grandpa's writing were the words "Professional terminators."

"Sable, this is why your grandpa died," Murph said softly. "He must have let Boswell know what he knew."

Murph turned a few more pages, and again Sable gasped. A lot of missing pieces fell together.

"What's that?" Murph asked.

"A transcript of a trial. Jim's trial, after he tried to kill me." Behind the transcript was a cashier's check paid to the lawyer who had handled Jim's case. "Boswell paid the defense lawyer."

"You know why, don't you?"

"Because Boswell was behind Jim's attack on me."

"Sounds like it."

"Then his attack on me might have been a reminder, just like that copy of the mortgage. Maybe he was trying to force Grandpa to do something he didn't want to do, or maybe it was a warning to Grandpa to keep his mouth shut. I always wondered why they had the trial so quickly." She leaned her head against the cold metal of the safe. "That was why Grandpa never wanted me in Freemont to begin with."

"Sounds as if Boswell might have lured you to Freemont for that very reason," Murph said. "To keep Josiah in line."

"Someone in this house is one of Boswell's hit men."

"I think we'd already figured that out," Murph said.

"Meaning he sent someone to continue the vendetta."

Murph touched Sable's shoulder. "They haven't gotten us yet." He put his arm around her. "Remember when we were talking about this on the bus on the way down here? You told me you could handle a gun."

"Yes."

"Could you shoot someone if you had to?"

"If I had to. How about you?"

"Yes, and I've proved it. I worked as a medic for a mining company that had holdings in Colombia. They sent me down there once, armed to protect myself against drug runners who were operating near our company. We . . . had a run-in."

"Did you have to shoot someone?"

"Yes. It was either him or me and my partner. I didn't kill him, but I injured him pretty badly. I'll never forget it, Sable. Believe me, shooting someone isn't easy, especially for someone like you."

"And you."

"And me. Think hard about this. What if our killer turns out to be someone like Jerri? Or Craig? Remember, we don't know who it is."

"But we have to protect ourselves, don't we? Boswell is so powerful." Her voice broke.

He drew her into his arms. "We're not quitting now, are we? Not just when we've found what we're looking for."

"We'll never get out of here with it."

"Hey, I'm supposed to be the pessimist here, not you, remember?"

"All of a sudden everything's changed."

He felt the soft warmth of her breath against his cheek. "Yes, things have changed, haven't they? I have even more reason to want to live now."

She rested her forehead against his shoulder.

"You know, this could become addictive," Murph said.

"You mean the terror and danger and running for our lives?"

"I mean learning to depend on each other."

"I think you're right." Sable stepped back from his embrace. Her gaze settled on one more thing in the soft glow from the flashlight. She reached into the safe and pulled out a small, leather-bound journal. She opened the first page.

It was a journal, in Grandpa's handwriting. The heading said, "Boswell's Enterprise."

"Sable!" came a sharp female voice from below. "Sable Chamberlin, where are you? Are you okay?" It was Audry. Time to go.

"Let's put these things back in the safe," Murph said.

Chapter 22

That evening, the light from glass oil lamps flickered on the shelves of the upper hallway, and a scent of vanilla drifted through the air, alleviating the odor of the oil. Two large lamps on shelves over the staircase illuminated the steps. Flames danced downstairs in the fireplace beneath a mantel decorated with three glowing candles. The house radiated warmth. Audry and Jerri had done a good job.

Sable walked down the stairway beside Murph. Except for a lingering headache, she felt fine physically. That strange and frightening episode of blindness had not returned.

Terminators. One of Boswell's terminators was in this house. The warmth of the house, even the comfort of Murph's hand guiding her, did nothing to thaw the icy tautness that accompanied every movement she made.

"I'm not hungry," she muttered to Murph.

"You haven't eaten since breakfast. You

will feel better with something in your stomach."

"You sound like Audry."

Murph chuckled. "I'm quoting her. She wants everybody to show up for dinner. She has a big surprise for us." The sound of chatter increased as they neared the back of the house.

"Are we ready for another surprise?" she asked.

His hand tightened on her arm, and he stopped and turned to her.

"What is it?" she asked.

"Speaking of surprises," he said softly, "I'm wondering more and more if maybe we should tell the others. This thing is getting out of hand, and others could get hurt. It isn't right to withhold information from them."

"But as you told Craig, it isn't right to endanger their lives, either."

"If we stick together we can reduce that risk."

She wasn't convinced. "Let's bide our time and see what happens tonight."

They stepped through the kitchen into the dining area beyond. Audry and Perry stood at the stove arguing amiably about the use of seasoning, while Bryce and Craig sat at the dining table across from

Jerri, sharing details of their excursion into the cave this morning. Simmons sat at the end of the table with his back to the wall, his narrowed gaze roving from Bryce, to Craig, to Audry, to each of the others, one by one.

"The fog was so thick I couldn't see a thing," Bryce said. "And then Craig just climbed up a ledge and fell through a hole and left me there alone."

"I didn't fall through a hole; I just moved a few rocks out of the way, and they fell down the other side, and you thought I'd fallen."

"He *left* you?" Audry exclaimed from the kitchen.

"I didn't leave him there for good, you know," Craig said. "I told him I'd be back. It just took me longer than I thought."

"How was I supposed to know that?" Bryce complained. "And I didn't know my way back, and I kept hearing water drip all around me, and sometimes it sounded like footsteps."

"That's why I don't like caves," Jerri shuddered theatrically. "Creepy places."

Simmons leaned forward, watching Craig intently. "I'm curious. What was so important that you'd leave a kid alone in a strange, dark place like that and —"

"Hey, I'm not a kid," Bryce said. "I'll be sixteen in two months."

Simmons ignored him. "So what did you find down in that passage?" he asked Craig. "You think there's something to that old story about treasure down there?"

"No treasure," Craig said. He looked at Sable, then Murph. "Ghosts, maybe, but no treasure."

"Ghosts." Simmons said the word with the same amount of disdain that Bryce had used the day before about the same subject. He sat back, flexing his shoulder muscles, as if trying to shrug away sudden tension.

"So how's the princess tonight?" Craig asked, indicating Sable as she took a chair across the table from him. "I thought you would at least demand dinner upstairs."

She made a face at him.

"How's the head?" he asked.

"Better," she said. "It's more like a hen egg than a goose egg now."

"Can we go down again tomorrow?" Bryce asked.

Murph laughed. It was a deep, rich sound that helped ease some of Sable's tension.

"Not tomorrow," Sable told him.

"Okay, here we are, folks." Audry came

bustling in from the kitchen with a huge covered platter. She set it on the table and stepped back. "You won't believe who cooked dinner tonight." She gestured grandly toward Perry Chadwick, who stood grinning broadly at the end of the kitchen counter, hands folded in front of him. "Our lowly water carrier. Would you believe it? Turns out he's a chef, complete with cookbooks! He finally told me that's what he carried here in that heavy suitcase, though I don't understand the big mystery."

"So that's why it was so heavy," Craig said.

"That and his toys," Jerri murmured.

"Toys?" Simmons asked.

"What you saw this morning when you went snooping through my things," Perry said, "was not a toy. It was a part of my photography equipment. I had no intention of leaving it up in that freezing bus."

"I was *not* snooping through your —"

"It turns out he was headed for a chef's challenge cook-off down in Branson," Audry said. "Oops, I almost forgot the peach preserve cobbler and homemade ice cream we made. I left the ice cream out on the patio." She stepped back through the kitchen and out into the hallway.

"Branson, huh?" Jerri leaned back to get a better look at Perry, her red hair gleaming bronze in the candlelight. "They're having a cooking contest in the middle of winter?"

Perry gave her a cool nod. "Complete with live television from Springfield's Channel 33. If I win, I get to travel to St. Louis for the regional next month."

"So why all the cookbooks?" Jerri asked.

"It's a challenge," Perry explained stiffly. "Just like those cooking challenges they show on cable. We won't know the ingredients until the contest begins. It's one of those."

Jerri gave a "no big deal" shrug, then turned to Bryce, who sat beside her. "How about you? I know Audry was on her way to a wedding, and Sable and Murph were coming here. Did you and your dad have something planned?"

Bryce frowned and looked down at the table. "Not really. He and my mom are divorced, and I was just coming down from Kansas to stay with him a few days. I just hope he isn't too worried about me."

Jerri's expression softened. "I'm sure he'll be glad to see you when you get there." She turned to Simmons. "And you're on your way to Harrison, Arkansas, Mr. Simmons?"

"Not by choice," the man grumbled. "My mom's in Fayetteville, but my sister wants me to go to her house in Harrison, get her car, and drive it to Fayetteville. That's what landed me in this crazy situation in the first place."

Sable felt Murph's sudden, attentive stillness beside her. That was it? The big mystery?

Audry came back through the door with an ice cream freezer and set it on the kitchen counter. She entered the dining room and whisked the cover from the large platter of food.

"Venison egg rolls made from scratch with mushroom sauce, with stir-fried vegetables on a bed of gingered rice."

Perry pulled off his apron and held a chair for Audry. "Time to dine."

Sable wasn't hungry, but she would force herself to eat. The food smelled like an Asian restaurant, and she loved Oriental. She sipped her water slowly as the others passed the platter around. She smiled politely at the appropriate times and studied her guests, one by one.

Audry beamed at Perry proudly, as if he were her own chick just hatched. "You could have told me you were a chef."

Perry chuckled. "Amateur. Don't forget the amateur. I have a lot to learn."

"You know what amateur means?" Jerri served herself and passed the platter. "It means someone who does something just for the love of it."

Perry patted his belly. "In that case, the evidence should have given me away. A bachelor living alone doesn't get this chunky on frozen dinners."

"Now, Perry, don't be too hard on yourself," Audry chided. "I bet you've worked off at least five pounds since we arrived here."

"Your coordination is improving, too," Jerri observed. "I saw you actually carry wood in from the pile beside the front porch, and you didn't fall on the ice."

Perry stacked four egg rolls on his plate. "I'm not doing as well as Craig, though. He practically skated all the way to the bridge and back today."

Sable's interest sharpened on Craig. "What was at the bridge?"

He hesitated between bites. "Just checking the condition in case we needed to get out. The ice is thick, and the bridge tilts dangerously. Your grandpa should have had that thing repaired years ago,

Sable. It must be at least a hundred years old."

"We seldom drove that way, except with a tractor to the field," Sable said.

They completed the meal in silence. It wasn't until after Audry dished out dessert that Craig spoke again.

"We'd have to do some chopping before we could risk a drive over the bridge. I thought I might go out and try my hand at it in a few minutes."

"Who said anything about leaving?" Simmons asked.

Craig took another bite of vegetables, shrugged, and washed the food down with a swallow of water. "Strange you should ask." He gave Sable a pointed look.

Oh, great. The decision was being taken out of their hands. Craig was going to tell them himself.

"I'm not going anywhere on this ice," Audry announced. "I've had too many bad experiences driving on ice in these Ozark hills. We just have to be careful. We can't afford any more emergencies."

Simmons took a final swig of coffee, set the mug down, and pushed away from the table. "Why are you all of a sudden talking about getting out of here?"

"Good question," Jerri said. "Sable, are

you sure you're doing okay? If we need to get you to medical care —"

"It's a possibility," she said. "I seemed to have some visual disturbances earlier, when I was in the cave."

"Somebody else was down there," Bryce said slowly. "I heard you, Murph. You told Craig somebody attacked you."

"What!" Audry squawked. "Attacked! Who attacked you? Sable, he's saying somebody pushed you down in that cave?"

"Okay, I'll explain." Murph put down his fork and folded his napkin. He pushed his plate back and cleared his throat. "Perry and Audry, thank you for dinner. It was delicious. I'm sorry we've had to put a damper on things. We had an extra spelunker down in the cave this morning."

No one spoke, but the tension thickened to near visibility.

"They jumped us in the crystal cavern." Murph explained the incident once again. "It's possible someone was exploring the pit and didn't want to be disturbed. When we arrived they might have felt it was necessary to jump us so they could get away without being seen."

Perry set his coffee cup down with a clatter. He leaned forward, eyes wide.

"That's pretty drastic action just to avoid a citation for trespassing."

Simmons sat at the end of the table like a storefront mannequin, his expression frozen. Only his eyes moved, gazing from face to face around the table in a panicked search.

"Is there another entrance to the cave?" Jerri asked. "Surely it couldn't have been one of us —"

"Someone also pushed me over the side of the cliff the other night," Sable said. "I didn't just slip on the ice. And that 'accident' Murph had in the woods yesterday was no accident. I saw what happened from the attic window. Someone threw a log at him from the ledge above."

"What's going on here, Sable?" Perry asked. "Why are you just now telling us about this?"

"We didn't want mass panic on our hands," Murph said. "And we knew someone was dangerous, but we didn't know who."

"And you do now?" Audry asked.

Sable folded her napkin and tucked it beneath the edge of her plate. "It could be any one of us."

"But I don't understand why," Audry said. "Why would anyone be trying to hurt us?"

"We can't go into great detail now," Sable

414

said. "But we have good reason to believe someone followed Murph and me here to stop us from finding evidence about crimes we think were committed in Freemont."

"Murders," Murph added.

"Murders!" Audry exclaimed. "Ar—Are you saying Josiah was murdered?"

Sable pushed away from the table. That was too obvious a slip to ignore.

Bryce swallowed convulsively as his gaze darted to the others at the table. "Somebody followed you all the way here from Oklahoma?"

"All the way into this house," Sable said. "I'm sorry to frighten you like this. Please, if you've seen anything that might help, tell me."

Jerri pushed her plate away, her normally ruddy complexion ashen. "That would put us in danger, too, wouldn't it?"

"I'm afraid it could," Sable said. "If the killer even thinks you've seen him — or her — do something suspicious, he could get nervous. From here on out we have to be very careful."

"That's right," Murph said. "We should all stay close to a group from now on. And I think we should lock our bedroom doors at night."

"Craig," Jerri said, "you don't have any chains for your tires?"

"No chains."

"Oh, that's just great," Perry spluttered. "We're stuck in the middle of the woods with a murderer. Where am I supposed to sleep? There's no lock on my door, remember? I'm in the sewing room. What am I supposed to do, nail the door —"

"Stay in the room with Simmons and me," Murph said.

Simmons suddenly focused his frigid gaze on Jerri. "Didn't you say you drove your route from Oklahoma City?"

"Yes," she muttered, leaning back in her seat, her round, freckled face pale with the burden of information they had just received. For once, the lines around her eyes made her look older than thirty-five. She rubbed her neck wearily.

"And nobody ever saw your photo ID." A hint of suspicion laced Simmons's voice. "And nobody actually heard you radio the dispatch office," he continued.

"I didn't realize I'd need a witness to prove it," she snapped, her deep voice tight with annoyance. "Lay off, Simmons."

"That's enough." Murph's steady voice calmed some of the frazzled tension that held the room in an ever-tightening grip.

"We're going to spend a lot more time in close proximity; fighting won't help matters."

Sable turned her attention to Audry. "We need to talk."

Chapter 23

Sable picked up a glowing oil lamp from a mirrored shelf in the dining room. "Audry, would you come with me to the family room?"

The normally talkative, strong-willed lady complied without a word. Sable led the way across the hall and into the cozy family room, where bookcases lined the walls and a useless television hovered in darkness in the far southwest corner. She placed the lamp on a tall sofa table along the wall to her right and closed the door.

Audry strolled across the carpeted floor and stopped to gaze out the window into the February darkness. "The moon's out," she said softly. "I can see the reflection of it breaking into prisms of light on the creek."

"No clouds?"

"Nope. I hope it stays like this. I checked the temperature about an hour ago. It's hovering just below freezing. You know how unpredictable Missouri weather is. It could be thawed enough for us to leave by tomorrow night."

"Don't get your hopes up. This hollow is one of the last places to thaw."

Audry fell silent for a moment. "We just need to protect each other until we can get out."

"Yes, we do." Sable strolled over to stand beside Audry at the window. "We also need to gather as much information as we can." She hesitated, then swallowed hard. "Audry, how . . . how well did you know Otis Boswell and my grandfather?"

Sable was close enough to hear the soft interruption of Audry's breathing.

Audry turned to her. "Boswell?"

"Otis Boswell. I think you know him, too."

Audry gave a sorrowful sigh. "So good ol' Otis is still in the picture after all these years, still stirring up trouble, I see. Why am I not surprised?"

"I was more than surprised when I saw an old picture of you with Grandpa and Otis," Sable said. "I was shocked and mystified."

"I . . . should have said something." Audry gently touched Sable's arm. "Believe me, if I knew anything that could help, I'd be the first to tell you. I'm no coward . . . at least, not that kind of a coward." She lowered her hands to her side and turned away. "I didn't even know Josiah was dead. It shocked me when you told me about it."

Sable waited. She knew, from Audry's reaction, that this wasn't going to be pleasant.

Audry squared her shoulders, breathed deeply, and turned to gaze around the room. She stepped over to a checkers table between two chairs. "All this is new, so different from the way it looked all those years ago."

"You were a friend of my grandparents?"

Audry shook her head. "Not exactly." She turned again to face Sable. "Never forget your grandfather was a wonderful man. He had his weaknesses." She spread her hands. "So did I."

Sable braced herself. "What kind of weaknesses are you talking about?"

A flush of color returned to Audry's cheeks. She stepped once more to the window, as if unable to meet Sable's gaze. "We were very good friends, dear. I don't think you would have liked . . . knowing how good."

For a long moment, Sable forgot to breathe. "No, I don't think so." She thought she'd prepared herself for this. She hadn't.

"I'm not going to try to excuse myself or your grandfather. We were wrong."

Sable swung away and strode toward the door, but she stopped before she reached it. She could not allow herself to get emotional about an incident that had taken place in the past. Not now, not with the danger they all faced. She couldn't let the past color the outcome of what was happening here now.

But Grandpa . . . ? She swallowed hard and took a deep breath. She turned back toward Audry. "How long did you and my grandpa have an affair?" She didn't try to keep the anger from her voice.

Audry winced. She turned from the window, her lips set in a straight line. "Not long, Sable. We both knew we were wrong. Your grandmother became sick soon after it began, and I know Josiah felt enormous guilt. So did I. Our guilt won't erase what happened, but it didn't happen again. As I told you, your grandfather was a good man. He learned his lessons well, and he learned them the first time."

"Did my grandmother know?"

"I hope not. I don't think Josiah would have told her. It wouldn't have done anyone any good — it would only have hurt more people."

"Did my grandpa —"

"He loved your grandmother, Sable. And he loved your mother very much."

"Obviously not as much as he needed to."

"Don't say that. As I told you, we had our weaknesses. We broke it off. It ended quickly."

Sable bit her lip and crossed her arms over her chest. "How did it happen?"

"I became acquainted with him when I taught your mother in high school. You're probably aware that Beth isn't the most athletic person — or at least she wasn't thirty-seven years ago. I spent some time with her after school a couple of days a week, and Josiah drove into town to pick her up, because your grandmother worked so many long hours at the restaurant in Eureka Springs. He was the kind of man who made people laugh, who put them at ease, because he genuinely liked people. I desperately needed to be able to laugh. I needed a friend. My husband was an alcoholic, and my marriage was failing rapidly. I confided in Josiah, and he was sorry for me. That was it. Nothing happened then."

"But I thought you said the affair —"

"Let me finish." Audry raised a hand. "I lost touch with your mother after she graduated, and naturally I didn't continue the friendship with Josiah. We moved away, and many years later my husband died of a stroke. I moved back to Cassville with my teenagers. I had to earn enough money to finish their education. My teaching salary didn't cut it, and so I took a part time job at a cafe in Cassville. That was where Josiah and I became reacquainted after all that time. He started coming in fairly often on my shifts, and your mother was no longer there to remind me that Josiah belonged to someone else. I was lonely . . ." She sighed and bent her head. "And now I'm so sorry. I never expected to be facing his granddaughter like this. I guess we always pay for our sins, even if we have to wait years to do it."

"How long did —"

"I won't go into any more detail about your grandfather and myself." An edge of steel strengthened Audry's voice. "But I will tell you that Otis Boswell found out somehow."

"You knew Otis before, as well?"

"Oh, yes, he was a great sports enthusiast. That picture you saw of the three of us was probably after a ball game. I saw them there often, sometimes together."

"So you didn't know Otis well?"

"Not as well as I knew Josiah, if that's what you're getting at," Audry said sharply.

"No. It wasn't."

"Okay." She spread her hands. "Well, then. I guess I'm a little prickly about the subject. I saw Boswell come into the cafe a couple of times when Josiah was there. Saw Craig's dad there too a couple of times. Reuben Holt."

"You knew Reuben?"

"Knew all the locals. It's a tight community, you know. They'd all sit together at the cafe while I poured coffee and tried to ply them with breakfast to improve business. You'd be surprised how much politics can be hashed over around a table with so many . . ." She stopped, blinked, then reached out to squeeze Sable's arm. "But you don't need to hear me jabber about old times. I'm sorry I had to tell you about things that are best left forgotten. I know Josiah would never have wanted his dear granddaughter to know this about —"

There was a sharp rap on the door, and Audry fell silent. Sable stepped over and opened it to find Craig standing in the hallway. The others hovered around the fireplace in the living room.

"Am I interrupting anything?" Craig asked.

"No, we were just finishing up in here," Audry assured him.

"Well, if you hear us moving furniture around upstairs, it's because we've decided to change the sleeping arrangements. The ladies will share your room, Sable. Perry is moving his cot into the room with Murph and Simmons. Bryce will move in with me downstairs. We all think it's safer that way."

"Agreed." Audry patted Sable on the shoulder. "Sorry to intrude on your privacy, dear, but safety comes before convenience. It sounds to me as if Dillon needs help guarding you."

While the men bustled between rooms and rearranged furniture Sable went upstairs. Her mind whirled in chaos. The pain she felt over Grandpa's apparent infidelity mingled with a fear that superimposed itself over everything else.

Was Audry telling the truth? Sable had already jumped to one too many conclusions about Grandpa's guilt. Should she believe he cheated on his wife just because a woman — who had been a stranger two days ago — claimed an affair with him?

But that would mean Audry had another motive for lying to her.

For a moment, Sable pushed all that from her mind. She would watch Audry as carefully as she watched the others. She could figure everything else out later. After they were safe.

She reached her room and glanced back along the hallway, every nerve attuned to each sound, each flash of light along the hallway, each thump on the floor. She was scared. They were trapped. They could not get out. Their stalker had them boxed in. The thing was, their stalker was also cornered, and cornered animals could be dangerous.

She stepped into her room and locked the door firmly behind her. The men were concentrating on the other rooms first, and she needed some time alone before she had a permanent crowd underfoot. She stood for a moment in the darkness. Who could be trusted in this house?

She lit a candle, leaned down, and shoved her hand between her mattress and box springs. The pistol was exactly where she'd left it after Simmons's near-drowning experience yesterday. She would leave it there for now; Murph was probably right

— she had begun to wonder if she really could pull the trigger. She wanted to find the faith to depend on prayer instead.

She straightened the comforter and strolled over to the window. The sun had set some time ago. There wasn't a streak of light left in the sky, and she had not yet grown accustomed to such early night — deep in this hollow, dusk always came earlier than it did in the open fields around Freemont, and dawn came later. Darkness was the worst time, when she couldn't see into the shadows.

A floorboard creaked in the hallway. She stiffened. "Who's out there?"

"Me." It was a deep, soothing voice. Murph. "Can I come in for a minute?"

Her hands shook as she unlocked the door. She knew she looked terrified.

He raised a hand to her face and cupped her cheek gently. "Are you okay?" His eyes were shadowed in the dimness of the candlelight, and she knew he was also suffering from the effects of the extreme stress.

"I'll be fine," she assured him. "How about you?"

A slow, weary smile crept across his face. "I think I can safely say that I've been developing a much closer relationship with

God in the past couple of days. I pray with every breath."

"Is it helping?"

"Yes, it is." He turned and locked the door, then took her by the arm and drew her closer. "I remembered something one of the guys with the ambulance service told me a couple of weeks ago. He's always spouting off about something, and so I didn't pay much attention to him then at the time. After we found that list in the safe, I remembered what I'd heard."

"What was that?"

"I didn't mention it to you because I thought it was too farfetched."

"Something else about Grandpa?" She wasn't sure she could stand to hear any more tonight.

"Not about him, no. He mentioned some rumors that had been circulating around town a few months ago. You know the doctor you replaced at the clinic?"

"Heidlage. They said he retired."

"Who said?"

"I think . . . Otis Boswell."

"Yes, and you know how well he can be trusted."

"Heidlage didn't retire? Don't tell me he died."

"Nobody knows exactly why he left, but he had apparently been concerned about the number of mining accident victims he'd been seeing at the clinic, and he complained to Boswell about it. Then he attempted to standardize emergency procedures for mining accidents. He started researching the past accidents and even went so far as to visit one of the mines. He spoke to several of the ambulance personnel, trying to get their input. Then all of a sudden he left."

"He quit? Or are you saying he was fired? Or . . . don't tell me he —"

"He gave notice and was gone in two weeks. He never said a word to anyone else, never explained why he was leaving."

"I know they've mentioned it a couple of times in the office. I didn't think much about it, either."

"Maybe it's something we need to think about. I reread some of those copies of workers' comp reports we found in the safe."

"You went up there alone? Murph, that's —"

"I took Dillon with me, and I took my weapon." He patted the bulge against his rib cage. "Just listen to me. I read all of them. None of them were serious, which means to me that those were just a little damage control."

"Damage control?"

"Anyone wishing to prevent an investigation by OSHA would keep reports to a minimum, particularly those for which the medical costs and sick leave could be paid out of company coffers. I've heard several of the men complain about the safety conditions, but they get good pay, better than most other miners in the country. For that much money, they'll keep their mouths shut."

"So you're saying someone from our clinic might have been paid to pull the reports we filed?"

"And Josiah found this out. Who knows, maybe Heidlage even told him about it, since Josiah was one of Otis's business partners. That could be when he started looking for a few details."

Sable touched the lump on her head, then sank down onto the trunk. "So now, instead of us being in danger because Grandpa broke the law, we're in danger because Grandpa was trying to uphold the law."

"Sounds likely."

"Okay. That feels better. But we're still in danger from somebody in this house, and right now I'm not willing to rule out anyone but you."

He turned from the window and stepped over to kneel beside her. "I'm sorry. Maybe I shouldn't have said anything. Why worry you further when neither of us can do anything about it right now?"

The gentle remorse in his voice, the kindness in his expression, touched her. "I would like to think it's because you respect me, and you respect my opinion." She forced a smile. "And maybe you're learning to shed some of that macho mentality."

He leaned closer, until she could feel his breath against her face. She didn't pull away.

He moved forward until their lips touched. His arms came around her shoulders, and he drew her closer.

"Sable, you in there?" It was Audry outside the door. "The men are ready to move in the mattresses. Don't forget you and Jerri and I are roomies tonight."

Chapter 24

The next morning, a bright dawn and cloudless blue sky provided welcome relief from a tense night. Once again, Murph had slept with the gun strapped to his chest. Finally, after lying awake for at least an hour, he opened his eyes to the squeak of bedsprings across the room, where Perry heaved himself from his narrow cot. There was a thump and a muttered oath when he kicked a piece of furniture with a bare foot.

Murph sat up in bed and looked down at the top of Perry's balding head from the lofty perch of the upper bunk. "Morning. Sleep okay?"

"Hardly." Perry bent over and rubbed his foot, then straightened and tucked in his shirt. "That cot sags in the middle. About halfway through the night I realized why. I had my suitcase stuffed beneath it in the sewing room, but when we moved everything in here last night, Mr. Simmons started complaining because I took up too much space. So to satisfy the sourpuss I left my cookbooks behind."

"That was quite a sacrifice." Murph climbed from his upper bunk and stooped to put on his shoes.

"Make fun if you wish," Perry said. "I've been poring over those things for days, living and breathing every recipe." Perry sighed. "I just knew I would win. And now I'll miss it all because of this blasted ice."

"I doubt it." Murph tied the shoestrings of his boots and straightened. "This storm must have hit Branson, too. They'll reschedule, don't you think? I'm going to check on the others, then stoke the fire and see about breakfast."

"Good. I'm going to go visit my books, if you don't mind. Your killer won't have any interest in me, I'm sure."

Simmons stirred in the lower bunk, poking his head out from beneath a thick quilt. The tangled kinks of his brown hair stuck out in every direction, and his eyes were muzzy from sleep — or lack of it. "We should stay in a group, right?"

Murph stifled a sigh. "I think it's a good idea for all of us to remain in the general vicinity and remain aware of our surroundings, but I don't think the three of us need to stick together like Siamese triplets; we just need to be more cautious."

"Sounds to me that if no one goes in the

cave, and no one goes outside on the ice under the trees, we'll be safe," Perry said. "I refuse to allow anyone to keep me from sitting quietly in my room."

"You'll be talking out the other side of your mouth when somebody bashes you in the head while nobody's looking," Simmons said.

"And why should they do that?" Perry asked. "Sleeping in a safe room is one thing, but I've never had the group mentality. If you want to be bosom buddies, feel free."

Grumbling, Simmons dressed, then trailed Murph and Perry from the room. Craig and Bryce had spent the night in Audry's recently evacuated room after some argument from Craig that someone needed to keep an eye on things downstairs.

The others had made it through the night without mishap with Dillon on guard in the upstairs hallway. By the time the others were dressed and downstairs, some of the tension began to ease.

Audry perked coffee and took out a big cast iron skillet to cook breakfast. Perry started pumping the many gallons of water needed for the bathrooms. It was life as usual on the Kessinger farm.

Simmons had suddenly developed the herd instinct. He avoided being alone in a room. Craig was cautious, watchful, and every hour or so he and Bryce went out to his Jeep in the garage to listen to the weather forecast.

While Jerri retrieved wood from the front porch — her activity of choice for the day — Craig tended the furnace in the basement. Bryce wandered from room to room, his brown eyes sober and watchful. Everyone, including Dillon, was accounted for, and Murph allowed himself to relax a little. For the moment, things were quiet.

He found Sable sitting alone in her mother's bedroom, which Craig had abandoned the night before to sleep upstairs.

"How about a game of checkers?" he asked.

She turned to him. "Look outside, Murph." She pointed out the window, then laid her hand on his arm. The automatic gesture encouraged him.

Late morning sunlight struck the hillside across the hollow, frosting the icy branches with rainbow dust. The effect was like a million tiny Christmas trees glittering in the distance.

"Isn't it beautiful?" Sable breathed, transfixed. "It's a wonderland. I don't think I've ever seen anything so perfect."

"It's beautiful, all right." Even more fascinating to him, however, was watching her enjoyment of it.

"Look, Murph, it's beginning to thaw." She pointed at the dripping icicles that hung from the eaves. "I checked the thermometer as soon as we came down this morning. It was thirty-two degrees, but now it's thirty-eight."

"Craig says the forecast is for increasing temperatures. How long do you think it'll take for it to thaw enough for us to get out of here?" Murph asked.

"Depends on the temperature. Down in this hollow, unless we have a real heat wave, we won't even be able to think about it until tomorrow, and even then it'll be dicey. Did you ever try to walk uphill on melting ice? We couldn't even stand up on it. I'm glad we have enough wood stocked up now, because I plan to stay inside." She reached up, as if to touch her pocket watch. She flattened her hand on her chest, sighing. "Why did they have to take my watch?"

"The only reason I can see is they knew it didn't work, and they wondered why you wore it."

"That is not a good reason to follow us

into the cave and rip it off my neck."

"Then somehow, someone knows — or at least suspects — that there is an item of vital importance inside it."

"The only item of importance is the watch itself. It came from Grandpa. It was a gift, and I want it back."

"Then we'll do what we can to see that you get it," he assured her. "But don't you think the silver and analysis might be of importance as well?"

"I don't see why. It doesn't say where that silver came from."

"It doesn't matter what's true, it matters what they suspect. If they think the silver is on this place, that would give them reason to take the map from the attic — and that clock face on the map — if you're sure that's what you saw — might have given the whole thing away to someone. If they find the silver, Boswell will know to fore-close on this place."

"He can't foreclose without giving us the opportunity to pay off the loan. Besides, all the map showed was the sinkhole, and Craig has found that," she said.

After another foray into the garage just before lunch, Craig walked through the open door of the bedroom, where Murph and Sable continued to sort through her mother's records and correspondence.

"Find anything?" He slouched into the cushioned chair beside the door.

"Sympathy cards," Sable said. "Grandpa had a lot of friends."

"Maybe we've been looking in the wrong place," Craig said. "I opened the garage door and used the light to look for some tire chains. That garage is packed with forty years' worth of old stuff."

"Did you find the chains?" Murph asked.

"One tire's worth. I'll keep looking. If we don't find anything else in the garage, we can check the attic. I want out of this place."

"But even chains won't work on the ice as thick as it is right now," Sable said.

"If it keeps melting, we might even get out of here tonight," Craig said. "It can't be too soon for me."

"What if someone doesn't want us to leave?" Murph asked quietly.

In the following silence, Perry called everyone to lunch.

Despite news of eventual freedom, lunch was uncomfortable, with short tempers and hurt feelings. Simmons snapped at Bryce for not doing his share of carrying water and wood.

"Water is my job," Perry said. "Bryce shouldn't have to do any of it."

"Well, if Perry can come and go upstairs any time he wants," Jerri said, "we should all be able to. He just uses the water excuse so he can go play with his toys. Audry, didn't you say you went back up to the attic this morning to look for some shoes?"

"I thought we were supposed to be sticking together," Simmons said. "I guess everybody's forgotten that one of us is a kill—"

"Do you mind?" Perry said. "We're trying to eat."

"Well, excuse me, but some of us are trying to stay alive," Simmons snapped back.

After lunch, Bryce retreated to the dining room to read by the light of the window. Perry complained that they were running low on wood for the kitchen stove because Audry kept the fire too hot. Murph and Sable held a checkers tournament in the family room, and Jerri and Craig got into a heated discussion about the benefits of modern medicine. Every few minutes, someone checked the condition of the ice outside and reported their findings to anyone who would listen.

By dinnertime, Murph was more exhausted than he had been in years. Sable had shown no aftereffects of her bump on the head, and the knot had gone down. She spent a great deal of her afternoon reading a Terri Blackstock hardback novel in the family room by the window — he'd checked on her several times.

Dinner was almost ready when Murph strolled over to sit down beside her. "Good book?"

She looked up at him, and he saw the quizzical expression on her face. She held the book open to him.

It wasn't a Terri Blackstock novel, unless Terri had decided to handwrite this one. With Josiah's handwriting.

He stifled a grin. She had placed the book jacket cover over the "Boswell Enterprise" journal.

"Learn anything?" he asked softly. They were alone in the room. Peace. Quiet. It wouldn't last long.

"Where are the others?"

"Kitchen, dining room, living room. Things are loosening up a little. I think Jerri made a foray into the attic in spite of Simmons. They're all getting sick of one another."

"That's because we all suspect one another." She closed the book and held it up.

"We guessed right. He kept notes about everything he did — wrote down the dates, included names. After the incident here when Jim attacked me, Grandpa went on a crusade."

"You mean he had his own vendetta against Boswell?"

Her eyes suddenly filled with tears. "His last entry was the weekend he came home for the last time. He was —" Someone passed the open doorway, and she paused before continuing. "He said he was going to send a package with copies of the evidence to Noah, then he was going to give Boswell another chance to clean up his act."

"That was his mistake."

"He was going to tell Boswell about his own conversion experience. He was —"

"Dinner will be ready in about ten minutes!" Perry called. "Get washed up. And if I hear one word about burned pork chops I'll send you flying across the room. And has anyone seen Jerri in the past few minutes? She was going to bring us more wood for the cookstove, and she hasn't done it yet."

Audry and Bryce ambled into the family room, followed by Simmons. "I think she went back down to stoke the fire in the basement," Audry said.

Perry stood at the open doorway with his arms crossed over his chest. "Well, do I have to be the one to go find her? I've got dinner to complete."

"Listen to the prima donna," Audry muttered, sitting down across from Bryce at the card table.

"I'll go find her," Murph said.

"You need me to go with you?" Bryce asked. "Audry doesn't know how to spell, anyway."

Audry leaned over the Scrabble board and fixed Bryce with a glower. "What do you mean I don't know how to spell?"

Murph left them to their argument. "You stay, Bryce. I won't be long." He called Dillon to go with him.

Enough light still filtered through the windows that Murph was able to climb upstairs without a flashlight. He didn't want to alarm the others, but he would feel better as soon as he found Jerri. She'd been yawning and complaining earlier about lack of sleep, and she might have come upstairs for a nap.

He stepped to Sable's door, knocked, then opened it. Empty. Methodically, he checked the other rooms. Dillon followed him into every room.

When Murph returned to the hallway

after checking the final room, he noticed the attic door standing ajar. Dillon's ears perked forward, and he whined. He walked up to Murph and nosed his hand, then whined again.

"What is it?"

The dog led the way up the attic steps, scratched at the door, and shoved it open with his nose.

Moments later, Murph found Jerri.

Chapter 25

"Gotcha!"

Loud laughter echoed through the room. Sable's eyes flew open, and she stiffened in the recliner where she'd been dozing. She looked over to find Bryce shaking his hands over his head in a victorious wave. "Two out of three, Audry. You'd better start brushing up on your vocabulary."

Audry pushed her chair back from the table. "I think you need to get Perry in here, you cocky little —"

Murph rushed in through the family room door. "Where's Craig?" His voice was loud enough to carry through the first floor of the house.

"I saw him outside through the window moments ago," Sable said. "I think he's knocking ice from the bridge. I know he wanted to do that last night. Murph, what's wrong? What happened?"

He paused for breath. "I found Jerri."

"What do you mean you found her?" Audry asked softly.

"She's upstairs in the attic." His eyes

444

sought Sable's. "She's dead."

Shocked silence blasted through the room, and then everyone spoke at once.

"Dead! When did she . . . What happened to . . . Who killed her? And how did . . ."

Perry came running in from the kitchen, wiping his wet hands on a dish towel. "What's going on? Did I hear you say something is wrong with Jerri?"

"Everybody be quiet for a minute," Murph said. "We need to find Craig and tell him to put whatever chains he's found onto the Jeep. We have no choice; we've got to get out of here. Now."

"And get ourselves killed in the process?" Perry exclaimed. "From what I've heard, that road isn't any less dangerous now than it was an hour ago, when we couldn't —"

"What killed her?" Sable asked Murph. "I need to go see —"

Murph stopped her at the threshold. "Not yet, Sable. It isn't safe. There's a bullet hole in her head."

"A bullet!" Audry cried. "Oh, no." She raised her hand to her face. Her eyes closed, and she swayed unsteadily. "This can't be happening."

Sable grabbed Audry by the arm and eased her down into the nearest chair.

"Someone shot her?" Bryce asked. "But we didn't hear any —"

"You looking for me?" Craig stepped into the room, unzipping green coveralls, his face red from exertion. "What's going on in here? Why are you all —"

"Murph found Jerri dead in the attic," Audry said. "She's been shot in the head." She covered her face with her hands. "Oh, poor Jerri. I can't believe this is happening." Her shoulders shook.

"Are you sure she's dead?" Bryce asked Murph.

"I'm sure," Murph said.

Simmons stood up from his chair. "How do we know we can trust what he says?"

"How long has she been dead?" Bryce asked. "When did it —"

"We're all gonna die right here in this house," Audry moaned.

"Stop it," Murph said. "We've got to slow down and think rationally. Craig, did you find the chains you were looking for?"

"I found them."

"We need to get them on those tires, and we need to clear the bridge of ice. You said it was badly slanted?"

"I wouldn't want to drive over it with that ice."

"You're not serious about leaving to-night, are you?" Perry exclaimed.

"Why Jerri?" Audry murmured. "Why would anybody kill Jerri? She was an innocent . . . They'll kill all of us before it's over."

"Not if we can help it," Murph said. "We're going to get out of here."

To Murph, it felt like a desecration to leave Jerri's body lying alone in the cold attic, but they had no choice. If they could get out of this place and call for help, the scene of the crime had to remain intact.

He only prayed no one else would die before they could escape.

Murph wasn't a policeman; he didn't know the correct procedure of what to do next — but then, he doubted many people in this same situation would have plans in place.

"Craig, you're the best on ice, I think," he said. "We need you to take the pickax out and start on that bridge."

"I've been working on that some already," Craig said.

"Good. At least one of us will come out with some coals from the furnace."

"How do you know you can trust

Craig?" Simmons demanded. "We let him out of our sight, he could —"

"You and I will go with him," Murph said.

"Fine, then we'll take the coals with us as we go."

"What about me?" Bryce asked. "I can help, too."

"You can stay here with the others." Simmons grabbed his jacket from a hook behind the family room door. "Come on, let's get to it. I want out of this dungeon before somebody gets us all."

"Right," Craig said. "The axes are on the front porch. Find another flashlight and watch your footing. It'll be treacherous out there tonight."

Craig opened the back door and stepped onto the patio. Simmons filled a bucket with ashes from the fireplace and followed him.

Murph leaned close to Sable, brushed her hair back, and whispered in her ear. "Get the .22 from upstairs. And take care of yourself, Sable. Remember what you said to me down in the cave yesterday?"

"I said lots of things."

"You said you didn't think you could stand it if anything happened to me." He lowered his lips to hers in a brief, gentle kiss. "Be careful. Don't let anything happen to you, because I honestly can't see myself without you. The moon is bright. Keep watch out the family room window, and if you see anything go wrong, get the others out of this house." He opened the door and stepped out into the cold stillness.

As soon as he disappeared into the night, Sable raced up the stairs. While she was loading the pistol, she couldn't help wondering again about the question Murph had asked her earlier: Would she be able to bring herself to shoot someone — actually shoot someone? Could she take a human life? And if she couldn't, would someone she loved die because of it?

The moon glared harshly from a star-studded sky, and the brightness was helpful. A cold wind blew an occasional feathery cloud across the moon, barely dimming the light. Murph turned once to gaze back at the silent house, visible through the leafless branches. For a moment he didn't see Sable watching from the door, but then the curtain lifted at the long window of the family room, and he saw her shadow. Reluctantly, he started on beside Simmons.

Even before he reached the bridge, he could hear a familiar *thunk, thunk* of an ax, and the tinkle of ice spraying against itself. Moonlight outlined Craig's shape as he labored at the far end of the slanted concrete.

"Could you use some help?" Murph called.

"Grab the pickax," Craig said without breaking stride. "It's chipping away pretty well. Got those ashes, Simmons?"

"Right here," Simmons said. Instead of carrying the bucket across the bridge, he set it down beside him, then stepped around Murph.

"There's a gravel pile at the end of the house, where Josiah was going to put in a driveway but never got around to it," Craig said. "We can use that if we need to for any rough spots."

"There aren't going to be any rough spots for you two."

Murph frowned and turned and found himself staring down a gun barrel of gleaming metal.

Craig's ax grew still.

"You shot her," Murph said.

Simmons smiled. "Is that really what you think?" His teeth looked wicked in the moonlight.

Murph didn't move, didn't reply.

"You two are working together, aren't you?" Simmons said. "You and Craig. I should've picked up on that yesterday when you went traipsing off into the cave together. You're covering each other."

Murph continued watching the barrel of the gun, as if it were a snake ready to strike. "What are you talking about?"

"I know what you're up to. You think you're going to have me all trussed up for the police. Who better to blame? The kid? Oh, yeah, he's scary. Or maybe it's the old lady, or the fat clown who can't even step out on the front porch without busting his face."

"Don't underestimate people," Murph said. "Where did you get the gun?"

"What I carry for safety isn't really your business, is it?"

"You carry a gun to your mother's deathbed?"

There was a whisper of sound behind Murph, and Simmons redirected his aim. His shadowed face revealed little in the dim light of the moon. Unfortunately, his back was to the house, and even if Sable could see them, she couldn't tell what was happening.

"Don't come any closer, Holt," Simmons

said, "or your buddy's going to join Jerri in the grave."

"What are you doing with that thing?" Craig exclaimed.

Simmons swung toward him. As if synchronized, Murph reached for his own weapon beneath his shirt, but Simmons caught the movement. He jerked his barrel up and came down hard against the side of Murph's head.

He struck again, and Murph sank to his knees as the night around him grew darker. He heard gunfire.

Then the blackness was complete.

Chapter 26

Sable pivoted from the family room window and raced toward the back door in the hallway. "Someone has a gun out there," she called to the others, "and some-one's been shot!"

"What?" Audry exclaimed.

"What happened?" Perry cried. "Who got shot?"

The three of them joined Sable at the back door. When she reached for the knob, Audry grabbed her by the arm. "Sable Chamberlin, are you crazy? You can't go out there!"

"Murph's out there." She pulled the .22 pistol from the pocket of her jacket.

There was a collective gasp.

"What are you doing with that thing?" Perry demanded. "What's going on here?"

"Murph needs help."

"No!" Audry's grip tightened on Sable's arm. "If you go running out there with a gun, the shooter could panic." She turned to Perry and Bryce. "We've got to get out of here now. Sable, where can we go? What can we do to escape that madman?"

"The cave," Sable said, fighting her own terror. Had they shot Murph? He could be lying out there dying right now. She couldn't just run away, not like this. She couldn't just abandon him.

But she had to get the others to safety.

"Perry, what about Craig's Jeep?" Audry asked. "Is it ready to go?"

"Not unless the bridge is clear." He laid a hand on Sable's arm. "Who did the shooting? Are you sure Murph wasn't —"

"Murph fell. I only heard one shot, but there's only one man standing out there now. It isn't light enough to —"

"Okay, so the cave," Perry said. "You're right, Sable, we've got to get to the cave. There's a rope on the basement landing and some flashlights."

"We'd better get a move-on." Audry nudged Sable back down the hall. "They could come back in here any second."

"No, wait, I can't go down yet," Sable said.

"Are you nuts?" Perry exclaimed. "Of course you're coming with us. Do you think the person who killed Jerri would hesitate at shooting you? Come on, Sable."

"No, go on down. Bryce, you can show them the way. Wait for me in the cave."

"What are you going to do?" Perry asked.

"Take some precautions. Perry, take one of those garden spades with you. We may get desperate enough to try to tunnel out of the sinkhole if it isn't big enough."

"The sinkhole?" Bryce asked. "You mean the place where Craig left me?"

"That's the place," Sable said. "We'll go there later. If I don't catch up with you guys pretty soon, Bryce, take Perry and Audry back to the breakdown cavern. You can all hide in the rocks. It's a big room, and —"

"I don't like this one bit," Audry said. "You need to come with us."

"I'll find you later." Sable disengaged herself from Audry's grasp and nudged them toward the basement door. "Now go. Hurry."

"You just be sure you come down and find us, honey," Audry said.

"We'll be okay, Audry," Bryce assured the older woman. "Are you still afraid of caves?"

"Not tonight. Tonight that cave down there is my friend."

As the others descended the basement steps, Sable ran up to the sewing room on the second floor. She checked the window, found it unlocked, and shoved it open. If they needed to get back into the house after they escaped the cave, this might work.

Murph couldn't be dead. He couldn't!

She left the sewing room and ran to the window at the end of the hallway. She looked down where she had seen him fall. Another figure was bent over him, but she couldn't tell from up here who it was. Both Simmons and Craig had been wearing dark coats. And yet, didn't she know her childhood friend better than this? Craig could never shoot someone . . . could he?

As she watched, Murph moved, bringing an arm up to his face.

Yes! One other figure straightened, and one remained prone, still. Dead? She wouldn't leave Murph alone. He was alive, and she would do everything possible to see that he stayed that way.

The left side of Murph's jaw screamed with pain, shooting tentacles of fire across his face and skull. Amazingly, the pain encouraged him. He wasn't dead, after all.

He tested the movement in his extremities and found nothing wrong, though the back of his neck and skull shrieked with agony when he tried to sit up.

Someone kicked his left shoulder, shoving him onto his back.

"Trying to make a run for it, Murphy?" Simmons mocked, leering down at him. "Want an extra hole in the head?"

Murph glared at the man's blurred, upside-down image. "You surprise me," he drawled. "I thought Boswell had more class than this. Are you going to hunt every single person down and kill us one by one?"

Simmons squatted beside him, the barrel of his gun barely two feet from Murph's face. "I won't have to."

Murph couldn't figure what kind of game the man was playing.

"Get up." Simmons shoved him again. "I'm not dragging you all the way to the house."

Murph glanced around. Simmons had apparently already dragged him several yards over the ice before giving up. Craig's prone body lay in a shadowed corner of the bridge.

The gunshot.

It took no more urging from Simmons to pull Murph to his feet.

"That's better. Just walk on ahead. We're going inside where we can talk."

Murph looked down at the gun in

Simmons's hand, and he prayed that Sable and the others had escaped to safety, preferably down into the hidden recesses of the cave.

Lord, please don't let Sable try to play hero tonight. Keep her quiet, and confuse this man more than he's already confused. And please give me wisdom. Fast!

He paused and turned to look toward Craig's fallen body at the bridge. "Aren't you even going to check and see if he's still alive?"

"I got him dead-on in the chest, and I'll do you the same favor if you don't move."

Oh, God, no! Not Craig. For a brief moment, Murph couldn't move. He'd stared death in the face many times in his career, but he'd never grown accustomed to it, and he always spared some time to grieve. These deaths, though — they were happening too fast. This nightmare just continued to spiral further out of control.

But as his grief caught him, Murph thought he saw Craig's arm move.

Simmons shoved him roughly. "I said get to the house!"

Murph turned away, managed a step on the ice, then another. "He's an innocent, you know." He felt the catch in his voice. *Lord, please let him still be alive. Help me to get back to him.* "Just a big kid. I wonder what flashed through his mind when the bullet struck him."

"I wouldn't know. Get a move-on." Simmons shoved Murph with his free hand.

Murph continued at his own regulated pace, praying for Craig, praying for Sable's safety, and praying that the house would be empty when they reached the back door. "What about you? What went through your mind when you thought you were going to drown in the creek?"

"What's that to you?"

"I just wondered how it feels, terrorizing the very ones who saved your life so recently."

No answer.

"Has it ever bothered you? I mean, wondering what would have happened to you if Audry hadn't dragged you from the creek? If Sable and I hadn't performed CPR on —"

"Does it bother you to think that if you don't shut up, you could be as dead as Craig in about half a second?"

Murph fell silent. When they reached the back door that opened to the hallway between the kitchen and the family room, he couldn't bring himself to reach for the handle. He turned and faced Simmons, and once more found himself staring at the barrel of a gun — except this time he recognized the shape of his own Detonics in the glow of moonlight. It was one of the smallest of the six-shot semiautomatic pistols manufactured, and it looked like a toy in Simmons's beefy hand.

"One move in the wrong direction," Simmons said quietly, "and you're dead."

"And if we go inside, someone else will die, won't they? I can't, in good conscience, do that. You'll just have to shoot me here."

Simmons kicked the door open with his right foot. The door slammed against the inside wall with a crash of glass. The sound triggered frantic barking from the depths of the house.

"Get inside!" Simmons shoved Murph forward.

Dillon came charging down the hallway.

"No, Dillon, stay," Murph told the German shepherd.

The dog stopped in front of the open kitchen door, his hackles stiff, fangs bared in a snarl.

Murph stepped into the house, moving as slowly as he felt he could without provoking Simmons. He peered down the hallway. At first glance, the place seemed deserted, and he felt a wash of relief. Maybe everyone was safely out of the way — and would stay there.

Simmons nudged him in the ribs with the barrel of his gun. "We need to have a little chat."

"We don't have anything to talk about."

Dillon continued to growl from the kitchen doorway.

"I think we've got a lot." Simmons prodded Murph with the gun again. "You know a few things you aren't talking about, not even to your doctor girlfriend. You're in this thing a lot deeper than she is."

"I don't know where you get your information, but —"

"Well, would you look at that." Simmons gestured toward the basement door, which stood conspicuously ajar. Too conspicuously, in Murph's opinion. "Looks like your friends took off on you. Guess you can't trust them any more than they can trust you."

From the hallway, Murph scanned the deserted family room as Dillon's deep growl continued to rumble from the kitchen.

"Dillon, quiet," Murph said, glancing at the dog.

Something about Dillon's protective stance alerted him. He saw a shadow slide along the floor from behind the breakfast bar.

Sable. *No.*

"You're not making much sense," Murph said quickly, moving to distract Simmons. "I'm a paramedic from Kansas, that's all."

"You trying to tell me a typical ambulance driver is going to carry a fancy little gun like this without a target?"

"Depends on whose ambulance I'm driving, and where."

"Your doctor friend may buy that, but I don't. Boswell likes to promise full payment after a job, then play two people off each other." There was a brooding pause. "Even me, it looks like," he muttered. "That way if there's an accident he doesn't have to pay."

The man's paranoia ran more deeply than Murph had first thought.

Simmons paused at the kitchen door, frowned down at the dog, and peered more deeply into the gloom of the kitchen as he continued to hold his gun on Murph.

There was a barely detectable whisper of sound behind the breakfast bar.

"Well, now, it seems they didn't all leave," Simmons said, raising his voice.

"Better come out of there before Mr. Murphy gets it in the —"

Murph ducked and jabbed toward Simmons with his right foot, catching him in the stomach. Simmons grunted as he squeezed off a shot where Murph's head would have been.

Sable rushed into view, holding the .22 pistol in her hands. Murph saw the terror that lurked behind those blue eyes as she fired a shot past Simmons's right ear.

The explosion shrieked through the house, and Simmons jumped backward in reaction. Murph pivoted and caught Simmons with his elbow. The force of the blow knocked the husky man against the wall. Murph tried to grab the gun from his hand, but Simmons kicked Murph in the gut, then fired toward Sable.

She screamed and stumbled backward as the bullet ripped a hole in the wall above her head.

Simmons shoved the barrel of the gun into Murph's face. "Try it again!" he shouted. "It'd be a shame to blow your brains all over this pretty kitchen and lose those nice bits of information."

Dillon snarled behind them.

"Call him off, Doc, or I'll kill your boyfriend and your dog."

"Dillon, stay." Sable's voice quivered with fear.

"Drop the pistol!" Simmons warned.

She hesitated, then laid the pistol on the kitchen counter.

He grabbed it and added it to his growing collection. "You try anything like that again and you'll be on ice like your buddy outside."

Sable gasped. "C–Craig?"

"Get over here with Murphy. Now!"

Bryce ran a few steps ahead of Perry and Audry as he led the way to the breakdown cavern. The sounds of their breathless panting seemed to echo from the walls around them, and he resisted the urge to beg them to breathe more quietly.

Shadows skittered around them, lurking just past each column, each stalagmite. The sound of dripping water whispered threats their way.

"One of us will have to go for help," Audry said. "The state park headquarters isn't too far away. I could —"

"No, you couldn't," Perry said. "I may not be the most athletic of men, but I'll die before I'll let an elderly woman risk her life to rescue me."

"Who're you calling elderly?"

"If anyone goes," Bryce said, stepping over a dry boulder, "it should be me."

"Bryce, can you find the place where you saw the fog?" Audry asked.

"Yes, it's not far from here. Do you want to go?"

"Not yet. I think we need to do a little spy work before we decide what to do next."

"Spy work!" Perry exclaimed. "You're crazy. What kind of spy work? What if we get caught?"

"Look here, Buster," Audry snapped, "Sable's not down here yet, and I intend to find out what's going on. If we can just find out what's happening, instead of sitting down here like a trio of helpless —"

"Okay." Perry raised a silencing hand. "If you do find out anything, and it turns out we have to go for help, I'll go."

"Right, that's all we need," Audry muttered. "Humpty Dumpty to the rescue."

Perry glared at her.

"Cut it out, you guys," Bryce said. "I'm going back to the basement and see if I can hear anything."

"I'm coming with you," Audry said.

"No," Perry said. "Bryce will make less noise by himself. Let's just stay quiet and find a place to hide."

★ ★ ★

Simmons herded Murph and Sable into the living room, looming ever closer to Sable in an obvious effort to intimidate her. Murph controlled the increased intensity of his anger with difficulty.

Dillon's threatening growls followed them, rising in volume any time Simmons made a quick move, then settling to a watchful rumble.

"If you can't make that dog shut up," Simmons grated, "I think I'll have me some nine-millimeter target practice. Won't that make a mess on this nice new carpet?"

"Dillon, quiet," Sable said.

The dog's growl ceased.

"Both of you sit on the hearth," Simmons said. "No, stay away from the utensils. There you go."

Murph prayed that the others had escaped, that they weren't also lurking somewhere in the house with misguided intentions of a rescue. What could Sable have been thinking?

Simmons settled across from them on the sofa, eyes narrowed, filled with dark anticipation. "Like I said, we've got some bargaining to do, kind of form us a little cooperative, exchange some insider info."

Murph swallowed. Hard. The only

reason he was alive was because Simmons thought he knew something. "Okay," he said slowly, "why don't you go first."

"Because I'm the one with the gun." Simmons raised the barrel to emphasize his point. "How much are you getting paid?"

"Fifty." Simmons didn't have to know that number simply reflected the most Murph had ever made in one year as a paramedic — working lots of overtime.

"Up front or after the job?"

"After." Murph felt Sable's sudden, focused interest. He tried to catch her gaze, but she avoided eye contact.

"You're *both* working for Boswell?" Sable exclaimed. She didn't sound as shaky now. She sounded angry. "So which one of you did kill my grandfather?"

Simmons's gaze slid over her in the firelight, then went to Murph. "You're not getting credit for that one. That money's mine."

There was a rush of air from Sable's throat. "And . . . Noah?"

Simmons smiled.

For a moment the pain and fury overwhelmed Murph with an intensity so great he didn't know if he could remain seated. He wanted to lunge across the space that separated him from this killer, catch him by his thick neck, and choke him. He wanted to knock the gun from his hand and then use it on him.

His fists clenched, and he concentrated on control. If he moved now, Sable could die. At the moment, he would be willing to risk his own life, but not hers.

God! he cried out in silent anguish, *don't let this killer get by with what he's done.*

"I think Sable has something I need," Simmons said slowly. "I think she'll give it to me."

"What makes you think that?" she snapped.

"Because you're one of those bleeding hearts who won't be able to watch your friends die, one by one, if you don't feel like cooperating." He flicked his gun toward Murph. "He could be next."

"Do you think you'll actually get away with killing six people?" Sable demanded. "Boswell won't lift a finger to help you. He'll feed you to the wolves."

Simmons shrugged. "In that case, six is no worse than one, is it?"

When Murph's heart rate slowed and his breathing grew even once more, he risked stating the obvious. "You killed Noah."

"The old man forced me." Simmons

gestured toward Sable. "She was already on her way to his house. He'd already blabbed to her. I couldn't put it off."

"You were the one in Noah's house that night," Sable said. "You killed him, then tried to kill me."

Simmons nodded. "Looks like I might get to finish the job."

Chapter 27

Bryce's feet slipped on the rocks. He grabbed at a limestone column to steady himself, peering through the gloom. Why hadn't he paid more attention when he came down here with Sable and the others? With all these formations, a guy could get turned around. He aimed his flashlight over stalactites and helictites, past boulders that seemed to merge into one big, confusing statuary.

The beam flicked over a soda straw formation. Yes! Sable had pointed that out. He walked beneath it, using it as a compass to point him toward the final passage that led to the entrance.

He reached the cave mouth and dropped to his knees to crawl into the basement. Instead of climbing the steps and taking a chance on making noise, he walked beneath the steps, directly below the door, where he could hear the voices much more clearly.

Sable remained tense, prepared to knock the gun from Simmons's hand the minute he looked away. But he never looked away. He was always alert, his pale blue eyes darting from Murph's face to hers and back again.

"Lay face down on the floor, Murph," he said. "You should know the game plan. Put your wrists together behind your back." He inched the barrel of the gun more directly in line with Murph's face.

Murph hesitated.

"Do it now," Simmons snapped, "or I'll put a bullet in your head. Hands behind your back. That's right. Now, Sable, would you do the honors? Take this cord and wrap it around Murph's wrists." He shoved the phone cord at her. "Do it!"

Slowly, she did as he said. They were going to die. Simmons couldn't allow them to leave this place, because then they could talk, which meant they could call the police.

"Tighter!" Simmons snapped. "And quit stalling, or you'll be doing it one-handed."

She pulled the cord tighter, though taking care not to cut off Murph's circulation. He gave further instructions, and she did as she was told.

Simmons gave a tight-lipped grin. "Finished. Now it's your turn. Pull that drapery cord down from the front window."

Again, she did as she was told. She could do nothing as he began to pat her down, but he had only reached her waist when Dillon stood up and stiff-legged it to sniff at the basement door.

"What's the matter, fella, have we got a snoop?" Simmons made Sable sit down, then tied a quick knot on the cord at her feet and wrapped the remainder of the cord around the set of fireplace tools. When he jerked the cord, the brass poker and shovel clanged against each other.

"Got me a built-in alarm here, don't I? Don't go away, folks, I'll be right back."

"We've got to get out of here fast." Murph jerked hard on the phone cord, and succeeded only in choking himself, tied up as he was like a trussed turkey. With his face against the carpeting, he couldn't see Sable; he could only hear her struggling.

"Can you reach the knot I tied?" she asked. "I tried to tie it close to your hands. That cord is slick; maybe it'll give."

Murph felt along the cord with his fingers, stretching the vinyl coated wire until it once more cut into his neck. He felt the plug end of the cord with the tips of his fingers and stretched until he could feel the knot. Stars shot around the edges of his vision. He stretched the cord until darkness overcame him and his fingers lost their grip.

"Murph! You've got to hurry!" Sable's sharp voice pushed the darkness back. "Try again."

As he reached once more for the knot, he heard Sable grunt, then a deafening clatter of metal. He turned his head, choking himself again as he caught a glimpse of Sable. She had fallen beside him and had dragged the fireplace set from the hearth.

"Turn over," she said. "Maybe I can reach —"

"You can't untie this stuff, not with your hands —"

"Mom always keeps a letter opener with a serrated blade behind the tool stand on the hearth so she can cut the twine around kindling when she purchases it. She doesn't do that too often, because someone usually cuts the wood for her." Sable grunted as she shuffled over the carpet toward the end of the hearth, rattling the poker, brush, and shovel behind her.

Choking himself again, Murph raised his head, and he saw the gleam of the letter opener in the flicker of firelight. "It's there. Is it sharp enough?"

"It cuts string; it should cut this stuff." She scooted backward. "You've got to direct me. I'll cut your cords first."

As he watched and instructed, she used the poker to drag the letter opener — with serrated blade — from the hearth, then scooted backward again to grasp it awkwardly in her bound hands. The equipment clattered with every movement.

"Turn over," she said.

Ignoring the pain in his arm and shoulder, he did as she asked. "Be careful as you cut, or Simmons will be able to follow a trail of blood even if we do get away."

"Trust me."

Murph braced himself for a sharp jab that never came. Instead, he felt the cord jerk and loosen. He pulled his arms free, unwrapped the cord from around his neck, and turned to find Sable cutting her own bonds.

She pulled the cords away and rubbed her arms. "Where's Craig?"

He untied her feet and helped her stand. "He's at the bridge."

"Simmons shot him?"

"Yes, but I think I saw him move."

"I'm going to get my medical bag and go check on him."

"Go ahead and get your bag, but we need to get to the cave."

"But if Craig's alive —"

"I'm the paramedic, I'm the one who needs to see to him, and I don't want you exposed out there. Right now, we need to do all we can to keep Simmons from making any more victims. We need to get to the cave."

"You mean you want me in the cave so you can protect me. You're still trying to do it all yourself."

"Sable, stop it. This isn't to protect you. I need you down in that cave. I don't know it, and neither do the others. Without you, we could all be lost down there. I should be the one to check on Craig." Murph picked up the poker and tested its weight in his hands, then shoved it through a belt loop on his jeans.

"That isn't much protection against an armed man," Sable said.

"He took our pistols."

"What about the shotgun upstairs? It was in working order when we found it."

"Done. Come with me. You too, Dillon. We need you out of the way for awhile."

They raced upstairs and grabbed the shotgun, pocketed supplies from Sable's medical bag, and locked Dillon in Sable's bedroom.

"It's for your own good," Sable told the dog.

His frantic barking followed them down the stairs.

When they reached the basement, Sable pulled her flashlight out of her pocket, but didn't turn it on. She touched Murph's arm. "We'll have to find our way in the dark. Hold onto me; I know the way by feel."

"What about the pit?"

"Don't worry, I'll stay well away from that."

As soon as they stepped into the overwhelming blackness of the cave, Murph felt Sable stop.

"Hear something?" she whispered.

He paused. Was that voices they heard, or dripping water? It was so hard to tell.

"No, go on."

They continued deeper into the darkness, feeling their way along the rough, wet cave wall. They had just reached the point where Murph believed the pit to be, when they heard a noise ahead of them — a low, angry voice. Simmons.

Sable gasped softly.

Was he talking to himself, or had he . . . ?

"What are you going to do to me?" came Bryce's clear, young voice.

"Add you to my collection," Simmons

said. "Don't worry, you've got good company upstairs."

Sable squeezed Murph's arm tightly. She urged him behind what felt like an outcropping of rock. Just as he stepped behind it he saw a flash of light. Simmons was coming this way with Bryce.

Murph tightened his hold on the shotgun.

He could hear Sable's breath coming fast and shallow, then heard her swallow in an effort to quiet her breathing.

Murph waited until Bryce came into sight, walking directly in front of Simmons.

Sable squeezed Murph's arm again. Simmons held the barrel of his pistol flush against Bryce's right temple. One sudden move could kill the boy. One rock thrown. One whisper of sound.

They could do nothing but watch.

Sable held her breath, and Murph knew she was thinking the same thing he was. What would Simmons do when he reached the house and found them gone?

Darkness descended again, the footsteps of captive and captor diminished, but for a few seconds longer neither Sable nor Murph moved.

"We've got to follow them," Murph said. "Let's go."

Chapter 28

Murph followed Sable through the darkness, which was barely lit by her flashlight. "Don't catch up with them," he whispered.

"We've got to try to get Bryce away from that monster," she said.

There was a soft *thunk,* like the closing of a door ahead.

"Hurry," she said, sprinting forward. "There's no telling what he'll do when he finds us gone." She reached the door to the basement and crouched down.

Murph caught up with her as an explosion of shouting echoed down to them from the house.

An echo of gunshot froze him in position. Bryce cried out.

Sable grabbed Murph's arm. "Bryce —"

"You're crazy!" Bryce cried, his voice reaching them clearly from the living room. "What did you do to Sable? Did you shoot her?"

Sable released Murph's arm and sagged against the basement wall. "He sounds okay."

Murph hustled her back out of the basement into the darkness. "He's not trying to kill right now," he said when they were out of earshot. "He's trying to terrorize."

"He's doing an excellent job of it."

"We've got to try to get Bryce out of there."

"How are we going to do that?" Sable asked. "Barge through the door and say 'boo'? The man's crazy! He's a lunatic. Any sudden moves and he could kill again. Easily."

"So that means we certainly can't go back through the basement," Murph said. "We need another way out of here."

Sable led him more deeply into the cave. "It'll have to be the sinkhole. Craig thought we could get out that way. I opened the window in the sewing room earlier. It opens out onto the mountain, and one of us might be able to climb up there and get inside, if we can traverse the ice. Simmons can't watch everywhere at once, and right now he has no idea where we are. We need to find that sinkhole, Murph."

"What about the others?"

"They're down here. I know where to take them to hide," she said.

"We should move quickly, then."

"Simmons might try to use Bryce as bait to draw us out," Sable said, ducking beneath a familiar-looking ledge. "But right now, he's vulnerable. He needs us in order to get into the safe, but for all he knows, we're somewhere outside or hiding in the house. Someone could come at him from any angle at any time."

"He knows he'll lose his advantage if anything happens to Bryce," Murph said. "Meanwhile, we can work on establishing our own advantage."

"And that advantage would be?" Sable asked.

"Our Divine One." Murph was overpowered, and he knew it. But God wasn't.

They walked in silence for a few more moments, then a scatter of pebbles startled Murph to a standstill. He swung his light toward the sound.

"Audry?" Sable called. "Perry?"

"S–Sable?" Audry's voice quavered from behind a ledge at the far end of the small cavern of marbled rust formations. She stepped out from behind the ledge, a coil of rope over her shoulder. Perry followed, mud streaking his face, a rip in the right knee of his slacks.

"Oh, Sable, honey," Audry said, "we thought that man had you for sure."

"We got away," Sable said. "Now he has Bryce."

"I know," Audry said. "We heard the whole thing, but we couldn't do anything to stop him."

"Come on," Sable said. "Let's hurry deeper into the cave. I know a much better hiding place for you."

"Where are Simmons and Bryce now?" Perry asked.

"They're back at the house."

"We tried to follow them," Audry said, "but these passages are confusing, and Perry got us lost."

"I did not get us lost. We had only gone a little way before we decided we hadn't been that way. We were also afraid we might put Bryce in more danger."

"You got us lost," Audry muttered. "Sable, we can't just hide down here in the cave. We've got to go for help."

"We will," Sable assured her. "But not through the basement."

"Think we can dig out that sinkhole you mentioned?" Audry asked. "We hid that little shovel we brought — it's farther back a ways."

"We may use it," Murph said. "Let's get moving."

"But what about Bryce?" Perry asked.

"We can't leave him with that bullet-head."

"We won't," Sable said. "If it comes down to it, I'll have to give the man what he wants."

"What does he want?" Audry asked.

For a moment, only the dripping water and the sound of their footsteps broke the silence.

"We can discuss it later," Sable said, skirting a low overhang.

Perry glanced at the shotgun Murph had slung over his shoulder. "Are you sure that thing even works?"

"I'm sure," Sable said. "Grandpa kept his things in good shape."

"What happened to that pistol you had?" Perry asked.

"Simmons got it."

"So now he has all the other weapons? That shotgun will be nothing against a small arsenal of handguns."

"He can only shoot one at a time," Sable said.

Perry shrugged and shook his head, then reached behind a stalagmite and pulled out a small shovel. "I'll stay away from the guns. Just show me where to dig."

"Not right now," Sable said. "Come on, keep walking. We can't waste time."

"Sable, I've already volunteered to go for

help if we can get out of here," Perry told her. "Don't even try to talk me out of it."

"I wouldn't dream of it. Audry, give Murph the rope. He and I have some prospecting to do as soon as we get you two safely hidden, in case Simmons comes back this way."

A few minutes later, breathing heavily, Perry tugged at the collar of his jacket. "It's hot down here," he complained as he trudged through the cave behind Murph and Sable.

"That's because you're wearing that heavy jacket," Audry replied. "Why don't you take that thing off?"

"I told you, I may not need it now, but I will if we get outside, and who knows when we'll end up outside? That hard ice sure sounds good to me now, and I never thought I'd say that."

They bypassed the rocky access to the passage that led to the sinkhole, and Sable led them to the place where she used to hide from her brothers as a child.

"It's dry here, and safe as long as you're quiet." She took the shovel from Perry. "Do you only have one flashlight between the two of you?"

"Two. This is the best one," Perry said, holding his light up. "I put new batteries in it this morning. We won't use the other one unless we have to."

"Good idea. Don't come out until one of us comes back for you . . . or unless . . ."

Murph took the shovel from Sable. "This is where I'll come back to get the rest of you."

"It's where we will come back," Sable said. "You're not leaving me behind, Paul Murphy."

"You need to stay with Audry and Perry. I know the main vicinity of the sinkhole. Give me the medical supplies from your pockets, and I'll see to Craig on my way back to the house."

"In your dreams."

"There's no use in both of us risking our lives out there."

"Cut the tough talk," Sable snapped. "I'm coming with you. Or rather, you're coming with me."

"Remember how we got here," Sable told Audry and Perry. "You may need to find your way later."

"Meaning what?" Audry demanded.

"If Murph and I don't make it, you need to get to the police. Tell them what happened here, and tell them to check out our former employer, Otis Boswell, of Boswell Mining. That's who Simmons works for."

Sable adjusted the rope looped over Murph's shoulder. "He knows some of the story, and the rest is in the safe up in the attic."

"Safe?" Perry stopped in his tracks. "What safe?"

"Sable's brothers will know about it," Murph said.

Audry squeezed Sable's arm. She gestured toward the weapons Sable and Murph carried. "You two be careful out there."

"We will."

Murph followed Sable silently for several minutes as she led the way back through the cave.

"I forgot to thank you earlier," he said at last, keeping his voice low.

"For what?"

"For believing in me."

"You're talking about that little word game you were playing with Simmons? Don't forget, I know how much money you make, and it sure isn't anything close to fifty."

"He didn't ask what Boswell paid me; he only asked what I got paid."

"Fifty?"

"Gross earnings one year when I worked a lot of overtime, including the pay I received for hazardous working conditions. I consider this pretty hazardous."

Sable paused, shone her light ahead, waited a minute, then went on. "That man's crazy."

"He's paranoid."

"Sure he is. If I'd killed innocent people the way he has, I'd be a patient in a state mental institution," she said.

"Don't forget how frightened he was after that incident in the creek."

"Most people would be."

"He was scared tonight, too, when we found Jerri."

"Yeah, scared he'd be caught." She turned, searched the way ahead of them once more with the light, and ducked beneath a low ledge.

"Here's the streambed," Murph said. "We have to crawl for about ten feet."

They dropped to their knees and followed the streambed around an outcropping of rock, into the fog.

"I wish we'd been able to bring a ladder along with this shovel and rope," Sable said.

"We'll find a way out," Murph said. "It'll be okay."

The darkness in the attic was barely broken by moonlight as the diminishing

486

sound of footsteps echoed from down below. Wondering was the worst thing, and Bryce didn't know how much longer he could stand it. Where were Sable and the others? Were they safe? They didn't know that muscle-bound jerk had hidden Bryce in a corner and was back in the cave.

Bryce struggled against the cord that bound his ankles and held his hands behind his back, but the cord stretched around his neck, cutting off his air. His arms hurt like mad from the unnatural position behind his back, but he couldn't lower them without choking. He searched frantically around the room for some way to cut himself loose, but he was stuck. He couldn't get away to warn the others. He felt so helpless, especially with nothing but Jerri's body for company.

Dillon scratched at the door in the hallway downstairs on the second floor, then howled mournfully. He'd gone crazy with barking when Simmons shot the ceiling.

Dillon howled again and scratched harder at the door.

Sable darted an uneasy glance over her shoulder. "Murph, how likely do you think it would be for Simmons to come looking for us?"

"Very. That's why I told you to stay put with the others. You can go back now if you want."

"Not on your life." But she hated to think what might happen if Simmons found Audry and Perry or managed to sneak up on her and Murph.

"You know," she murmured quietly, "if I have to be trapped in a cave with a killer on the loose, I'm glad it's with you."

"Why?"

"You make a bigger target."

She saw the whiteness of his grin when he looked at her over his shoulder. "Would you be quiet?"

A sudden echo of sound barely reached her ears over the noise of their footsteps.

Sable grabbed Murph's arm. "Shh! Stop and turn your light out for a minute!"

There was a click, and blackness descended.

They stood in absolute darkness and listened for a long moment. All they heard were the sounds of their own breathing and the echo of dripping water.

"Are you sure you heard something?" Murph asked.

"No. Just wait a minute longer."

They waited.

"It was probably the water," Murph said

at last. "Let's go on. You keep watch behind us."

Murph's light came back on, and he stepped into pale drifts of fog. It thickened rapidly, reflecting his light back at them until they could barely navigate through the narrowing passage. Swirls of mist ebbed and swayed in ghostly patterns, taunting them as it hid formations that suddenly emerged in front of them, blocking their path.

They managed to find their way about fifty more yards down the passage, then once again Murph stopped and turned out his light.

"Did you hear something?" Sable whispered.

"Water. Listen."

This time the sound of water was louder and more definite.

"That's more than just a few drips of seepage," Sable whispered. "That's a steady stream." She felt a stirring of excitement. "Murph, have we found the sinkhole?"

Murph turned his light back on, cupping his hand over the beam to reduce glare. They followed the sound of water a few more yards, until they came to the thickest mist and felt the movement of icy air on their faces. Murph aimed his light upward. "Looks like the place Craig described."

"We'll have to climb."

"That's right."

Sable leaned the shovel into a small depression in the wall of the passage.

Murph aimed his light all around them, then stepped over to the cave wall and tested the dampness of the clay embankment. With the shotgun in its sling over his left shoulder and the fire poker dangling from his side, he handed Sable his flashlight and climbed a ten-foot-high bank.

Sable waited until he reached the top, then tossed him the flashlight, and followed. They didn't need the shovel, after all. It looked as if Craig had knocked some rocks out of the way.

Murph straightened and stood, placed the shotgun beside him on the ledge, and reached down to help Sable the final few feet to the ledge.

He indicated the sinkhole above them, which opened into the night sky with a rough diameter of perhaps two feet. From that opening dangled several long roots from a bush or a small tree.

"If these roots are strong enough," Murph said, "I can use them to pull myself up through the hole, then drop the rope down to you."

"Or you could lift me up, and I could tie the rope around the tree or bush that belongs to those roots."

"I'm going first. We don't know where this thing comes out."

"So what's your point?" Sable asked.

"My point is it could be dangerous. I'm bigger than you, so I say who goes." Murph secured the rope around his shoulder, stuffed her medical supplies into his larger pockets, and stepped up on the clay embankment. "Hold your light for me, and I'll stick mine in my pocket."

Sable glared at him, but she did as he asked. Now was not the time to turn militant. "Just hurry."

"I'll leave the gun down here. You can hand it to me before you come up," Murph said.

He reached up for one of the thick roots near the sinkhole. The root held him. He heaved himself up, arm muscles bulging as he reached for another root closer to the hole. The root snapped, and he dropped to the cave floor with a grunt.

"I liked my plan better," Sable said. "Give me that rope and give me a boost."

"One more try." Murph readjusted the

rope over his shoulder and once more stepped up the slanted clay wall.

This time the roots held. He reached the opening and pulled himself up with a scattering of dirt and pebbles.

A falling rock missed Sable's head by inches and hit the cave floor with an echoing *thwack*. She turned a fearful gaze back down along the passage, but she saw nothing.

Murph looked down from above. "This comes out by the creek, all right. A couple more feet, and the creek would have been in the cave. The bank is steep and slick."

"So you know where you are?"

"I can get my bearings. I see a corner of the house from here."

"Good. Now just tie the rope and go on down to Craig. I'll sling the gun over my shoulder."

He hesitated, his misgivings obvious on his face from the glow of her flashlight.

"I've got it, Murph. Craig already suspects you. If he's still alive, and he sees you coming after him with a shotgun slung over your shoulder, what's he going to think? Just hurry and go."

Murph switched on his flashlight and withdrew from the mouth of the sinkhole.

As Sable waited for the rope to be

dropped down, she cupped her hand over the face of her flashlight to prevent glare from the fog. A moment later, the rope unfurled directly beside her.

When she reached for it, the beam of her flashlight reflected against a black vein of some kind of deposit in the cave wall a few feet past the sinkhole.

She reached for the shotgun, grasped the rope, then hesitated. With a quick sweep of her light, she found the vein once more.

It wasn't galena.

She caught her breath and stared at it. She almost reached out and touched it, but she heard a scuffling sound from somewhere in the darkness behind her. She had to catch up with Murph.

She turned off her light and stuck it in her back pocket, looped the shotgun sling over her shoulder, then grasped the rope up high. Wrapping a loop around her foot, she used that to push herself up, ducking her head to avoid the fresh shower of loose dirt and rocks that fell on her. She reached up again, then held the rope and froze. A light flashed through the mist from the passage below.

She heard the scattering of loose pebbles and breathing, then the scuff of shoe leather against hard clay.

She hugged the rope, suspended in the mist, suddenly afraid to exhale.

The rope bit into her hands, and her grip slid with the moisture that had collected. She reached for a better hold and was horrified when another shower of dirt and pebbles scattered noisily across the floor below her.

The light below scattered the misty darkness once again.

She dropped to the cave floor and swung the shotgun from her shoulder, disengaging the safety. No time to escape. She would have to stay and fight.

As the footsteps returned and the light grew brighter, she scooted behind a stalagmite and pressed herself against the cave wall where she had seen the black vein.

A glimpse of moonlight filtered in through the sinkhole. She heard the sound of ascending footsteps coming closer. She waited, wincing when the light grew brighter, pressing herself against the wet stalagmite.

The footsteps quickened for a few seconds, then stopped, still out of sight. It was then that Sable remembered the rope, hanging down through the mist. The beam from a flashlight focused on it, and then slowly circled the upper cavern.

She held her breath and squeezed between a stalagmite and the cave wall. If she stayed put, she might be shielded by the fog, and it was just possible he would pass by.

She waited as the steps drew nearer. Light penetrated the white mist with an eerie glow, once more illuminating the vein. Sable got a good, close look at it, like a black wire twisting through the rock around it.

Silver turns black when exposed to air. . . .

The footsteps drew closer. She tightened her grip on the shotgun, raising it.

For a moment she was hidden by the glare of the mist. But Simmons stepped around the edge of the stalagmite.

He was barely three feet from the barrel of the shotgun. His eyes widened. She pressed her finger against the trigger.

Chapter 29

Murph emerged near the foot of a hill to the sound of rushing water just below. The moonlight bounced against a cascading swell of a creek; he could feel the droplets on his face. He'd been right when he told Sable how close the creek was to the sink-hole. Flooding along this creek had obviously caused the erosion.

After tying the rope securely to the bush he'd used for leverage, he had dropped it back down the sinkhole. From there he had awkwardly scrambled down the final few feet of the hill alongside the creek, glad of the large pockets in his carpenter jeans.

He could see the house and the warm glow of the oil lamps through the windows from here. The mountain encircled the house, leveling at the second story, then reaching up to the attic. Sable's idea to open the upstairs window might work, if Simmons had not discovered it.

Murph only wished he knew where Simmons was right now.

Against his will, he left Sable to climb

out herself. She would not thank him for waiting, and she was right — if Craig were alive, he would need immediate attention, and he would need to get to warmth quickly.

Take care of her, Lord. Protect her. I know You can do a much better job of it than I could. He hurried along the creek bank toward the bridge and saw the distinct outline of Craig's body in the moonlight.

He glanced back, expecting to find Sable scrambling down the hill behind him. What was taking her so long? Was she having trouble climbing the rope with the shotgun over her shoulder? He should have insisted she hand it up.

But he was learning quickly that one did not force Sable Chamberlin to do anything against her will.

He turned back, then halted and glanced toward the bridge. Above the chatter of the creek, he'd heard — or thought he heard — a low moan. Or was that Dillon howling from Sable's bedroom?

Shadows of boulders merged with the moonlight. He didn't dare turn on his flashlight; it could be seen from the house. He crouched at the edge of the bank and hesitated only a few seconds before the moan came again.

"Craig?" he called.

Another moan, mumbled words, then, "Help me . . . trouble."

Murph had been trained to use every precaution to protect himself in dangerous situations — after all, who would rescue the injured if the rescuer ran into trouble? Simmons could be using Craig as bait.

Murph glanced along the creek bank once more. Sable still hadn't emerged from the cave.

"Murph," Craig called. "That you?" His voice was weak. Strained.

Murph decided not to wait. He stepped down along the steep bank, catching at frozen stubble and rocks to slow his descent. Once out of sight of the house, he switched on his flashlight and saw Craig's supine form more clearly.

The man held his gloved right hand over his heart. Blood stained the glove and glistened from a wound in his chest.

Murph released his hold on a rock and slid the rest of the way down. "It's okay. I've got you."

Simmons remained frozen in her sights, mist swirling around him, enhanced by the glow of his flashlight. He no longer looked frightened.

"Go ahead," he said, in an "I dare you" tone of voice.

"Unlike you, I don't shoot people in cold blood."

"But this isn't cold blood, is it?" He sounded almost taunting, almost as if he wanted her to pull the trigger. "I'm a threat to you, a threat to all your friends. I killed your grandpa, and I killed Noah."

Why was he antagonizing her like this? "And Jerri," she said. "Don't forget Jerri."

"I didn't."

"You didn't forget her, or you didn't kill her?"

To her amazement, he took a step toward her. Her finger tightened on the trigger. She had to pull it. Had to! "Stop."

He darted and rushed. She squeezed the trigger hard. Nothing happened. The gun didn't fire.

He grabbed it from her and slung it across the cavern as he raised his pistol to her face. "There we go. That's better. You have to have a firing pin for it to work." He chuckled. "You should have checked for it before you brought it down."

He'd taken the firing pin.

"Why don't we head back toward the house? We have some things to discuss."

"No, we don't."

"Oh, you'll discuss it, one way or another." He aimed his light at the cave wall. "Looks like you found the treasure. Silver, is it?"

"You took the map from the attic."

"Nope, but it doesn't matter right now, does it? A fella can't very well mine something from someone else's property. Not until that property's his."

That was what he'd been doing down by the creek when he'd almost drowned. He'd been looking for the sinkhole.

He stuck the flashlight into his rear pocket so that the beam reflected from the ceiling, giving the cavern a more muted glow. "Climb down. Any sudden moves, and I'll shoot you in the head and find what I need some other way."

Sable didn't tell him that there was no other way. Dynamite wouldn't budge that heavy old safe. If he needed the information inside — and he did if he was working for Boswell — he would have to go through her or Murph to get it. Nobody would figure it out any other way. She hoped.

Craig leaned heavily against Murph. "He shot me, Murph," Craig wheezed. "Others safe?"

"He's got Bryce in the house. The rest

500

are in the cave." Murph unzipped Craig's coveralls and checked the bullet wound — high on the left side of his chest. He pulled the stethoscope from a deep pocket and listened to Craig's breathing. As he'd feared, the bullet had collapsed the lung, but at least it wasn't getting any worse — no tension pneumothorax. Good breath sounds on the other side.

Craig was talking, so his airway was clear. His heart rate was a little fast, and his blood pressure, when Murph checked it, was holding pretty normal. That meant he hadn't lost too much blood. Yet.

"Okay, hold tight, Craig," Murph said. "I'm going to roll you over and see if there's an exit wound on your back."

There wasn't.

"Is it bad?" Craig asked.

"Not as bad as it could be. You must have started to turn away when he fired so that it didn't catch you straight on. That, plus the heavy coveralls gave you some protection."

"I'll live?"

"You will if I have anything to do with it."

He rolled Craig back over and pulled out a handful of 4" x 4" gauze pads and a sheet of Elastoplast.

"What's that?"

"Pressure bandage. It's going to hurt, so brace yourself. You might have a broken rib or two from the impact of that bullet."

He placed the pads on the wound and anchored them with the Elastoplast.

Craig groaned, leaning against Murph's shoulder. "You know what you're —"

"Yes. I'm a paramedic. Trust me." He rechecked the sound of Craig's breathing. "Let me know if your breathing gets difficult. Now hold on tight. I've got to get you to the house. Can't have you hypothermic."

"I was wrong about you. I'm sorry."

"I'll gladly enjoy all the groveling you want to do after we get you to safety. Now shut up and hold on."

Simmons forced Sable ahead of him through the passage, holding the flashlight in one hand, the gun in the other.

Every time the barrel of the gun touched her shoulder she had a flashback to the last time she'd been attacked in the cave. She could not allow herself to panic. She had to be prepared for any opportunity, any weakness he might show.

"Why did you take my watch?" she asked and was gratified by the calmness of her voice. She didn't feel calm.

For a moment he didn't reply, then, "What watch?"

"You followed us into the cave and grabbed the pocket watch from around my neck."

"You've got the wrong guy. Now shut up and walk faster. I figure your buddy Murph has probably reached the house by now."

She did as she was told. "So you were looking for the sinkhole when you fell into the creek."

He didn't reply.

"Did someone really try to drown you, or did you just lose your footing and fall?"

He shoved her forward roughly. "Go."

"Lord, keep her safe. Keep all of us safe." Murph crouched in the shadows of the house, barely daring to breathe. He'd made it to the back of the house with Craig — no easy task. Craig was about as much help as a dead fish, and a wrong move could start him bleeding again — could kill him. All Murph could do for Craig right now was get him inside the house out of the cold.

Now if only Dillon didn't bark again and give him away. For all Murph knew,

Simmons could be back down in the cave, searching for them. But what if he wasn't? Murph couldn't take any chances.

Sable had told him which window she'd raised, and he found it quickly, wishing he had that pickax he'd seen lying next to Craig down at the creek. He stepped gingerly on the slanted hillside and was relieved to find no ice. Craig was enough of a burden — it would have been impossible to carry him up the steep slant if there had been an inch of ice, as well.

When he reached the window he eased Craig down. "Hold tight just a second."

He ran his hand along the wooden sill. The window was open, the bottom of the frame even with Murph's chest.

He hefted Craig up to the window sill and eased him over onto the floor of the sewing room. Craig landed with a grunt.

"Sorry." Murph braced with his arms, then gave a quick thrust with his feet to hoist up and over. He caught himself and balanced in the frame of the window, careful not to stumble onto Craig.

"Okay, Craig, we're in a mess. I've got to get you to a hospital soon."

"Can't," Craig said. "Got to help the others."

"I know. Simmons has Bryce, and he

may even be down in the cave now, looking for the others."

". . . man's crazy . . . don't let him get away with this." Craig struggled to get up, but fell weakly back against the sewing counter. "And Boswell . . . get Boswell. You have a gun?"

"Not anymore." Murph eased Craig against the wall. "Lay still until I can get you to help. Keep your feet up."

". . . not going anywhere."

Murph felt Craig's pulse and rechecked his breathing. Little change.

"I'll get you out of here as soon as possible," Murph promised.

He went swiftly through the room, pausing only when he landed on a squeaky board. He stepped past Perry's open case, stopped, and aimed his light inside. Cookbooks. He reached down and picked up the thickest of the set. It was too light. He replaced the book, selected another one and hurried out into the hallway. He desperately needed to know what was happening to Sable, and for a moment, he almost climbed back out the window to go in search of her.

Dillon barked and scratched from inside Sable's room. Immediately, there came a series of muted thumps from overhead.

Murph froze. Jerri's body was up there, and it wasn't her ghost making that noise.

Cautiously, he crept down the hallway to the attic steps and opened the door. He aimed the beam of his flashlight toward the place where he'd heard the thumps.

There was a grunt, more thumps. Murph negotiated the obstacle course, then saw a body.

Bryce lay face down in the far corner of the attic. He was tied with cord from the drapes. Simmons had wrapped it around Bryce's wrists, ankles, and neck. The teenager looked like a securely tied calf at a rodeo.

Bryce struggled within the confines of the cord that held him until he could turn his head enough to see who was coming toward him. Murph removed a rag from his mouth.

"Hurry! Simmons is down in the cave. Get this stupid cord off of me."

"We've got to hurry back down," Murph said as he fumbled with the cord at Bryce's wrists. "Sable might still be down there."

Murph. Where was he? Why had she foolishly told him to go on without her?

Maybe he had missed her and was coming back to find her. She just hoped he could take Simmons by surprise.

Except Simmons was ready and waiting for surprises. He wouldn't hesitate to kill her if he thought she was trying to escape.

"If you need me so badly," she said, ducking beneath a ledge, "why did you try to kill me the night we arrived?"

"I didn't."

"You're not the one who pushed me?"

"I didn't say that. I said I didn't try to kill you." He shoved her forward. "Move! We don't have time for a gabfest."

She stumbled, righted herself, then kept moving. "So why did you push me?"

"Because Murph moved."

So he *had* been after Murph. "You didn't push us in the cavern?"

"Don't know what you're talking about."

They walked in silence for another moment, then she asked, "How did you get into the business?"

"Family."

"Boswell's a relative of yours?"

"A guy doesn't buy loyalty like mine with money. He buys it with blood."

"He's your father? Uncle?"

"I don't guess it's occurred to you that the more you know, the less likely you are to live."

For a moment she focused on placing

one foot in front of the other, trying to think of Murph rescuing Craig at the bridge, of Bryce in the house, of Audry and Perry waiting in the darkness. But she couldn't resist one more question — one that wouldn't get her killed.

"Doesn't it even disturb you a little that Murph and I saved your life, and now you're planning to take ours?"

He didn't answer.

"I mean, if someone had pulled me from an icy creek, restarted my heart, breathed life into my lungs, I think I would have had a slightly different reaction to the whole thing."

"You might."

"Anyone would. How could you live with yourself?"

"Saving me was your choice, not mine. I didn't have any say about it. And don't bother sending me a bill."

"Don't worry," she snapped. "I'll turn it into workers' comp."

"You do that."

She remembered something Noah had said once, something that had surprised her. He'd said that in order to do the right thing, the right way, a person did it for God alone. If you wanted to do good, you didn't do it for public acclaim, but because it was the right thing to do.

But how could saving Simmons's life be the right thing to do when he killed people for a living? As a physician, she healed for a living. As a paramedic, Murph rescued people for a living. But when a healer saved the life of a killer so he could continue killing — what was right about that?

"I didn't kill her," Simmons said quietly.

She continued walking, showing no sign that he'd startled her. Had he read her thoughts? Had she unintentionally spoken those thoughts aloud?

Help us, Lord. Help me.

They were nearing the breakdown cavern. It wasn't much farther to the house, and if Murph had been successful, they would surely be coming back down for her any time. What would Simmons's reaction be? She would have to be prepared. Simmons was holding her arm lightly now, loosely enough for her to jerk away if she wanted to. If only he didn't have his finger on the trigger of that gun! She couldn't forget his quick reaction in the kitchen earlier.

They neared the house, and she peered into the darkness ahead, straining her ears for the sound of distant footsteps, of voices. Had something happened to Murph?

Simmons tightened his grip on her arm. As he stepped up beside her, something moved directly beside them — a quiet rustle of clothing and footsteps on the hard clay floor.

Something struck Simmons in the side. He grunted and stumbled sideways. Sable yanked her arm from his grasp. She swung around and jerked her knee upward — perfect shot.

He buckled forward with a cry of pain.

Sable dropped to the ground and rolled out of his reach, her flashlight clattering uselessly on the rocks a few feet away.

The blast of a gun reverberated through the cave. She took advantage of the noise to make her getaway, groping blindly along the path, tripping on stalagmites, grazing her shoulder on the cave wall. She dove behind a rock just before Simmons's light came on.

"You're a dead woman!" he shouted. He shone the light around him, its glow reflecting against stalactites and fallen boulders. "You'll never get out of here alive!"

His footsteps came toward her. She lay paralyzed, praying silently for help, for whoever had hit Simmons once to hit him again. Was it Murph? Where had he gone? She shrank deeper into the shadows, closer to the pit of her nightmares.

Chapter 30

Simmons's steps drew even with the boulder where Sable crouched in the shadows. She held her breath, pressing against the cave wall. Its jagged edges scraped her right arm.

Lord? Where are You? Now would be a great time to do something.

As the beam of Simmons's flashlight crept closer to Sable's hiding place, a rock smacked the cave wall and bounced onto the path.

Simmons squeezed off another shot. The percussion stunned Sable like a jolt of electricity. The bullet ricocheted. Shards of limestone shattered onto the path beside her.

Simmons snapped off the light, throwing the cave into darkness.

From where Murph crouched on the far side of the passage, he heard Simmons's labored breathing. Cautiously, he inched forward, preparing himself for hand-to-hand combat — with the aid of the fireplace poker he had carried with him all this way.

When Simmons switched his light back on, Murph lunged with the poker. Simmons lurched sideways at the last moment, and the poker struck his shoulder instead of his skull. Simmons stumbled backward, raising his gun.

Sable leapt from her hiding place and tackled Simmons at the back of the knees. His legs buckled.

Murph slammed into him from the side. The gun and the poker flew through the air and bounced from the cave wall. The flashlight dropped to the ground, and Murph's foot spiraled it sideways. The cave flickered with strobes of light, casting odd shadows on the surrounding stone. The wayward beam gave just enough glow for Murph to see his opponent.

Simmons punched Murph in the gut. Murph buckled. Simmons hit him in the face. As Murph recoiled from the blow, Simmons spun around and grabbed Sable by the throat.

She gasped, kicking at him, trying to claw his face. He dragged her toward the pit.

Murph jumped him again, driving him forward and knocking him off balance, slugging him in the face. Simmons grunted, stepped back, and launched a kick that caught Murph high and hard on the chest, knocking the wind out of him.

Sable couldn't get her bearings. Her heel caught on a boulder. She lost her balance and tumbled closer to the edge of the pit. A rock gouged her right hand.

Simmons threw Murph aside and stumbled across the rocks toward Sable.

"No!" she screamed.

He shoved her downward. She grabbed at an embedded rock and held tight. Feeling around with her toe until she found a foothold on a rock below, she clawed her way back up.

As she neared the top, Simmons tried to kick her, but she ducked. His foot connected with the flashlight he'd dropped. It flew over the side of the pit, slammed against Sable's right shoulder, then shattered far below.

Darkness. Sable clung tightly to a cold, damp slab of rock at the edge of the pit. Her grip loosened from the rock. She slid back a few precious inches. Her feet slipped from their hold. Her bruised hands weakened as they grasped at the dislodged rocks.

She heard grunts and labored breathing

as Murph and Simmons continued the struggle nearby. She couldn't hold on much longer. She closed her eyes in terror.

Someone shouted to them from the direction of the cave entrance. Bryce. Light reflected against the edge of a boulder, and Sable saw Murph and Simmons grappling on the ground.

Bryce shouted again, racing toward them through the dimness. Simmons rolled away from Murph and grabbed a fist-sized rock. He drew it back. Bryce shouted and leapt, hitting just hard enough to knock Simmons away.

Murph grabbed Simmons and jerked him to his feet. "Sable!"

"I'm here! Help me!" She couldn't hold on. Her fingers dug into the loose gravel and mud.

Bryce scrambled over the rocky terrain toward her.

Simmons wrenched free and spun back on Murph. There was a snap of metal, and the wicked glint of a switchblade caught the light in Simmons's hand. He lunged forward, and the blade sliced the air. Murph stumbled backward.

A lightning-quick, muffled ping echoed through the cave. A red starburst spattered across Simmons's chest. He gasped and stumbled backward, staggering against the rocky teeth of the pit. The glow of a flashlight outlined the shock on his face.

The switchblade clattered to the ground as Bryce reached down for Sable and grasped her hand. Simmons's body pitched forward and knocked Bryce aside, barely missing Sable in an arched dive. He hit the rocky bottom with a sickening thud as Bryce scrambled to keep from falling as well.

Sable's hands slipped. The jagged edges of limestone scraped her flesh. Loose dirt and pebbles gave way beneath her feet. "Help me!"

Murph lunged forward and grabbed her by the arms. He swung her away from the pit and clung to her, enfolding her in his arms as Bryce scrambled up beside them.

Breathless and shaking, Sable collapsed against Murph, tears of relief streaming down her cheeks.

"It's okay, Sable, he can't get you now. You're safe, you're . . ." His voice trailed off, and Sable felt his body stiffen once more. "Who shot him?"

Sable raised her head and saw his frown of confusion.

"N–no! What are you doing?" came Bryce's frightened voice from somewhere beyond them in the darkness.

Murph's breath stopped for a moment. "Bryce?" he called. "What's wrong?"

There was no answer. Murph helped Sable to her feet and held her steady as they walked back toward the path.

Bryce stood in the shadow of the ledge, his eyes wide, his face frozen in shock.

"Bryce, what —" Murph stopped abruptly. His hand tightened on Sable's arm. Beside Bryce stood Perry Chadwick, his high forehead creased in a frown, his thinning hair frazzled across his forehead.

The glow of Bryce's flashlight outlined the dark shape of a weapon in Perry's hands. Sable frowned and blinked and took a step closer. It couldn't be . . . but it was aimed at Bryce. For a moment, the sight was so incongruous, the impact of it didn't register.

"Perry?" Sable said, confused. "What's going on? Where did you come from? How did you find the gun?"

"This, my dear, is a beautifully crafted mini-Uzi, complete with silencer. Please don't refer to it as a gun." Perry's voice dripped with disdain. "It's the top of the line, my pride and joy."

"But . . . I don't understand," Sable said. "Bryce isn't —"

"Please don't start asking a bunch of

silly questions." He spoke as casually as if he'd been cooking in the kitchen. "You know what I want. Do you want me to tell you what happens to Bryce if you don't give it to me?"

"Let him go, Perry," Murph said. "You're not going to kill an innocent kid."

"He's a teenager. Teenagers are never innocent. They get on my nerves almost as badly as dogs." Perry kept his gaze trained on Sable. "Are you going to give me the evidence your grandfather collected against his poor, long-suffering partner? Don't try to tell me you don't have it. You gave yourself away earlier, remember? Your grandfather gave you away with that confession letter."

"But Grandpa didn't confess," she said.

"Whatever. Too bad he didn't make the combination more obvious in his note; then we could have avoided all this extra fuss."

"Where did you see the letter?"

Perry gave a sad sigh. "It wasn't as if you hid the thing. Sable, dear, you simply must use a little more cunning in these endeavors. You're like an open book." He shrugged. "Unfortunately, not quite as open as I needed, but I mustn't blame you for everything."

Once again, she had made a horrible misjudgment of character. "Let Bryce go and I'll give it to you."

Perry smiled, a cold smile that barely stretched across his full lips. "Bryce stays where he is. He makes a great insurance policy. I need a hostage, and I need those papers, Sable."

She was defeated. She couldn't risk the life of a fifteen-year-old boy just to avenge her grandfather. Maybe she wouldn't need the evidence and proof that Grandpa had gathered against Boswell. If they lived through this . . . but that was the thing. They wouldn't. Perry couldn't let them live.

"Perry, please. Think what you're doing. I can't believe you'd shoot Bryce in cold blood."

Perry moved closer to Bryce, as if to suggest that he would have no problem pulling the trigger. "And I can't believe you would gamble his life away for a few pieces of paper."

"What have you done to Audry?" Murph asked.

"Don't worry, she's hiding in the dark like a good little old lady, waiting for clumsy, heroic Perry to return. I took her flashlight. In case you needed it, of course."

"Let Bryce go, Perry," Murph said. "Take me if you need a hostage."

Perry shook his head. "I'm a smart man, Murph, contrary to the image I have led you to know and love. Too bad Simmons didn't use his head a little more. He opted for the old-fashioned, muscle-head approach, but that won't cut it anymore. So much is demanded in our profession. Acting . . . photography . . . prospecting for silver. Oh, by the way, the map was a great help. Thank you so much for sharing it with me."

"And the watch?" Sable asked.

"That, too, could help in the end. If only it had contained a certain series of numbers, it might have saved us a great deal of trouble."

"How did you know about the watch?" she asked.

"I have eyes like you wouldn't believe."

"Eyes?"

He gave her a tight smile. "Too bad for Jerri she saw too much."

"Photography equipment," Murph said.

"That's right," Sable said. "Audry mentioned that Jerri had seen your 'toys' in the sewing room. Surveillance equipment?"

"Only the best."

"That's why Dillon noticed someone

had been in my room," she said. "You'd been planting your equipment."

Perry raised the Uzi and took another step, until the barrel of the gun was barely six inches from Bryce's head. "The papers, please, Sable. Now."

"What good will it do us?" she asked. "We've seen you, we know what's happened. You'll have to kill us all, anyway."

"Perhaps you'd like to see me start now — with Bryce. Come on, Sable, you're a physician. You're supposed to do no harm."

She turned slowly toward the house. *Keep him distracted if possible.* "Those books," she said. "You wanted us to see what was in your case, didn't you? You staged the whole thing, made a big deal out of it so we'd be too suspicious not to look. You left your case unlocked, even after that big show of outrage at Simmons."

Perry's face broadened in a smile of satisfaction. "I could've been on the big screen."

"We didn't open the books, though," Murph said. "Were they hollow?"

"Oh, very good. When did you discover that? No one ever does. Cookbooks bore most people."

Sable noticed the almost casual way Perry held the menacing, dark gray Uzi.

"No wonder you insisted on wearing that heavy jacket down here in the cave," Murph said. "It hid the gun very well."

"You knocked me down in the attic, too," Sable said, piecing more things together. "You used the window in your room — the sewing room — and climbed over to an attic window. That was why it was so cold when I returned. Is that how you killed Jerri?"

"You can't blame a guy for taking advantage of every opportunity. I overheard you tell your Mr. Murphy about how you crept out that window to the attic when you were a child. Oh, and how did you like my night vision goggles in the cavern? Didn't you love that ghostly glow?" He said it like an industrious kid bragging about a new toy.

Ghost eyes. She hadn't been blinded by the fall after all. There had just been very little to see. Night vision goggles.

They reached the low ledge above the cave mouth that opened into the basement. "You go first, Sable. Murph, you're next. And don't forget who stands to lose if you try anything." He patted Bryce on the shoulder.

The boy recoiled from the man's touch, then swallowed and met Sable's gaze with poorly concealed fear. She attempted to convey reassurance with a nod, then turned and knelt to crawl into the basement. Murph came directly behind her, followed by Bryce and Perry.

Perry's aim never wavered. There was no awkwardness in his movements. He straightened and brushed at his clothes with his free hand.

"So what are you going to tell Boswell when you return to him with the evidence?" Sable asked. "You can't tell him you killed a member of his family."

"I won't have to tell him a thing, will I? All I have to do is present what he's looking for — in exchange for a large cash donation, of course. By the time he discovers that his dear, faithful nephew has had a little accident, I will be long gone, never to be seen again."

"But what —"

"I'm sorry, this conversation is terribly interesting, but if you keep stalling, I'll be forced to blast our young friend's head to bits." A sudden harshness in Perry's voice gave a cutting emphasis to his last words.

As Sable turned toward the basement steps, Murph caught her arm and squeezed. He squeezed again. She frowned up at him. As she did so, a streak of white caught her attention from the mouth of the cave.

For a second, the cave's ghost had never seemed more real. But this was a very substantial ghost, in the form of a very angry woman in her sixties, wearing a white sweater and black slacks, stained with dirt.

"Okay," Sable said quickly. "I'll take you to the attic and give you the papers you need, but why don't we work out a deal." She continued to talk to cover the sound of Audry's movements. "If you're going to disappear anyway, never to be seen again, why don't you give us a fighting chance?"

"And how would I do that?"

"You can start by handing over that ugly-looking gun of yours," Audry said from the shadows. "And before you make a wrong move, let me remind you that Simmons lost his pistol back there in the cave, and I found it."

Perry froze. His eyes narrowed.

"Don't think I don't know how to use this thing, either," Audry warned him. "I taught classes in gun safety for ten years. So. You kill Bryce, you die. It's as simple as that." The click of a safety release reinforced Audry's words. "There were a lot of things

I didn't notice about you. Not until you left me back there in the dark. Or so you thought."

Sable remembered the penlight Audry had used on the bus the night of the wreck. Perry didn't know she always carried it with her.

A look of iron-hard anger flashed across his face, then was once again camouflaged behind his bland expression. "I should have known, Audry. You are a woman of many talents. However, I can still cook better than you."

She pressed the barrel of the gun against his skull. "What am I going to have to do to make you drop that gun?"

He continued to aim the Uzi at Bryce for another long, agonizing moment, then sighed and lowered his arm. The Uzi fell from his hand with a heavy thud. "Don't shoot, Audry. I'm not that desperate."

Murph snatched the weapon from the ground and hefted it in his hand.

Audry stepped aside to allow Perry to precede her to the basement steps. "Don't try anything funny. My quick reaction time won me a couple of awards in shooting contests not too many years ago. Now, Sable, suppose you tell me what on earth happened since our last episode."

"We've got to get Craig to a doctor," Murph said. "Simmons shot him. I think the Jeep is ready to go. I'll do a little more chopping on the bridge before we cross it. I don't want to take any chances on the ice, especially now that we've come this far." He glanced at Sable. "I'm driving."

She shook her head. "I'm driving."

Sable grinned in the rearview mirror at Murph as she cautiously maneuvered Craig's Jeep onto Highway 86 and turned toward Cassville. Perry was trussed like a Thanksgiving turkey in the far back beside Murph. Audry sat with Craig's head on her lap in the back seat, while Bryce sat up front with Sable. They had left Dillon at the house.

"Now do you mind telling us exactly what is going on?" Audry asked.

"You were right about Boswell," Sable told her. "Only it was worse than you thought. It seems he's got his own little pocket of organized criminals ready to do his bidding. He hires strike breakers, killers, and anyone else he can buy. He framed my grandpa when the deal on the Seitz place fell through — and it fell through because Grandpa checked it out. He had the ore tested and discovered it matched perfectly the grade of ore in one of the working mines, because it was the same ore. Then he used his own shotgun here at home and experimented down in the cave to see what a limestone wall salted with ore would look like."

"Told you it was Boswell," Craig mumbled. "I never trusted that man."

When they reached Cassville, they took Craig, Audry, and Bryce to the hospital, then drove three blocks to the police station to deliver Perry Chadwick. Sable and Murph told their story and promised to stay around for more questioning. The police would have to contact the Missouri Special Crimes Unit to investigate the deaths in the cave.

The FBI was already on its way to pick up Otis Boswell. It looked as if Perry would be more than willing to testify against his boss to try to save himself. The evidence Grandpa had left in the safe would be enough to stop Boswell for good.

Sable and Murph returned to the Jeep in front of the police station.

"A couple more warm days like today, and that ice will all be just a memory." Murph gestured toward the sparkling-crystal tree limbs that overhung the building. He put an arm around her shoulders, drawing her closer — but tentatively, as if afraid she would pull away.

She leaned toward him, nestling against the solid bulk of his chest. The warmth of his arm generated its own special kind of comfort. Sable realized that she felt at home there, close by his side, protected and warm.

A car whispered by on the road, its headlights turning the limbs of nearby trees into prism reflections.

A limb crashed somewhere in the shadows, shattering the sweet stillness. Sable shivered, pressing closer to Murph's side.

"I feel as if I'm living in a crystal world," she said. "Everything is made of crystal — the forest, the road, the building behind us, and the people. Especially the people. It sometimes seems as if it could all break into a thousand fragments at the slightest movement."

"It won't. God's creation is more substantial than that. People change, but God doesn't."

"It's going to take awhile to learn to depend on that."

"It'll take your whole life. It's okay, though. God's had a lot of patience with me over the years."

"I wish I had your spiritual strength."

"My spiritual strength? You're kidding, right? I'm the one who keeps trying to rely on my own strength. You said it yourself. My macho side keeps trying to take over."

She took a deep breath, watching the reflection of lights that outlined the tree limbs. "I guess we'll both learn, given more time. Meanwhile, I could sure use some encouragement."

"What kind of encouragement?"

"Oh, you know, a strong friend nearby, who can remind me about God's love and provision, and who can pray with me . . . you know . . . pull me out of the deep places, and help me dodge bullets . . . stuff like . . . that." She fell silent. Was she being too forward?

"How about that private practice you wanted to build?" Murph asked. "Are you still interested?"

"Of course. It's been a dream of mine for years."

"Mind if I share it with you?"

"You're not worried about starving? A solo practice is a risky proposition these days."

"My biggest concern is staying near you." His arm tightened around her. "I'm not going anywhere."

Acknowledgments

As is the case with every novel, the reader can't blame the writers alone for the finished product. Many other friends, colleagues, and family members must shoulder some of the responsibility, and, we hope, some of the thanks for *The Crystal Cavern.*

As always, we would never be able to settle down and write if not for the loving support of our parents, Lorene Cook and Ray and Vera Overall. Thanks, Mom, for all you do.

Our thanks also go to those who have had a part in the editing process: Liz Duckworth, Mike Nappa for Barbour Fiction, Barbara Warren of the Blue Mountain editorial service, and Jackie Bolton, who tries hard to screen everything before we turn it in.

A special thanks to our friend and colleague, science fiction novelist Randall Ingermanson, for helping us smooth some of the rough spots.

We also wish to thank Paul Gibfried, former boss and expert in metallurgy, whose insights guided my efforts in the study of mining in our area.

Thanks to Kent Alexander, whose knowledge of mining also helped guide our story.

Finally, thank you, Robin Lee Hatcher, an amazingly talented friend and colleague with a servant spirit. We appreciate your words of wisdom.

We belong to a wonderful support group of fellow novelists — who happen to be Christians — called ChiLibris. Every day, they touch us, give us encouragement, guide us in the right direction. Knowing you all has been one of our greatest rewards in writing.

About the Author

Hannah Alexander is the pen name of Cheryl and Mel Hodde. Together, this husband and wife team has published nine novels, including the Healing Touch series. In 2004, they were awarded the Christy Award for romance for their novel *Hideaway*. They make their home in the Missouri Ozarks and can be found on the web at www.hannahalexander.com.